Enchanted to Meet You

CARA STOUT

AVON *a*

For Mom,

who always listens to my stories first.

I love you.

HarperCollins Children's Books, a division of HarperCollins Publishers,
195 Broadway, New York, NY 10007

HarperCollins Publishers, Macken House, 39/40 Mayor Street Upper,
Dublin 1, D01 C9W8, Ireland

Avon a is an imprint of HarperCollins Publishers.

Enchanted to Meet You

harpercollins.com

ISBN 978-0-06-348047-6

25 26 27 28 29 LBC 5 4 3 2 1
First US paperback edition, 2026

Originally published in Great Britain by Penguin Books, 2025.

1

IMOGEN

I love the smell of burning polyester and hot dogs in the morning. I just didn't expect the flames to reach so high.

My boss flings the restaurant's glass door open with a shout. "Imogen, what the hell are you doing?" His striped hat falls from his head as he rushes outside.

"Giving you back this uniform." I lean against the cement planter to admire my handiwork. "I think it looks better this way."

I've dreamed of doing this since the moment they thrust the drab fabric into my hands. But mostly after the night manager decided it was cool to berate me in front of the whole restaurant for accidentally putting the wrong topping on a hot dog.

The thrill of seeing a dream come true brings a warmth to my heart.

It could also be the fire.

Customers huddle around the window to view the show, while my boss grabs a hose.

"You'll pay for this." A weak stream of water sputters toward the flames already licking a flower box under the window.

A delighted grin etches my face. This is worth all the nights I came home smelling like a deep fryer. Plus, I'm doing my coworkers a favor. Clearly, they didn't bother to make these uniforms flame retardant—health and safety at its best. At least now everyone knows what type of people they work for.

You're welcome!

I've quit countless terrible jobs over the last seven months. When I turned sixteen, I was told that now was the time to enter the workforce and learn responsibility . . . *Gross.* This might be the most dramatic exit to date, however. Okay, *fine.* It is *one hundred percent* the most dramatic. But they made me wear a foam hot dog on my head and hand people coupons for questionable meat. I'll consider us even. I'm typically easygoing, but a girl can only handle so much. I wasn't going to sit around and wait to be yelled at by a middle-aged man in striped shorts, with a bad attitude.

"Well, this was fun." The flames fizzle out, a wisp of steam curling from the charred pile. "But it's time for me to say farewell." I enjoyed the show, but I'm not dumb enough to stick around to see what consequences come from my arson.

Water drips from the front of the boss's uniform. "How many jobs is this now?"

I bite my cheek, keeping a snarky *screw you* to myself.

"You're going to run out of places that'll hire you soon. I took a chance on you, Imogen." He pushes a hand through his thinning hair. "Should've known better. Serves me right."

I unzip my backpack, then throw my name tag inside—all that's left from this job. It lands with a soft thud next to the rest of my collection. I keep the name tags from the places I've worked. Morbid, maybe—it's also getting heavy. My mom says they represent my failures, but to me, they're stepping stones to my future. Wherever that might lead.

I look up to find my—*former*—boss staring between me and his phone.

Is he going to call the police?

My gut clenches. Explaining why I quit another job is stressful enough without a prison cell added into the mix. I raise my hands. "Don't worry, I'm leaving." I slip on my bike helmet.

Maybe I didn't think this through. Title of my memoir.

"You can't keep making people regret offering you a chance. This job isn't perfect." He fishes the smoldering fabric from the trash can with a shovel. "My uniform chafes like no other. But not everything is perfect. We don't live in some fairytale where happily-ever-after magically happens. You need to learn to accept that, or you'll end up alone and penniless."

"Better than being stuck here for the rest of my life." I peel out of the parking lot, bike wheels skidding, without a second glance.

Farewell, hot dogs, you won't be missed.

Perfection is possible—I've witnessed it firsthand. My best friend, Divya, already knows what her dream career will be. My parents have been happily married for decades.

I know fairytales aren't real. I'm not naive. But I do know one thing: I won't find perfection with a hot dog on my head.

The ten-minute ride home is enough to fester the nerves in my anxious stomach. My mom only works part-time, but she always has activities scheduled. Let's hope she chose today to make herself scarce.

Mom's blue sedan greets me in the driveway.

Ugh. I don't know why I thought I'd suddenly develop good luck on the short ride back home.

At what point does my somewhat chaotic journey of self-discovery and my duty to use what opportunities my parents have given me collide in a fiery wreck? How long before they start to wonder where they went wrong?

I can't stay outside all day, and not just because I might pass out from the smoke lingering on me. I steel my shaking hands and head inside. A few balloons and a handmade sign greet me in the entryway.

"CONGRATS ON YOUR FIRST WEEK!"

Oh boy. My chin drops to my chest, my limp arms barely holding my bag from hitting the ground. A congratulations sign after one week on a job seems like overkill, but I guess my parents thought it was worth a celebration with my track record.

"Imogen, is that you?" Mom's voice carries from the kitchen.

"Uh—yeah. Sorry. Bathroom." I bolt for the stairs. Pain blooms on my knee as I stumble up them, not stopping until I'm safely behind my bedroom door. I throw my bag onto the ground, ripping off my clothes and the lingering scent of failure.

The walls still have the remnants of the boy band posters from middle school, and even their smoldering stares feel like they're judging me. I'd be mortified to bring a boy to this room. But luckily for me my love life is more abysmal than my job history, so it's a nonissue.

I had one almost, *maybe*, probably-doesn't-count boyfriend, but that lasted barely a month. And a series of terrible dates over the last year that I'd very much like to burn from my memory. I may not know what perfect feels like, but I certainly know what it *doesn't* feel like. Growing up reading fairytales, I was conditioned to strive for a happily-ever-after. Maybe that's a personality flaw, but why should I settle for less than I deserve?

"Aren't you supposed to be at work?" Mom asks when I come downstairs a few minutes later.

My shoulders sag as I lean on the kitchen island. "I can tell you with certainty that I'm not supposed to be at work right now."

She yanks various knitted items from her bag on the counter. She's not a crafty person, and the odd-shaped designs prove it. After six months in her knitting club, she's yet to produce anything remotely usable, but she keeps trying. *Clearly, that gene skipped over me.* I went to a pottery class with her last year, and nearly gave the instructor a black eye when my clay flew off the wheel and smacked him in the face. Needless to say, I never returned.

"Did you quit another job?" She tiptoes around the words, her voice kind but weary.

I don't make eye contact, intensely focused on the leftover pasta sauce I'm picking off the counter. "This time, no. I got fired."

"Imogen . . ." She doesn't finish her thought. She doesn't have to. Mom taught for nearly thirty years, and as someone who found so much passion and fulfillment in a career, she doesn't understand why I can't do the same.

I grab ingredients from the fridge to make a sandwich. "Mom, I hated it. Everything smelled like oil, and the night manager was creepy and obviously has anger management issues that need addressing. Plus the uniform itched! Also, as I learned today, their fire safety is awful."

She frowns but doesn't comment on the fire thing. "Reasons to leave are always plentiful, but so are reasons to stay."

"I'm not like Dad. I won't stay at a job that's slowly killing me for thirty-plus years just to get a cushy pension." I slap bread onto a plate, lathering it with mayo and mustard.

"Sweetheart, you know your father and I love you. But you're getting older, and real life is going to come knocking sooner than you think. Having a solid job history and useful skills will do wonders when applying for college or a future career." She fluffs her short gray hair. "You said this summer you were going to get serious."

"I know, it's just . . . hard." I rip a piece of cheese in half, trying to pull the slice from its plastic package, my hands unsteady. "And I always have a job—always. I'll find a new one in a week."

Her voice is soft, not angry—it'd be easier if it were. "Finding jobs isn't your problem. Keeping them is the area you need to work on."

My fingers dig into the soft bread as I squish the sandwich together. *Serious* and *Imogen* are not words people often use in the same sentence.

Mom runs a hand through my hair, and her lavender soap masks the burnt-plastic odor clinging to me. "Sweetheart, I want you to have a wonderful life, like your father and me."

My eyes squeeze shut. I blame the sting of tears on the smoke exposure. But the pain in my chest is harder to write off.

What do you think I've been searching for?

Nothing is quite as sad as an abandoned mall—except perhaps the person sitting on the ground with their rusty bike in the middle of the afternoon on a Thursday, staring at it. Or perhaps even more so, this is not the first time said person has been found here.

Said person is me.

The mall closed two years ago, not long before I started high school. You can still see the "EVERYTHING MUST GO" signs scattered on the dusty tile floors if you peek through the windows.

It only seems fitting, now I'm jobless—once again—that I lounge on the weed-filled cement with a sandwich and chips, studying the crumbling facade of my childhood.

It's late May, but the unrelenting summer heat made an early appearance. I tuck my red waves behind my ear. After chopping a good portion of my hair off last week, it now hits right above my shoulders. This shocked no one. Whenever I get antsy, I cut it or dye it a wild color.

My head snaps up as tires crunch on the cracked cement full of rocks and broken glass. Divya hops off her hot-pink bike, fashionable as always in her bright-orange-and-yellow sundress. The black braid slung over her shoulder shines in the sun, and her bronze skin glows like she walked off an ad for a beach vacation. My perfect best friend—said with zero sarcasm.

"I don't know why you love this place. The vibe is so depressing."

I manage a half-hearted shrug, finishing my last bite of sandwich.

"Imogen." She chooses to stand beside me, rather than joining me on the rather gross ground. But I'm feeling gross, so we're a perfect match. "I thought you had work today? Imagine my surprise when Find My Friends said you were here?"

I clear my throat, wiping crumbs off my pants. "I did."

"And you smell like burnt plastic because . . ." Divya's dark eyes bore into me, many years of friendship not letting me get away with vague answers.

The hot cement sticks to my bare legs as I shift positions. "I set my uniform on fire." Lighting that match and watching the flames burst into life was more satisfying than almost anything I've done. A sad statement I won't say out loud.

Divya huffs softly. "Imogen, you didn't."

"I'm surprised it hadn't caught fire before."

"But it didn't catch fire." She steals a chip. "You *set* it on fire. Big difference."

After months of explaining why I've lost jobs, I should be better at it. "I hated it, Div." My voice grows louder as I list my complaints. "I had to wear the stupid hat and—"

"And the one before you said smelled like feet."

"It did."

"It was a shoe store. What did you expect?"

I play with the rock chips near my feet. "Well, I won't be blamed for not wanting to work with smelly feet or where the boss yells at me for no good reason." Easy justifications to give when I know the real underlying cause of my aversion to holding a job. But excuses always come easier than the truth.

"Of course you shouldn't." Divya takes my hand. I blink up at her beautiful face. The sun shines behind her like a halo. "I know you're afraid you'll end up like your dad."

A lump strangles my already heavy breaths. I keep my gaze straight ahead. My dad had a heart attack seven years ago. He was in the hospital for weeks; we almost lost him. The doctors didn't say his job nearly killed him, but it did. I vowed I'd never get stuck like him.

Divya continues, "Maybe you purposely choose places you know you'll hate, so you have an excuse to quit?"

"What if that's it? Maybe I don't really want a job. Maybe"—I stand—"I want to sit in the mall parking lot and remember what it feels like not to be a total failure." I wrap my arms around my stomach, hands twisting into my shirt.

I've had nearly a dozen jobs since turning sixteen. This nagging voice in my head always whispers, "What if there's something better out there for you?" and to get it to stop, I have to do something new. I hope one day I'll find my passion, my place, my perfect fit, and it'll shut up. My dad's career is a dumpster fire, but Mom's wasn't, and when Divya graduates and gets her dream job, it won't be.

If they can find their forever, maybe I can too.

"I'd never call you a failure, Imogen."

"I've failed at everything." Even when I actually try, which makes it all that much harder. I rub at the pressure in my chest, my gaze dropping to the ground.

"No, you won that sloppy joe–eating contest in eighth grade."

I smile despite myself. "My crowning achievement. I peaked at thirteen." Divya and I became friends in elementary school. I broke my crayons in kindergarten art, and she let me borrow hers. She's been saving me ever since.

"I know what will cheer you up." She smiles. "How does summer at a theme park sound? It wouldn't cost you a thing. In fact, they'll pay you. All the buttered popcorn and turkey legs you can eat."

I raise an eyebrow. "Sounds fake. You know you aren't supposed to click on those emails, right?"

She grabs a pebble off the ground and throws it at me. "How do you think I met that foreign prince? I only had to send him my Social Security number." We laugh, and I feel lighter, like I always do when she's around. "No, this isn't an internet scam. My summer internship at the media company is offering a cash prize to the intern who can write the best investigative journalism piece by the end of next month. This could be a huge boost to my college apps next year."

Being an investigative reporter has been Divya's life goal since she figured out they existed. She broke her first story in middle school about the cafeteria using fake meat in the burger patties.

Shocking? No. Gross? Extremely.

"Remember Fairytale Gardens?"

"How is that even a question?"

Fairytale Gardens is a theme park located about forty-five minutes away. We've gone once a week, every summer, since I can remember—sometimes twice a week, if my begging worked. When I was eight, they did a one-time, three-day-long summer camp, which might be the highlight of my entire life. To this day, it's still my favorite place ever.

I watch vlogs in the offseason just to get my fix. My favorite were the ones with the fictional queen and her sons. They showed the behind-the-scenes life of the "royals." However, a few years ago they stopped, and I've missed them ever since. Still, the guests do a good job with the POV shots of the rides, where I can pretend that I'm speeding along the coaster track, heart pounding as the drop nears.

"What do you say to undercover work?" Divya asks.

"What do you mean?"

"I want a story that's going to blow the rest of the competition out of the water. Which means I need someone on the inside to get me the real dirt." Divya frowns, pulling an envelope from her bag and handing it to me. The first thing that stands out is the large "FINAL NOTICE" stamped across the front in red letters.

I open it, withdrawing the paper inside. I try to decipher what I'm looking at. But, like always, Divya explains it for me.

"I found this notice from the bank yesterday. It says my parents will have to turn their restaurant over if they can't pay the money owed. But if I can win, I know the prize money will be able to help hold off the collectors until we can get the rest of the funds. And who knows, if I can get some traction on the news story, I might be able to get other writing jobs."

"They can't lose the restaurant. We always celebrate our birthdays there—it's tradition. And your mom makes the best Indian American fusion desserts in town. People will riot if they can't get them."

"I know, but I guess it's not enough. I can't let them lose everything they've worked for." Divya's normally bright eyes dull, filling with tears.

Divya's family has always welcomed me with open arms, and are the most generous people I've ever met. When my dad was in the hospital, they let me stay at their house for as long as I needed, while Mom was taking care of him. They had me assist at the restaurant as a distraction so I wouldn't be alone with my fears. If this is going to help them, I'm all in—whatever it is. I never thought I'd have a way to pay them back, but now I do.

I squeeze her hand. "We won't let them lose anything, okay? So, it's you and me?"

Her shoulders sag. "Just you. I have my internship. I can't have two jobs and help my parents at the restaurant."

"Yeah, poor you. That fancy internship is really bringing you down in life." I wink.

A grin peeks out and she bites her lip to suppress it as she slides the bill back into her bag. "So, I can't go."

"I don't know, Div. You're the mastermind, not me."

"I need you."

I need you. Not what I usually hear from people. That's normally my line.

Divya shoos a fly away from her face. "Besides, you're the best woman for the job. You know Fairytale Gardens better than anyone."

"What's the piece?" I don't have anything else going on. Plus, I haven't visited Fairytale Gardens this summer and I did always fantasize about working there. Honestly, I'm disappointed I didn't think about applying myself.

"Rumors are circulating about the owner—that he isn't on the up and up, like it seems."

I mime twisting a mustache like a cartoon villain. "And you'll uncover his dastardly deeds?"

Divya twirls her braid. "I was on Reddit and got talking with a charity that used to receive donations from Fairytale Gardens, but those contributions stopped in the last few years."

"Maybe they picked a new charity."

"They did. But my whistleblower thinks those are shell charities. That they don't exist."

"They're probably just bitter. Do you want to ruin the childhoods of kids who enjoy fairytales and roller coasters by exposing the park?"

Childhood is already fragile and fleeting enough.

"I had a bad experience with Snow White as a child."

"This is revenge for Snow White?" I tease.

She wears her serious face: lips pressed tight, deep lines between her eyebrows. "It's about the truth. I need you,

Imogen. I can't do this without you." A lie and we both know it.

"Why not just call the authorities? I'm sure they could handle it. We can come up with another story."

"Pff," she scoffs. "And have them take all the glory from finding the bad guy? No way. I'll break the story and then we can bring them in. And it's like I said, I need an exposé that'll eclipse all the others—I know that this is the one."

"So, what, I just walk around wearing a wire and hope someone confesses?" I'm a "jump and hope a net is there to catch me" kinda girl, but even this is a stretch for me.

"You'll just need to look around, snap some pictures of anything suspicious. Talk to the workers, and get them to spill. I know you can do it—people love talking to you. So, are you in or out?"

Divya may have a problem with fairytales, but I don't. My best memories are summers spent on roller coasters and meeting princesses. Nostalgia is a magical concept—it makes you hope.

And if I lack one virtue in my life, it's hope.

Divya relying on me is a switch in our friendship, but I owe her for all the times she saved me. It gives me the warm and fuzzies to know I could be helpful for once. And Fairytale Gardens really is my happy place.

"I'm in."

2

TRISTIAN

"Tristian, are you just gonna sit there and let Tyrone kill me?" My twin brother, Garrick, shoots daggers at me from the sofa. Tyrone cracks a smile as he lets off another cannon right into Garrick's video-game counterpart. Tyrone is sixteen, like Garrick and me, and we've been going to school together since kindergarten. His family owns a karaoke bar down the street that Garrick likes to show off at. "Dude!"

I ignore my brother's ranting about sportsmanship and focus on my phone, where I've been for the last hour while they embarked on their video-game crusade, along with my younger brother, Aldrich. I play sometimes, but it's not really my thing. Scrolling through my phone, I reread my upcoming summer program itinerary for the five hundredth time.

I've been dreaming about going to Europe since I was little and I got my first history picture book for Christmas. I love the idea of places that've been around for hundreds of years and still stand, like living, breathing pieces of the past. It's the closest I can get to time traveling. So, when my history teacher told me about the summer trip to Europe, where you could spend six weeks learning and traveling to all the cities I'd dreamed about and earning some college credit, I couldn't turn it down.

But I can only tune out the yelling for so long. I glance back at Garrick—who shares most of my DNA, but not my face, since we're fraternal twins—as he tosses the control to Aldrich with a dramatic sigh. "Tyrone, don't you need to be back at work?"

"You're such a sore loser." Tyrone grabs his soda off the table, leaning back into the couch. "You're lucky we've been friends since we were five, or I might take offense."

"Tristian"—Garrick throws a pillow at my face—"can you take your eyes off your screen for a quick sec to have my back? When he says I'm a sore loser, it's like he's saying that to you, too, since we're practically the same person."

"We are definitely not the same person." And not just because Garrick has bright blond hair and mine is brown. Garrick is a star—he's always the first to jump onstage or make a fool of himself just for the attention. I would much rather stand in the background and let the eyes pass over me. Unfortunately, being part of the family that owns Fairytale Gardens theme park means everyone around here knows our names.

I grab a slice of pizza off the table, slipping my phone into my pocket. Garrick isn't wrong about one thing: I should enjoy these last few weeks with my brothers. We usually spend all summer together at FTG, the nickname for the park. Over the years, our roles have changed, but we're always heavily involved.

We've been playing face characters for years, knights and princes in shining armor. Then last summer Garrick stepped into learning more about the food and beverage department, and I had a brief stint in maintenance—I'd wanted to see how everything ran. But while Garrick thrived in his role, my interest quickly fizzled out when I realized it was more about fixing leaking pipes and changing light bulbs. Or at least that's the most they let me do.

"Will you bring me back a stein from Germany?" Aldrich asks. He's two years younger than Garrick and me, and has the same bright blond hair as Garrick. They got it from our mom. Pizza gets caught in my throat, and I swipe Aldrich's soda to wash it down.

"I would like my weight in chocolate," Garrick adds.

The heaviness I've carried around for the last two years lifts a little as I picture myself walking those cobbled streets. I've spent my life wrapped in fairytales, in fictional adventures, thinking this faux castle and rusty park was all I could ever want—but then Mom died, and I realized all I ever was, was a fake prince trapped in a life I never got to choose.

I know I'm only sixteen, but it feels like my whole existence was planned out before I was born. I want to have my own adventures, see places created by legends long past, and create a future my father didn't craft.

And in three weeks, I'll get a taste of that.

This experience will give me options outside of being stuck in my family's castle-shaped shadow for the rest of my life.

"I know I don't say it often"—I keep my eyes down, stomach clenching as I push my can around the coaster—"but I'll miss you guys."

"Stop, you're making me blush." Garrick shoves a breadstick into his mouth.

I swallow my pizza in three large bites, the crust scratching my windpipe. "Game of darts?" I suggest, trying to lighten the mood. "Loser buys the next pizza?"

"Nah, you Walshes always kick my butt at those," Tyrone says.

All the years playing carnival games at the park have given me a leg up. "I'll do it with my eyes closed. Give you a fair fight."

"I'd avoid that bet," someone says behind us.

My shoulders clench to my ears before I turn around. I'd know that voice anywhere. Ivor.

My older brother stands in the doorway to the living room with his hands in his pockets, wavy brown hair perfect as always. "Tristian, can we talk?"

Gut twisting, my initial reaction is no. My love for my oldest brother has long been buried under years of resentment. It might as well be my father before me.

"I'm in the middle of a game." My jaw tightens as I try to maintain eye contact.

"This will only take a minute, T." His face doesn't give anything away.

Garrick and I share a look—that twin telepathy at work. *Run while you still can*, I imagine Garrick saying. But I've already had enough crap from Ivor and Dad about going on this trip, so I don't want to rock the boat any more than needed until I'm safely on that plane.

Ivor follows me out the sliding door and onto the balcony. The warm night hints that summer will come early this year.

The video-game music and laughter fade as Ivor slides the door closed behind him. I lean against the railing, crossing my arms, then unfolding them to hang loose at my sides. "So, what's up?" I keep my voice light, but the hesitation peeks out.

Ivor stays near the door, hands shoved deep into his pockets. Our relationship hasn't been the same since Mom died. When I declared I wanted more than the family business, he saw that as me abandoning them and all our parents had built. Ivor runs Guest Relations and Experiences, while playing a prince on the side. He's fulfilled in those castle walls; the path laid out for him is one he embraces with open arms. The choice to forge my own way wasn't a dig at him, but he took it as one. I could've tried to smooth it over, but my pride wouldn't let me backtrack.

His eyes move over the space before he turns to me. "I'm sorry to do this, T, but you can't go on your trip."

The sharp edge of the rail stings my palms as I press my hands into the side, my body tense for a fight. That's how all the sparse conversations over the last year have gone. "Ivor, I know you want me to stick around and play prince again this summer, but Dad already agreed to let me go. It's done."

"It's not, actually."

My eyes narrow as a buzzing starts in my ear. "What do you mean?"

"Dad never signed your permission form. He didn't give his authorization, and since you're sixteen, you can't go without it."

My jaw tightens. "What the heck, Ivor? I gave that to him months ago, and he said I could go." I run through a thousand scenarios in my mind. I saw confirmation that he sent it, didn't I? Suddenly, I'm doubting whether I did. I was swamped this last month with finals at school. Did I somehow miss this freaking colossal mistake?

"He said he needs you in the park." Ivor drops his gaze to the deck, pushing his foot across the wood, a nervous tic he's had since we were kids. Ivor is ten years older than me, but I've been the same height as him since I turned fifteen. "But I know you wanted college credit, so we can do some paperwork and call this an internship. Ted was the head of marketing and he just retired, so that department needs some attention. You could do that."

As one of the last family-owned theme parks in the nation, when people came, they stayed awhile. My whole family has worked here in various jobs. As Ivor got older, he slipped into roles with more responsibility, and now the same is expected for me.

"I don't care about marketing. I don't care about FTG. I had this summer planned. Dad can't do this."

"He can, and he is." Ivor rubs the back of his neck, pausing for dramatic effect, I assume. "FTG is in trouble. We open full-time this weekend and are already in the hole from last year. We can't afford to hire a new marketing manager. Not yet, anyway."

"Ivor . . ." I shift from foot to foot. The smell wafting from the Royal Fare restaurant across the way makes my stomach rumble in the quiet space. Our house is located on the outskirts of the FTG property. That's why it feels like I eat, sleep, and breathe fairytales—fake history at its finest. Truthfully, that's where my love of history started. I used to study all the facts about Carpathia, the land where the Fairytale Gardens story takes place. Until one day I realized it was all make-believe.

"I really want to go." I drop my voice, hoping some part of the big brother I used to know is still there. I could get Garrick to forge Dad's signature—he's been doing it since we were kids—but that's never been my thing. I would be too worried about getting caught and sent home from the trip with my tail between my legs.

Dark circles rim Ivor's eyes under pinched brows. He acts like he wants to apologize but switches mid-thought. "You owe us."

"Don't do that." I grab the railing to give my hands a reason not to shake with anger.

The wood cracks as he steps beside me with a sigh. "Fairytale Gardens is your rightful place. You don't belong gallivanting off in Europe. We've always spent the summer together."

"That's the point. I wanted to see more."

"The park has struggled with attendance, the financials aren't great, and Dad's unwell," Ivor says when I've gone quiet. "It's his heart."

"I'm not a cardiologist."

"He misses you." My laugh is hollow, and he arches a brow. "He does."

"He said that?" It's not that I haven't seen Dad every day, but we barely share a handful of words. The longest conversation we've had in the last two years was when I asked him about going on this trip. I thought we'd made some headway. Joke's on me, I guess.

Ivor runs a hand over his impressive beard. "He didn't have to, I can tell. Ever since Mom died—"

"Don't!" I cut him off. "Don't use Mom as a guilt trip to force me to stay." I already missed my chance to go to Europe last year because I wasn't ready.

"Why do you think Dad started Fairytale Gardens? Why he created the Carpathia royal family and their story?"

"To make money."

"Because family has always meant more to him than anything. Carpathia survived because the family worked together." Ivor's unwavering faith in our father, in Fairytale Gardens, makes my stomach curdle. I can't understand why he trusts a man who doesn't deserve it.

"Carpathia is a fairytale created by a man who wanted to profit off childhood innocence and overpriced food." The words taste bitter on my tongue. At one time, I loved Fairytale Gardens. I've spent all of my summers here. It was my second home; sometimes my first.

But as I got older and my mother's health weakened, I saw my father for what he really is: a greedy man. After Mom died two years ago, he got worse—cold and angry. I couldn't wait to get away and see the world, especially after having dreamed about far-off places since childhood.

"You need to forgive Dad for whatever slight you think he inflicted on you. Everything he did, he did for us. Fairytale Gardens is your home, always has been, always will be. It's not a monster holding you back from life. The problem isn't FTG."

Ivor places a hand on my shoulder. "Tristian, you're my brother, and I love you. The park is in trouble, and we can only save it together."

When you've spent your whole life being told you are a heroic prince, it's a hard habit to break. And Ivor is building me up to save the day. I resent the part of me that wants to.

Ivor is wrong, though. Fairytale Gardens doesn't hold any answers for me anymore. But the livelihood of my whole family is wrapped up in the park, and if it fails, they'll lose everything. And despite the rift between us, I can't let that happen. Besides, without Dad's permission, there isn't much else I can do.

"Guess I don't have a choice." I shrug.

Ivor flashes the royal prince grin. "That's the spirit."

3

IMOGEN

After masterfully convincing my parents that the only job I found was at Fairytale Gardens—and adding that since I already loved the park, I couldn't possibly want to ditch it—they agreed I could work there for the summer.

I was shocked, actually.

Maybe they truly believed that this was the only place I might consider sticking around. So, that's why a week later, as the June sun shines high in the sky, Mom and I are driving the forty-five minutes to Fairytale Gardens. I brighten the very dull car ride by belting show tunes the whole time. *Wicked* never sounded so good.

"Are you sure you'll be all right staying on property?" Mom asks after the gate attendant tells us to drive back to the cast housing.

My smile could light up a whole room. "Of course. You know Fairytale Gardens is like my second home. Plus, it's only for five weeks. Think of it like summer camp, but I'm getting paid." That's how long I have to crack Divya's story. "Will you take the long way around? I want to see the gates."

The same zooming butterflies I have every summer when we finally arrive after dreaming about it all year have overtaken me.

A large—more chipped than I recall—baby-pink sign reads "FAIRYTALE GARDENS' and below in gold, "*A magical world awaits*."

Pastel colors and light sand decorate the park beyond the turnstiles admitting guests. I lower my window to generic fanciful music blasting from speakers—an upbeat, cheery tune, if not repetitive. Large trees and shrubs soften the entrance; flowers edge the pathways, a bit overgrown in places, but it adds realism.

Still, my heart gives a leap at—

A loud honk sounds from the car behind us.

"Crap, sorry." I wave out my window as Mom drives away toward the back before we cause pileup at the entrance.

The magic disappears once we're through the gate to the employee parking lot and cast housing. The only time I've seen this part of the park was the summer I was eight and I came for the three-day camp. The place feels bigger in my memories, slightly less splintered and aged, but the mind tends to gloss things over. Several rows of brown and yellow apartments no one has touched since the eighties surround cracked asphalt. That's where I'll be staying. I wonder if it's as glorious as I remember.

"Thanks, Mom." I'm unbuckling my seat belt and reaching for the door handle as Mom puts her hand on my cheek, forcing me to look at her.

"If you need anything, just call." Her smile is bright, but I see the hesitation in her eyes.

"This one is going to work out."

Mom nods. "Still, if you need us."

Leaning over, I pull her into a hug. "I love you, Mom."

"I love you too, Imogen."

I grab my suitcase from the back and we say our goodbyes. I'm watching Mom's car pull away as my phone vibrates. "Were you tracking me?" I say to Divya.

"Yes. Find My Friends, the world's greatest invention."

"I think penicillin would argue otherwise." I press the phone between my shoulder and cheek, grabbing my tote bag off the ground, where I abandoned it.

"Have you gotten to orientation yet?"

"Almost." I spot a sign telling me where to drop my suitcase off until I get my room assignment. It's so bizarre being here as a worker; it's like seeing how a magician performs a magic trick. Somehow, way less magical.

"Imogen, you can't be late."

You and I both know I am more than capable of it.

Slinging my tote over my shoulder, I push my sunglasses up my nose. The sun blazes overhead. If the temperature is this high in early June, I'm not excited for the rest of the summer. Technically, I don't know how long I'll stick around, despite what I told Mom. When I complete Divya's story, I have no reason to stay, other than my love for the park. But I plan on being long gone before the story breaks. Something grips my insides tight when I think about an exposé rocking Fairytale Garden's world. But this place is amazing. I can't imagine anything ruining it for good. I'm just helping stop the bad guys.

I hear shouts in the background of the call as Divya clicks on a keyboard. "Fairytalers must report to orientation at three." She reads the welcome email to me again for the one hundredth time.

"Do companies think cutesy names for their employees will make us forget we're at work?"

"Can you focus? I don't want your tardiness to get you in trouble."

I roll my eyes, even though she can't see. "Yeah, don't want my fake job in peril."

"The park job is fake, but you can't get fired on Day One, because then my story is a bust." The strain in Divya's voice gives me pause. She's usually the self-assured one. I recall how badly she needs this to succeed to save the restaurant.

I head toward the offices and break room near the hedge blocking the park from view. "I won't get fired, and I'll keep my real purpose secret. No one keeps a secret better than me. I never told a soul about the time you hid the frog we dissected in the potted plant in science class, and for three days no one could figure out why it smelled."

"Yes, thank you for your continued loyalty."

"Div, I'm about to head in." I stay a few paces from the brown stucco entrance with a giant sign over the glass double doors welcoming the Fairytalers for the year. The excited chatter from the groups entering filters back to me. And if I strain, I can hear the music from the park and smell turkey legs—or maybe that's in my mind . . .

It's happening. The giddiness is trickling to my core.

"You got this, Imogen. I love you."

"Love you, too." I slide my phone into my bag, exhaling a long burst of air. "You got this, Imogen," I repeat to myself.

Stepping inside is like magic. The doors open into a space filled with colorful vintage posters and pictures from years gone by in the park, as well as a layout of the building. The left leads up a flight of stairs to the costume department and offices. To the right is the break room. It smells like lemon floor cleaner and cotton candy. I drop my suitcase off with the others in the designated area and head to the break room.

"Welcome, welcome!" A bright-eyed white man in a Fairytale Gardens T-shirt stands at the open break-room door. "New recruit?"

"Yes." I throw on a charming smile. Partly for show, but mostly because I'm bursting with joy.

"Awesome, welcome to the family."

I press my lips together to keep the cringe off my face, but I'm not sure it works.

He doesn't skip a beat. "Come in, and we'll get you settled." He holds a box with T-shirts identical to his. "Take one and put it on, then grab a seat anywhere."

Harsh fluorescent lights hang from the drop ceiling, with one window overlooking the parking lot. An expansive mural of the Carpathia countryside covers a wall—it's the most incredible thing I've ever seen. I snap a picture, for when I beg Mom to let me paint it in my room later. I'm going to spend every lunch break discovering new details. White-and-brown speckled linoleum squeaks under shoes as people shuffle into the plastic chairs lined in rows, facing a large pull-down screen at the front.

I choose a seat near the back, slipping on my T-shirt. About two dozen people sit here, a mixture of ages, but the majority skew toward my age or a little older. The excitement I felt at returning turns into a gnawing worry in my gut.

What if seeing behind the scenes ruins the happy memories I've kept all these years?

The closed door calls my name, but I force myself to look up front, pushing down the familiar urge to run away. Worrying is not my vibe. Regret is more my style. So, I'll wait for that moment to arrive.

"Welcome, newest Fairytalers, to the Fairytale Gardens orientation. Or, as we call it for short, FTG. I'm Michael, and I'll take you through today's adventure." Michael flips on a projector. "First off, FTG is a family, and we support each other. Second, you need to know the story that inspired FTG and that has been the cornerstone of our park for the last twenty-five years." He clicks a button, and a video begins to play.

The simple animated film tells the story of Carpathia, the fictional land Fairytale Gardens is based on. King Osgar and Queen Isobel ruled the kingdom of Carpathia peacefully. But one day a terrible blight from the nearby lands attacked the kingdom.

People died. Crops failed. *You know, the usual stuff.*

The king had three sons, and he sent the middle son, the bravest, Prince Winthrop, along with his knight to fight the plague. Long story short, the prince defeated the blight with the help of a fairy princess from a neighboring forest. They fell in love, saved the day, and everyone lived happily ever after.

I snuggle my tote bag closer. The sharp edges of the Fairytale Gardens storybook I brought with me dig into my arm. It was a souvenir from the first time I visited at three years old. My mom read it to me every night until I memorized it.

"This story is our bread and butter. Our founder, Bartholomew Walsh—you'll get to know him as Barth—created it, and everything you'll see in the park originates from it." Michael looks on the verge of tears.

I'm used to orientations, and, while fairytale-themed, this one isn't much different.

"Before I let you free for the day," Michael says at the end of the hour, "please check the list at the front for your job assignments and apartment numbers. Your training begins tomorrow; see the time next to your position."

Divya cast a wide net when applying. I'd love a spot at the carnival games or as a ride attendant. I told her we'd have a heated phone call if I got stuck cleaning toilets all summer.

She tried to convince me nothing was more fairytale appropriate—just ask Cinderella. I love a fairytale, but I don't want a crappy prince who can't remember me without a glass shoe.

I scan the page for my name.

Turkey stand. Huh.

While I enjoy a good turkey leg, I'm a little disappointed. When I thought about working here, I imagined whimsical princess dresses and crowns, or at least a pirate hat. I find my apartment number and debate taking my stuff up, but I have an hour to kill before the welcome dinner, and I'm dying to get into the park.

4

IMOGEN

Fairytalers enter the park through a secret hollow apple tree with a glistening gold trunk. I'm let into the back of Carpathia, the land housing the park's crowning jewel, a sand-and-stone castle adorned with copper turrets and spirals. The design is Arthurian, with various fairytale clichés thrown in.

Guests chat as they walk past me, studying colorful maps and pointing to their destinations—screams echo from the rushing roller coasters out of sight. I've been caught in the whirlwind of orientation, but it settles on me that I have another job to do: discover if Divya's whistleblower was right.

How will I do that? And more importantly, is it true? The jury's still out.

I can't imagine Fairytale Gardens harboring a dark underbelly as I walk through the tunnel under the castle and into the Village Center. Kids scream with delight, and delicious popcorn and caramel apple scents drift from nearby stands. The highlight of my childhood summers and I'm helping destroy it. I ignore the acidic burn in my gut. I reassure myself with the thought that I *could* help clear their name, too.

Maybe I'll be the hero at the end of the story.

I slip on my sunglasses, the sun unrelenting on the hot pavement, and snap a few pictures to send to Divya. I'd wear a hidden camera and microphone 24/7 if she had the budget. She told me a dozen times she wanted to come. But with her equally important internship happening at the same time, she couldn't be in two places at once. Luckily she has me, a friend with zero future prospects, to do the legwork for her.

At least I can be useful to Divya's and her family's future, while having fun in the process. Even though knowing this story rests on my unqualified shoulders makes my stomach churn, I won't let that discourage me from making the most of this excursion.

The park bustles with afternoon guests. Throngs cluster around the Village Center to get their picture with the castle. The pulse of so many bodies and untamed energy let free makes me giddy. The first ride I ever went on was Pirate Adventure. Tradition dictates it's my first stop.

Four specific areas spread out from the Village Center to comprise Fairytale Gardens. The Perilous Sea is directly to the left when you enter. Pixie Forest is to your right. Straight ahead and to the left, Glacier Peaks, and to the right, Carpathia and its castle. I could walk these paths with my eyes closed, but I don't.

Trampling a child on your first day isn't a good look.

A large ship carved from wood, with a sign warning off the faint of heart, greets me over the walkway to the Perilous Sea's entrance. In the center sits a massive human-made lake representing the sea. The smell is less fresh ocean air and more harsh chlorine and wet cement.

The land has carnival games and a few rides, including Pirate Adventure and Sea Monsters' Swing. A sizable crowd waits to meet one of the famous Carpathia mermaids. Ahead is a restaurant I dined at once and never again—I threw up popcorn shrimp when I was six. All attractions are watched overhead by the gondola ride Flight in the Clouds, which transports you to different lands.

I jerk to the left to avoid a face full of cotton candy as a text from Divya pops up in response to my pirate picture.

Divya
I don't get the pirate obsession.

Imogen
One word: Orlando Bloom.

Divya
That was two words.

Imogen
Two more words: Captain Hook.

Divya
The cartoon with the curly hair and puffy shirt?

Imogen
No, the one with eyeliner and leather.

The line for Pirate Adventure is forty minutes, and I spend the wait texting Divya my favorite ride-to-movie adaptations.

A sadly underrated genre.

Pirate Adventure is a dark ride, but not scary. It tells the story of Captain Stormbreaker and his quest to locate a hidden treasure long thought lost. Like all fairytales, he finds the gold and doesn't murder or pillage anyone.

The welcome dinner is rapidly approaching, but Sea Monsters' Swing calls my name. A voice—sounding a lot like Divya—tells me not to waste my time on more theme park rides. I should check for evidence in the main office, in regard to the suspect charities. I huff as I drag myself in that direction to assume my investigative reporter persona.

Magic lives in this park, bringing me back to carefree days when I believed in the impossible. It doesn't have the clean, shiny, new aesthetic other magical parks do, but that makes it special. It feels lived-in, loved. For a girl who set fire to her last job, I'm oddly optimistic this endeavor might turn out okay.

Strolling down the Village Center, I people watch. Despite the chaos, calm washes over me. A worker holds a giant bundle of balloons as kids run around her, begging their parents to buy one. That job is only slightly better than toilet duty.

Watching the exhausted parents of over-sugared children reminds me that I told my parents I'd send them a picture when I got settled. The picture is proof I didn't run off to join a cult. Not that I ever would—they require way too much commitment.

I line the balloons behind me in frame to take a few selfies with the castle in the background. The rich aroma of roasted turkey legs calls my name.

"Rod, I told you not to give her ice cream *and* cotton candy." A middle-aged woman with a southern accent glares at a tired man. "She'll never sleep." As the woman speaks, a tiny child charges from behind her and slams right into my legs.

I stumble back over the curb I'm perched on and smash into the worker with all the balloons. It'd be messy and super embarrassing if the balloons just floated off, but the universe takes it a step further. The balloons don't fly away; they are attached to the woman's belt. Instead, my arms twist and tangle with the strings. The woman screams as we tumble to the ground, cotton candy perfuming our descent, before we land with a thud.

Pain radiates up my hip, and a burning sears my palms where I managed to keep my head from banging into the pavement.

"Sorry! Here." I try to help the woman with her balloons, but she grunts a mumbled swear in response.

"Need a hand?" A voice comes from above as a shadow falls over me. I push away the balloon strings. The cement scorches, but not as much as the flush over my neck and cheeks.

"No." I straighten my sunglasses, crouching as I collect the spilled contents of my tote. "I've got it—really." I grab my lip gloss, wallet, and phone, pressing them into my chest as I reach for the Fairytale Gardens storybook I've been carrying around with me, but another hand gets it first.

"That's mine." I lunge for it, teetering close to falling into the guy—I see it's a guy because I finally glance up. "You?" His familiar face shocks me into stillness.

Curious eyes study me as our gazes meet for the first time. Tristian Walsh looks a lot different than the first time we met ten years ago. When I was a kid, I lost my parents in the park and was taken to Barth's office to wait. Tristian was there—this little kid dressed like a prince. We sat and played with a toy model of Fairytale Gardens until my parents came to pick me up. He was so kind and made me feel safe when I was terrified. I never forgot it, and every year since I've looked for him in the park—watched him change roles until he became the starring prince once more. I never spoke to him again, but I've lost myself in those ocean-blue eyes from afar on more than one occasion.

Tristian's chiseled jaw tightens as I stare. *Oh crap, did he say something?*

"What?" I snatch the book from him. Now I wish I had left that stupid storybook at home. Dang me and my sentimental heart.

He pushes brown waves off his forehead, but they cascade back like a shampoo commercial. "Do I know you?" His voice is deeper than before, the words a contrast to the bright fairytale around me. Butterflies zoom about my stomach.

"Nope." I grab my tote bag, which he's picked up, and shove my stuff into it, the handle ripping in my haste. My cheeks burn, and I try to stand, but I'm still attached to the strings and trip backward. His hand flies out to catch me. I yank away once I'm stable physically—emotionally is yet to be determined.

"Wait." Tristian removes a group of balloons from my arm, returning them to the woman.

"Well, thank you." I flash him my best smile, despite the embarrassment coloring my cheeks the longer I stand here. I attempt to push past him, and the crowd that has gathered to watch the show. Is it my performance or the Character Carriage approaching?

Maybe both.

His eyes sparkle as a knowing smile plays on his lips when he notices the Fairytale Garden T-shirt I'm wearing. "Do you work here?"

If I wish with enough force, will an earthquake swallow me whole?

I clear my throat, forcing my shoulders to relax. *Be cool, Imogen.* "Yes. And you're still around too, it seems. Once a prince, always a prince, huh?"

Interest fades from his features, replaced by a hard line between his brows. "Hardly. I have ambitions outside of this place." He rubs the back of his neck.

My face smarts from the invisible slap, but I don't let him see it. I smile extra bright because he bristles when I do. "What can I say? I'm a sucker for a happily-ever-after. Now, if you'll excuse me." I gather what little dignity I have left and push past him—or try to, at any rate. The gathered crowd has surged forward as the carriage begins its path around the center.

He doesn't physically stop me but jogs to reach where I'm

squeezing past a couple holding two large ice cream cones. "Hold on, uh—you."

He doesn't remember me. I shouldn't be shocked. I was an unremarkable girl in a sea of faces who made no impression whatsoever on the golden prince. Even if that moment of comfort he provided has always stuck with me.

"Stop. You need to go to first aid."

I turn back, spinning on the balls of my feet, as he collides with the man holding the ice cream cone.

"Dude!"

"Sorry." Tristian holds his hands up in retreat. "Let's go over here." Tristian takes my elbow, leading me away from the crowd and toward the castle.

"I told you, I'm fine." I jerk away, cradling my bag tighter.

"Really? Because the blood running down your leg gives me pause."

I try to ignore the flush his attention conjures, stopping for the first time to take stock of what hurts. Below my shorts on the back of my upper thigh there is a cut about an inch long. *Ouch.*

"I'll take you to get it looked at."

"It's not that bad." It only stings a little when I move. "It looks worse than it feels." The bright red blood against my pale skin is at odds with the charming music and fairytale castle around me.

"The first aid is right inside the castle. It'll only take a second to get a bandage."

"I don't need you to save me." I'm perfectly capable of handling any mess I create. Or running from it—whatever's easier.

He pushes again at his waves to remove them from his forehead, but like the bands of teen girls that follow him around, they won't stay away. "What's your name?"

I frown. I should not be engaging in this. But it's not like I can go this whole time without telling anyone my name. "Imogen." I watch his face, hoping maybe that'll spark a memory, but it stays blank.

Fine, that's totally fine. It's better I stay forgettable.

"I'm Tristian—but it seems like you already know that."

I don't dignify him with a response.

A family with a stroller glares at us as they try to get up the narrow entrance to the castle. Tristian inches closer, his arms reaching to either side of me to lean on the guard fence behind. He huffs. Whether from the family or me, I'm not sure—but I feel it on my warmed skin. Why does he smell good? Woody and slightly pepperminty. I'm sweating. If he takes a good whiff, he'll inhale perspiration and anxiety.

He moves back when the family leaves, hands in his pockets, head tilted to the side. "So we're clear, if you bleed to death I did try to help."

I roll my eyes, patting him on the chest. "You're off the hook, Prince Charming." I scoot past him.

"Are you going to take my advice?" His voice echoes around me in the castle's tunnel.

I glance over my shoulder. "Not my style." I give a small wave as I walk away.

5

TRISTIAN

Blood trickles down her toned leg as she saunters away. From this brief encounter, I can tell she's a free spirit—the polar opposite of me—and like a lot of people around here, she seems to know me. Had we met before? I rack my brain, trying to drag up any memories of her, but nothing surfaces. Her red hair and sparkling green eyes seem like something I would remember. And the fact that she is too stubborn to walk ten steps to first aid . . . I doubt Imogen is the kind of girl you forget.

Once a prince always a prince, huh?

Everyone assumes that's what being a Walsh means. FTG is all you'll ever amount to. If Ivor isn't lying about the internship, then I can at least pretend this summer is worth something more than crowns and sword fights. I'll take the (probably fake) marketing internship and make my mark. Even though I have zero idea what exactly marketing entails.

I notice my hands are shaking and quickly shove them into my pockets before heading into the castle tunnel once I wager I won't run into Imogen again. They designed the castle and its grounds to look like they had withstood centuries of battles and weather, built from the sturdiest stones. Nowadays, it looks worse for wear. The same sentiment goes for the whole park. Everything needs a fresh coat of paint.

In the early days, Dad would never have let the park become so worn down. He walked the lands every morning, his assistant trailing after with a clipboard—and me behind with my wooden sword—listing any necessary repairs that were needed.

He checked under every cart and behind all the trees to ensure there weren't any hidden problems. I made it a game to uncover issues to save the day in Dad's eyes. The park sparkled; the shine of the copper turrets gleamed on a summer's day. Everything felt like it belonged in this land, important and cared for.

But those days are gone, both for the park and for me. It stays exactly the same and I need a bigger space to grow in.

The densely packed crowd squeezes to pass inside the castle, through the path toward the land of Carpathia. Dingy, chipped tiles cover the wall and ceiling. Some guests venture off to the Royal Fare restaurant or the shops, others to meet characters. I keep walking back into the sunlight.

Ivor's voice greets me as I pass Knight School in the corner, followed by the unbothered tones of Garrick. Of course, it's not them; they're in character. Ivor, the eldest prince, Thornton, and Garrick, the valiant knight Kendrick the Kind. They're onstage teaching young kids how to sword fight. Garrick is a show-off, so he's happy to stick around FTG forever, playing a fake hero.

My brothers and I learned to fight the moment we were old enough to hold a wooden sword. Garrick even became an accomplished fencer in middle school. I stop briefly to watch them onstage.

Any distress Ivor hinted at is gone. He smiles broadly, eyes keen on Garrick as they walk in a slow circle, swords drawn. "One must always remember to keep your eyes on your opponent. You must anticipate their attacks." Ivor's gaze fixates on Garrick's sword.

"True words, Your Highness. I, however, find myself distracted by the lovely ladies come to see our show." Garrick winks at the audience. I smirk. Garrick's a big softie on the inside, but his charming exterior is so bright I don't know how any of us can see most of the time.

Ivor advances, using Garrick's boastfulness as an in, but Garrick didn't nearly become a junior Olympic fencer by luck. He doesn't get distracted with a sword in his hand. Lunging out of the way, he hits Ivor in the shoulder as he goes. The crowd gasps and then cheers.

The swords aren't real, merely lightweight fakes, but the metal makes an excellent sound when it hits the chain mail armor. Garrick gives a wry smile, pushing bright blond hair off his sweaty forehead. "Perhaps you should stick to the castle, Your Highness. Let the professionals do the fighting."

"Hey, Tristian," a voice says from my right. I glance down to see Aliana, who's a foot shorter than me.

"Hey." I shift my weight back and forth.

"I didn't expect to see you this summer." She twirls a dark curl through her fingers. "Last I heard, you were going to Europe."

"It didn't work out." I shrug, trying to keep the disappointment out of my tone. "Ivor gave me a marketing internship instead." I can't make myself sound excited, no matter how hard I try.

"Sounds right up your alley." Her lips twist into a knowing smile. I've been friends with Aliana for years; she knows I want to see the world and learn more about its history.

For the characters in my father's stories, family duty is always the first priority—but I'm not the fake prince everyone sees me as. I have dreams and goals of my own. The thrum of my pulse increases with each clang of the swords, spots invading my vision. I close my eyes, taking a few deep breaths before opening them. Cheers erupt from the crowd when Ivor hits Garrick. The whole act is preplanned, but they do an excellent job of keeping the suspense on who will win.

Ivor—it's always Ivor.

Inching closer, Aliana's fingers drop from her hair to curl around my bicep. "Well, I'm happy you're here, love. FTG wouldn't be the same without you." Her touch is a familiar note in a song I haven't listened to in ages. But the melody is off. It grates at my nerves.

Aliana has been a family friend since middle school, when her older brother worked here. She plays Princess Lilyana of Arkmane, Prince Thornton's wife—a role she insisted on having since that's her favorite character in the story. Her family is Venezuelan, and she told me about trips she'd taken as a child to see them. The beautiful places she visited. I hate to admit that it made me jealous.

Aliana was my first kiss. And while it was only a one-time thing during truth or dare three years ago, Aliana hasn't hidden that she would like more. But her crush has always been one-sided. She's a great friend, but we don't have that spark. That didn't stop her from letting everyone think we were an item. I could've shut it down, but the playboy prince reputation got around and I just let it morph into its own beast.

Truthfully, I liked the idea that people thought I wasn't an option. It was easier than having to open myself up for real to a girl.

I unfold her fingers from my arm, letting her hand gently drop as I step away. "It's good to see you, but I need to meet with my dad."

"Good luck." Another roar from the crowd erupts as Ivor wins the fight.

The entrance to the Fairytalers section hides behind a tree. I slide around it, and the magic falls away. Faint music follows me as I travel the asphalt road, past the apartments. I'm bunking with Garrick at FTG. Despite his ability to get on my nerves—it started when we were in the womb—I'd rather that than be stuck at home with Dad.

My father's office is in the main building. I take a deep breath before heading inside.

"Tristian, sweetie." My father's secretary shimmies from behind her desk to hug me. She smells like roses and cough drops. Milly has been Dad's assistant since I was a kid. Silver streaks her dark hair, but her gray eyes still shine.

"How are you, Milly? How're the kids?" When Dad was too busy for me, Milly let me sit and color at her desk.

"Same as ever. My hip acts up in the rain. The kids are good. James is in culinary school in Tuscany. Lord knows, he didn't get the cooking gene from me." I fight the rush of jealousy when I hear this. "And Reed had a second baby. Do you want to see a picture?"

"Of course."

I know she's stalling when she's shown me all of those and moves on to pictures from earlier this year, when she took the family on a trip to Bora Bora.

"Is Dad in?" I can't sit here all day.

She hesitates before nodding. "Go on in. I'll hold his calls." I give her another hug before knocking on my father's door.

"What?"

"Hey, Dad." I step into the dark office, closing the door behind me, even though my legs scream at me to run the opposite way.

Despite the sunny day, Dad has the desk lamp on, a concentrated glow over a stack of paperwork. Heavy curtains obscuring the large windows add to the dungeon aesthetic.

"Tristian." He links his fingers together over a protruding belly. He's the kind of man who spent his life in decent shape, but it's slowly dripping away. A gold watch shines on his wrist, and a bronze nameplate on the desk reads "Bartholomew Walsh." The only objects in this whole place still shining like new.

Behind him, hung on the wall between two windows, is a painting of my family—except it's not. I always thought it was the family he wished he had. They painted us as the Carpathia royal family, in our capes and crowns, with swords valiantly at our sides.

As a kid, I thought we were royalty, the way my dad talked. I idolized him and couldn't wait to grow up and be like him. But as each year passed, I realized what that truly meant. He was a man consumed by a dream—an image he'd do anything to keep.

"I came to make sure Ivor told you about our arrangement." I force myself to look him directly in the eyes, to maintain focus. I can't let nostalgia get the better of me. It's a slippery slope that'll drag me in and make me believe all kinds of fantasies.

"He said you'll set up an internship for me to get college credit. So at least I can get *something* real out of this summer." The chair in front of the desk stares me down, but I choose to stand, hoping it gives me authority. Because in this room I have always been that little boy trailing behind his father.

"Yes, Ivor said you'd do something with that. But that will have to come second to your role as Prince Winthrop."

Of course, he thinks prince duty is more important than developing a skill to help me get out of here. A force builds behind my eyes, a muscle twitching underneath it as my heart rate increases. "Dad, I wasn't even supposed to be here. Why didn't you—"

"Tristian"—he stands, his full height not yet altered by age—"this park is your legacy. I know education was always important to your mother, but you belong here. Your vacation can wait."

I grit my teeth, hands curled into fists to keep the vibrating anger at bay. "It wasn't a vacation." Heat rises in my cheeks, the fury this man brings out in me boiling to the surface. "I was going to study places and people. Let me do the things I want with my life." He got to make his dream a reality; why can't my dreams hold the same weight?

"Tristian, you're a prince, heir to all of this." His arms swing wide. "I spent my life building Fairytale Gardens for you and your brothers."

"I know you did, Dad, but this is your dream."

"Your family should be your dream. Your poor mother—rest her soul—she only ever wanted her boys to stay together."

"Don't," I say, but it's barely a whisper. I swear I smell a whiff of Mom's perfume like she just left the room.

"You can't run away from your legacy."

"Dad, I—"

"I have a meeting." His hand on my shoulder steers me through the door. "I'll see you at dinner." He closes it behind me. I shake my hands to expel the residual agitation, and release a heavy sigh. Milly gives me a tight smile as I head downstairs. When I pass the break room, Aldrich steps out.

"Tristian!" He envelops me in a hug.

I rub my little brother's messy blond curls, and he elbows me in the ribs. "Did you see my new costume?" Aldrich fixes his hair, his prince costume bunched in the sleeves.

Despite my anger with my father, and my disillusionment with Fairytale Gardens, it's nice to see Aldrich excited. "Fits like a glove. Welcome to the prince club." I try to keep my voice light. I don't want to rain on his parade just because I'm stuck in a downpour.

He shrugs. "I can't wait to sword fight at Knight School." His unabashed grin actually makes me forget I'm pissed at this place.

"Well, when you lose to Garrick or Ivor, we can have a ride-off to commiserate. Sound good?"

His face lights up. "You sure you can handle it? Last time you nearly puked all over a fairy."

"Stomach of steel, little brother."

We've been doing ride-offs since we were kids. Who doesn't love barreling around on a coaster until you puke your guts out?

Aldrich leaves to change, and I stand in the hallway of my childhood, surrounded by relics of a life I don't know where to fit into anymore.

6

IMOGEN

I went to the first aid.

Not because the prince commanded me to. Because blood threatened to stain my sandals, and it's almost impossible to clean blood off leather. My brief time at the shoe store taught me this life lesson. They bandaged me up and I'm as good as new.

Logically, I know there's no reason Tristian Walsh should remember me. But my stung pride didn't get the logic memo. He's crossed my mind so many times over the years, I'm a little ticked he doesn't at least vaguely recall our moment. Too bad the impression I made today is unlikely to be one he'll ever forget. Me, sprawled on the ground as blood gushed from my leg . . . it's not how I expected a meeting with him to go. Not in all the wildest fantasies I created.

And oh boy, were there plenty to go around after each summer.

But to make things easier on me, I'll just steer clear of him. Tristian Walsh and his face will not be a problem.

I mingle among people streaming in for the welcome dinner. The smell of roasted meat and potatoes fills the air as I get closer to the break room. My stomach grumbles with the anticipation of food, but I take my time examining the pictures and posters from over the years plastered on the wall. Companies love to brag about their good deeds; I hope to find something linked to the charities they've donated to in the past. Divya will snoop on her end, but I'm on location for hard evidence.

Leaving the food and laughter in the break room, I head up one level. Photos of costumes and old rides line these halls. Unhelpful. I go up another flight.

This one is more fruitful. I find a display on the wall dedicated to the organizations Fairytale Gardens has worked with. My breath quickens as my adrenaline kicks in. I get why Divya loves investigative reporting.

It's exhilarating.

Many of these charities I've heard of, so I know they're real. I snap a few pictures to cover my bases and send them to Divya. The last section is smaller, partially obscured by a desk. I'm halfway behind it when a woman exits the door beside me and moves to sit at the desk.

I jump with a yelp, phone slipping from my grip, but I catch it before it hits the floor.

"Did you need help, dear?" The white woman has black, silver-streaked hair and a kind expression. She looks vaguely familiar. I think she was there in my core Tristian memory.

Eww. I'm not calling it that.

I lick my dry lips to keep my words from getting stuck. "Oh, no—I'm fine." I squeeze my phone. The broken tote bag hangs off my shoulder by one strap.

"The welcome dinner is downstairs."

"I was headed there, but got distracted when I saw all the great work the company has done with charities over the years," I say with awe, like I just discovered this fact.

The woman's gray eyes drift over the display, sadly too far away for me to get a decent look. "I believe the family is quite proud of it."

"Milly"—I read the word on the nameplate—"can someone recommend a charity to donate to? I'm really passionate about saving the rainforest. Could you direct me who to talk to?" I put on my best casual smile.

"All the charities go through Mr. Walsh." She nods to the door she exited from.

Barth Walsh. *Huh.*

Guess Divya will take down a big fish. "Cool, so—"

The phone on her desk rings. "I'm sorry, dear, I need to see to this."

I take a last look at Barth Walsh's door before retreating downstairs. It's a start, at least.

I'm heading back down to the break room when a high-pitched laugh floats up the stairs. I pause, eyeing the landing below me. A girl with dark curls and tanned skin is running her hand up a familiar guy's arm. He leans against the wall, expression inscrutable.

"Tristian"—the girl brushes her fingers over his bicep—"don't think I will let you sulk all summer." After lingering a few seconds longer, she retracts her hand and runs her fingers through her shiny hair before disappearing.

Aliana.

We go to the same school and she never stops talking about

Fairytale Gardens and her ties to the family. We aren't friends, but word travels, and it's well known that she and Tristian were *the* couple for a few summers. Despite all the girls wanting Tristian, Aliana won him. Not that there'd been any real competition. My cousin goes to the same school as the Walshes and he told me there was one girl Tristian supposedly liked, but then an anonymous video went viral of her puking all over herself and she never spoke to Tristian again. Despite rumors, Aliana denied she was responsible, but the implied threat was enough to stop anyone else from vying for Tristian's attention.

Which makes me dislike and fear Aliana, despite having little interaction with her.

I attempt to backtrack, but I trip and have to catch myself on the stair railing, my bag banging against the wall with a thud. Tristian's head turns my way. Not wanting to be caught eavesdropping, I square my shoulders and head down like that was my intention all along.

Nothing to see here. Move along.

I gift him a bright smile as I walk into dinner, releasing my breath once I'm on the other side of the break room.

Opening the summer season with a welcome dinner for all the Fairytalers is a tradition, we were told. FTG operates from April through October on weekends, but from the beginning of June through August they open every day. It's their busiest time of year, when most of the staff work, so they start it with a party. Not all Fairytalers can join, since the park is open, but the room is already packed. The chairs have been moved since the orientation, to be replaced with food buffets and communal dining tables.

I take a plate, trailing behind a guy dressed as an elf, and fill it. Because I spent my time in first aid and snooping upstairs, most seats are filled when I've loaded my dinner. And by most I mean all. I scan the room, pressure building against my rib as I grip the plate I overfilled.

"You look lost." Michael from orientation steps beside me, twirling a soda bottle.

"That's just how my face looks."

"Don't worry. I got you." He points to a table near the front. "Aliana has a spot open by her." She holds court at a table with a brown-haired white girl and two boys I recognize as Walshes.

"I'd rather eat in the bathrooms next to Ogre Escape." And that roller coaster has two nausea-inducing upside-down loops.

Michael glances over. "What?"

"Nothing. Thanks." *I'm a fully capable human. I can interact with people who I don't care for with ease.* I repeat this mantra to myself as I weave through the compact space of chairs and bodies, activating my most pleasant smile as I reach the table, my new colleagues quiet as I stand behind the empty seat.

"May I?" I nudge it with my knee.

"We were"—Aliana starts, but the older Walsh, with bright blond hair, interrupts her.

"By all means." He pushes the chair out with his foot.

"Thanks." I slide into the seat, grabbing a chicken leg to give my hands purpose. "You're Garrick, right?" I remember the lopsided smile. He's a Walsh and Tristian's twin. It's not weird I know this—everyone who comes to the park can read the plaque in the gift shop talking about the Walsh family.

"One and only. Have we met? Because I'm certain I'd remember."

Flirty charmer? *This I can handle.*

It almost distracts me from Aliana's staredown across the table, her heart-shaped glossy lips pursed in a frown.

"I'm Imogen."

Garrick puts out a hand, and I shake it with the one not covered in chicken leg. "This is Aldrich, my little brother." He points to the other blond, holding a slice of watermelon. "Raina and Aliana."

I focus on eating my food while they chat about park gossip. I add in a comment here and there to lessen the awkwardness of my sudden arrival into their group.

When I'm nearly done, and ready to bolt, I catch Aliana staring at me. "Do we go to school together?" she asks.

"Uh, yeah, actually." Plot twist: the person I did not expect to know me, does, and Tristian—who I hoped might remember me—is totally clueless.

"Weird." She leaves that odd comment hanging in the air as her eyes flick over my shoulder, perking up. "Tristian, I saved you a spot, but"—she waves at me—"do you know . . . sorry, what's your name again?"

"Imogen," Tristian says before I can respond. A spike of pleasure runs over me at the frown Aliana gives him. "And that's all right. I wasn't planning on staying."

"Sit down." Garrick stands, yanking Tristian into the chair beside me that he vacates before he grabs an empty stool for himself.

"We were just saying how happy we are you decided to stay." Aliana leans forward.

"Thanks." Tristian squirms, his forearm brushing against mine.

Be cool, Imogen. He's just a person. A very hot, princely person, but a person all the same.

"Stay?" I let my attention land fully on him.

A furrowed brow clouds his blue eyes. "Yeah, I was supposed to—it doesn't matter." I assumed he never went anywhere else. That he always just paraded around, playing a character, just like I've seen him do every summer the last few years.

"Why would you leave? This place is magical."

He sighs, fingers drumming on the table. "I doubt you'd understand."

I catch Aliana's lips twitch up from my peripheral, and my body tenses on instinct, expecting a fight, but it doesn't come.

"I can't believe this is my last summer," she muses, eyes coasting over the room.

"Last summer?" Tristian and I say at the same time.

Aliana's face flickers with amusement. "I know everyone is really busted up about it."

My fingers dig into my thigh, a burst of pain radiating from my cut. "Where are you going?" I force away any wobble trying to escape when I speak, my voice unnaturally low as I attempt to sound cool and at ease in a group I idolized from afar.

"I'm going to work at my dad's dental office."

"Really?" Tristian's jaw is tight, and I recognize the tone of jealousy I've heard in my own words before.

But what would he have to be jealous about? He gets to be a freaking prince at the best place in the world. I cannot imagine a better future being planned out for you.

"You know my dad is a dentist. The Walshes aren't the only ones with a legacy."

Tristian responds by picking at a hole in the tabletop. I might not have a doctorate or castle to live up to, but I get wanting to please your parents.

"What about you . . . Imogen? Is this a layover before bigger things?" Aliana's tone is innocent, but my gut twists regardless. She's so perfect it makes me squirm.

"Well . . ." I glance to the exit, calculating the time it'd take me to get to the bus stop and pretend this never happened.

"Can I get everyone's attention, please," Michael says, saving me from answering. "Let me introduce our fearless leader and founder, Bartholomew Walsh." The room fills with applause as a white man in his late fifties comes in from the hall, along with another brown-haired, bearded man.

Barth smiles, but his hands clench into fists at his sides. "Welcome, Fairytalers. It's always a pleasure to see bright new faces at the start of the summer. I hope you enjoy your time with us and that you find a little magic to take with you." The cadence of his voice tells me he's recited this speech many times. Any meaning it may have held has long since slipped away.

"For the newcomers, let me introduce my sons." He motions to my table for the boys to join him. "Ivor"—he points to the tall, bearded man who came in with him—"Garrick, Tristian, and lastly, my youngest, Aldrich."

They wave and smile. Tristian is the only one whose smile is made of glass. I'm getting the feeling I might have pegged Tristian wrong all these years.

"Family is the heart of this park." Barth exchanges looks with his sons. "And we welcome you into ours. Thank you." He leaves before the applause stops.

Chairs scrape the floor as people exit the break room. I jump up, using the chaos to escape to the apartment I've yet to see.

"You found the first aid." Tristian's voice stops me before I can make a clean break.

"Is that your way of telling me you're checking me out?" I rest my hand on my hip, to disguise the fact I was about to hide in my room and make every effort to never cross paths with him or anyone from that table again.

A girl in fox makeup walks behind us, forcing us closer together. "I promise you, it was all in the name of health and safety."

Focus, Imogen. "A true gentleman. I'm sure you'll have no trouble fitting back into those princely shoes."

He shoves his hands into his pockets with a low growl.

"Why do you do that?" I don't know why I'm still here. My escape is moments away; I should seize it.

"Do what?" His woodsy smell is mixed with chocolate now.

"Make an mm-humpf"—I mimic his grunt—"when anything about being a prince is mentioned."

"Reflex."

"Okay, sure, buddy, whatever. A piece of advice, maybe you should keep the bah humbug vibe to yourself. Kinda brings down the magic."

His laugh is humorless. "I know your type." He pushes toward me, tapping the storybook poking out of my broken bag. "You hold on to fairytales long past their expiration date."

I ignore the dig, prodding my finger into his chest. "And I know your type. Boring and grumpy. Only reads highbrow literary novels and watches war documentaries. Heaven forbid you let yourself have an imagination." I don't break his gaze.

"You better go. Might be a fairy godmother outside poised to grant your wish." He blinks and turns away.

I flip my hair over my shoulder with a grin. "Great, if you sprout warts and a tail, we'll know it worked."

The balmy evening air hits my already flushed cheeks when I step outside. *What a jerk.* He works in a theme park literally set around a magical story; you'd think he'd have a bit more whimsy about him. He might look like Prince Charming, but if he keeps opening his mouth, he'll ruin even that.

I push Tristian Walsh to the back of my brain as I drag my suitcase to my assigned apartment. All my focus needs to be on Divya's story. Tomorrow is a new day. I'll start fresh with a clear head. The bag gets stuck on a few steps—a wheel broke off last year and I never got a new one—and when I finally arrive at the apartment on the second floor, the lock requires a few jiggles but I get it open. The place smells like mold and mothballs, with a hint of—I want to say Cheetos. The interior is decorated with white walls in an open living room/dining room/kitchen combo—small but cozy—with two bedrooms in the rear and a shared bathroom. The furniture is a dusty rose, with faded flowers printed across it.

I turn on the AC before I examine the cramped bathroom. Its blue tiles are the height of eighties fashion, but at least it's clean. Both empty bedrooms look the same, so I grab the one with the green theme, removing clothes from my suitcase and tossing them into the dresser. I know there's a pool party tonight. If Divya were here, she'd tell me to stay home and rest for my first day tomorrow. But she isn't, and besides, it's research—scoping out the suspects.

"Why does it smell like pennies and nachos in here?"

I freeze, my swimsuit dangling from my hand when I hear the voice in the living room.

No, please god, no.

I pop my head out of the bedroom and look at my new roommate.

Aliana.

7

TRISTIAN

"You can't tell me you wouldn't have missed this if you left?" Aldrich plops onto the lounge chair next to mine, water droplets spraying from his wet hair. The music pumps loud, Aldrich's voice lost in the beat.

The welcome dinner is Dad's official park business, but the pool party is the real celebration. I used to count down the days until it arrived.

The park closed about thirty minutes ago, and the last of the Fairytalers trickle in as Aldrich rambles on. Even though the sun has set, today's record heat remains. The terra-cotta-colored cement is warm, and fake tropical trees and bushes surround the water. If you squint, they almost hide the apartments, and you can pretend you're on vacation.

Water splashes in voluminous waves off the slide as people speed down it. The pool is compact but large enough to allow rowdy Fairytalers to let off steam. Warmth spreads across my chest as I rest a hand behind my head and sip my drink, the familiar scene playing out before me. "Yeah, this I would've missed. How was your first day as a prince?"

The signature Aldrich smile that reminds me so much of

Mom blasts across his face. "Dude, it's the freaking best job in the park." The grin droops slightly. "But there were a few guys from school who were giving me crap for the crown."

I clap his shoulder. "If anyone comes at you, find me or Garrick. We'll make sure it doesn't happen again. We've always got your back."

"Thanks, T." The smile returns and I think my big brother status is still intact.

Two guys play chicken in the pool; the larger one yanks the skinny kid, who didn't stand a chance, into the water. That's usually me and Garrick. I went to work on more than one occasion with a bruise sustained in off-hour activities.

A heaviness replaces the warmth as the picture clears. I wanted away from this. I can't allow nostalgia to take me back to my place in the Walsh line, and away from the future I'm trying to carve out for myself.

I take a longer swig of my drink.

Garrick leans against my chair, tipping it back. My feet hit the ground. He pushes Aldrich over so he can sit, Tyrone taking the chair opposite. Tyrone hasn't worked here, but he never misses a pool party.

Garrick grins, scanning the pool with eagle-sharp eyes. "I was flirting with a fairy during my meet-and-greet, and I was feeling a vibe. Do you see her?"

Tyrone chuckles. "Dude, you always think you feel a vibe."

Garrick slings an arm around Aldrich's shoulders. "Look at my face. It's a curse, honestly."

"That's what I think whenever I look at you, too." My drink catches in my throat as I bust out laughing.

"*Tristian*," Garrick yells as I spit soda on him. "Don't hate just because I got this face and you're stuck with that one."

I shake my head, fighting my grin. I hate letting Garrick know he's funny too often. We have to keep that ego in check. Across the way, I spot Imogen. My eyes snag on the bandage before I snap them back up. At least she took my advice.

"I see you have a summer romance in mind, too." Garrick's eyebrows lift.

"What?" My drink sloshes on my chest as I jerk upright.

"The redhead from dinner—Imogen. She seems cool. Go for it. Because if you don't, I might."

I push down the sudden urge to shove Garrick into the pool.

Resting my hand behind my head, I peer at the sky, taking steady, deep breaths of the chlorinated air. "I'm not looking for anything this summer other than making it through." That sounded convincing, right?

Garrick shakes his head. "Just because you returned to your own personal hell doesn't mean you have to pout about it."

"I'm not pouting." I rearrange my face into a neutral look and loosen the vise grip on my drink. "I just won't be pursuing any summer romances. They never work out."

"Who said anything about working out? This isn't about true love and marriage. We'll leave that to Ivor. This"—he grabs my head to force my gaze across the pool—"is about fun. You do remember fun, don't you?"

I shove his hands away.

He continues unfazed. "Besides, as older brothers it is our responsibility to teach Aldrich."

"Run while you can," I faux-whisper to Aldrich, who smirks. "I'm getting in the pool."

The warm water is moderately cooler than the air outside. I dive and miss a body by an inch. Here it's difficult for people to perceive me any other way than just another Walsh cog in the machine. Anonymity was part of the appeal of leaving this summer and getting lost in the history of the world. I could be anybody I wanted or nobody at all.

I push my hair back, breaking the surface. The slide tempts me, but they take it three people at a time—an accident waiting to happen. I debate telling them off, but that's Ivor's job. He's the responsible one, the authority. Garrick's the fun one, the loose cannon; Aldrich, the little brother, kind to a fault. What does that leave for me?

Long legs dangling off the side of the pool snag my attention. I follow the smooth lines to a bright blue bikini, and Imogen's smiling face. She gives me a quick salute.

My body tells me to swim closer as my brain throws up a stop sign. But like everything at FTG, the choice is made for me as waves push me closer.

Her red hair is in a half ponytail, delicate strands framing her face. "Did you get confused?" she calls over the buzz of activity.

I glide through the water until I bump into her leg. "What?" I lean one elbow against the pool edge. My gaze wanders over the spatter of freckles across her nose. I didn't notice them earlier. Clearing my throat, I try again. "What?"

A glint twinkles in her eyes. I grind my fist into the rough cement, biting a groan.

"I assumed you got lost and wound up here by mistake." She waves at the people. "This is a party—fun. You didn't give off the fun vibe earlier."

The mass of bodies pushes me closer to her, my hand grazing her thigh as I attempt to keep upright. I jerk away, embarrassment rushing over my cheeks.

Tristian, get it together.

"Why aren't you in the pool?" I talk to occupy my brainpower.

She lifts her leg to point at the cut.

"Does it hurt?" I might hate my princely facade, but it was sort of nice to play the dashing hero in real life.

"Not really."

The water ripples as I flick my fingers over the surface. "I'm sorry."

"What?" Her eyes narrow in confusion.

Licking my lips, I rotate to face her, angled so she can hear me over the party. "I'm sorry."

She leans on her legs to close the gap between us. "About?" She draws out the short word.

I run a hand across my forehead. "You're going to make me say it?"

"You started the conversation." Her nails tap along the cement.

A groan escapes me. "I was a jerk earlier. I'm—it's been a long day." Week, but I don't want to get into specifics.

"Everyone is allowed a free pass—once."

I nod, grateful for her grace. It's a nice quality. My eyes drift to my brothers and Tyrone, who have started a limbo game.

When I look back, I catch Imogen checking me out before she quickly glances away.

"Imogen!" Aliana's voice snaps me back to reality as her donut floaty hits me in the side. "Oh, sorry, love." She yanks down her sunglasses to study us.

A muscle twitches in Imogen's tight jaw. "Did you need something?" Leaning on her hands, she kicks water, narrowly missing Aliana's face.

Aliana's eyes follow the line of my arm to where it rests next to Imogen. "I call dibs on the shower first."

"It's all yours." Imogen's curled toes press into the wall.

"Right. Tristian"—Aliana's attention shifts to me—"want to go down the slide?"

"I'm good." The last situation I want to be in is anywhere with Aliana that might give her, or anyone else, the wrong idea. There are enough rumors about us without adding more fuel to the fire.

Her fingers curl around the handholds on the floaty, tongue flicking across her teeth before she purses her lips. I've never had a problem with Aliana, she was more than pleasant to me, but she likes to push boundaries to see what she can get away with.

"Fine. I'll see you tomorrow." She gives us one last examination before floating away.

"What was that about?" I ask.

Imogen's mouth squeezes into a straight white line. "That"—she presses two fingers into her temple—"would be my new roommate."

A laugh bubbles in my throat. "No!"

"Yes! Just my luck. But *perfect princess* Doctor Barbie will not get me down." Hair falls onto her face as she shakes her head. A bright smile lights up her features.

Why is she so happy? I've seen her twice before this, and both times were disasters, yet she's smiling. Maybe she could show me what that's like. Since Mom died . . . No, I can't do that here.

I open my mouth to keep the conversation going, but a scream from the slide stops me from continuing. A group lugs a person from the pool. I jump out of the water and fight past stunned people frozen in place as I jog over.

"What happened?" My mind laser-focuses on Raina on the ground. She's been playing the role of Princess Arden—the most important character in the Fairytale Gardens story—since last year. Her face contorts in pain as she grips her ankle with both hands.

"Ah," she hisses as I try to examine it. "I twisted it. I—ah, no, don't touch it." She bats me away when I put my hand on it.

A crowd gathers as everyone tries to sneak a peek. "You need to see a doctor. It's already swelling." I help her stand, and her two friends grab under her arms, taking her away toward the apartments.

I spin around to Imogen, watching me, mouth slightly open.

"What?" I didn't realize she'd followed.

She frowns. "You're good in a crisis."

Flashes ping through my vision to when we found out my mom was sick. How Ivor, the calm one, always in control, completely broke down. And Garrick did what Garrick does best: ignored responsibility like the plague. While I assumed the big brother role.

Chills run over my wet skin as my throat tightens. "You never know how strong you are until you have to be." I grab a towel from the stack by the pool and hand one to her.

"Thanks." She bites her lip. "Tristian—"

"I'll see you around, Imogen." I trudge away before I let my traitorous brain think about her any further. I hope I don't see her again. I'm supposed to hate being stuck here. If I enjoy myself, Dad wins.

"Tristian, are you—Tristian . . ." I ignore Garrick's protest as I head to the apartment.

8

IMOGEN

The day starts bright and early for me at nine.

I left the pool last night after Tristian's hero moment so I could get back before Aliana and hide in my room. I avoided her, texting Divya until I fell asleep. But I can't dodge her for the whole summer, so I need to cowgirl up and get over it.

Aliana left around six a.m. She must be one of those baffling morning people who find the strength to exercise each day. But now she's in the kitchen, drinking coffee.

"Morning." I keep my voice light as I step around her to grab a mug from the cabinet.

"It's really strong."

"What?" My hand tightens on the cup.

"The coffee." She points to the machine behind me. "The stronger, the better."

Unsurprising.

I prefer my coffee blond, with whipped cream and caramel, but I won't admit that. "Cool. Strong is great." I pour the dark liquid into the white mug.

"And we don't have any cream or sugar. I like it black." She clicks her nails against the counter, a challenge in her unwavering stare.

"It's fate we're roommates because that's how I take mine, too." I grin, taking a large gulp. Her eyes never leave my face.

Her coffee preference shouldn't irk me so much, but the insecure girl in the back of my brain can't get past the fact that she dated my crush, and that she always looks like she just walked off a photo shoot. The embodiment of the unattainable I strive for but never quite reach.

There's a part of me that wants to be her friend. I'm all alone here and could use an ally, but I'm not too proud to admit I'm intimidated by her. Honestly, Aliana is just way too cool for me. In fairness, Divya is also way too cool for me, but I've known her so long she's stuck with me now.

"Is that so?" A sculpted eyebrow lifts in doubt.

I swallow a second time, in hopes my saliva will dilute the bitter brew. "Great." I drink another sip for good measure. "You can make it every day." I suppress a cough.

She deposits her mug in the sink. "Not likely." Plucking her bag from the couch, she walks out the door without another word.

Once her footsteps fade away, I check the cupboards and fridge for cream and sugar, but they're empty. Pouring coffee down the drain is a terrible way to start the day, but I can't drink this.

I didn't bring any food, so I need to grab breakfast from the break room before my shift. According to the clock, I'm already due in the costume department, but arriving a few minutes late will be fine. I'll say I got lost.

A text from Divya comes through as I walk to the main building ten minutes later.

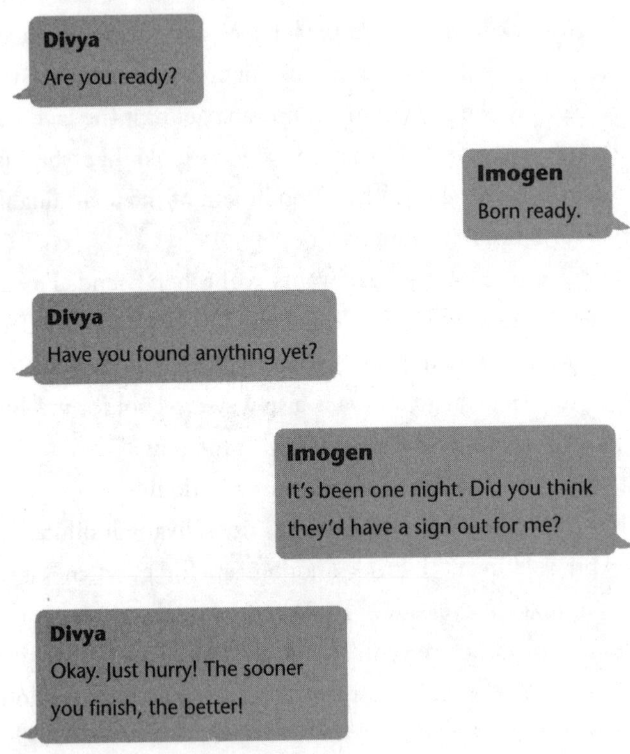

Better for who? The minute I get Divya's information and leave, I'm back to applying for jobs I hate to please my parents. I owe Divya for a lot over the years, so I know I can't stall forever, but a few days won't hurt anyone.

I peel the banana I got from the break room as I head to the second floor to pick up my uniform. Harold Yoo is in charge of the costume department. He has thinning gray hair and the bushiest eyebrows I've ever seen in person.

"What was your name again?" he asks for the fourth time.

I twist strands of hair through my anxious fingers. "Imogen Rogers."

The room is a mix of burnt smells from the iron accented with fresh laundry detergent. Clothing racks line all the walls, colorful fabrics drape over the two tables, and a sewing machine sits in the corner. Cardboard boxes hide the one window in the back.

Three floor-length mirrors rest in a half-hexagon shape on a platform next to Harold's desk. His puzzled expression reflects in them. "Mm-hmm." He spins his chair to type into the computer. "You need to go to Maria's office on the third floor."

I pinch the skin at the base of my throat. "Maria?"

"She's in charge of casting. Your assignment must have a problem."

Pressure pushes at my ribs, my mouth dry as a desert. *Oh, crap, have they already figured out I'm undercover?*

"OK, thanks." My calm expires in the hallway. I wipe away the sweat mustache, flattening my hands on the wall at the bottom of the stairs. If I get fired, it'll be no different than the last string of jobs. I'm not worried. But if I screw up Divya's story on Day One, I'll never live that down.

Imogen, you've negotiated your way out of worse situations. I continue my internal pep talk as I jog up the stairs. Milly smiles from her desk as I pass, following the signs to Maria Nolan's office.

I knock on the door with her name.

"Imogen?" A tall white woman in her early fifties steps out a moment later. "Come in." She has flat, solid features, her dark blond hair twisted into a bun. She looks like Aldrich—not a Walsh but perhaps their mother's side.

The office is cramped, with a desk in the center and corkboards featuring different face characters scattered throughout the room. "I'm Maria. This is Yvette Ortiz." She indicates a short Latina woman with bouncy curls, held in place by a black headband and a scrunchie, sitting in front of the cluttered desk. She looks a few years older than me.

"Please, have a seat." I take the chair next to Yvette. Maria sits in the one opposite. "Imogen, I'm sure you're wondering why I called for you." Her smile eases my knotted stomach only slightly.

"A little." My hands squeeze together so tightly they turn white. I force them flat against my legs.

"I know you're supposed to start at the turkey stand today, but we had an accident—Oh, nothing serious," she adds when my eyes widen. "Raina, a princess, broke her ankle last night."

"At the pool?" She nods. Tristian running to the rescue is not a scene I'll soon forget. "Do you need me to make a witness statement? Is she suing?"

"No need. But she's out for the summer. And, in fact, she was our backup princess from last year." Her lip twitches.

"Okay . . ." I frown, not sure where she's going.

Maria's eyes crinkle at the sides when she smiles. "We want you to take her place."

"Take her place?" I glance at Yvette, silently typing on an iPad, then close my eyes, processing the request, before opening them again. "You want me to play a face character?"

"Not just any character." Maria twirls a pen in her hand. "Princess Arden of the Wellspring."

I look between them. *This is a joke.* No way can I be Princess Arden of the Wellspring—the most important character of the FTG story. I can't be the most important part of anything.

"Why me?" My stomach does a backflip as another idea tickles my brain, vibrating through me—a long-held childhood fantasy come to life.

"For one, you're the only person with a background in theater," Yvette says.

I frown, racking my brain for what the heck she's talking about. Then I recall the résumé Divya submitted for me and how she made some *colorful* embellishments—such as saying my role as "featured townsperson number two" in our school play was actually a leading role. I'm an all right actor, but I don't think I'm star material.

But I've never had a job like this before . . . That alone might stave off the familiar itch to run away to greener pastures. And honestly, what girl wouldn't want to be a princess? I always loved to watch the carriages with the characters ride by in their fancy gowns.

Still . . .

"You should find someone else." I stand, the chair wobbling in my haste. As much as the idea thrills me, I'm not here to play a princess. I need to lie low, not put on a ball gown and parade around the park. Slipping away unnoticed after getting the info I need is the whole plan.

"Well, the thing is, your measurements are the closest fit to the costume—we double-checked. We need our princess. No time to search for another. We have a gal that works part-time, but she's only the understudy from last season. Just between us, she doesn't have the drive to do it full-time."

And they think I do?

"I'm sorry, I don't . . ." I taper off as my voice gives out.

"It will only be temporary until we find a new girl," Maria suggests. "Think you can manage that?"

I let out a gust of air. "Okay . . ." My resignation is tinged with excitement. It might be fun to play pretend. "I'll do it." I've rushed into plenty of situations that ended horribly. What's one more?

"Excellent." Maria gets to her feet, followed by Yvette. "We have no time to waste. Yvette, take her to costuming, get her fitted and ready for the stage."

"Wait—I'm going on right now?" Tightness tugs at my chest, my brain yelling *abort*, *abort*!

"Are you familiar with the Fairytale Gardens origin story?"

My eyes dart to Yvette for rescue, but she's oblivious to my panic. "Yes, but—"

"Excellent, then it'll be a walk in the park. Plus, Yvette will be here the whole time for moral support."

I scramble after Maria, who's already out the door. "I need time before I—"

"Dear." She stops me short, and I dig in my heels to keep

upright. "As I said, we don't have a princess and guests come here expecting to meet her."

I force calm into my voice. "You have other characters . . ."

"But only one Arden."

I search out Yvette to garner support, but she is typing on her tablet.

"Imogen . . ." Her voice softens. "Trust me, I've done this for twenty-five years. I've yet to find a princess that didn't fit."

Well, Maria, there's a first time for everything.

9

IMOGEN

The banana and black coffee swirl around my gut as I text Divya in all caps while following Yvette to the costume department. She doesn't respond.

"Don't take this the wrong way," Yvette ponders when we reach the second floor. "But you don't seem happy about this promotion."

"No, I am—I guess. It'll be fun to try something new."

New is my favorite pastime. I consider that an admirable quality, but it's more a detriment to my life than a positive.

"I don't know if I'm cut out for this." I feign intense interest in a wall scuff, so I don't have to meet her eyes. "Especially with zero training."

Yvette grabs a thin booklet from her bag, shoving it in my face. "Not *zero* training. Read this while Harold fits the costume. Besides, cut out for it or not, no one would choose turkey legs over a ball gown."

"If they were starving, they would." I flip through the scant pages. It summarizes Arden's life, and gives facts about her character and answers to commonly asked guest questions.

Harold peers from behind a rack of flouncy dresses. "You're back."

"We need her costumes fitted. She's due onstage in"—Yvette consults her trusty iPad—"an hour." My stomach does another flip.

"She's our new princess?" Harold takes in my crossed arms and stiff smile, frowning.

"I'm as shocked as you." I press my palm to my forehead.

What does a brain aneurysm feel like?

"Give me a minute." He picks up dresses as he wanders toward the back.

I bite my cheek, pulling on my earlobe. I don't get nervous at new jobs. I've had too much practice for them to affect me, but this one is testing my limits.

"Getting the opportunity to play a face character is a big deal. Seize it," Yvette offers.

My problem is I'm not good at important things. It's easier to brush off failure if you know it won't last to begin with.

"How long have you worked here?" I change the subject.

"Four years. I started at the popcorn stand. It took me a year to move into casting. I worked hard." Her chin juts out, eyes daring me to fight her on it.

"I don't doubt it." Yvette doesn't seem the type to take any crap, and I appreciate that in a woman. She seems like just the person I want to get to know. "I'm sure people won't think I earned the crown."

Face characters are the most sought-after jobs. *Cutthroat* is a better way to describe it. They're at the top of the pyramid.

First, they get the best costumes—fancy gowns and shining crowns—no overheating in a furry death trap or an itchy polyester polo. Second, while I'm not one hundred percent sure, I'm guessing they get paid the best. You know, money to keep that face in camera-worthy shape and whatnot. I make a mental note to get the details on the salary. If countless jobs have taught me anything, it's to make sure you're getting what you're worth.

And lastly, you get to brag for the rest of your life that you used to be a freaking royal. It's a legacy that will last forever in guests' pictures of their treasured vacations.

Yvette shrugs. "Who cares what others think? Kill it, and they won't have anything to talk about."

I keep waiting for the moment at a new job when everything clicks. When I know I've found my place. Divya knew right away her career would be perfect—Mom, too. And from the way Dad tells it, he knew pretty quick his was *not*, but he stayed and then got stuck. That pressure suffocates me with every new gig.

This job isn't real. I just have to last long enough for Divya to get her story. And if I'm going to fake it, dressing up as a princess is not a bad way to do it.

Harold and Yvette help me get into costume. While not comfortable per se, at least it's got a faux corset. The soft velvet fabric is dusty pink with braided-rope details around the neckline and along the bottom of the full but contained skirt. The sleeves are puffy and remind me of the cotton candy they sell in the Village Center.

"Not bad," Harold says with a mouth full of pins. "I need to take up the skirt and let it out a bit at the waist and shoulders. Shouldn't be too extensive."

"That's the reason I got the job." Cinderella probably felt like this—only qualified because the glass slipper fit.

Harold helps me step in front of the mirror, and for a moment I'm breathless. If I squint, I look like a princess. It sure beats a foam hot dog and polyester pants.

"Magical, huh?" I jump at Yvette's voice.

"It's heavy." And I don't mean the dress.

"All right, the first rule you should know—" Yvette sits to the side of the mirrored platform while Harold makes alterations. "Don't touch the guests, unless they touch you first."

I nod. "Consent, got it."

"Also, never, *ever* break character. That's a biggie. And trust me, plenty of people will try to get you to slip up."

The costume smells faintly of cotton candy. "What if I—"

"Turn." Harold spins me to face him.

"What if I do break character?" I peek over my shoulder at her.

Her nose wrinkles. "Don't. Maria might appear nice, but she's got a bite."

My swallow catches in my throat. "Yvette . . ."

I can't do this. I set my last uniform on fire. I shouldn't be allowed to wear a crown.

"The most important part is to have fun—the guests are excited to see you."

Excellent—more people I can let down when I fail.

Harold tugs at the bottom of my skirt with a satisfied sigh

twenty minutes later. In that time, I've gone from mild panic to full body sweats with each word of advice.

"Your princess is complete." Harold steps away and helps me off the platform.

Hell no, your princess is not complete. She can barely walk in heels.

"Are we going *now*?" I can't wipe my sweaty palms on my gown, so I flap them in the air like a bird.

"Almost. First, you need a wig and a crown." Yvette glides out the door, and I assume I'm supposed to follow. I move double-time to catch her, lifting my hem so I don't trip. A bloody nose is not a regal accessory. We go down the hall a few doors until we reach hair and makeup.

Yvette knocks on the slightly ajar door. "Hello, Pierre?" The room smells like hair spray and burnt hair.

"Yvette, sweetie, have you brought my new Princess Arden?" A tall man with green hair and a nose ring steps into view. "Aren't you the cutest? Have a seat." His voice is lyrical, like he's about to burst into song with every word. He thrusts me into the black leather chair in front of the mirror. "I'm Pierre, by the way."

"Imogen." I clasp my hands in my lap. Yvette stands in the corner typing on her tablet—it might be her power source. I'll have to check for a cord connecting them.

Pierre throws a smock over my dress. "All right, Imogen. I'll do a quick makeup look—Arden isn't very high maintenance—and get you in the wig. You aren't allergic to anything, are you?"

"No." I tug at the collar of the smock. It's already hard enough to breathe.

He selects different colored foundations to test. "Excellent. A girl a few summers ago didn't tell me she was allergic to red dye. Poor thing's face swelled like a chipmunk."

Pierre's regime is extensive. If this is low maintenance, I'm afraid to see his definition of high maintenance.

"Stage makeup can feel a bit heavy at first, but you'll get used to it after a few days. We have to make sure it's on good. Can't have you resembling a melted candle in everyone's vacation pictures."

It takes about thirty minutes to finish, and if you can get past the thickness, I don't look half bad. I wiggle my nose to ease my itchy face.

Next comes the wig. "Don't worry—we cleaned it."

I wasn't worried until now.

The wig has long, thick, blond curls, with braids pinned around the top, perfect for the tiara to sit on. I hope I have the neck strength to hold it.

"Is it stable?" Pierre asks after he's attached the tiara.

I move my head around. "Seems like it."

That makes one of us.

"Excellent. Drop it off when you're done. It needs to go back on the form." He points to the faceless head on the counter, and I thank him before he shoos us away.

Yvette snatches my phone as I take a picture to send to Divya. "You can pick it up with your clothes after the shift." She slips her tablet into her bag, giving my phone to Harold to store with my stuff as we pass the costume department. "Ready?"

"No." I take a deep breath. This'll be fine—fun, even. I straighten, flipping my curls over my shoulder and regretting the sudden movement in the heavy wig. "But not being ready has never stopped me."

Her face softens for the first time. "Well, you look great."

I force my rapid pulse to slow with a little motivational pep talk. *I got this.* I've started enough jobs to fill several résumés. What's one more?

"Come on, princess. Your prince awaits."

"My prince?" I've been thrown in so many directions this morning that I haven't had time to catch my breath.

"Yup, don't want to keep Tristian waiting."

10

TRISTIAN

Prince Winthrop hangs in front of me, or the shell of him. The costume I'm meant to parade around in all day dangles on the rack. I've sat here for twenty minutes, forcing my coffee to last a little longer so I don't have to put it on. The second I slip into the prince's leathers, don his sword and crown, I'm right back where Dad wants me.

People here can't see Barth Walsh's son doing anything different. Maybe I can't even see it myself.

"Tristian, why are you still here?" Ivor walks in and wastes no time. "Aren't you due at Knight School for the morning performance?"

"Is that a question? Because you know the answer better than I do."

Ivor begins changing into his prince attire. "Put the costume on and go sword fight. You always liked fighting the best."

I dig my nails into the arm of my chair. He's right, I did, and I hate he knows it. "Ivor." I stand. "I thought you said I could do a marketing internship, yet here I am, still playing dress-up."

"We need a Winthrop." Ivor rubs a cloth over his sword

to shine the hilt. "Can't market a prince if we don't have one." He slips the weapon into his belt, then snatches my costume.

He sighs when I continue to glare at him. "Tristian, I didn't know Dad was going to spring this on you. I'm sorry about that, really. I'd have given you a heads-up if I'd known." When I don't respond he adds, "I'll have someone get you into Ted's old office tomorrow. He had all the marketing plans on his computer when he retired."

I stare at the costume before yanking it from him a little too hard. "Fine." I shake the leather jacket off the hanger. "But to get college credit, I need to be an actual intern."

He slaps my back. "Duly noted." He slips his arm through a gold crown before leaving me alone again.

I mutter to myself as I get undressed.

Once in my prince's best, I take a leisurely stroll to Knight School. *Let them start without me.* As much as I'd love to blame Ivor for making me promenade around with a stupid fake crown and bejeweled sword, it isn't totally his fault. I said yes of my own free will. And maybe he didn't know Dad was going to make me a prince again, but he didn't do anything to stop it either.

"About time." Garrick jumps off a barrel when I enter the backstage waiting area. "I thought I'd have to fight myself."

"I'm happy to let you." I roll my shoulders to relieve the growing tension.

Garrick selects two weapons off the rack with a grin. "Come on, T. Show your twin brother if you still got it." He tosses me a sword and saunters onstage.

"Prepare to lose, dear friend." Garrick lashes with his blade to strike mine.

The crowd gasps and I nearly drop my sword. Fighting used to be my favorite part of the job, but as the audience follows my every movement, my steps falter and I become unsure of my next move. My arms tingle and I shake them to get it to stop, but my whole body feels like it's vibrating the longer I'm onstage. The darkness creeps in around the edges of my eyes as my vision tunnels. The familiar feeling of panic only makes me panic more. I can't get a deep breath.

To keep myself from tipping over the cliff, I circle Garrick, the crowd fading from view behind my back. The tightness in my chest releases its hold slightly at the reprieve.

This show feels like it always does, never changing, but that's what makes me panic—what if I can never change either?

"Don't be so sure." I repeat the familiar lines, pushing the fuzzy feeling in my body to the back of my mind. The sword is awkward in my grip.

Garrick lunges, and I let him hit me in the leg. I buckle to the stage with a painful thud. I manage a hit on his arm. We have a few variations to the show, but it stays the same for the most part.

After losing, I scowl. If I do get my hands on the marketing, maybe I'll change Winthrop's fate.

"Well fought." Garrick helps me stand and turns to the dispersing crowd. "I hope you gracious spectators learned a few tricks today. If you wish to fight as well as me, please sign up for the training class within the hour."

With the sales pitch done, we hurry offstage. "One day, I'll win." I secure my weapon on the rack and replace the decorative sword in my sheath.

"Not likely. Kendrick the Kind doesn't lose—at least, not to you."

I glance at the clock. "Crap, I have to go." They booked my onstage performances so tight I'll be lucky if I get a break before dinner.

Short on attendants, I escort myself across Carpathia to Pixie Forest. I ignore the sweat trickling down my back. Prince Winthrop the Worthy used to be easy to play. He smiles brightly, gives hearty laughs, and is always the dashing savior, never selfish.

A few guests follow me as my path intersects with them. I smile, adding a soft cadence to my typically rough voice. "Thank you for gathering on this beautiful day. I shall return later to converse with you." With a final jaunty wave, I head toward the edge of Pixie Forest.

"Prince Winthrop," comes a voice from behind me. "Wish I was a grown dude dressing up all day. Must be nice." A couple of guys my age perched on a fence laugh. The comment isn't directed at me, but it is about me.

My fingers curl around the sword at my side as my jaw tightens. Around me, people take pictures, a mob ready to pounce. I reposition my face into an easy grin, even as an invisible fist squeezes my heart. I walk away, quickening my pace, blood pounding in my ears. When I round the corner onto the walkway between Carpathia and Pixie Forest, I take a second to breathe.

The crowded park looms behind and ahead, but here it's secluded. Most people don't know this shortcut exists, leaving me as alone as one can get in the middle of a theme park.

My costume's leather and heavy fabric seals to my skin in the heat, making me claustrophobic. I rip off my cloak and throw it to the ground with trembling hands. My crown tumbles off as I lean forward, hands pressed into the fence. I kick the wood with my boots.

"Tristian." Yvette comes over.

"Yeah?" I clear my throat of the hoarse word, squaring my shoulders to bring me to full height, before trying again. "Yes?"

"We're late for the carriage ride." She gestures to the oversized gold-and-white carriage around the bend in the trees.

Today's ride will suck more than most because I'm alone. My Princess Arden, Winthrop's bride, is noticeably absent. Raina broke her ankle.

"Lead the way." Seizing my fallen cloak and crown, I follow Yvette, closing my eyes and breathing deeply as I approach. I mentally prepare myself to put on a facade.

"Hey." My eyes pop open at the familiar voice. Sitting in the carriage, dressed in full costume, is Imogen.

"What—uh?" I turn to Yvette.

"Winthrop, meet your new Princess Arden."

11

IMOGEN

The best way to describe my prince is bewildered and pale. Or at least that's how he looks when he sees me in the carriage.

"I'm as shocked as you." I tug at the neckline of my dress.

"I doubt that." He grips the side of the carriage. The horses shake their reins impatiently as we wait for Tristian to load. I, too, would like to get this show on the road.

"Tristian." Yvette steps in. "We need to go."

I scoot over to make room for him. It does little good. The size of the bench would make a love seat blush. He scratches his chin with his thumb. "Ivor put you up to this, right? No, wait, it was Garrick, that jerk."

"This isn't a joke." My wig itches and I try to alleviate it without knocking the whole thing off. When I move it too much, I inhale hair spray. "Will you get in the carriage, please?" I flash a friendly smile for good measure.

He looks to Yvette for confirmation, and she nods. He pushes hair off his forehead, mumbling as he steps inside.

"Careful." I wrench my skirt away before he stands on it with grimy boots. "Harold will kill me if I get this dirty."

Yvette signals to the driver, and we're off.

I reach for the side to steady myself when we lurch forward. My other hand grabs Tristian's, his body stiffening in response. "Sorry." I withdraw it, like I touched a hot stove, curling it in a fist in my lap. "Okay, other than feeling like I'm going to puke, this is kinda fun." I beam at him, which he welcomes with a frown, so I grin wider before he looks away.

The carriage rolls into the streets of Carpathia. The familiar regal music plays as the guests cheer. The smells of turkey legs and candied apples mix with the rustic aroma. This close, Tristian's ever-present woodsy scent—a mix of balsam and cedar—is intoxicating. I'm a princess, he's the prince. I'm allowed at least a little pining for him.

Right?

Then he ruins the fantasy I'm crafting by opening his mouth.

"You're supposed to wave." He twists toward me as his hand glides in a practiced rhythm.

"We're supposed to smile, too, but you're doing more of a grimace." I raise my hand, displaying my brightest grin for the kids screaming our names.

His sword digs deeper into my leg when he moves. "I'm not grimacing." He mimics my smile, but it doesn't reach his eyes. "You caught me off guard, is all."

Licking my lips and swallowing does little to cure my cotton mouth. "You weren't the only one." The carriage makes the first circle by the castle as Glacier Peaks takes shape. "They threw a gown on me, pinned on a wig, and shoved me out the door."

"Don't move your mouth."

My bright grin drops, my mouth opening into an O. "Dang, tell me how you really feel." He's killing my delicately applied princess vibes.

He sighs, annoyance thick on his words, but his face remains pleasant. "I didn't mean it like that. I meant you need to keep a smile on your face, speak with minimal movement from your lips. Watch me." I study the micromovements that don't interrupt his smile.

He has nice lips.

Imogen—eyes on the prize, not the prince.

Forcing my attention on the crowds, I replicate his technique. "I'll practice keeping my mouth shut."

"Arden! Winthrop!" Kids and adults alike yell at us from the side. Their faces light up when I wave. The small action makes their day. I know because I used to be them. I loved seeing the characters come to life in front of my eyes.

The carriage performance takes ten minutes before we circle back to Pixie Forest. Our final act is Winthrop giving Arden a kiss on the cheek. Only, I move for him to kiss me on the left, while he goes for the right, and our lips nearly collide. We narrowly miss what would've been a disaster. And clearly Tristian agrees, because he vaults out of the moving vehicle to prevent it.

After taking a few steps, he rakes a hand through his hair and turns, extending the other while I struggle with my skirt, trying to exit.

"Thank you." I add an extra layer of syrup to my words as I take his hand. "You are the kindest prince in all the realms."

He rolls his eyes and I'm satisfied. "What's next?" Tristian's fingers tighten around the pommel of his sword. Screams drift from Mushroom Spin to our right, infiltrating our haven in a patch of trees.

Yvette clicks on her tablet. "Meet-and-greet in the Pixie Pavilion."

My fun grinds to a halt as a cold sweat stings my skin, despite the heat. "With actual guests?"

Tristian pops his neck. "No, with mannequins."

I peg him with a glare. "You don't need to be a jerk. Some of us are new to this, not lifers." His lips press together as he ignores me.

Yvette mutters in Spanish. "We just need to get through a few of these, and then it's lunch. Can you manage?"

"I'm fine." I pick invisible lint off my dress.

Tristian stares over my shoulder. "Me too."

Neither of us sounds convincing.

"Prince Winthrop the Worthy and Princess Arden," booms an announcer's voice as we walk into our meet-and-greet in the Pixie Pavilion. Little kids wave and squeal our names, jumping as we enter. I try to embody what I remember about Arden, a fairy princess, defender of Carpathia.

A large white fabric tent blankets the area, covered in vines and leaves, flowers and fauna, and fairy lights drip from the sides. The ground is painted like moss-covered rocks, alongside a few real ones. The soft sounds of nature and a babbling brook echo from out-of-sight speakers.

Tension consumes Tristian's body, but he smiles as he extends an arm. I loop mine around, praying I don't fall on my face.

"Greetings, my friends." His voice is light as he gestures to me. "My lady and I are delighted to see all of you this fine day."

My throat tightens, and I know it would come out very un-princess-like if I spoke. I settle for a passable curtsy, my back stiff as a board, so I don't lose my tiara or wig.

For all his huffing, Tristian is a natural. In a sparkling moment, I glimpse the prince I pined for—the one with the kind smile, who stayed with me when I was scared and alone. Which one is real? I remind myself it doesn't matter. He's nothing more than a distraction I can't afford.

He leads me with little effort to the two crown stickers on the ground. Once we settle into our spots, Yvette sends the first guests over.

A child no older than five stumbles as he races to us, hands full with the stuffed doll replicas of our characters. His parents follow behind, phones at the ready to capture the moment.

"Okay, even you have to admit that's adorable," I whisper from the side of my mouth.

He tilts his head toward me, lips grazing my temple. "No, I don't." The prince's facade flies into place as he crouches. "Hello, good sir! Arden, my dear, this figure is the spitting image of you."

The doll has a purple stain on its dress, and its eyes are missing, both redrawn with marker.

"And you, my love." I kneel, too, patting the head of the Winthrop doll the boy clutches to his chest. "Head full of stuffing."

Two can play that game.

Tristian's eyes flash with danger. "Now, *dear*," he begins, as Yvette clears her throat a few feet away. Tristian and I don't break our stare-down.

To my immense satisfaction, he concedes first, smiling at the uncertain boy. "Would you like a picture?"

"What happened to the horse?" The kid grips the dolls tighter as they begin to slip.

"Horse?" Tristian tilts his head.

"The one that helped save the kingdom. Did it get to live with you after?" His round eyes fill with concern.

"Of course it did." I can't let this child leave worried about a horse. "In fact, most nights Trist—" I barely catch myself. "Winthrop sleeps in the stable with him to keep him company."

"Which works out," Tristian butts in. "Because Arden snores terribly. I'd rather sleep with the pigs and the horses." The kid giggles. His parents look confused.

"Even better for me." I stand. "Gives me more time to get to know Sir Kendrick the Kind—"

"Okay," Yvette interjects. "Let's get a picture."

Tristian poses like a cardboard cutout. I link my arm around his last minute and beam at the camera. "Nice to meet you." I wave wildly as they walk away.

"You can't do that." Tristian angles toward me to hide us from the crowd.

"Do what?" I smile, raising my eyebrows innocently. "I was playing along."

"By saying you wanted to hook up with Garrick." His foot drums at a steady pace, his annoyance requiring an outlet.

I tap my finger against my lips. "I didn't say those words. Maybe you just heard what you wanted." I shrug and push him away as a new group approaches.

Luckily, the next few guests keep it short and sweet. They pose for the photo op and move along. The little kids are my favorite, with their unfiltered excitement as they sprint to us and throw their little arms around our legs, embracing us in a hug so pure I nearly burst into tears the first time it happens.

"Can you say it?" Two girls stand before us, a few years younger than we are. They blush head to toe as they fawn over Tristian.

"What is it you wish me to recite?" Tristian's smile is unbelievably fake. I don't know how he doesn't fall face-first from the plaster it must take to keep it attached.

"The vows!" they squeal. I cringe at the high pitch. "They're like the most romantic thing we've ever heard."

Tristian's smile suddenly becomes real. "Ah, yes, *the* vows. Arden, won't you do me the honor?" He runs a hand under my chin, chills covering my body. "I always love hearing them from your precious lips."

I twist fake hair around my finger as I bite my cheek. "Vows?"

"Our wedding vows, of course. I know you remember them by heart." The smirk on Tristian's face might have been handsome, if I didn't want to throw a pie at it.

But I won't let him see me sweat. "Of course I remember them. How could I forget?"

I one hundred percent do not remember Arden and Winthrop's vows.

Tristian motions to the girls. "Don't leave us waiting."

Ugh.

What do people who love each other say at their wedding? "They started . . . uh . . . like so . . ." I shoot a glance at Yvette, but she's deep in conversation with a couple in line.

Tristian leans in, a hand behind his ear. "Sorry, love, I can't hear you. Do speak up."

Sweat builds on the base of my spine, and my thick stage makeup is about to slide off.

"You know." I spin to the girls, my eyes bright. "I have the best idea. Would you please say them for us? I would so love to hear them from the other side." I grab Tristian's arm with both hands, digging my nails into the leather.

The girls hesitate at first but give in and recite them for us. I clap loudly when it sounds like they're done.

"Clever." Tristian pries my hand from his arm as the girls leave.

I mimic him, tracing my finger under his chin. "You're going to have to do better than that." A muscle ticks in his cheek, and I swear he fights a smile.

The end of our thirty-minute meet-and-greet approaches with hardly any incident—other than my lack of knowledge about fairy spells and Tristian calling one of his brothers by their real name. The final guests are a couple in their early twenties.

"My girlfriend's a huge fan," the guy says to me. "Right, Marilyn?" She smiles and shakes my hand. "So, I thought this would be perfect."

"Oh no." Tristian covers his mouth, teeth cutting into his bottom lip.

The guy drops to one knee and removes a box from his pocket.

"Oh." I clasp my hands over my chest in the excited way Arden would.

"Marilyn, I know we've only been dating three weeks." Tristian and I exchange a glance. "But, will you marry me?"

Marilyn freezes, eyes wide—an understandable response—and says . . . nothing. The crowd around us watches intensely.

"Perhaps she's cursed," I suggest. "Her voice removed."

Tristian catches on with a vigorous nod. "A curse indeed. You should seek help from the fairies." Neither of them moves.

"Marilyn?" The guy attempts to put the ring on her shaking hand.

"I—I don't want to marry you." Marilyn looks at me like I should agree with her—which I do, but Arden wouldn't tell her to run away.

"I do believe you have your answer." I try my best to keep a pleasant expression. I'm Arden right now, but sorry, I'm with Marilyn.

"True love isn't a force to take lightly," Tristian chimes in. "It does not always appear at first sight. Perhaps you should take more time before you embark on this quest." He pats the guy on the back as he helps him stand.

"Is this because of Dave?" The guy doesn't move, eyes narrowed as he accuses Marilyn.

"Dave, my boss? What would this have to do with him?"

"You work late." The tips of his ears tinge bright red. "You two are probably having an affair."

Omg.

"Okay." Tristian tries to intervene by stepping between the

couple. "Perhaps you'd like to take this conversation somewhere private?"

"Screw you, prince boy." He shoves at Tristian's chest, but Tristian remains in place, as sturdy as the castle behind us. "This is between my girlfriend and me."

"I don't think she's your girlfriend anymore." *I can't help myself.* The dude needs to hit the road.

"I suggest you leave." Tristian remains relaxed, but rests a hand on his sword. Like he'd fight a guest. Although I wouldn't mind a demonstration of his sword work.

"News flash, bro. This isn't a real kingdom. You can't order me around."

Tristian leans down, voice low. "No, but my family owns the theme park, and I can have you hauled out if that's the way you want to leave."

The guy rams the ring box into his pocket, then scratches his neck as he gives Tristian a once-over. He looks like he's about to leave, but on second thought, twirls around, cocks his arm, and punches Tristian in the jaw. Marilyn, Yvette, and I gasp collectively, along with the rest of the crowd.

"Security!" Yvette yells into her walkie.

"Some prince." The guy spits on the ground.

Tristian touches his jaw gingerly. "Screw it." He pulls his arm back, but I grab his fist before he can retaliate.

"Prince Charming doesn't beat up the guests," I hiss.

Tristian turns, eyes wild, brown waves plastered to his sweaty forehead. "I'm not Prince Charming." He tugs free and knocks the guy back with an uppercut as security barrels into the tent.

12

IMOGEN

"Let me get this straight."

Twenty minutes later, Ivor paces in front of Tristian and me, the stuffy air in Maria's office making it difficult to breathe—or perhaps it's Ivor's tone. "You punched a guest."

Tristian adjusts the ice pack against his jaw. He's hunched over, with his elbows resting on his knees. "He hit me first."

Ivor halts, glaring at us. He's still dressed in his prince costume. "God, Tristian. In what universe do you think it's okay to strike a guest? In front of other guests, no less. Children were present!"

Maria sits in her chair, fingers in a steeple grip against her tight mouth. Tension laces the room. I shift in my chair, the squeak piercing in the silence.

Tristian drops the ice pack and uses his hand to move his jaw. The skin is bright red from the cold and the punch. "If I hadn't stepped in, who knows what he might've done next."

"Security was on its way. The situation was under control. This is a marketing nightmare." Ivor pinches the bridge of his nose. "Do you know how many comp tickets I've had to hand out, so guests wouldn't post the videos they took? I had to grovel and explain that you were only trying to be the valiant hero. You're incredibly lucky you have such a good reputation. I have enough on my plate with complaints about price increases, I don't need you adding to them."

"What Ivor means," Maria interjects, "is that we have an image to maintain. It's not okay for the guests to see the cast, especially Winthrop, breaking character like that."

"The guy was out of hand." I speak up. Tristian's clenched fist has me worried I'm about to be in another brawl. "Plus, like, only five people saw it."

I had more of a crowd at my arson attempt.

"Who are you?" Ivor acknowledges me for the first time.

"Oh, uh, Imogen." Under Ivor's stare, I feel like I've been sent to the principal's office.

"She started today," Maria adds.

"Imogen, you're new, so I'll give you some leeway." Ivor's lips purse like he's sucked a sour candy. "But let me make it clear, under no circumstances do you punch a guest."

"What about trip them?" I try to lighten the mood. Tristian stares at the ground, but his shoulders shake with a chuckle.

"Aunt Maria, perhaps we need to give them a training refresh. I can't have them onstage if this is what happens." Ivor glances at the clock on the wall. "Just stick to the carriage rides and wave from the castle's balcony for the rest of the day."

"Ivor." Tristian stands. "Let me focus on the internship. That'll get me out of your hair."

I frown. *Internship?*

"Did you do this on purpose?" Ivor asks.

"Did I make some dude propose to a girl who clearly didn't want to marry him? Yeah, Ivor, I did. You caught me. Planned the whole thing to mess with you."

If I could sink into the floor right now, I would. Maria looks like she'd join me.

"You complain about wanting to be your own person. If that's the case, then you need to grow up and take things seriously." Ivor storms out.

"Well, I don't know about anyone else." I smooth my skirt as I stand. "But I could use an extra-large turkey leg for lunch."

Tristian doesn't join me and says less than a handful of words as we do three more carriage rides and a couple of sessions waving from the castle.

Despite the absolute mess this morning and the dressing-down from Ivor, I had a fun day. My chest bursts with joy as I look around. The dreams I played in my head are actually real, and that realness still shocks me. I keep waiting to wake up and have a hot dog on my head.

"That went well," I tell Tristian at the end of our day. The evening guests will have to live without Arden and Winthrop.

Tristian grunts a response as he yanks off his sword in one long move and hits the wall.

"We didn't have any more brawls. Ivor should be happy." I pepper on a little more sunshine to clear the storm clouding his features.

"Ivor isn't happy about much involving me." He takes the stairs two at a time, and I jog to keep up with his long legs.

"Maybe you need to bake him a cake."

He stops mid-step, and I slam my hand into the wall to avoid falling backward. "Bake him a cake?"

"Yeah, everybody loves cake." I've pissed off my parents enough times to know an *I'm sorry* cake goes a long way. "Make it chocolate for extra points."

"You're something else." He starts back up the stairs.

"Thank you." Those stupid, inconvenient butterflies decide to start dancing in my stomach again.

Get the memo: we don't like him.

Fine. I sort of do, but he's off-limits.

"That wasn't a compliment," he says as we enter the costume department. Thank god he opened his mouth again and ruined the moment.

"Sounded like one." A box with my name sits on a shelf, and I find my street clothes inside. I remove the container with his name, tossing it to him.

"I must've said it wrong."

He disappears behind the changing curtain, one of three against the wall, and I take the one next to it. My elbow pushes the fabric between us open slightly as I try to unlace my gown, and I freeze. Tristian's top half is bare, with strong lean muscles and lightly tanned skin.

My witty retort catches in my throat. *What was I saying?*

He might not think he's Prince Charming, but he's got the looks to claim the title. I yank the drapes closed as he glances up.

"Well, I, for one, had fun today." A hot, blotchy flush covers my cheeks as I try to keep my voice unbothered.

"I'm shocked." His muffled voice doesn't hide the sarcasm.

I remove my wig, the tiara clattering to the ground as my head screams in relief. Slipping into my street clothes is anticlimactic. I got used to the gown and crown, and my heart drops a little to give it back. Stripping off my uniform is usually the highlight of my day, but not here.

"You seem the type to love everything," he adds.

"Ha!" I bark. "Sorry, it's just I know about a dozen former bosses who'd argue otherwise." Discovering things to complain about in a job is my number one talent.

"A dozen?" He comes out right before I do.

I sling the gown over my arm, the wig hanging off my other hand. "A dozen-ish."

His hair is ruffled and sticking up, due to the hair spray. It makes him look semi-normal. He catches me ogling and I make a quick turn to keep him from seeing my pink cheeks and probably heart-emoji eyes.

"I pegged you as the girl who stays at a job, no matter what. Always finding the bright side."

I'm taken aback by these words. That's the opposite impression most people have. They think I hunt for the worst in any place—searching for an excuse to leave.

And they'd be right.

It's my MO. But at Fairytale Gardens, I feel the bright side seeking me. It's probably Divya's doing—if it weren't for her story, I'd have already found the exit.

I grin because it really bothers him. "What can I say? I love a fairytale."

He shakes his head, studying my face. He's about to respond when a voice explodes from upstairs. "Uncle Tristian!" A small boy bounds down the carpeted steps.

"Bradley." Tristian drops to a knee, arms open wide. The young boy, around four, jumps on him. He runs a hand over the kid's curly Afro.

"Uncle Tristian, you have to come see me fight! Daddy taught me the swords." He draws out the word *swords*.

"I will, buddy. I can't wait." He stands, and the kid keeps his hand tight on Tristian's. "This is my nephew, Bradley. Ivor's son."

Bradley observes me with deep curiosity. "Why do you have a wig?"

Leave it to kids to get right to the point.

"Stole it from a mermaid in a fight." I twirl the hair into the air. "It was my prize."

His eyes narrow. "Mermaids don't fight." He peeks at Tristian for confirmation.

"Have you ever tried to take a mermaid's treasure? They don't take kindly to that," I say, with an exaggerated shake of my head.

"Are you a pirate?" He drops Tristian's hand, treading forward.

I put my finger to my lips. "Shh, we can't let everyone know. Piracy isn't legal in these parts."

He breaks into a grin. "Uncle Tristian, can I be a pirate?"

Tristian hums as he massages a hand over his tender jaw. "You'd make an excellent pirate. Also, your dad would hate it, so all the more reason to do it." He winks at me. This is a different side of Tristian—his genuine smile makes my heart melt.

Stop making me feel things!

One second he's a grumpy jerk, and the next he's this loving uncle. *Pick a lane, bro.* I need to know where it's safe to drive. I can't afford a car crash. Divya would never forgive me. I mean, she would because she loves me, but *I* would never forgive me for wrecking this assignment.

"Bradley!" a voice calls from the top of the stairs, as a tall Black man jogs down them. "Sweetheart, I told you to—oh, Tristian, hi." Two deep dimples accentuate a kind smile.

Bradley darts over to him. "Papa, she's a pirate." He points to me.

"Remind me not to tell you where I buried the treasure." I cross my arms.

"Is she? I'm James Walsh, Ivor's husband." Bradley looks like a mini version of James, even down to the tiny dimples.

"Imogen. I'm—uh, new." I can't say I'm a princess out loud. It sounds ridiculous enough in my head.

"Did a kid throw up on your wig?" James asks.

I examine the wig, resisting the urge to smell it. "No, but I can't wait for that experience."

He laughs warmly, rubbing a hand over his shaved head. "I worked here one summer, and it happened three times."

"It's a rite of passage," Tristian says defensively.

"Also the reason it was only one summer." James grabs Bradley's hand as he tries to sprint up the stairs. "We'll leave you to it. Nice to meet you, Imogen. Tristian, please come around more."

"I'll try." He hugs Bradley before they leave.

"Cute kid," I say as silence settles in around us. Faint noise trickles from the break room, but here, we are alone.

"Yeah." His eyes drift down the stairs.

I should walk away right now. Leave Tristian alone and bring my focus to the mission. But I want to stay a little longer. "Did you have him show up on purpose?"

"What?" He frowns, looking back at me.

"People use kids or animals to appear more likable."

"You don't think I'm likable?" His face gives nothing away.

"I think you don't know what you want to be."

If I wasn't studying him, I might've missed the moment his face fell before he slipped the mask back on. "Oh, I'm plenty likable." He takes a step toward me. "Trust me."

"Yeah?" I lean in, a breath away now, warmed by the drop in his voice. A heartbeat feels like an eternity as I give those butterflies a moment to enjoy this. "I'll believe it when I see it." I pivot, tossing my wig over my shoulder.

If I'd stayed a moment longer, I might've let him show me how likable he can be.

13

TRISTIAN

I've had bad days at the park. There was the time I nearly broke my leg when Garrick dared me to jump off the Jousting Horses. Or when my pants fell down in the middle of a sword fight. Or worse yet, the first time I put on the costume and walked onstage after Mom died.

Today doesn't come near the last one, but it's a distant second.

I punched a guy. Sword fighting might be in my DNA, but I'm far from a violent person. I've never even been in a real fight. Chalk it up to the anger of being in Winthrop's shoes again, of Imogen's annoyingly upbeat response to everything. When that man took a swing, a foreign part of me took over. Blood rushed in my ears, my vision narrowed, and then he was on the ground—I barely remember what happened.

My aching jaw is a nice reminder, though. I work it carefully with my hand as I head to the apartment. I want a hot shower, a burger, and to sleep for the next week.

My traitorous brain brings Imogen front and center as I recall the day. She stunned in her dress—and actually killed it with the princess knowledge, all things considered. I was pretty impressed. Maybe I should have told her that. But the second I saw her in the carriage, I almost ran for the hills. Because part of me wanted to sit with her, and not just because it's literally my job.

The muggy air in the apartment hits me in the face when I open the door. Garrick always keeps it boiling. I drop my stuff on the small dining table and flip on the AC with more force than needed.

"Tell Jack he can't order five different kinds of mustard." Garrick exits the bedroom in gym clothes, cell phone pinched between his ear and shoulder. "Because it's a theme park. People can live with one mustard."

Garrick isn't actually in charge of anything, but he's been helping more with food and beverage. I think it's his way of honoring Mom—that was her baby.

"Did another kid puke on you?" he says, hanging up the call.

"No—not yet." I clench my jaw.

"Then why do you look like crap?" Garrick's messy curls fly everywhere as he pushes a hand through them.

"Ivor lectured me." I sit in the rickety chair and rap my knuckles against the table. My chest burns, the pressure ramming against my skin. "I need to get out of here." If I don't, I might explode.

"Excellent idea. You know I'm always up for a prison break. Tyrone can get us a karaoke room and free cheese fries." He grabs water from the fridge, offering me one, but I shake my head.

"I know you always got my back, G. But I was talking a little further than Tyrone's bar."

"Just say the word and I'll sneak you out under my coat."

"Really? You don't have a guilt-ridden speech about family and responsibility?"

He leans against the counter, twisting the water cap. "You're confusing me with another brother." Garrick is the laid-back one, who doesn't care about anything. He encouraged me to go on the program in the first place. He doesn't mind staying at FTG: not out of family duty, but because he didn't want to try for anything else.

I manage a laugh, but cringe when pain shoots through my jaw. "Imagine the look on Dad's and Ivor's faces if I just didn't turn up to work."

"I would get it cross-stitched on a pillow and give it to you for Christmas."

The dark cloud brewing all day dissipates the longer I'm with Garrick. "But Ivor and Dad . . ."

He flips the water bottle, catching it before it hits the ground. "You've always considered them one and the same." Garrick's face turns serious. "They aren't the same, Tristian."

There's a pang in my chest, and I press my thumb into it to make it go away. "It's not that I wanted to leave you guys this summer." I love my brothers. I just wanted an adventure and a life I made, not one copied from a storybook.

"*I* know. You didn't pick FTG." He swings a banana toward the park.

"And you did?" Garrick is the most outgoing of the four of us, the free spirit. He's the closest replica of the knight he plays.

He finishes the banana before he speaks—stalling. "I never

wanted anything. It's why I didn't go to the Olympics for fencing. I didn't care enough. This seems as good a place as any to stick around."

"And you're happy? You don't mind?" I fill a towel with ice. It stings when I press it to my jaw.

"Nope, they can bury me with the other dead body on the pirate ride."

"There isn't a dead body on the ride. That's a myth." I grin, even though it hurts.

Frown lines cross his forehead. "Then how did I see a ghost?"

"Too much rum?"

"Or not enough." He finishes off the water. "So, were you going to tell me about punching a guest, or was I supposed to pretend you got a bruised jaw from your new princess?"

I tilt my head. "How do you know about either of those things?"

He grins. "You thought you could have a brawl, and no one would talk about it. I heard about it from Aldrich, who heard it from Aliana. Who I think heard about it from an elf—or the popcorn-stand girl."

I groan, resting against the counter. "Do we have any pain meds?"

Garrick grabs the bottle from the cupboard, shaking it. I reach for it, but he yanks it away. "Nope. I want the story first. And don't skip any details. I want to know about every twitch on Ivor's face when he yelled at you."

"It wasn't that exciting."

"Not even the princess?" He wiggles his eyebrows.

"Imogen is . . ." Funny, exciting, the polar opposite of me. *No*, she's a distraction. One I don't need to get into. "Garrick, give me the pills." I grit my teeth and immediately regret the surge of pain across my mouth. Lunging, I rip the bottle from his hands, and head to the bathroom.

"Hey, T?"

"Yeah?" I flip on the shower; it takes ages to warm up.

"I know you don't want to be stuck here forever, and I respect that. But do me a favor and don't let something good slip through your fingers just because you think what you want is somewhere you've never been."

An image of Imogen's kind smile as she talked to the little kids, her spinning in her dress when she didn't think I was looking, flashes through my brain before I shut it down.

Fairytale Gardens is quicksand, and it will drag me under if I let it. I might be stuck here for the summer, but I won't let anything deter me from reaching my dreams one day.

14

IMOGEN

Yvette does her best to cheer me up at dinner, promising me the first day is always the roughest. But even she couldn't pretend that a prince punching a guest is a usual first day hiccup.

"I've seen your résumé." Yvette picks at her fruit cup. "I'm sure on that extensive list there must've been other first days that rival this one?"

I stab my fork into a fry, pointing it at her. "Okay, I feel like you're trying to make me feel better, but also, when you say *extensive* in that tone, it undermines the sentiment."

Yvette's chin dips to her chest as she attempts to hide her grin. "I swear, I'm only trying to help." The laugh bubbles up as she speaks, the words cracking as she fails to conceal it. "But seriously, you worked as a magician's assistant?"

This break in her otherwise professional exterior softens me, and I'm laughing, too. "What? It's a real job."

"You get a page for the résumé, and *that's* one of the jobs you included?" She snorts when she laughs, and I like her more with every word. I miss Divya, but it's nice to know I might have a friend here.

"I thought it'd be a useful skill at a theme park." I shrug, tossing a fry at her. She catches it in her mouth, and I applaud.

"Well, if I need someone to saw in half, you're my girl."

I leave Yvette after dinner and head back to the apartment. Aliana isn't there. I've missed a call from Divya, so I settle into the couch—the culprit of the Cheetos smell—and prop my feet on the coffee table as the video call rings through.

Her face pops up on the screen, a pen wedged into her hair. She's at her internship. Honestly, she'd probably live there if they let her. She's wearing a bright orange suit jacket and silky purple top. It startles me to see the difference between us so starkly. She's on her way to a real adult job and I'm still playing at a theme park. I did have fun today, but that thought sobers me a bit.

"So, a princess, huh?" Surprise laces her tone, even though she'd messaged me a bunch of exclamation points in response to my text.

I grip the phone tighter. "I know you wanted me to lie low, but I wasn't sure how to get out of it." My stomach clenches, anticipating her response. Divya hates when plans veer off track. She could accuse me of not taking the job seriously.

Wouldn't blame her.

"Don't worry. You just need to be more careful. Besides, maybe this can work to our advantage." She props the phone against the computer so she can type.

"What are you thinking?" I study her composed face. I want to be like Divya, strong and confident in everything I do. If she was with me, we'd already have the information we need.

Her attention stays on the computer screen. I'm used to her multitasking. "You're Princess Arden, right?" I nod, even though she isn't looking. "That means you have a prince."

"*Yeah.*" A knot forms in my gut. "Tristian Walsh."

"Your summertime crush." She spares me a wink.

I slide off the couch, circling the cramped living room and kitchen. "You're exaggerating."

By the look on her face, I suspect the calm, nonchalant tone I attempt fools no one. "I seem to remember several conversations over the summers about Prince Charming."

The living area exhausted, I take my pacing to the bedroom. "He's too hot a commodity for me. I don't need the competition. And he's like top tier grumpy status." Although, when he looked at me today, I felt like the only thing in the room.

But he's not my type. He'll barely crack a smile, and he's too pretty—which he also knows. It's a dangerous combination.

"Anyway." Divya picks up the phone. "Play nice with him. Maybe he knows something useful."

I plop onto the bed, kicking off my shoes. "Doubtful. I've gathered that he's not a fan of the park. I heard on the grapevine that he is supposed to be doing some summer program in Europe, but it fell through."

Her heels click on the tile as she wanders through a hallway and into a kitchen. "Great, then he shouldn't care when we expose the truth."

"You want me to use him?" I bite my cheek. Tristian may not be my park bestie, but the idea of exploiting him makes my skin crawl.

"I want you to be his friend, and if he happens to tell you

useful information, well, that's not your fault." I'm graced with a great view of the ceiling when she puts the phone face up on a counter, as the hum of a coffee maker grates from the speaker.

I curl into a ball on the blanket. "From this angle, I can see straight up your nose." The joke doesn't quell the dull ache across my rib cage, but I can't argue with Divya. I'm here for her, after all. As much as I love playing a princess and everything about FTG—that's not the reason for my employment. I just need to keep reminding my brain of that.

"So, princess?" she nudges when I've gone silent. "Kind of your dream gig."

I fight a grin. "Yeah." I snuggle the blanket to my face. "I wish you were with me, Div."

My heart aches with her so far away. We've always been a team. I'm the sidekick, and she's the hero. I don't know if I can get her the answers she wants on my own.

"I know, but you got this. You don't need me." Her confident smile is a helium boost to my deflated balloon.

Despite the pressure of a new job, I enjoyed myself today. At no point did I want to make a run for it—even when the brawl broke out. And I'm excited to train tomorrow. When have those words ever crossed my mind? The FTG nostalgia envelops me like a warm hug from a loved one you haven't seen in ages. . . .

"Did you listen to a word I just said?" Divya interrupts my brain's ramblings.

"I'll be honest with you, no." I cringe, giving her an apologetic smile.

"Scientists should study your ability to completely ignore the world around you."

"*Anyway*, what did you say?"

"Can you break into Barth Walsh's office?" Her casual tone makes it sound like she wants me to pick up takeout, not commit a crime.

I nearly drop the phone on my face. "Yeah, right."

She's returned to her desk. "I'm serious. I've looked into the charities—they were all created in the last two years. They have websites, but not much on them."

I startle—heart pounding when Aliana's high-pitched voice trails in from the living room. I jump up and shut my door.

"So, they're real?"

I click the volume down on the call as Divya continues. "They appear real enough on the surface level. I'm still digging, but you're there for a reason. So you can see what I can't."

"And you think"—I keep my voice low; the last thing I need is Aliana overhearing—"I'll find it breaking into Barth's office?"

She shrugs. "You can try."

I sit against the headboard and stare at the door. "Doesn't this violate some code of journalistic ethics?"

"Not if you're the one doing it." She picks up the phone. "I need you to focus."

"I am focused." I snap my eyes back to the screen.

"No, not just right now. You can't get lost in the clouds."

My nails dig into the palm of my free hand with a sharp sting. I know what she's getting at. She thinks I'll flake. I want to argue with her, but there's no fault in her logic. She has years of evidence to support it.

"You can manage that for a few weeks." She examines her nails before glancing back at me. "Which works perfectly because I want you in and out ASAP."

"I know. I'll focus one hundred percent." I unclench my fist. *There's a first time for everything, right?*

But as I give my promise to Divya, one I want to keep, the voice in my head—the one I imagine resembles the purple devil emoji—whispers to me. It tells me this is too hard, too much responsibility, and it shouldn't be this difficult if it's meant to be.

I nearly rip my skin off waiting for Aliana to go to sleep. Four hours pacing one's room will do that to a person. Each moment added another weight to my shoulders. I managed to call my parents and let them know the new job is going great. They tempered their enthusiasm. Guess they're learning. At last, around midnight, Aliana went to her room. I waited another hour to be sure she was asleep.

Creeping into the hall, I press my ear to her door. A fan's whistle is the only sound. I walk on my tiptoes through the dark living room, clamping my jaw to conceal a yelp when I stumble into the coffee table with my shin.

I open the front door in micromovements, but since this place was last serviced in the eighties, the hinges come with a sound effect. A loud squeak permeates the air around me.

My heart slams into overdrive; drumbeats only I can hear overpower the screeching door. I bite my tongue, eyes darting toward Aliana's bedroom. I'm about to attempt breaking and entering; she's the last person I want to catch me.

Screw it.

I let the loud wails of the hinges go to town as I wrench the door open and slip out. If it's going to perform a screaming opera, might as well make the song as short as possible.

My breath eases when no one follows me from the apartment as I walk across the parking lot to the main building. It's open all night; you just need a code to get in. If caught, I'll say I was going to the break room. Also, thanks to my recon earlier, I know they don't have security cameras. The park's covered with them, but I guess they figure the office isn't at risk.

Works for me.

I pass no one on my way. FTG's lights are faint behind the trees. It's the quietest I've ever heard the place. As someone who prefers loud chaos to quiet reflection, the eerie silence sends goose bumps over my bare arms. I force my breath into an even rhythm as I let myself into the building.

I wait at the bottom of the stairs for several agonizing minutes and listen for any movement on the upper floors. The only noise comes from the clicking air conditioner and my raging heart.

When I reach the second floor, I wait again. I could create a lie about why I'm on this level. I left stuff in the costume department—forgot to return my wig. But I have no reason to be on the third floor, especially at one a.m.

After a few minutes, I'm confident I'm alone. However, it takes another moment to convince my legs to move. There's something about empty buildings that conjures ghosts around every corner, real or imagined. For my purposes, tonight, I'll take spirits over the living.

The third floor is the darkest. The parking lot lamps filtering through the side windows are the only light source. Barth's office is locked and since I haven't deduced how to get in, I slide my attention to Milly's desk. With her gone, it gives me a chance to study the charity pictures on the display wall behind it that I couldn't get to yesterday.

Many of the donation recipients are well-known groups. I snap a few more pictures to cover my bases. The last section is smaller. It has a few charities listed and a smiling kid holding a giant check with a decent sum of money. Three charities have received donations in the last year. That's when the whistleblower stopped receiving their contributions.

The organization names are unfamiliar to me, but that doesn't mean they aren't legit. I take pictures of these too, cringing with every camera flash, and send them to Divya.

Next, I search Milly's desk. Barth seems like an old-school guy. I'm guessing he relies heavily on his assistant. I don't know what I'm looking for—I doubt they left me a folder marked "incriminating documents." But that'd be very helpful.

I click the keyboard to wake up the computer, and a screen prompts me to sign in. I scan the sticky notes lying around, but nothing jumps out as the password. I move on to the drawers. As I reach for them, I stop short.

Should I have brought gloves?

But they don't even have cameras. I doubt they're out here dusting for fingerprints. I relax slightly, letting out a deep breath and shaking my arms to get the feeling back.

The first drawer holds nothing of value: a couple of cough drops, a stack of photos, and three gift cards to Starbucks. I wipe my sweaty hands on my shirt before crouching to get into the lower drawers. Every little sound sends my nerves into overdrive. I lick my lips, blocking the voice in my head yelling to get the hell out.

The next two drawers have lots of papers, but nothing useful. However, in the last one there's a leather planner marked with the previous year's date. I flip through it for anything noteworthy. There were two meetings early last year, three weeks apart. Barth met with each of the charities—or was supposed to anyway. I can't confirm just from this. A few months later, it shows Barth went on a business trip.

Perhaps using the charity money? I snap a picture and send it to Divya. She can sort out the details.

This is a sliver of proof that Barth was actively participating with the charities. There's a chance they fooled him, right? He might not be aware they were fake. But I've heard how people speak about Barth. Nothing gets past him. His innocence might just be wishful thinking.

As I slip the planner back into the desk—hopefully where I found it—I spot a loose key under it. I examine it as I stand, glancing toward Barth's office. Worth a shot. Running my hand over the cold metal, I slip the key into the lock.

The lock clicks, the door sliding open with no resistance.

Thank you, Fairy Godmother.

I'm about to step inside when feet scuffing on tile stops me. I yank the key out, pulling the door shut with as little noise as possible. I don't have time to put the key back, so I tuck it into my pocket.

I make it down one flight of stairs as Tristian walks up from the first floor. *Crap.* Each muscle in my body simultaneously decides to go on strike, freezing me in place. Even my heart takes a few beats to pump again.

His eyes run over me, pausing on my guilty face. I slip on an innocent smile. "Fancy meeting you here." I pray he doesn't hear my erratic heart.

"Imogen? What are you doing here? It's nearly two a.m." His tone is more curious than demanding, but it doesn't calm my shaky breaths.

I keep my tone light and friendly. "What are you doing here?" I point to a bag slung over his shoulder.

His rumpled hair pokes at odd angles, and his weary eyes have dark shadows underneath. "I asked you first." He levels me with an unwavering stare.

I reach into my pocket for my phone. "I left this in the costume department after Yvette took it from me." I'm adding so much sunshine to my voice I might blind us both.

"And you came by at two in the morning to get it?" His lips purse as he frowns.

My stomach tightens, but I keep my face nonchalant. "It has my sleep app. Couldn't go to bed without it."

Tristian raises an eyebrow. "They lock the costume department."

I shrug. "Harold must've forgotten—lucky me."

"Sure," he mocks, not buying my story.

I attempt a hair flip, but I smack myself in the face instead. "Are you going to turn me in?" I try to sound unbothered. Too bad my racing heart betrays my casual tone. "Doesn't seem the princely thing to do."

I can't tell if he clenches his jaw in anger or to hide a laugh. "You should go to bed."

I should, but I'm curious. "Will you tell me your story?"

"If I have to explain myself, so do you." A dare flashes in his eyes.

"That bad, huh?" I click my tongue.

"About as believable as you coming to pick up your phone." He wears a wolfish grin as he leans toward me. "So, I'll spill my secret if you spill yours."

I hear Divya's voice in my head urging me to go home before I can divulge any secrets. Still, the curiosity surging through my veins could serve us well. I *want* to know what he's doing.

For Divya, of course. Intel.

I study him a second longer. Unanswered questions percolate until one almost bubbles over as his challenging gaze holds mine.

No.

It's not worth the questions he'd ask in return.

"I'll see you tomorrow, Tristian." I saunter past him, chin held high, even though I nearly trip down the stairs.

Day One helping Divya find her story is a bust. Let's hope the next one is more fruitful.

15

IMOGEN

Whoever decided to start construction at six a.m. should be forced to ride Ogre Escape on a loop for twelve hours. I shove a pillow over my face to tune out the pounding rattling my sleep-deprived brain. I didn't get to bed until two thirty. The banging doesn't stop, and instead a yelling voice joins it. I throw the pillow off to glare at the ceiling.

"Imogen!"

I sit up, regretting it instantly as dizziness consumes me.

"Imogen, it's Yvette."

Pushing the blankets off me, I stumble from bed, grabbing the wall to keep upright.

"Yvette?" I rip open the door to see her and Aliana. "What's up?"

"Training. Remember?"

I rub my eyes to clear my vision because I hope this is a dream. When I open them, they haven't disappeared. "I do remember, but why are you here at six a.m.?"

Her lips press into a thin line. "Because the park opens at ten, and I need you ready to go by eleven."

I take a deep breath. The door is the only one of us

responsible for keeping me vertical as I lean against the frame. "I don't know how well I'll absorb information right now."

Aliana gives us both a once-over. "Not so easy being a face character, huh?" she says before departing.

Yvette steps into the room and twists open the blinds. The sun peeks through the slats. "I'll have coffee and pastries in the tower for you."

"With cream and sugar?"

She pivots toward me. "Put on your shoes, and let's go."

I'm still wearing the black leggings and T-shirt from last night's break-in. I grumble my agreement, slipping onto the bed to pull my sneakers from under it. "I must warn you, I'm not a morning person."

"You'll be in good company. Tristian wasn't too happy when I woke him either."

I jerk up, pain shooting through my skull. "Is he here?"

"He'll meet us there."

It feels like I'm going somewhere I'm not allowed. But I trail behind Yvette up a winding staircase to a room at the top of the castle. This truly feels ripped from the pages of a fairytale. The wood floor creaks beneath our feet as she lets us into a door labeled "Training."

The rounded space tucks into a turret of the castle. A vaulted ceiling houses large wood beams connected to the roof, while wide oak planks with scuffs and dings decorate the floor. A few mirrors and different vintage signs cover the wood-clad walls. Fresh bread and roasted meats from the Royal Fare restaurant below accent the timber smell.

Tristian sits in a window seat. The sunrise casts pink and orange hues on his face. He has a paper cup in one hand and a croissant in the other.

But what draws me in is the coffee-rich aroma. I stumble to a table along the wall, pouring myself a cup with extra cream and sugar. I take a long sip. The warm liquid provokes a groan as I grab a Danish.

"Wow," I mumble, mouth full of pastry, stepping to the window next to his. "You can see the whole park from here." The eyeline is high above the trees, and I can peek into all the lands, except Glacier Peaks, which hides behind its fake mountain. "*Simba, everything the light touches is our kingdom.*"

Tristian sips his coffee, ignoring my comment.

"What, not a *Lion King* fan? Okay, noted. How about *Pinocchio*? The whole boy on strings thing seems right up your alley." I am egging him on a little, but the silence is too much this early.

He responds with a furrowed brow. "Are you always so perky at this time of day?"

I shrug. "When the view is this good, it makes up for the ungodly hour."

Scoffing, he picks at his flaky untouched croissant. "Are you ready to learn how to be a royal?" he says after a beat of uncomfortable silence.

I nibble at my sugary Danish, watching Yvette set up a projector on the far side of the room. "I thought we did a *great* job yesterday." I feel a tiny bit perkier now that sugar is coursing through my veins.

"With any luck, they'll fire us." Tristian's hand curls around his cup as he mumbles through gritted teeth. "Then Dad can use some of that money he hoards to create a robotic Winthrop that will do exactly as he commands."

Hoarding money, you say? I file that nugget away for safekeeping.

I finish my coffee in a few gulps. "That's the spirit. Not only did I get woken at six a.m., but I also have to cheer up Prince Charming."

"Why do you keep calling me Prince Charming?" He rubs his eyes, fighting a yawn.

"Because"—I take an aggressive bite of pastry—"you seem to really hate it."

My head aches, and I want to sleep, but annoying him makes me feel better. I'm eyeing a second cup when Maria strolls in.

"Hello, dears," she sings, eyes bright. "We have limited time, but fear not, I've trained princes and princesses since Tristian was in diapers. I'll get you shipshape."

"I could do this job in my sleep." Tristian leans forward to rest his elbows on his knees. "In fact, I wish I was sleeping."

Maria gives him a knowing look over her shoulder. "Then perhaps you should stop punching guests and upsetting the boss."

He grumbles under his breath, and I hear "Ivor" and "not my boss."

"I think we got put in time-out." I pat him on the shoulder.

Tristian lounges against the window, finally eating his croissant. For a guy who punched a guest yesterday, he should be more stressed. But he apparently wants to get fired. My breath quickens as I picture Divya's face. I can't let that happen.

"No time to waste." Maria claps her hands. "First things first, you need to get in costume." She heads to a partitioned area near the wall. "Come on," she says when I don't follow.

Maria flourishes a less intricate ensemble before her and Yvette helps me into the dress. "Arden wears this costume for her fairy life, rather than royal duties."

I slip on the white underdress, followed by the brown skirt, leather belt, and laced corset top. The corset isn't too tight—a blessing because I'm already struggling to breathe. Leaves, roses, and a few woodland creatures embroider the soft gray fabric. It laces in the front, and delicate bows tie over my shoulders in a single strap. The white dress's short sleeves fall over my shoulders to expose the top.

"Arden's clothes aren't always as elaborate as the other princesses'." Maria tugs the corset a little tighter. "She's a far more down-to-earth royal. It's why the people love her."

"In the story or the park?" I adjust the front.

"Both—Arden and Winthrop are the heart of the Fairytale Gardens story."

No pressure.

Yesterday was a fun new job, a dream come true—today is a new responsibility level. Arden is the crux of the whole fairytale. If I screw this up, it's a lot worse than messing up a hot-dog order.

"Don't worry, Imogen." Yvette places a hand on my shoulder. "You did fine yesterday. Maria will just fill in a few blanks in your knowledge."

“And Tristian will be right by your side. You couldn’t ask for a better partner—once he stops assaulting guests,” Maria mutters, gliding back into the main room.

When I’ve centered myself, I step from behind the curtain. Tristian has changed into his prince outfit, hand on his sword. “You look . . . good.” His words come out in a rough cough.

“Don’t strain yourself with the flattery.” I smirk, putting on my best bravado.

“For you, my love, never.” Maybe it’s delirium from lack of sleep, or the coffee kicking in, but Tristian’s smile looks genuine.

“You plan on getting into another fight?” I point to the sword.

“Never know. It’s best to practice with it. It’s bulky and pokes out at an odd angle. If we don’t get used to it hanging there, it could throw you off onstage. But I promise, I am very adept with my sword.”

I don’t doubt it.

“Now you have the outfit,” Maria says, smacking him on the back of the head, clearly having overheard us. “It’s time we learn to walk in it. Tristian, take her in a few circles around the room.” Tristian offers his arm, and I loop mine around it as she barks advice like a drill sergeant.

Maria observes with sharp eyes, ready to catch any mistake. “Shoulders back. Your left hand should rest delicately on your stomach or be looped around Tristian’s arm. The other can lie on top or do a small wave. Like so.” She demonstrates the motion.

“Smile.” Tristian leans in, breath tickling my cheek. “You look like you’re going in for a root canal.”

I'd prefer complex dental work right now. I'm all for playing princess, but training to do it on less than five hours of sleep is a nightmare. A constant dull ache permeates the base of my skull. I run my tongue over my teeth and lips to cure my dry mouth and attempt a smile.

"Less teeth," Maria corrects me from the opposite side of the room.

"I've never had any complaints before." I draw my mouth closed.

"You have a nice smile—it's just too happy . . ." Tristian tilts his head. "Try to appear more pleasantly content."

"I'd describe myself as the exact opposite of *pleasantly content* right now." I squeeze my eyes shut, willing my developing headache to take a hike.

"Then it's perfect practice for when a kid cries in your face as a parent forces them to take a picture with you."

I press my side into him. It's a nice place to lean. I could get used to this.

Ugh, no. Stop.

After a few more rounds, Maria puts us in chairs, and we practice for the carriage rides. She turns on the music used during the parades.

"While in the carriage, we want you to look natural." She says this while I sit, stick straight, with my neck aching from holding my head high and my legs plastered together. "Exchange a few words with your prince, smile, laugh—you're in love."

"In love?" I glance over at Tristian, my heart fluttering in my chest as he blinks slowly. Those long lashes should be illegal.

"Deeply, madly." He leans in, a warm breath caressing my ear. "Imagine our secret dalliances in dark corners of the castle."

My cheeks flush, while a cheeky grin spreads across his face. The lack of sleep has him more at ease than yesterday. It's like the Tristian I always imagined existed. A longing grips me.

What if I let myself give in for just a second?

"Tristian," Maria scolds. "We want a nice blush on her face, but we aren't trying to scandalize the guests."

"Or are we?" He winks at me. I could get used to this Tristian.

No, Imogen.

No getting used to anyone. Even if I like being the recipient of his attention way more than I should. A romantic entanglement will only lead to royally screwing up Divya's story. My loyalty is to her. Anything that puts that at risk isn't worth it.

We spend more time on my facial expressions. Pleasant and interested without insincerity. Who knew my face gave away so much? This could explain why I never kept a customer service job.

"Not bad." Maria nods approval, while Yvette turns off the music. "You've made great progress. Take a quick break while we get the slideshow ready."

"Slideshow?" I follow Tristian to the table.

He pours a coffee and hands it to me. "As you witnessed from Ivor's anger yesterday, staying in character is important. Soon, you'll know Carpathia's and Arden's histories backward and forward."

"Like what our wedding vows are?" I nail him with a stare over my cup.

"Yes." He turns back to the table, adding cream to his cup. I spy the smile he attempts to conceal. A different one than the prince wears—softer, less perfect.

I lean over him to grab a sugar as he turns right at the same time, making his lips brush my temple.

He clears his throat, taking several steps back. "You did good yesterday—I'm the one who screwed it up."

I ignore my fluttering heart and shake my head. "No, you didn't. That guy was asking to be punched. Anyone would've done the same." I rip my sugar packet too hard, and the grains fly through the air.

He hands me another without comment. "Not you. You tried to stop me."

Tristian will always pass for a handsome prince. His ocean-blue eyes and wavy brown hair are an easy comparison. But right now, I see the real him: the worry clouding his face, the way he gnaws his bottom lip. I thought I wanted to know Prince Charming, but my gut tells me the real guy is a whole lot more interesting.

"All right, Your Royal Highnesses." Maria breaks the moment, and Tristian slips back inside his princely persona. "Time for a history lesson." Yvette stands by a rickety projector with a clicker in hand.

The projector smells like it might catch fire at any moment, but I try to put the thoughts of death in a smoke-filled room aside and pay attention.

The presentation goes over every detail about Arden, and

her life before becoming a princess—how she joined forces with Winthrop to defeat the blight, and their nuptials following the victory. There's an in-depth history of Carpathia and its royal family. I glance over at Tristian a few times; he's mouthing along with the dialogue. He blushes, head dipping low when I catch him.

"I hope you took notes." I stare at the booklet Maria gave us. It's the same one Yvette gave me yesterday—that I already lost.

"What is Arden's favorite flower?" Maria quizzes.

"Um . . ." I flip through the book frantically.

"Poppies," Tristian whispers under his breath.

"Poppies—the purple ones," I add quickly, proud I remembered at least part of the answer.

"And what vows did she say to Winthrop on their wedding day in front of the kingdom?"

I share a look with Tristian, his face saying, *I told you so.*

I paid extra attention to that part of the slideshow. "She didn't say vows at the royal wedding, but she did at their secret nuptials the night before."

Very romantic.

"Can you recite them?" Yvette pipes in.

"Thine love will always spring from the truth within my heart . . . uh . . ." I flip through my booklet. "Oh—and even when my heart stops, and my body returns to the earth from which it came, my love for thee will grow eternally in the flowers and the trees."

"Very good." Maria's phone rings, and she steps away to answer it. Yvette takes the opportunity to put away the projector.

"You'll never forget those now." Tristian leans back in his chair; the wood creaks dangerously. "Our guests are hopeless romantics. At least once a day, someone will ask us to recite them."

"I've never told anyone I loved them. I can't wait to profess my love to you in front of an audience." I tug at my corset laces.

Have they gotten tighter while I was sitting?

Tristian's brows lift as he says softly, "I love you."

"What?" I cough, choking on my spit—very princess-like. I cringe, a spike of familiar anxiety racing through my body.

"I thought we should practice saying it." His blue eyes locked on my face sends a burning across my skin.

"Oh, right." I know it's pretend. I don't love him. I barely know him, and he doesn't love me. Still, my voice catches on the words. I clear my throat and try again. "I love you, Prince Winthrop."

"That sounded totally natural and not at all like I'm holding you at gunpoint." He breaks the tension with a laugh.

16

TRISTIAN

I haven't trained since I started playing a face character at fourteen. So, this refresher course is painful enough, but add to it that we've been at it for two hours, and it's only eight a.m.—I'm coasting on fumes.

Imogen smiles at me, and the lack of sleep makes me return it, that hard thing in my chest dislodging a little. Maybe being here isn't so bad after all? I'm dying to know why she was wandering around the offices last night. However, if I get her to confess, she'll make me return the favor.

Then I'd have to admit I was searching for pictures of Mom among the hundreds on the walls. One part of me is happy I stayed and get to feel her everywhere I go. Though admitting all that is the same as conceding to Ivor and Dad, to the life they think I should live.

"Now, I'm sure I don't need to emphasize this point any further, but since we're here . . ." Aunt Maria wraps a hand around her necklace. My mom used to wear one just like it. I swallow the lump in my throat. "Please refrain from fistfights with the guests. No matter"—her voice sharpens as I open my mouth—"if they deserve it or not."

When yesterday's guest swung at me, every minor annoyance I'd held in about FTG raged to the surface, and I saw red. In hindsight, it was childish, and my fist hurts almost as much as my jaw. Still, pissing off Ivor was a nice bonus.

"So we won't carry on about that anymore. I know you learned your lesson." Aunt Maria runs a tight ship, but she's got everyone's best interests at heart.

"I want to focus on the most important task, meet-and-greets—pictures." Her heels click against the floor as she circles around us. "These photos will hold fond memories for a lifetime."

I'll never get over the idea of being immortalized in family pictures.

Maria motions for Yvette to be our stand-in photographer, the iPad her camera. "Let's practice a few poses."

"I prefer this pose." I position Imogen behind the guest—a mannequin—and step in beside her. "Because if they throw up, they do it away from us."

Imogen winces, regarding the plastic person with suspicion. "You all talk about throwing up a lot. I expect constant bombardment." Her back stiffens as she tries not to fidget. Maria already called her on it three times.

"Depends where we are. Pray it's not near a thrill ride." The three cups of coffee do little to alleviate the pressure behind my eyes.

"Talking in a picture," Maria cuts in, "is not flattering."

Imogen's face scrunches as she suppresses a laugh. Her reddening cheeks and twinkling eyes slowly eat away at my annoyance. I admire the way she just jumped right into this whole experience. Her resolve to make the best of any situation is something I wish I had. Training sucks, but she makes it marginally more entertaining. If I weren't so tired, I'd stop myself from enjoying this, but I don't have the energy to fight it.

I think bland, pleasant thoughts as we move through the poses I know all too well. Maria imparts a few more tips, and overall we get a passing grade.

"Do you think we'll make it through the day this time?" Imogen sits in the window seat after Maria and Yvette leave. We've got an hour before our first appearance.

"You'll be perfect." I undo the sword at my side and place it on the table.

Her laugh makes something warm in my chest. My hardened outer shell melts every time she makes that soft sound that feels like a summer's day. I'm not sure how to feel about it.

"Let's not go that far." She raps at the glass with her knuckles. "I heard you weren't supposed to be here this summer."

I glance toward the door. I should stop by the marketing office before I get shackled into prince duty for most of the day—I might not care about marketing, but I should probably try to do something. Still, a few more minutes with her won't hurt. Even though she's fully invested in the FTG culture, she doesn't have the same tarnish I feel for the rest of the park.

"I wasn't. I was going to study history around Europe, but my dad vetoed it at the last minute. Ever the tyrant king." I run a hand over my leathers to smooth them.

The sun dances across her face, giving her a glow. "That sucks. I'm sorry. But there are worse places than FTG to be stuck at. Trust me." Her intense gaze doesn't leave my face.

"Maybe for you, but this isn't how I want to spend my summer. But it's not like I ever get a choice." I still have a seed of hope Dad will change his mind. I know the deadline for signing up has passed, but they don't leave for another month. Even if that's a long shot, it's keeping me afloat.

She trails her fingers over her neck, dancing along the ruffled edge of her top. I swallow hard. In another time, this might be the perfect setup for me to ask her out. We could go play carnival games and I'd impress her with my amazing skills. But doing that would further tie me to the place I'm still hoping to escape from.

"You said something yesterday about interning?" she asks.

"Ivor handed it out as a consolation prize for having to stay. He said he needed help with the marketing, and I could be the intern. Doesn't matter that I have zero interest in marketing." I clench my jaw, ignoring the pain.

"I might not know anything about internships, but this doesn't look like what a person would do with a marketing one." She waves to my fallen sword.

"Actually, I'm headed to the office right now." I grab the weapon and march toward the door like a man on a mission, even though I don't have the slightest clue. "See you at the carriage."

"Wait." She follows me down the stairs and out the castle's side entrance, so we can bypass the guests. "Why didn't you turn Ivor down, if you hate marketing?" She's out of breath when she catches up.

If I still believed in fairytales, I might say this is the beginning of my story—the wayward prince about to start his hero's journey. "I don't hate it. I just don't care. But my family needs me. My father . . . hasn't been the same since my mom died." I detach myself from the words to make them easier to swallow.

Her voice drops. "I'm sorry." She pats my shoulder awkwardly. "Everyone around here sings her praises."

"Thanks." I run a hand over my mouth to cut myself off from divulging any more. I'm not here for summer camp bonding. "What about you? Why are you here?"

We arrive in the backstage parking lot. People scurry by us, hurrying to their morning shifts. I keep my course for the office. Ivor didn't get me the key, but I know Milly has one. She's got all the keys to the kingdom.

Imogen nibbles her bottom lip, taking her sweet time to answer what I thought was a softball question. "My life was aflame. I needed to reset." I hold the door for her into the main building. I catch another whiff of her perfume as she walks past—spicy, like cinnamon.

I relate to the need for a change of scenery. "Not shocking, given your colorful job history." I spare her a smile as we head to the offices.

"How do you know about my job history?" Her eyebrows rise in shock.

I turn away to stop myself from fantasizing about kissing her. "After our whirlwind courtship yesterday, I browsed your file. I mean, a guy shows up to his royal carriage and suddenly has a new bride, it's only proper I get to know you better."

Imogen plays with the ties on her shoulder straps. "Mm-hmm. In fairness you should give me a peek at yours," she counters.

"It'd put you to sleep. I've worked here since I was twelve. I'm surprised Dad didn't shackle me to the castle when I asked to leave." Okay, he wouldn't do that, but I'm annoyed and it felt good to say.

When we get to the third floor, Milly is in deep conversation with my father and a security guard. Imogen stops short next to me. "What's going on?"

Dad's voice rises as I approach the desk. "I don't give a damn. This is a violation. We should have installed cameras. Who cares how much they cost."

"What's up?" I attempt to shove my hands into my pockets, but my costume doesn't have any, so I grab the hilt of my sword to make up for the fumble.

"Tristian." Milly's smile is tight. "We just had a little security concern, is all."

"Oh?" My eyes roam over the space, but nothing seems amiss.

A muscle twitches in Dad's jaw. "Someone broke into my office."

"Sir, we don't know if that's the case. Perhaps you forgot to shut the door when you left," the security guard says, examining the lock. "There's no sign of tampering."

"I've never once left my door open in two decades." Dad's face is flushed, his hands curled into fists.

I glance at Imogen, hanging near the stairs, face unreadable. She was here last night—I don't know if she was on the third floor, but she was in the building.

A reflex from deep inside almost makes me spill her secret, like I might win Dad's approval if I do. But the churning in my gut keeps me quiet. I have no idea why she was here. Outing her would only get her in trouble, and I don't want to lose another princess.

Besides, what do I care if someone broke into his office? It's not my problem.

My leathers tug on my shoulders as I lean on the desk. "Sorry to bother you then, but I need the key to Ted's old office. I know you must have a spare."

Milly searches a bottom drawer and withdraws several sets of keys. "It's here somewhere." She flips through them. "Oh dear." Her face turns sour.

"Something wrong?" I ask.

"It appears the key to Mr. Walsh's office is missing."

This gets Dad's attention. "See." He points to the mess of keys in Milly's hands. "I told you it was a break-in. I want a full investigation. Report back when you've found the culprit. And get me a security camera." He stalks into the office, leaving the rest of us in awkward silence.

"Maybe if Dad wasn't so concerned about only making money, he could've invested some back into park improvements," I say to Milly.

Milly offers a tight smile before sliding the key across the desk to me. "Anything else?" Her eyes wander to Imogen behind me.

"No. Thanks, Milly." I nod, walking back to Imogen. "Are you coming with me or . . ." I didn't want her to follow me a minute ago, but now I have a burning question.

Imogen tucks a strand of hair behind her ear, biting her lip. "Uh, sure."

17

TRISTIAN

I unlock the door and flip on the light to the dusty office. "So, do you have anything to add to the whole break-in situation my father is losing his mind about?"

Her brows knit together. "Why would I?" She stays near the door, arms crossed over her chest.

"Just thought since you were here, you might've seen the culprit."

"Are you accusing me?" she asks, voice void of her usual sunshine.

I hold up my hands in retreat. "No." I genuinely don't think it was her. The story she gave me was likely a lie, but I can't see why she'd be in Dad's office. It's not like there's anything worth stealing in there, unless she's in the market for an oversized painting of my family.

"Because you were here, too. It could be you, for all I know."

"It wasn't me."

"Well, it wasn't me either." Her tone is fierce.

A twinge of guilt stabs my chest at the anguish on her face. "Sorry, of course you didn't do it. My dad probably left it open and forgot." He wouldn't want to look like a fool and would blame everyone else before taking responsibility.

She nods, eyeing up the door like she's ready to bolt.

"Do you want to help me?" I say quickly before she can make an excuse to leave. I don't know why I ask. It's just that when she's around the world seems a little brighter.

She presses her lips together, studying me. "Help with what? I don't know anything about marketing."

"That makes two of us." I offer a laugh and she grabs on to it like a lifeboat.

She beams once again, sitting on the opposite side of the desk; the coldness melts away as the sunshine reappears. I fight the smile tugging at my lips.

"Well, if that isn't an airtight argument, I don't know what is. What's first?" she asks.

I start Ted's computer, knowing it's probably password-protected, and I won't get any further than sitting in this chair. The computer prompts me and I type in random words—nothing. I look up to find Imogen staring at me. I take out my phone as a distraction. "If I can't get on the computer, we should at least check out FTG's socials as a starting point." I grab a sticky note off the desk with a handwritten list of passwords for all the major sites. I can tell right away Garrick wrote it. Either he left it for me or set it up for Ted.

Imogen leans forward on the desk, hands resting under her chin. "Excellent plan, marketing man." Her face turns red as she holds in her laugh.

I twist in the chair, so I'm angled toward her. I pull at the loose laces of the sneakers she's still wearing as her feet tangle over my legs. "Did you rhyme on purpose?"

"Obviously. Feel free to use my skills in your captions."

I find myself studying her, wishing I had the ease she projects so effortlessly. "Do you follow FTG on social media?" I ask, switching my focus back to my phone.

She gets up, leaning over my shoulder to see my screen. Tendrils of her red hair tickle my cheek. "Honestly, I try to avoid social media. It makes me spiral."

I know the feeling. Every time I see a picture posted from a trip, my blood pressure rises. It's like their joy is an affront to me.

"I'm supposed to help with marketing, but FTG's socials are abysmal. It's mostly just tagged posts from Garrick or random shots of ads." I follow FTG on all the major socials, but I never really paid much attention. Garrick is the real star—I leave that stuff to him.

"Let me see." Imogen grabs the phone as she sits on the desk. "We can fix this."

I try to snatch it back, but she twists to the side, pushing me away with the toe of her shoe. Resigned, I lean back in my chair. "I thought you weren't into social media?"

"I can at least figure out a hashtag and a filter." I watch her tap her fingers against her lips in time to a silent song as she scrolls through the page. "All right, so we just need to update Instagram and TikTok. Those are going to be the best ones to promote the park. What?" she adds when she looks up to see me staring.

I shake my head. "How are you so good at everything?"

She frowns. "I'm definitely not."

"Okay, maybe not. But that doesn't stop you from jumping right in and trying. This is meant to be my gig and I couldn't even snap a few pics for Insta because I was pissed off."

I startle when she places a hand on my shoulder. "It's fine to be pissed. This wasn't how you wanted summer to be, and I get that. So, why don't you let me help you? Teamwork makes the dream work, or whatever—I'm not into sports."

There she goes, making me smile again. "Show me what you got."

She nods, clicking away on my phone.

"Can I have the phone back?"

She playfully slaps my hand away. "I'm fixing a few things."

"Should we make you an intern, too?"

Her face lights up. "I actually think my parents might die if they found out I had an internship."

"Not your style?" I joke, feeling lighter already just being around her.

She doesn't respond, just does this cute little half smirk. "Done." She hands the phone back to me a few minutes later. "I changed the passwords to 'TlovesFTG4life!' but feel free to change it."

I scowl, but it doesn't have much heat behind it.

"I knew you'd love that. Oh!" She jumps up from the desk. "As our first posts, we should do a day in the life."

"Huh?" My eyes narrow at her sudden excited burst. I'm not going to like what she's about to say.

"All day, we post videos and pictures of what a day is like for our characters. People love that. It's like the vlogs FTG used to post." She beams with pride, like she discovered a new planet and gets to name it after herself.

My stomach flips at the memory of those videos. They were Mom's idea. They weren't anything serious, just fun little clips with me and my brothers as we pretended to be our fictional counterparts.

I shake my head. "No way. I'm already stuck playing a prince. I don't need to add social media star to that." Even if re-creating something I did with Mom might make her feel closer.

"Wow, so you think you're going to be *so* impressive that you'll become an instant star? Interesting." She bites her cheek, suppressing a huge grin. "Please, do tell me more."

"That's not what I said."

"Hmm, that's basically what I heard." Now her smile feels mocking.

"I'm trying to take this seriously. I don't want to make it into some farce." I feel splotchy red spots appearing on my neck, the sign my emotions are getting the better of me.

Huffing, she runs a hand through her hair. "I was joking. Okay? I know you want a big ol" serious job. I promise we will make sure you don't come off as fun in any way."

I groan, slouching into the chair. "Why don't we ask Garrick to do it? He loves attention."

"It'll be great. We can even say our vows." She winks and grabs my hands, dragging me from the room.

An hour later, after hair and makeup, I still haven't convinced Imogen to give up on the idea. The concept isn't flawed—hell, it's brilliant—but I don't want to do it.

"Phones don't exist in Carpathia." I shrug on my cape as we wait for our cue to start the carriage ride. "If we take selfies, it'll ruin the whole illusion."

Imogen gives me a deadpan stare. "All day we take pictures with guests—most of those taken *on phones*. This is the same thing."

Dang it. She's not wrong. Helping her into the carriage, I lean against the door. "Point taken."

She bats her eyelashes and grins smugly. "Tristian." The wig hides her long neck, the massive curls covering the delicate lines. "Get in here. We're doing this." She pats the seat. I hold off as the music signals our entrance.

"Yvette, snap a picture, please." Leaning in, Imogen places a hand on my arm and smiles for the camera. Last second, I grab her chin to turn her face toward mine.

"Got it." Yvette gives a thumbs-up. "You'll make all the people swoon."

The carriage lurches forward. Lines crease Imogen's forehead.

"What?" I wave to the emerging crowds. "It was less posed."

The wind throws a curl across her face. "We spent all morning learning how to pose."

"Maybe we should switch it up. This park could use a bit more real." The uptilt of her smile twists my gut.

Imogen forces us to do several videos before our meet and greet. "If you want to punch someone today, let me know beforehand, so I can tell Yvette to catch it on camera."

"Funny."

No fights break out in the meet-and-greets. We follow Aunt Maria's rules and create enough content to satisfy Imogen's agenda. The day has flown by. I haven't thought about Europe or about how much I hate it here—okay, maybe I did once or twice between Imogen-shaped distractions. The panic still found its way in when I slipped out of Winthrop's head into mine. But it was manageable.

"I love this one." Imogen pushes the phone to me as we sit in the costume department after our shift. The video shows us with a little girl dressed as a fairy.

"Not bad." I scratch at my leftover stage makeup. I can never get it entirely out of my eyebrows.

"Not bad? Tristian, look at all those views."

The count is higher than I would've guessed.

The door creaks open as Garrick and Aliana come into the room. Imogen stands, slipping her phone into her pocket. "I know this isn't the summer you planned, but I have a feeling you could be pretty good at this if you gave it a chance." She drops her knowledge before disappearing out of the room.

"Dang, I wanted to see a fight today." Garrick hooks his sword on the wall rack. "Why'd you have to go and conform?"

I tear my eyes away from the door. "I didn't want to give Ivor a heart attack. So I played the good boy."

Garrick fakes a gagging motion.

Aliana dumps her costume on Harold's desk after changing. "Whose idea was the TikTok?"

"Imogen's."

She pouts. "Huh, smart. I saw it on my *For You* page."

Pride surges in my chest. The FTG story might have decayed for me, but Imogen brings out a part I didn't totally hate.

18

IMOGEN

The sun bakes the back of my neck. The far side of the castle is mainly in the shade, just not the part where we have to stand and wave. Yvette has separated Tristian and me for the afternoon character meet-and-greets.

"You're stepping on my skirt." Aliana's voice drags me from my delirium as she yanks the fabric from under my shoe.

I huff, trying to remove the delicate strands of wig hair from my face without grabbing at it and ruining my already questionable stage makeup.

"Guests like group pictures with the princesses," Yvette told me earlier, when I protested about this arrangement. But Yvette was not to be persuaded, which is why I'm with Aliana on the first-floor balcony.

The short cement guardrail scratches my hands as I move to avoid Aliana's absurdly large gown. The dark burgundy fabric has white and silver accents.

My dress is more elaborate than yesterday, a soft robin's-egg blue color with gold and navy-blue flowers sewn into the bodice. The shoulders are puffy with the same blue fabric, and white chiffon billows over my arms. Today's wig is more intricate—braids weave into a bun at the base of my neck.

The guests stand several feet below us, and I lean over to see them.

"Watch the wig. If it falls off, I'm not getting it for you." Aliana has offered helpful tips like this all afternoon. I would take her harsh tone more personally if I didn't hear her talk this way to literally everyone. Even the people I know she likes. I think it's just her default setting.

"It's practically glued on. It's not going anywhere." I tug on the back all the same. Despite the heat and the putrid smell from the bathrooms across the way, Aliana remains the perfect princess. Her delicate smile is the right amount of teeth, and when she leans down to hear the tiny guests, her back remains straight as a flagpole.

I mimic her movements as best I can before the impostor syndrome consumes me.

I'll never be as good as her.

Over the last few days with Tristian, I thought I did well. Except he wasn't trying hard to be good. Aliana looks effortless. She might have helpful tips, but you'll catch me jumping off this balcony before I ask her for any.

Yvette is frowning when we meet her after we're done.

"What's wrong?" I ask, pushing my wig off my neck to get some air.

She shoves her iPad into her bag. "Staff meeting."

"Why?" Aliana takes a sip of water.

"Something to do with security." She shrugs. "We need to be there in five."

I hang back as the two of them head toward the break room, feet refusing to move. My stomach does backflips, and my fingers are icy cold as I wrap my hand around my wrist.

"Imogen, come on. It's mandatory," Yvette calls when she notices I'm not with them.

A sour taste coats my mouth, and I swallow, throat thick, attempting to alleviate it. I follow them, making an excuse about the bathroom when we arrive, before darting upstairs to the costume department.

Harold is there, and I ignore his quizzical look as I fumble to get my phone, scattering my clothes all over the floor. Scooping them into my arms, I deposit them in the box, phone already pressed to my ear, calling Divya as I scurry into the quiet hall.

"Hey," Divya answers after a few rings.

The noise increases from downstairs as a large group of Fairytalers head to the meeting.

"I'm leaving." I cup my hand over the speaker to hide my words from the passersby.

"What? Why?" There's only mild alarm in her tone.

"They figured me out. *Ugh*, I knew this was a bad idea. I told you." My sentences are rapid-fire as my heart rate increases.

"Slow down and fill me in."

I tell Divya about Barth's door being left open, even though I was sure I closed it, and that he's launching an investigation.

"Now they've called a meeting, and they're going to expose me. My stuff is still in the apartment, but I don't have time to pack." I'm rambling. "But does it really matter? I can buy new clothes."

"Imogen, calm down." Divya raises her voice to talk over me. "If they thought it was you, they would've hauled you out of there already, not set up a meeting."

I press my palm into the wall, hunching my shoulder and turning around as someone walks by. "What if they want to make an example of me?"

I actually liked it here. I don't want my last memories of this place to be me being dragged out in handcuffs.

"Then I'll pay for your bail."

"*Divya*," I hiss.

"You're fine. Just go to the meeting and play it cool."

The sweat glistening on my forehead and the blood pounding in my ears are the opposite of cool. I hang up with Divya, taking a deep breath before heading into the meeting.

Yvette saved me a seat right next to Tristian. I give them a tight smile, slouching into my chair—which is very hard in a corset.

"I'm sure you're all curious why you're here." Michael stands at the front, Barth next to him with his arms crossed, a scowl very reminiscent of Tristian marring his face.

I try to take a sip of water but choke on it. Yvette hits my back, and I hold up my hand in apology. Tristian offers a puzzled look but nothing else.

"We've had a serious breach of trust. Two nights ago, Mr. Walsh's office was broken into. We're still investigating the situation but wanted to give the culprit a chance to come clean. If the person, or persons, responsible fess up, we won't press charges. If not, we'll be forced to follow legal action."

A gaping hole widens in my unsettled stomach. I was here for the fun of it. Never once did I assume I could get in any real trouble. Suddenly, the stakes are a lot higher.

The Fairytalers glance around with confused looks. I curl my hand into the folds of my gown, tensing my muscles so tight they start to shake. I keep my face inquisitive. I give Tristian a shrug, like, *Huh? Who could it be?*

He asked me about the break-in yesterday, and I covered my tracks well enough. He didn't seem to think I was involved. But what if Tristian casually mentions he saw me that night? They'll want to talk to me and I don't think I'd stand up to police interrogation. I'd spill my guts and Divya would be exposed and that would ruin everything for her and her family. Still, right now, no one is accusing me. I just need to keep it that way.

When no one fesses up, Michael continues. "If any of you saw anything, please report it." He looks over to Barth, who nods but stays silent, staring us all down. I focus intently at a spot just past Michael's shoulder so I don't have to make eye contact. "You're all dismissed."

"Are you okay?" Yvette asks when I don't get up.

I blink, uncurling my hands, which ache from my iron grip. "Yeah, just hungry."

Tristian pulls a granola bar from a pouch at his side and hands it to me. "This is for show. Mom was the responsible one. Dad can be careless when it comes to certain details."

"You don't think the break-in was real?" I nibble on the bar, not because I'm actually hungry but because it keeps my hands busy.

"Highly doubt it. Nothing to steal in there but a bunch of worthless fake relics. Dad's money is spent on less tangible things."

"Like?" I ask. I didn't want to use Tristian for info, but if he's offering it up freely, there's no harm in hearing it.

Tristian shrugs. "He's gone on plenty of trips to other theme parks to scope out the competition, and Dad's such a king himself, obsessed with image, I'm guessing he's flying first class and staying in the nicest hotels."

"But you've never gone with him?"

"Yeah, right. Like he'd let us," Tristian scoffs. "Probably doesn't want us getting any ideas of what else we could be doing with our lives."

I gnaw the inside of my lip. *Huh.* Sounds like Tristian might not be too broken up about exposing his dad's underhanded dealings. If Barth is responsible, maybe Prince Charming would be happy for an excuse to break out of the kingdom.

Tristian might be off my scent, but Barth is still on high alert. I need to be more careful. I'll have to take a few days off from snooping until everything calms down.

Day Five at Fairytale Gardens starts with a photo shoot. The weak light of the soft morning sun is still strong enough to make me squint.

"Tristian." Garrick sits on the curb in front of the castle. "Can I wear sunglasses?" He uses his sword as a hockey stick to hit rocks. All the main characters are here in full costume. Most of us linger at the castle's base, while Tristian speaks to the photographer.

"Tristian!" Garrick yells again.

"What?" Tristian spins to look at him, raking a hand through his hair, eyes narrowed.

"It's bright. I can't see." Garrick holds a hand up to block the sun.

Tristian rolls his shoulders. And even from my place several yards away I can see his clenched jaw. He turns and converses with the photographer for several minutes.

"Fine, everyone angle the other way." He directs us to new positions. "Imogen, will you stand here?"

I situate myself next to him. "You're doing great." I give him a thumbs-up. Since the warning about the break-in I've been on my best behavior. So far no one's come and dragged me from my room in the dead of night to throw me in the dungeon. Not that there is a dungeon.

That I'm aware of.

He lets out a quick breath. "I'd have better luck wrangling monkeys. But you inspired me to get involved."

I try to temper my smile. I like the idea of inspiring someone—especially Tristian Walsh.

"What's wrong with the old photos?" Ivor polishes his crown on his cape. "This is a waste of money."

"Those marketing photos are from five years ago." Tristian's words are tight as a vein in his neck bulges.

"So?" Ivor pushes.

"*So*, you said I was the marketing intern, which means I'm

taking charge." He nods to the photographer. "Let's get this over with."

"Did you speak to Dad about—"

"Ivor!" Tristian's sharp voice cuts through the group chatter. "If you want Dad to run everything, you shouldn't have offered me this role." Ivor and Tristian have a silent battle with their eyes before each turns away. "Take the photo."

After thirty minutes, the photographer signals the group portion is finished and we'll move on to the couple and individual shots. Tristian and I are first. "Let's go to Pixie Forest," Tristian tells the photographer.

"This was a great idea—a refresh is just what the park needs. We can put them on Instagram, too. They'll look great with the fantastic new ads you showed me." I try to cheer him up and replace the sour lemon pucker he's sporting. "For not knowing what a marketing intern is supposed to do, you seem to be hitting all the marks."

He shrugs halfheartedly, footsteps dragging as we walk. "I could see Garrick from the corner of my eye. He looked bored, and Ivor looked pissed. I'm sure my face didn't come off much better."

"Well, I smiled how you taught me, so I'll look fabulous, if nothing else." We take a seat in the meet-and-greet alcove. My joke does little to lighten the gloom on his features. "Maybe they can Photoshop a smile on your face?"

"It just—" He stops short, dropping his head into his hands. I see a slight tremble as he leans on his knees.

"What?" My hand hovers over his back. I want to be comforting, but we've been balancing on the line "coworkers who bicker but in a fun (possible even a flirty?) way" and I'm not sure where we stand.

Should I pat it? Is that weird? I decide to keep my hands to myself.

"Ivor asked for my help with the marketing and, like a fool, I thought that would mean something. But he'll never listen to me." He gazes at his feet, his voice flat. "No one here cares about my opinions."

"That's not true." I nudge him with my knee, and he glances up. "Aldrich and I hung on your every word."

His body sags, shoulders rounded forward. "Great. I can order my little brother and the new girl around. I'm really going places."

I run a hand down his arm, sliding it with ease over the buttery soft leather. His body stiffens as his Adam's apple bobs. We hold each other's gaze for a second before turning away.

"Are we ready yet?" he asks the photographer.

"Two minutes. Just fixing the lighting."

I fiddle with the ends of my wig as I study him. "Here's my unsolicited advice. Have fun. Making yourself miserable the whole time will only make it worse. And who knows, you might surprise yourself and enjoy it."

He scoffs. "If you really believed that, I doubt your résumé would be so long."

My stomach twists at the truth in his words. If I hated a job, I'd get out the second I could. But those places weren't Fairytale Gardens.

19

IMOGEN

I'm six days into my run as Princess Arden, and while not perfect, Tristian and I have found our groove. And by groove, I mean we haven't started any more brawls. So, when Yvette mentions the park staying open late for the Fairytalers, I thought I'd earned the night off. Granted, six days isn't impressive, but I've quit jobs in less than a day—so this is a stellar performance in my books. My parents even sounded pleased when I talked to them at lunch. It feels nice to be doing something right.

> **Divya**
> Anything yet? I'm antsy. Lol.

The text sits uneasily in my gut, a lump of lead on an otherwise magical day. I need to keep the mission as the primary focus—it's just hard when I wear a tiara and have a prince at my side. Also the investigation is still ongoing, so I'm walking on eggshells, sure that my good luck is about to expire like Cinderella's at midnight.

At one point yesterday, Aliana made a weird comment that

maybe someone was stalking around at night and I held my breath for a solid minute waiting for her to accuse me. But then she switched to complaining about the unreliable air-conditioning in the apartments and didn't even spare me a second glance.

"You came." Tristian lounges against the railing next to Mushroom Spin. His prince attire is long gone. A gray T-shirt and khaki shorts have replaced it.

I miss the leathers.

The park closed an hour ago. "I never miss a party." I brush a strand of hair behind my ear, gracing him with my signature sparkling smile. "I should be more shocked you showed up, Ebenezer Scrooge."

A muscle ticks in Tristian's jaw. "You're *so* funny."

"I know." I beam. "You should try it sometime."

It's a warm night, and the park lights blink out the stars. A few rides in Pixie Forest have stayed open for the Fairytalers to ride without the guests disturbing us.

After spending all day confined to a meet-and-greet stage, or the carriage, I relish the fresh air. Even if it does smell like stale popcorn and disinfectant. The bright red and blue spotlights from Mushroom Spin dance across the ground.

"I hate this ride." Yvette fidgets beside me, followed by Aliana and her gaggle of fairies.

"It'll be . . . ," I start.

"Don't you dare say fun. It will not." Yvette frowns, hands searching for a tablet she doesn't have.

"Entertaining," I finish, like I was always going to say that. Yvette and I have been texting the last few days and she's hilarious when she wants to be. I even made plans to hang out with her and her girlfriend later this week.

"I'll kick your ass." Aldrich perches on the entrance gate.

"You wish." Garrick leans against the opposite fence, a leg kicked up behind him. "I haven't lost a ride-off since—well, never!" Tristian turns away from us, but I can tell he's a little pale, even in the colorful lights.

I recline, forearms resting on the warm bar forming the line. "What's a ride-off?"

Aldrich's face lights up. "We've done it since we were kids. We get on the wildest ride, and the last person to quit or not throw up wins."

I lift an eyebrow, watching Tristian from my peripheral vision. After pressing against him all day, pretending to be deeply in love, my body seeks him out without my permission. It's really annoying, actually. I'm a modern woman. I don't need a prince.

Want, well, that's another story.

"What do you win?" I try to focus.

"There isn't a prize." Tristian runs a hand through his hair to hide the shaking. I've seen a range of faces from him—the charming prince, the pessimistic downer, and the genuine heart—but I haven't seen fear. Until now. Or at least extreme discomfort. It makes me want to participate in this game even more.

"Where's the fun in that?" I tap a finger against my teasing smile. "If we do play"—I brush past Tristian as I move to the entrance—"there should be a prize."

"Oh, you're playing?" Tristian's eyes lock on mine with a challenge. The park sounds fade into the background.

Heat rushes from my head to my toes. Okay, I'm not imagining it this time—he's for sure checking me out. I push my shoulders back, attempting to look way cooler than I am.

"Sure," I counter, not breaking his stare, even though my brain is screaming *omg, omg, omg*. "Unless you're afraid a girl will beat you?" I exaggerate a frown by thrusting out my bottom lip. Is this flirting? Am I doing it right? Wow, I'm terrible at this. I wish my wingwoman Divya was here.

Garrick throws an arm around his brother's shoulders. "You can play with us any day." He winks.

My attention doesn't waver from Tristian. "What's the prize?"

The wily grin conceals Tristian's unease with a practiced hand. "It's more interesting if the loser has to do something."

"Yes, a punishment." Aldrich claps his hands.

"I'm so proud of you." Garrick fakes a sob as he slaps Aldrich on the back. "The losers have to"—he taps his chin—"jump into the Perilous Sea."

"No way—that water is disgusting." Aldrich gags, shoving Garrick away.

"Sounds like fun," someone mutters from the back of the line. Several Fairytalers have gathered around. It's the way of the Walshes. They're the flames, and the rest of us are the moths. A tug in my gut makes me stop.

I don't want to be a moth.

Just another girl hopelessly infatuated with the handsome brothers. As much as the flame feels good now, it'll leave me freezing when it disappears.

"You should be worried, little brother." Garrick brushes

invisible dirt from his shoulders. "I don't lose. What do you say, T?"

Tristian speaks to me when he answers. "I'm in."

His face makes me want to run headfirst into the flame.

"Sorry, guys." Yvette holds her hands up in retreat. "I'm out." I should walk away too, get on the kiddy train and behave myself. But that was never going to happen.

A few others join the game, Aliana included. I ignore the pain in my ribs when I think about Aliana and Tristian together. It shouldn't bother me as much as it does.

I'd like to pretend I'm not extremely invested in the outcome of this game, or that I'm only trying to win so I don't have to jump into questionable water, but really I'm just far more competitive than I like to admit.

I pick a mushroom that smells the least like bleach, hoping that means no one threw up in it earlier. Other than that, I have very little strategy to winning. My whole life has been one giant spiral. Spinning should be easy, right?

I grip the edges of the mushroom spinning out of control, my clammy hands struggling to keep hold. My stomach rolls as I whip to the side, my hair catching in my mouth and obscuring my vision. Divya's disapproving face flashes through my mind, but a sharp turn flings me forward, and my chest hitting the center console evaporates the image.

Yvette cheers me on from the sideline as two people wave in defeat and the ride slows to let them off. A few minutes later, Aliana quits, along with three others. It's me and the Walshes left. I should've known the odds were against me.

I wish I'd skipped dessert earlier, but I couldn't turn down caramel brownies—that'd be a crime. They slosh in my gut with every new rotation. Garrick's never looked better. Tristian is a little worse for wear. Aldrich stares off into the distance, mouth plastered shut.

"You can stop any time," I yell, hair caught in my mouth again, as my mushroom whirls by Tristian's.

"If you want to swim with me, you only have to ask." Tristian acts nonchalant, but he's pale as fresh snow.

"I took a spin class last semester." Garrick grins, arms slung beside him on the mushroom's rim. "Spinning is my specialty."

"That makes no sense." The music swallows my voice.

"Doesn't have to. I'm still going to win." Garrick props his feet on the side of the ride vehicle. Aldrich remains silent, face unreadable.

"I really hate him." Tristian's fast voice whirls past me. If he doesn't improve soon, I may have to forfeit to get him off in one piece. I can't have a disoriented prince by my side all day tomorrow.

"Garrick!" I come up with a new tactic. "Is that building on fire?" I point behind him, and he flips his head around quickly, interrupting his rhythm. Two minutes later, there's a gagging sound, and he waves in defeat.

"Dirty play." Garrick stumbles off his mushroom. "I respect it."

"Can we outlast Aldrich?" I ask Tristian as they start the ride again.

Only a minute passes before he shakes his head. The ride slows to a stop. "What kind of prince would I be if I didn't fall on my sword for a lady?"

My foggy brain takes a second to realize he's quitting. "Wait, you're out?"

He walks close to me. "Please beat Aldrich." The deep rumble of his voice makes my skin tingle. I shake my head, my arms and legs limp noodles. The ride spins again, but I lost my tempo, distracted by Tristian.

Nausea rolls through me as my stomach clenches. I clamp my mouth shut, grinding my teeth to stay on the mushroom. It's too late. I raise my hand in defeat. The ride stops, and through blurry vision I watch Aldrich's face break into an all-consuming grin.

"Yes!" He jumps out, dancing across the floor to rub it in Garrick's face.

"Here." Tristian offers his hand to steady me. I'm not here to flirt with a hot prince, but it'd be easier if he weren't all chivalrous. My brain is a pile of mush, spun to its limits. The sensible part of my mind—which was already lacking—has left for the night.

"This is a terrible game." I press the back of my hand to my mouth, worried my dessert might make a reappearance. "I can't believe you talked me into it."

His body vibrates in laughter against my side. "Yeah, I talked you into it. Sure, let's go with that version of the story." He brushes hair off my face, and I freeze, not sure if I want to push him away or pull him in closer.

I straighten my posture. *What would it be like to kiss him?* His warm hand rests gently on my arm, his thumb making slow circles. I can smell his minty gum, and if I just rise up on my toes I could meet his lips.

I've kissed exactly two guys, and neither was anything worth repeating. But with Tristian there's more than just wanting to smash our lips together. It's this feeling like it might actually mean more—and that is really overwhelming to my commitment-resistant brain.

But as my fantasy takes over, it morphs into what Tristian's face would look like if he found out I lied about breaking in. The sweet smiles I manage to drag out of him would be locked away behind his stony facade. Then the picture changes into an image of Divya. The disappointment I'll have to face if my impulses interfere with the reason she sent me here.

I swallow hard, skin tight as I step away. I pivot on my heels to follow the crowd headed toward the Perilous Sea.

This area is darker, shut for the night. The only lights come from the front entrance and Pixie Forest. I stand on the sea's edge as the others prepare themselves. Garrick dives in first—not shy about showing off.

"Is this safe to swim in?" Yvette eyes the dark water.

"It's mostly a swimming pool." The bravado I displayed moments ago wears thin.

"Yeah . . . I saw a kid throw up here this morning," Yvette mutters. "You don't have to do this."

A few people hesitate to get in, but adrenaline takes over, and they go for it. In the dim light, I can make out the outline of Tristian's lean, muscular body as he slips into the water a few yards away.

"Yes, I do. You should go—pretend you've seen nothing." She hesitates but leaves me alone.

Luckily, the barrier around the sea is short, because falling over a fence is not a good look. I remove my shoes before taking a running leap in. My breath leaves my body as the cold water hits my skin.

"Holy crap." I kick my feet to stay afloat. It didn't look this deep from the shore. I can't touch the bottom without dipping my head underwater, which—gross. Hard pass.

How long do I have to stay to make good on my bet? A few minutes should do it.

I'm only wearing shorts and a T-shirt, but even the minimal fabric clings to me, making my movements sloppy. Garrick and the others have swum to the center, splashing and screaming. I don't spot Tristian. Not that I was actively looking for him.

I pivot, ready to head back to shore, when something seizes my foot. "Ahh!" Tangy water splashes into my mouth as I try to swim away from the thing trapping me. But the more I struggle, the tighter the slimy thing's grip becomes.

"Hey, hey, stop." Tristian swims from my left. "What's wrong?"

"There—something—it's got my foot." I pant in shallow breaths.

"Okay, hold still." His sun-kissed curls shimmer in the dim light.

My heart rages in my throat. "Are there animals in here?" I should've asked this beforehand. I kick my legs faster, images of giant sea monsters and snakes escalating the panic in my tight chest.

"Stop." Tristian grabs my arm, a firm hand encircling my wrist. "There are no animals. It's seaweed."

"Seaweed?" I stop struggling, the pressure in my chest easing.

"I have to untangle it. May I?" He points to my leg.

I lick my lips and take a second to calm myself. "Yes, please do. Now." I slow my kicks so I don't hit him in the face. He lets go, and I try to keep afloat.

Tristian dives under the water, and realization slams into me that he's going to be touching my bare leg. I might be fully clothed, but said clothes are skintight at the moment, and with him so near I might as well be naked. My body reacts on its own, my leg flailing.

"Hey." His head breaks the surface; he's rubbing the water from his eyes. "You almost kicked me in the jaw."

I clench my teeth in a grimace. "Sorry—I—close your eyes."

It's hard to determine his expression in the spotty light, but I swear he smiles. "What?" His voice teeters on the edge of a laugh. "I can't see if I close my eyes."

"Yeah, that's the point." I know the logic is flimsy. The clothing is exactly the same as when we were on dry land, but in the dark, with the water surrounding us, this is getting a whole lot more intimate than I'm ready to digest right now. I try to swim away from him. The seaweed has other plans and it yanks me back. "*Ugh.*"

Water splashes my neck as he moves toward me. "Imogen, do you want to get out of this water?"

I sigh. "Yes, of course I do."

His fingers graze the back of my hand. "I promise, I'll be a gentleman. But if you prefer, I can go grab Yvette or Aliana to do it instead, if that makes you more comfortable."

My stomach twists as my heartbeat increases. I do trust Tristian to keep his hands to himself. "It's okay, you can do it. Just hurry up. I don't want to be seaweed food." My voice is rough.

"I don't think that's how seaweed works, but I'll be quick." He smirks before diving under the water once more.

I try not to fidget as his hands slide along my calf to loosen the seaweed. I dig my fingers into his T-shirt to stay afloat. With a final tug, I feel the release. He breaks the surface. "You're free."

"Thanks," I say, out of breath. My hands rest on his shoulders, our knees bumping together. "It's not so bad when aquatic life isn't trying to drown me."

He glances at the rest of the Fairytalers, who have returned to shore. "I'd worry less about the fake seaweed and more about the chemicals they dump in here."

My breath hitches when his hand grazes my waist. His eyes widen before he quickly pulls away.

Shaking his wet hair, he clears his throat. "We should—it's late." He pushes away from me to swim toward shore.

I take a second to return my breath to a normal rhythm before lifting myself from the water.

Despite the warm night, I shiver as the light breeze tickles across my wet clothes. I wrap my arms around myself to keep warm.

"C'mon, I know where we can get some dry clothes." He fluffs his hair.

I could totally just go back to my apartment and get dry there, but I want to spend a little more time with him. "Lead the way."

20

TRISTIAN

I lead Imogen toward a stairwell between the Perilous Sea and Glacier Peaks. The muggy night air hangs around us, chlorine and bleach perfuming it. The Fairytalers' distant laughs echo from the other side of the sea.

Imogen sucks in a breath. "Where are we going? Because this seems majorly sketchy."

I laugh. Even when we're talking like we're in a horror movie, she still seems excited to be there. "My dad's old office is hidden in the mountains overlooking the Village Center."

Lifting myself on my tiptoes, I run my hand along the top of the doorframe. At first, I think it's not there, but then my fingers close around the cold key. "Garrick hid a key here years ago. We used to use it to sneak in and have extra breaks."

The door lets out a squeak when I push it open. I have to force it with my shoulder to get it wide enough to let us in. This was where Dad worked before they built the main office. Now it's used for storing old merch, and is probably home to a few tiny creatures. The dust swirls around as we disturb its resting place, dredging up the smells of wet cardboard and stale air.

"There should be some old T-shirts around somewhere. Will you get the light over there?" I point to the far wall.

She nods, inching through the room, careful not to trip on the plethora of boxes. I hear a click, and a faint, flickering light fills the room. "Wait a sec." Imogen glances around, face scrunching. "I've been here before."

"Really?" I crouch to riffle through a cardboard box on the floor with light blue T-shirts adorned with pink embroidery, reading "Fairytale Gardens Theme Park." "Was this in another one of your late-night excursions?"

"Ha-ha." She throws an old Winthrop doll at me. "No—dang, I actually forgot it was this place. I guess I just assumed it was Barth's new office."

I grab out an oversized tee and toss it to her. "When were you in Dad's office?"

She runs her hands over the stitching, tracing each letter slowly as she speaks. "It was ten years ago. I got separated from my parents, so while they looked for them, Barth brought me in here to wait." She slips the shirt on, looking up at me through long lashes. "You were there, too, actually."

I blink, the T-shirt still in my hand as I drip on the wood floor. "I was?" I've met her before? How could I forget that? Even if it was ten years ago, Imogen Rogers is not a person you forget.

She pulls on the hem of the shirt. "We played with a toy castle. You kept me from being scared." She whispers the last part.

I close my eyes, trying to pull on the threads of the memory. I spent a lot of time in here as a kid. Milly would let me play while Dad worked. As I dig deeper, I conjure up a pint-sized Imogen. Just as sunny as the one in front of me. "You wouldn't let me be the prince. You said you had to play both the prince and the princess, so I was stuck being the horse."

Her face lights up, those bright eyes shining in the yellow light. "You remember."

I nod. I came into the office after Garrick ran off to help Mom in the kitchen. I saw her sitting in the oversized chair, tearstained cheeks bright red. I offered to play because I didn't like seeing her sad.

I rub the back of my neck, offering a sheepish grin. "Sorry it took me so long."

She shakes her head. "It's okay. I didn't expect you to remember. I was just one in a sea of thousands I'm sure you helped along the way." Her red hair is curling at the ends as it dries, surrounding her face like a picture frame.

My chest is tight, heart thumping against my ribs. "You were never just one of the crowd."

The smile playing on her lips does little to ease my pounding heart.

"We should probably . . ." I wave with my free hand toward the apartments. *Wow*, how does Garrick make it look so simple to talk to cute girls. One look at Imogen and it feels like my mouth is full of marshmallows. She makes everything seem so easy, even when she thinks she's floundering.

She opens her mouth, as if to say more, but closes it. "We should." My skin prickles as I watch her flick off the light and step out the door.

The park is quiet. The rest of the group has already left. "Do these nighttime romps happen often?" Imogen fills the silence as we walk. I'd noticed she did the same thing each time I slipped into my head over the last few days.

The T-shirt smells like mothballs and chlorine, the scent making me sneeze. "Garrick's suggested it a few times over the years. Today was your lucky day."

She surveys me with a soft smile. "You're the one who got to feel me up underwater—you're the lucky one."

The rumble starts deep in my gut, traveling up and filling my chest, bursting out like I'd held it in for decades. Once I've started, I can't stop.

Imogen's brows scrunch together. "I didn't realize I was that funny."

"There's a lot you don't realize about yourself," I whisper. Her smile drops, lips twisted. "What?"

She pulls the tee up to partially cover her mouth. "Focusing on myself is not my favorite pastime."

Really? Because I'd like to make it mine. But instead of hitting her with that truth bomb, I ask, "Why's that?"

"I'd prefer to focus on this." She waves to the castle as we approach.

The relic holds a lifetime of memories neatly stored in an eighty-foot stone-and-plaster structure. Some I want to hold on to forever, and many I'd prefer to forget.

"What are you thinking?" She breaks the silence.

"How much I hate this place." The words fall out like they've wanted to for the last six days.

"The castle or . . ."

I stop short. "Or, and—all of it. I hate being stuck here, and

I hate myself for hating it." A guttural groan escapes me, hands shaking. "Sorry, this wasn't supposed to—anyway." I plaster on my fake smile, but she returns it with a frown.

"You don't have to do that." Her low voice fills the air around me like a warm embrace.

"Do what?" I strain to keep an even tone as the heaviness pushes at me from all angles.

She surprises me by squeezing my hand. "Pretend. Put on the smile and the voice."

"What voice?" I focus on her fingers wrapped around mine.

"Your 'prince' voice. It's okay to hate your job. I've been there . . ." The last words drop off as she clears her throat.

The park is dark, but I don't need light to see it crystal clear. "It's this place. I'm only one thing within these walls, around the Fairytalers." Pressure strangles my lungs, crushing against my chest, making it hard to breathe. I rub at the bare skin with my free hand to make it stop.

"I'm your partner, right? We're a team when we're onstage. I need you to have my back in case I royally screw up."

"Pun intended?"

"Obviously." She smiles, and I mirror it. "You have my back, so I'll have yours. Which means you don't need the fake prince facade."

"Some would argue that's all I am." I see my father's smug face.

"Nobody is all one thing. Take me, for example. I . . ." She taps her chin, and I stop myself from reaching out. I could kiss her right now, if she'd let me. "Oh, I am a horrible singer."

"What does that have to do with anything?" Her random thoughts are becoming my favorite thing.

I want to keep her talking because when we stop, we'll both go our separate ways, and this stripped version of us will disappear. When the fairytale music comes back on with the morning sun, this person I let her glimpse will disappear. It's how I survive.

"You see me and think, *wow*, she is probably stellar at everything."

"Do I?"

"Why else would you keep staring at me?" The joking is gone, replaced by a surprising vulnerability.

"Why else?" I match her tone.

She clears her throat. A faint blush creeps up her cheeks at my gaze. "Anyway, you say you're just a fake prince, but I know there's more to you."

I don't believe her, although I appreciate the effort.

"I bet if we dig deeper, we'll find more," she says.

"Do you want to keep digging?"

A million unsaid things pass across her brilliant eyes. But she goes with, "I . . . I need to go to bed."

Disappointment settles as she steps away. It's how this night should end. But my shoulders still sag the farther she gets from me. Shoving that regret deep inside, I follow behind her. A glance over her shoulder is the night's finale as she disappears into the apartment.

I need to stop the distractions.

FTG will lure me into its fantasy, if I'm not careful.

21

IMOGEN

It's halfway through the day and we've managed to avoid the subject of last night's *excursion*. I really thought we'd turned over a new leaf. I mean, he actually remembered me—which was shocking. But what if I'm projecting? The closeness we shared in the company of the stars might be more in my head than reality.

Whatever the case, we've been super awkward all morning. I suddenly have no idea what I'm supposed to be doing with my hands. I'm overanalyzing every word that comes out of my mouth. I should probably think about them before I say them, but that would be too un-Imogen-like.

Every brush of our hands, each exchanged smile, even just for show, twists my stomach into knots. Last night it felt like the first time I had talked to the real Tristian, no mask. It was nice to witness who he is, not who he wants people to see him as—or what the park demands he be. But that doesn't mean there's anything more between us than a friendship. Which is cool, but also . . . I might kinda like him. A little.

"I knew you'd be a natural." He removes his jacket as we exit the meet-and-greet stage and head to the Royal Fare restaurant.

"You're full of it. We both thought I'd be a disaster." I nudge him in the ribs as I shimmy past him. I'm turning up my brightness to max capacity in the hope it hides my awkward undertones.

This position came with expectations, which scared me, but they might make it worthwhile. At my other jobs, I was replaceable, a dime a dozen. Here, I feel special. It gives me a fuzzy feeling in my chest.

"What if we try going off script today?" I suggest. "I was thinking it could be cool for our next series of posts."

Tristian gets the door for me when we reach the castle. Clinking glasses and clanging pots greet us from the kitchen in the next room. "I don't think so. I was hoping I'd get to stay behind the camera and we could give Garrick the spotlight."

"Why? You were so good last time."

"I'm not you." That all-too-familiar dark cloud slips over his features.

"Who is?" I twirl in my skirt. "But you're not half bad when you want to be."

"You're going to keep on at me until I give in, aren't you?" His furrowed brow makes his stage makeup crack.

"I will only accept your full surrender."

He shakes his head. "Not going to happen."

I shrug, lifting my eyebrows. "We'll see."

He's made it no secret that he wants away from FTG, but that his family—mostly his dad—is never going to let that happen. But what if I could? Not *me* exactly, but Divya's article. If we can expose the park of wrongdoings, that might give Tristian the out he so desperately craves. Without the pressure of his family's expectations, he would finally get to decide what it is he really wants to do.

I know we've only known each other a short time, but I can see Tristian is a trapped bird. It's a feeling I know all too well. Maybe I can set him free.

Yvette hands us each a roll with ham and cheese. "You're on in five."

"They wash down better with this." Garrick enters the hallway with three mugs of juice.

I sip mine as Ivor walks in, staring into the bubbles to avoid eye contact. My confidence is mediocre when it's Tristian and me onstage, but surrounded by these longtime face characters, impostor syndrome kicks in. I take another mouthful to cure my dry throat.

Garrick drains his drink before he yanks on his helmet, straightening his armor as he enters the dining hall, Ivor behind him.

"Ready?" Tristian asks, facade slipping into place. I turn in to him automatically—an invisible string tugs me toward him. Last night unlatched a gate between us, one I can't help nudging open a little wider.

With a nod, I take his arm, counting my breaths as we walk into the Royal Fare banquet hall.

This is my first time here this summer, but it looks the same. Various types of wood decorate the walls and floor, while colorful fabrics hang from the ceiling. A dozen tables complete the space. The other face characters are already making their way to each one, greeting guests and taking pictures.

As Yvette leads us to our first table, the scent of roasted meat and hearty gravies wafts over. "Good afternoon, my friends." Tristian's inviting attitude is like a friend in a room full of strangers. But still, I notice the slight shake to his hand, the clamminess of his palms the longer we're in front of the guests.

"How are you enjoying your visit to our lands?"

"The beef's a little salty." The dad pokes at a bloody cut on his plate.

"Modeled after my dear older brother, no doubt."

I press my lips together to keep in character.

"Everything is lovely," the mother says. "Kids, take a picture with them." Two little girls run eagerly to us, but the older boy slouches, dragging his feet.

The pattern continues for seven more tables—a brief hello, a little chat, and a posed picture. But with each interaction Tristian's words become more clipped, and I can feel his erratic heartbeat when I lean against his chest. He needs a distraction.

"Tristian." I pull him to a stop before we reach the next table.

"Yeah?" His brows knit together in concern. Perhaps he thinks I'm about to bail—speed away with the gown and tiara, never to be seen again.

There's no exposé yet to release him from this torture, so I'm going to help him in a different way.

"I know you hate most of FTG, but you must enjoy something after all these years. What's your favorite part?" I play with the front of his vest, mimicking a newlywed couple madly in love.

His frown deepens. "This isn't the time."

"Humor me."

He rolls his shoulders. "Uh . . . I don't—sword fights. Why are you grinning?" He looks dubious at my sudden giddiness.

Guests fill every table in the busy restaurant. I shrug. "The people would probably love a show with dinner, even if it's not in the script."

Tristian glances to a few tables away, where Ivor is absorbed in a conversation with a child. "Would you hold my crown?" Tristian's whisper tickles my ear.

"I'd love to."

He steps away, tapping Garrick on the shoulder. "Sir Kendrick, what do you say to a little show with dinner?"

Garrick tilts his head, confused, but smirks when Tristian draws his sword. "Why, dear friend, you know I never turn down a demonstration of prowess."

"What is happening?" Yvette's lips twitch upward, despite the deep creases in her brow.

Palpable energy fills the room. My insides vibrate with excitement. "A show." I clasp Tristian's crown close to me, taking a step back. "Oh, take a video."

Yvette's gaze darts around the room.

"Come on, Yvette, it might be fun." I drag us into empty chairs. When I was younger, my favorite thing about the park was that anything could happen. The unknown surprises made every moment an adventure.

"For you." Tristian blows me a kiss, whipping his cloak back. The sound of the two swords clashing draws the attention of the restaurant.

"What are they doing?" Ivor hisses in my ear.

"Sword fighting." I cheer when Tristian knocks Garrick to the ground.

"Put that phone away," Ivor scolds. Yvette fumbles with her phone, slipping it into her pocket at his gruff tone. Face beet-red, Ivor stalks toward them. "Enough." He steps in between them, his sword hitting theirs. "Weapons must remain sheathed at meals."

"Rules are made to be broken." Garrick leans back, resting heavily on his hilt, breath labored.

"You're done," Ivor whispers, so only his brothers can hear. "Please, everyone, return to the feast." He walks away and goes right back into the scene like nothing happened.

Tristian rejoins me, breathing heavily as he slides his weapon into its sheath. He brushes a stray tendril of hair into my braid. A round of oohs and aahs echoes from the nearby tables.

"Don't encourage them," I whisper as he slides a hand down my cheek. Tingles run up my spine as if this wasn't all pretend. We're onstage—none of this is real, I remind myself.

He presses our foreheads together, staring into my eyes. "Who says it's for them?"

I turn away, hiding my smile, as Yvette leads me to the next table.

22

TRISTIAN

I've sat in the makeup and hair department since my shift ended forty minutes ago, staring at the message on my screen—a reminder of the upcoming flight in two weeks. I really should have gotten off the email list about the program, but part of me still hoped I might get myself there.

I shove my phone into my pocket. My nerves are as built as they'll get.

I've put in some good effort as marketing intern—as fake as it might be on Dad's end. I got a new ad up and running; not the best in the world—the University of YouTube can only teach you so much—but considering this is my first attempt I'm kinda proud. The analytics are showing some great traffic. Although less than ideal, I also managed the disastrous photo shoot. I got the initial images back, and as I suspected—we look miserable.

The other complication I did not anticipate is Imogen. When I ran into her on the first day, I thought our paths were unlikely to cross again, but they intertwine further all the time. After our nighttime swim, it's getting hard to write off the looks we exchange as strictly friendly. But maybe that's all they are and I'm jumping to conclusions. Imogen is kind to everyone she encounters—even Aliana. So, maybe I'm overthinking this whole thing?

That's fine. The voice in my head sounds firm, reassuring, like the prince I pretend to be. But as I knock on my father's office door, the scared little boy inside makes his way to the front.

"Tristian." He doesn't lift his eyes from the desk.

I thrust my hands into my pockets, gut twisting as I shut the door. "Hey, Dad." My stilted voice grates against the thick air.

"What do you think of the new posters for the Starlight Ball? I had a few mocked up. Don't know if the font is big enough." He holds up a poster in light blues and purples, white snowflakes around the edges. The font is a little small, but worse is the large picture of me—well, Prince Winthrop.

"If you'd consulted me, I could have helped. I've been up late the last few nights planning. It might've been nice for me to handle this." My posture is rigid, my hands curling into fists as I shift them to cross over my chest. Erratic energy makes me squirm, but I tense to stay steady. I don't want Dad to see me uneasy and think he has all the control, like he has for so many years.

"I had Milly sort it out." He squints to read the fine print.

I suppress the harsh tone lacing my words. "Dad, about that summer program I enrolled in . . ."

"Tristian," he scoffs, dismissing me like he's done so many times before.

"Dad, this would be a life-changing experience for me. Colleges will be impressed to see that I've done a bunch of different extracurriculars." I frown, fighting against the tension headache searing pain between my eyes. "I've been doing what's expected of me and I can see the park is doing just fine, and *will* do just fine without me. The trip starts in two weeks, so there's still time for you to sign off on it."

He lays the poster on the desk, hand skimming the edges. "Tristian, we talked about this. Your family needs you. You can't abandon us to gallivant around Europe."

Heat flashes across my chest. "My future doesn't lie in these walls. You know I want to study history, and this trip will mean I can see it firsthand."

He snorts, rolling his eyes.

I pause before the shaking overpowers my voice. If I want him to see I've outgrown these walls, I can't look weak.

He comes over and places a hand on my shoulder, rare contact for a man who's shown none since the day my mother died. I was the one who held Aldrich while he cried over Mom's grave. Dad retreated into himself like a scared turtle. None of us were allowed past his hard shell.

"You're a Walsh. You act as if this park is a ball and chain." The pressure from his grip tightens. "This is your legacy. Do you know how many people would kill for this? And you want to throw it all away? Do you hate me that much?"

"I don't . . ." It sounds like the end of a sentence; it could be one. I let it drift off, unsure. I don't hate him—not most of the time.

"This isn't up for discussion." He retakes his seat, grabbing my mom's picture off the desk, and stroking the gold frame. Her bright smile always reminds me of Aldrich's. I try to find myself in her features, but the face I see in the mirror every day reminds me more of my father. "I lost your mother too soon. So, we have to stick together. That's what she would've wanted."

"All I ever wanted was a chance to make my own way."

I leave him with his memories.

"Imogen, hey." She is standing behind Milly's empty desk, examining the pictures on the charity wall.

"Oh." Her lips part in surprise. "Tristian—I thought you went home." She pushes wayward strands of hair off her face.

"Not yet. What are you doing?" I join her at the wall.

"Nothing, really. Just looking." She flicks her bottom lip.

Thick dust covers the glass housing the pictures and awards. "You and my dad are the only ones who look at this wall."

"I didn't know FTG was so big into charity donations. I don't see you in the recent photos." She studies me from her peripheral vision.

"Nope." In the past, my brothers and I would pose with different recipients of the money FTG donated for the causes, but after Mom died everything fell by the wayside. She was the one who always encouraged us to get involved.

"Hmm." She taps two fingers against her lip rhythmically.

"What?"

Her hand drops, and a smile replaces her puzzled stare. "Nothing." She shrugs, changing the subject as fast as she brought it up. "Did you see the announcement in the break room?"

I shake my head. "No. Did they close the park?"

"Dark. But no, the Starlight Ball." A groan escapes me and she scrunches her nose. "Contain your excitement. You might burst a blood vessel."

This night keeps getting better and better. "It's a cash grab that requires us to learn new lines. What's not to be excited about?" I exaggerate a tight smile.

Imogen tilts her head. I try not to squirm under her stare. "But the Starlight Ball is the best scene in the Carpathia story! It's to celebrate Arden and Winthrop saving the kingdom." Her eyes drift off, glazing over in a memory. "I never got to go. My mom shared your philosophy—she thought it was overpriced."

"Well, now you can go. FTG grants miracles every day." My sarcastic tone doesn't diminish her glow.

"Stick around. Maybe you'll get yours too." She pats my chest before walking toward the stairs.

"We would have to dance." I follow her toward the chatter on the ground floor.

She spins on me when we reach the second floor. "Do you not want to dance with me?" Lowering her voice, she leans into my personal bubble. She doesn't touch me, but her hand hovers near mine. It feels like an electrical current is running between us.

A snarky comeback is hot on my tongue, but then I soften. "I'd love to." I enjoy the pink tint my words give her cheeks.

"Too bad you hate all that fairytale stuff—could've been fun."

My heart pumps loud in my ears. I want to jump on a plane and fly thousands of miles away from this stupid park and the prince I share my skin with. But, right now, I want to keep talking to Imogen.

"Can I show you something?"

Her green eyes flicker with amusement. "Sure."

The air is muggy with the threat of rain in the darkened sky when we get outside. The unpruned trees hit against the side of the apartments as the wind picks up, leading the way for the storm off the dark horizon.

"Hello, Tristian." Milly rolls down her car window, pulling to a stop alongside us.

"Nice ride." She drives a black Range Rover SUV. "Dad must have given you a hefty bonus this year."

She shakes her head with a wave of her hand. "Don't tell your aunt."

"I like her." Imogen watches Milly drive away.

I scratch the back of my neck, leading her toward the edge of the park's rear entrance. The air is thick, the kind you can feel when you take a deep breath. The rain will be a welcome break from the stagnant summer heat. Summer thunderstorms were always my favorite.

"Where are we going?" Imogen's curious voice edges with skepticism.

I ignore the pit in my stomach as we enter the park access gate. Instead of heading into Carpathia, I steer away from the golden tree. "I escape here when the world feels too crowded."

I proceed into the hidden walkway as thunder rumbles in the distance. The decommissioned tower is three levels of intricately carved wood painted and cladded to resemble an outpost watchtower for the kingdom of Carpathia. The exterior is pockmarked with holes and cracks from years of rocks and debris being thrown at it in mock battles. A spiral staircase wraps around the outside, missing more steps than is wise to attempt climbing. But that never stopped me.

The bottom level comprises three swing sets, a rock wall, and a small zip line. The second floor has large faux moss hanging off the side—most of which is missing because Garrick used to rip it off and fling it at us. The top is my favorite. Broken and useless spyglasses are fixed to rusted railings. The precarious footing makes it the most private place on the property.

"Oh." Her voice is low as we get closer. "Yeah, no—that'll collapse if I breathe too hard near it." She backs away with her hands raised.

"It won't." I saunter up the stairs, avoiding the busted ones, glancing over my shoulder. "Probably."

"I love the confidence." She watches me take a few more steps before following—testing her weight on each one. "I guess I see the appeal," she admits when we reach the top. The park sparkles ahead of us through the trees. "The reward certainly outweighs the risk."

I laugh sharply.

"What?" She twirls a spyglass toward her, abandoning it when she sees the broken glass on the eyehole.

"Nothing." I rub my chin. "No one who knows me would ever say I take risks."

"Well, if it makes you feel better, I take foolish risks all the time, and they're hardly ever worth the reward." She leans over the railing but doesn't touch it.

"Is working here a risk?" With her profile to me, it gives me access to study her uninterrupted. The blackened stormy sky silhouettes her. She could be a portrait hung in the castle—no, that's not right. A hundred artists wouldn't be able to replicate her. That fire behind her eyes, the way her lips twist ever so slightly . . . it can't be copied.

"This risk, so far, has been . . . worth it. I always loved this place. It's like a hug from an old friend."

"From birth, I was told fairytales. For part of my life, I actually thought I lived in one. I don't know . . ." I take a deep breath. This is more honest than I've been with anyone in a while. The words remove a heavy weight that's been a burden on my chest for a long time. "Gradually as I get older, I'm becoming more and more disillusioned with fairytales—the message that good always wins, and happily-ever-after waits for you at the end of the book.

"Still, every time I walked into this place, I got some hope rekindled. Then my mom got sick, and died." I fight past the hitch in my voice. If I stop now, I won't start again, and I need to get this out. "Her death had no higher purpose, no launching the hero into a journey—she was just gone. And I wanted out of this story."

Imogen angles her body toward me, both our faces half in shadow. My shoulders sag as I grip the guardrail.

She places a delicate hand on mine. The touch is a whisper, unsure, but enough. "Maybe you're the hero who takes a little longer to find his journey."

"You think I'm a hero, huh?"

"Not at all." She looks at me through hooded eyes, a smile

tugging her lips. "Clearly, I'm the hero of this story." Lightning cracks across the sky, illuminating us for a second, followed by a rattling boom of thunder.

"Okay, hero." I move toward her. "What's your journey? Who's the big bad villain you have to defeat?"

She stills, teeth cutting into her bottom lip, before turning away. "Probably myself." Her arms wrap around her stomach like she's cold, despite the muggy night. "That wouldn't make for a very thrilling park ride." Lightness seeps into her voice, but I recognize it now as the veneer she slides into place when she hides a real emotion.

I'll play into her facade. "Not unless you turn into a dragon." I clench my hands, shoving them into my pockets to keep from reaching for her.

Onstage, we touch and flirt with ease. Long glances are encouraged. I have to remind myself it's not real. The rain will drive us inside soon, but maybe I can squeeze in a few more moments before writing myself out of her story.

"How do you feel? About being Arden? Easier or harder than you thought?"

She taps her arm. "Both. It's easy to talk to the guests, but hard to stand with a heavy wig on my head." The wind picks up, the crisp smell of rain and electricity heavy in the air. "You're lucky you don't have to wear one."

"We used to mess with Ivor, saying he'll have to wear one to keep playing a prince when he goes bald." Ivor used to joke along. He was one of us.

She takes a deep breath, eyes closing. "You think the park will be around when that happens?"

"Who says he's not bald now?"

She's so magnetic, her personality just as beautiful as the outside. Each nerve in my body slams into hyperdrive. It would be so easy to give in and kiss her. Just to see what it felt like.

Her eyes pop open like she can read my thoughts. "Seriously, do you believe FTG has what it takes to stick around?"

"I used to say yes, because where else would I go? But sometimes I find myself wishing it would fall apart. Then I wouldn't feel guilty about leaving." Thunder swallows the words at the end.

"You shouldn't feel guilty for wanting more than what your family expects from you. God knows I've done my fair share of changing."

"How's that working?"

"Not great." She blinks her glassy eyes. "I'm sure it's only a matter of time before I mess up this perfectly crafted fairytale."

Hand shaking, I gently wipe away the tears.

"You don't need to be perfect." Her brows scrunch together; she worries her bottom lip. "Really. Perfection is unattainable—it's boring. Maria may have a formula for Princess Arden, but the best performers always add a bit of themselves into the role."

"I'm not a performer." Her head shakes. "I'm not sure I'm anything."

"We're all performers. Some just hide the performance better."

"Tristian . . ." Thunder booms and a raging downpour engulfs her words.

"Come on." I turn to head down the stairs, but her hand holds me in place. The rain falls in heavy sheets as she stares at me.

"Imogen?"

She stumbles, bumping into the rail as she pulls away. "Sorry." She blinks, waking from a dream. "I . . . just—we should go." Stepping past, she's careful not to touch me as she takes the steps two at a time.

"Imogen." The rain obscures my vision, the pounding on the cement deafening as I chase her into the parking lot.

"I'll see you onstage." She doesn't look back, darting up the stairs to her apartment. I press my fist into my lips, not bothering to move as the rain soaks me to the bone.

23

IMOGEN

Uggggbhh.

I slam my back into the door to shut it. Sliding down, I bang my head against the solid wood. My hands scrape across my face to rid myself of Tristian—the ghost of a kiss that didn't happen, but one I really wanted. The urge to let myself fall under his spell was like nothing I've ever felt. The warmth of his touch made me feel like, for once in my life, something might work out for me.

When I started, I didn't even blink an eye at having to conceal my true intentions to everyone, but now . . . god, I knew Tristian was likable. I just didn't expect to be thrust into his arms and forced to play his adoring princess every day.

It's getting harder to pretend I'm not lying through my teeth. I could tell him the truth. He basically admitted that he wants the park to fail so he has an excuse to leave. Maybe he could help me? He's pretty wary of his father. Telling Tristian I think Barth's shady might not come as a shock.

What am I saying? It's too risky to get Tristian involved.

I blame the rain.

Tristian had stood there, blue eyes dark and piercing. It would've been so easy to take the last few steps and see what it felt like to kiss him. To finally confirm if the exchanges we've shared were something more. But before I could act, the guilt had sunk in. If I get wrapped up in Tristian, I would be putting Divya's story in jeopardy, and that cannot happen. She's my priority.

I should pride myself on having self-control. Even if that restraint has left a cold sting on my skin.

"You look like a drowned cat." Aliana sits with her arms slung over the back of the couch. I suck in my cheeks to contain a scream. The shower is calling my name, so I ignore her, depositing my wet shoes by the door to dry.

The hot water does little to wash away the vision of Tristian. After switching into sweats, three missed calls from Divya greet me when I check my phone. Along with a text from Mom. I send Mom back a quick message, letting her know it's going great, and that I'm totally not spiraling. I don't actually add that last part.

Pulling my knees into my chest, I stare at the screen. I haven't been in touch with Divya in a few days, other than texts. She'll want answers. I wish I could give her a big break, but all I have is a guilty conscience. The fairytale has gotten in the way of my real purpose for being here. The fancy gowns and shimmering tiaras were a beautiful distraction. Not to mention Tristian and his stupid, handsome face.

It feels like it's time to implement my favorite tactic: avoidance.

That's how I usually solve a problem.

But I can't throw my phone in the dresser and ignore Divya. She'd probably show up at my door, looking for answers. My thumb hovers over her name on the screen. One more night won't hurt. The phone is almost in the drawer when Divya calls, again.

I push out a deep breath through my nose. "Hey." I sit back on the bed.

"Where have you been?"

"I thought you had Find My Friends?"

Her bright yellow living-room wallpaper accents the background. "I do—but I'm not running surveillance on you twenty-four seven."

"Just on the odd days."

She pops a chocolate in her mouth. "It's more economical. Speaking of economics . . . any more info on our wayward charity funds?"

"Wow, great transition." I glance at the door. When I finished showering, Aliana was in her room. Part of me wishes she'd overhear. If she outs me for my spying, I won't have to do it anymore. Of course I'd have to leave the park, and my life as a fake princess would end.

Then there's Tristian.

"Imogen."

"Yes, sorry, thought I heard an intruder." I scoot back to rest against the pillows. "You know I've had to lie low with the investigation ongoing."

"No worries. They caught the guy."

I frown. "What guy? I'm the guy, and last I checked I'm still here."

"They fired him this morning. It's why I was calling you. He was skimming money from the tills, and they just assumed he was responsible for the break-in as well."

"And you know this *how*?" I'm boots on the ground and I hadn't heard.

"Don't you check the Fairytalers' Discord?"

"There's a Discord?"

She rolls her eyes. "Yes, it's been blowing up the last two hours."

"I was . . . busy." I offer an apologetic shrug, leaving off I was busy with Tristian.

"Well, it's great news for you, because with the fire averted you can get into Barth's office tonight. It's great timing—go while the guards are down."

"It's pouring rain." The heavy storm thrashes against my window, wind rattling the panes.

"That'll cover your movements."

"And leave a trail of water to track me with." They might have caught *a* wrongdoer, but I'm still worried Barth won't let it go.

"Fine, when it's not raining, will you try? You've already had to put it off too long."

I tug my fingers through my wet hair. I've never cared if I got fired from a job or got caught doing something I shouldn't. But I'd be lying if I said I didn't want a little more time before that happened here.

"Imogen? What's up?"

"Nothing."

"Don't *nothing* me. I can always tell when you're off."

I bite my lip, forcing down a swell of guilt. "It's . . ." I glance toward the park I adore that's just out of sight. "I love FTG and I'm having trouble seeing a bad side."

When I look back at the screen, Divya's confident air has disappeared. Her lips twist to the side in the same way they do when she's worrying about acing a test. "*Oh*, Imogen. I didn't . . . I guess I kind of forgot what this place means to you. I was so wrapped up in trying to save the restaurant and jump-start my future I didn't—"

"Stop, Divya. It's fine, *really*." My voice is too high to be believable. Because she's right. I didn't think it through at the start either. That by coming here I would destroy my favorite place in the world. I only focused on helping my best friend.

I watch the wheels turn behind Divya's eyes. "You know, I haven't found anything more about Barth or the charities, so maybe it really is just bitter people with a grudge spreading rumors—like you said. Why don't we call the Fairytale Gardens investigation a bust and I can scrounge up another story closer to home. There's still time before the contest is over."

"Divya, you don't need to do that. I want to do this. Because you're right, something shady is going on here. Tristian has already dropped hints about his father's spending habits. I just need to dig a little deeper."

My childhood love of some rusty rides and fairy princesses is not nearly as important as helping save Divya's family restaurant and the people who have been there for me when I needed it most.

"Only if you're sure." She's trying to hide her hopefulness.

"When the rain stops, I'll break in to Barth's office."

The rain stops an hour later.

I wasn't lying when I told Divya I wanted to keep going with the investigation. Still, I'm not sure if there is anything to find. But I'm going to do everything in my power to show Divya I tried my best to get her story vetted.

Then, if there really is nothing to discover, I will be free to pursue other things, possibly Tristian-shaped, without the guilt of letting Divya down.

The ground glistens, and I have to weave to avoid large puddles in the potholed pavement, but, like before, I make it to the main building without incident. There were two security guards out tonight, but neither seems very interested.

Each second I'm exposed escalates my racing heart. I still have the key, and slip into Barth's office with ease, closing the door behind me. I really thought he'd at least get the locks changed, but apparently that's not high priority.

All that talk was just for show. Guess I understand what Tristian means.

Drapes cover a large window, and a grand wooden desk sits in the center with a computer. Maybe he keeps his passwords by it, like I do. Behind the desk hangs a huge painting of the Walsh family dressed as their fairytale counterparts. The subjects in the portrait smile, blandly pleasant, like I was taught. Tristian's mother is the obvious center of the picture and not just because she's in the middle—the men all angle toward her. She was the heart of this family, of this place.

I shake my head, spinning away from the desk. I didn't come to admire art. I turn my attention to the bookshelves and filing cabinets. There might be evidence on the computer, but I picture Barth as a hard copy guy.

After rummaging through file folders for fifteen minutes, I find nothing beneficial. Several documents have Barth's signature for donations to the various charities, but these are the legit ones. The newest organizations still elude me.

A safe sits in the corner of the room, but I can't find any papers with the code for it. Not wanting to risk my luck, I leave empty-handed.

The coast is clear, my exit in sight, when voices trail from the break room. I slide into an alcove near the first-floor bathroom, stomach in my throat. I peek around the pillar to see who it is. I needn't bother—I recognize them all too well.

"Just like old times." The door blocks part of my view as Aliana lounges on a table, Tristian sitting on a chair in front of her. I thought she was asleep in her room when I left. "Being here isn't so bad, right?" Aliana's voice is low, spoken in a tone those with history share.

"It has its moments," Tristian says. His face is half cut off by the doorframe, making it hard to read his whole expression, but he's smiling.

Bile burns my throat and I swallow a few times to get rid of it. I've tasted jealousy before, but never this strong.

I need to get out of here.

Aliana slides forward on the table. A few more inches and she'll fall into his lap. "I'm always here for you." Her face disappears from my view, leaning forward as her hand rests possessively on his leg.

Tristian's chair scrapes the tile as he shifts. "Aliana . . ." His voice fades away, the blood pumping in my ears muffling the words. Fine by me. I don't need to listen to the sweet nothings he whispers to her.

My vision blurs with bright spots. I glance toward the front door. They'll see me if I make a run for it. The other way out is in the rear of the building. It's an emergency exit tied to a door alarm.

Screw it.

I don't want a front-row seat if they're about to make out on the break-room table. I skid across the floor. My wet shoes squeak as I slam into the back door. Pain shoots across my shoulder from the impact, but I don't slow.

A wailing alarm screeches through the night. I don't stop until I'm safe in my room. My heart hammers as I collapse in my bed, chest aching too deep to soothe.

I knew better. The thought brings a fresh stabbing to my heart.

He is the dashing prince everyone wants. Girls line up miles long to get a moment of his attention. Because he feels like the sun, the glow of his admiration is a warmth that caresses you head to toe.

And like a chump, I fell for it. I just thought the attention meant something more this time around. Or maybe I only saw what I wanted to see. The power I thought I held with his gazes was never really mine.

But I'm taking the power back now. I was granted a gift tonight. A reminder that Tristian Walsh is a charmer I can't let distract me. Divya is my best friend, and she's entrusted me with a job—I won't let her down. I almost let a stupid crush overpower my friendship responsibility. I won't let that happen. Tristian can have secret break-room liaisons with whoever he wants.

Just not me.

24

TRISTIAN

"Ivor." I've managed to corner him in the break room before the breakfast meet-and-greet at the Royal Fare restaurant. "Did you see the billboard?" I put up the new one where I knew he'd pass it coming to work.

Another bullet point to my résumé: I had a call early this morning with the marketing director of a major hotel chain to see about getting our ads linked with their websites and locations nearby. I'm not sure if it's going to come together, but it felt freaking amazing to be spoken to like an adult and not just some theme park kid.

I do my best to treat Ivor like I would a colleague. The annoying colleague who steals your lunch from the fridge, even though it has your name on it.

Ivor takes his sweet time pouring one pack of sugar into his mug. "I did."

I pinch the bridge of my nose. "And?"

"It looked really good—expensive." He steps around me. "But effective."

Fairytalers crowd the hall as they arrive on shift. I weave past them to follow Ivor to hair and makeup. "Thanks . . ."

I trail off because I'm shocked by the praise—as microscopic as it is.

His expression is strained. "Maybe you should consider pursuing it? The park could use some shaking up."

Wait, was that another compliment? Did I like it? A weird sludge swirls in my gut. What if I could actually do more with this marketing thing? History is packed with real-life stories I could spend a lifetime learning about, but FTG has some history of its own to tell.

The three chairs are occupied when we get to hair and makeup. Garrick and Aliana sit in the two closest to the door, chatting while Pierre finishes Aliana's wig. Imogen waits in the one near the far wall, head buried in her phone.

Ivor waves me off. "Garrick, move—you're done." Garrick raises his eyebrows at me but vacates the room.

"Hi." I turn my focus to Imogen.

She mumbles a greeting without looking up. My brows pull in as I perch on the table in front of her.

"I see you dried off." I offer a reminder of our previous evening—which promptly reminds me how I fell asleep with visions of us finally kissing. I'd very much like to make that a reality if she'd let me.

"Yup." Her eyes remain downcast, scrolling through TikTok.

Does she regret letting it get that close? I'm not even sure we *were* going to kiss. Perhaps I'm overthinking it and that wasn't on her mind at all. And now I've made this super awkward by thinking she wanted to kiss me when clearly it was just platonic.

I cross my arms, fisting the soft leather of my jacket. "Any new ideas for us?" I point to the phone, trying my best to be just a friendly neighborhood pal. *Wow*, I'm using words like *pal*. Someone *please* put me out of my misery.

She glances up this time, surveying the room. "Not my job." Pushing away from the table, she scoots past me. "See you at breakfast."

"Imogen, what—" Hair spray assaults me as I run out the door following after her. I cover my mouth in a coughing fit. She doesn't stop. "Hey." I catch her after my lungs have rejected the spray.

"What?" She uses her arms as a shield across her chest. The delicate flowers on her wig and tiara juxtapose her cold words.

Fairytalers rush by, taking little notice of us, but I drop my voice anyway. "If this is about last night . . ."

She tilts her head to the side as a fake smile slides into place. "What about last night? Did something happen?"

"I . . . uh . . . maybe?" I raise a cautious eyebrow, hoping to coax a genuine grin. I get nothing. "No?" My cheeks flush as I try to backpedal.

Her passive shrug stings as she barely makes eye contact. "So many ladies fall at your feet. It must be hard to keep them straight." Slender fingers pick at her corset strings.

Frowning, I take a step back. "Sorry, you lost me."

For a single moment, the real emotion underneath peeks out. Hurt? But like a shooting star, it's gone as quick as it came. Imogen's jaw tightens in response when Aliana's laugh filters from the makeup room.

I release a sharp breath when the puzzle pieces click into place. "Did you have another nighttime excursion?"

"Did you?" Her tight lips are a thin slash on her otherwise impassive face.

I went to the break room last night to escape the confines of my room. Insomnia is a monster I can't fight my way past, no matter how good my sword work is. Getting up and walking around is the only thing keeping me sane when the night drags on.

Aliana found me and we got to talking about the old days, and my mom. She was trying to coax me out of despair when the alarm to the back door went off. We didn't see anyone. I almost forgot about it.

It was Imogen—dang—I should've guessed. She must have seen Aliana and me. That's what's turned her sunny disposition icy.

The bitterness in her expression only thinly veils the real sentiment beneath. She hated seeing Aliana and me together. Which means I didn't overthink what could have happened last night. She's as tethered to me still as I am to her. The thought sends a thrill into my chest.

And as good as her facade is, I can tell she's hurt. The slight twitch in the corner of her mouth, the way her throat bobs like each swallow is painful. A primal urge to fix the misunderstanding surges through me. To comfort her with the knowledge that what happened last night between us meant more to me than a passing tryst.

It's a simple fix to explain that nothing happened. Aliana was comforting an old friend. I could clear this all up with a few words. Warmth spreads throughout my body at the idea of what that admission could lead to.

That intoxicating impulse is why I decide in this moment not to tell the truth.

I shrug, resting my hand on my belt. "I'm a busy guy." The words burn like acid. I bite my tongue to stop myself from retreating. To force the lie into existence and make it my reality.

She opens her mouth, then closes it, eyes dropping to the ground. Her hands ball into fists. "See you at breakfast." She spits the words out.

I feel like a jerk. Watching her walk away with thoughts of me and Aliana weighing her down is a knife to my stomach. But as much as it was great to hear Ivor's praise and see that my place here might be bigger than I realized, I *do* still want to leave FTG. To rid myself of this fairytale. Imogen will only drag me in deeper until I'm so far under that leaving this place never crosses my mind.

The morning is brutal. I flub my lines several times. Imogen, on the other hand, never lets her disguise slip. The guests think she's madly in love with me. But her stilted touch, and forced smile, tell me all I need to know.

Good. Great. *Freaking fantastic.*

This is what I wanted. So, why do I want to punch a wall as I leave the Royal Fare restaurant? A text from Aldrich, asking if I can meet him at the Perilous Sea, saves both my downward spiral and the castle from needing to be replastered. I head that way.

"We aren't playing darts," Aldrich declares as I walk with him to the carnival games.

I roll my eyes. Despite the irritation left from my crappy day, a smile tugs at my lips. "If you don't practice, you'll never beat me." We stop in front of the balloon dart game and I signal the operator to give us each a set of darts. "Come on, I'll show you the trick."

The games are rigged. To beat them, you have to know the tricks, and if you don't, best to just enjoy the experience and not expect to win the stuffed Winthrop doll.

But if you've spent your life here, and know which balloons they underfill and which are blown up enough to actually pop, you stand a decent chance. I only have two years on Aldrich, but two years is a lot of time to practice.

The colorful balloons sway in the light breeze. "Aim for the ones on the edge," I instruct Aldrich. He gnaws on his bottom lip, eyes narrowing before he sets the dart sailing. It bounces off and hits the ground.

"First one's always a write-off. You got this, Al. Give it another try."

It takes several more attempts before he catches on. "Did you only win because you knew how to cheat?" he asks.

"Cheating would imply the game was fair to begin with." I grab my set of darts, bursting three balloons in a row.

"Did you want the prize?" the kid operating the game asks, pointing to the Winthrop doll.

I cringe, those beady fake black eyes staring me down. "No, thanks. Aldrich, you can think of a better reward than that, I'm sure."

"Ice cream." His face lights up, eyes drifting to Glacier Peaks and the ice cream parlor hidden within.

"Great, you can buy me one."

"Nah. I want a fair chance. Let's pick a different game."

After this morning, it sounds like the perfect distraction.

Aldrich decides ring toss is the great equalizer to bet on, since we both suck at it and there's really no way to cheat. Despite my best efforts, Aldrich manages to win. I am both annoyed and proud.

"First the ride-off, and now carnival games—Tristian, you've really lost your touch." He laughs, cheeky grin wide on his flushed cheeks as we walk to Glacier Peaks.

I shove him and he narrowly avoids colliding with a trash can. "Nice try, little brother. But I'm just waiting for my moment to shine." The words hitch in my throat and it takes me by surprise.

The ice cream parlor's decor mimics arctic caverns and glaciers. Now, I enjoy ice cream as much as the next guy, but Aldrich's obsession with it is on a whole other level. I went with a single scoop of strawberry with chocolate sauce and he ordered The Mountain—which is meant to serve four. After thirty minutes at our table, it looks more like a bog.

I can't decide if Aldrich eats his remaining ice cream in that disgusting way on purpose or if I'm projecting my annoyance.

"You sure you don't want some?" He pushes the sugar-coated mess toward me for the fifth time.

"Aldrich, I swear to god, if you ask me again, the ice cream is going on your head." I pinch the bridge of my nose. The sickening sweet aroma of cream and sugar doesn't help my pounding head, and the unease in my stomach is developing the longer we sit here. The games gave me something to focus on, but now my thoughts wander back to Imogen and my lie.

He plops a spoon into the melted mess with a smirk. "Don't be mad because you lost."

"I can leave you here." I push my chair back with a squeal.

"Come on, T. It was a joke." Aldrich frowns, hands up in defeat. "I won't offer you any more ice cream." Garrick and I were always the closest. But just like I wanted to be like my big brother, Aldrich wants to be like me.

"Fine." I lean back in my chair, knuckles pressed into my mouth. Most of the tables are empty. A few rowdy kids jam coins into a jukebox in the corner.

Aldrich licks caramel off his hand. "What was up with you and Imogen?"

My eyes jerk up. "Nothing." I keep my tone even.

"Okay, because it seemed like you two were in a fight."

"We had a misunderstanding." The words are clipped.

"And you didn't fix it?" He grabs another spoonful. Most drips into the bowl.

The waitress passes, and I ask her for a straw. "This'll be easier." I flick it at him.

Ripping the paper off, he shoves it in the goopy puddle. "So, you didn't fix it?"

I sigh. "No, I didn't."

"Why not?"

"Aldrich, why do you care?" Heat flashes across my skin,

my gut seizing as he insists on continuing this unwanted conversation.

"Because"—he slurps the ice cream—"you seemed happy with Imogen. It was almost like having the old Tristian back. The one from before . . . ya know."

The anger in my mouth turns to ash. Any harsh words bottling up slip away.

Before.

Before Mom died—before everything changed. I scoot in my chair, leaning my elbows on the table. "Imogen . . ." Imogen, what? I press my palms into my eyes, a frustrated growl escaping. "She adores this place and loves to point out all the things she loves about it to me *constantly.*"

"And that's a bad thing?" He frowns in confusion.

"Yeah, because she's right." I shake my head, thumb scratching over my skin. "She makes me remember what I loved about FTG."

"T—"

"I have places to be Al—a life outside this park. If I let her hate me, let her think I'm a playboy, she'll move on. It's hard enough thinking about leaving you guys, but if I have a girlfriend, too . . . It'll just be another excuse to stay put."

Aldrich finishes the dregs of his ice cream. "I get it—I guess. But I can see it in your face. You like her, and, Tristian, if I've learned anything since Mom died, it's that life is short. Why would you push away someone you might like because they aren't where you thought you'd find them?"

I cock my head. "When'd you get so smart?"

He tosses his spoon into the bowl. "Well, I got you and Garrick for brothers, someone had to pick up the slack." I kick him under the table.

The truth in Aldrich's words doesn't leave me unfazed. But Imogen wants FTG; she loves it. I want as far away from it as possible. Our stories don't align, and maybe it's best they stay that way.

25

IMOGEN

This last week has made me reconsider the whole Fairytale Gardens life. My first seven days were like stepping into a nostalgic dream. But as my time here has dragged on, the familiar flight instinct is creeping in.

Tristian and I play the perfect couple onstage—every step and word to the letter Maria instructed.

It's been awful.

My stomach drops to the floor now every time I have to smile at him. The second we step offstage, we part ways like we're running from a tidal wave. I'm unsure how to describe what's going on between us. Last week I'd have said we were friends . . . possibly more. Now we're coworkers. Full stop. Not even the kind you grab a burger with after-hours.

Sure, there'd been an almost kiss. But I'm guessing he's almost kissed plenty of princesses. I was just dumb enough to think with me it would be special.

Yvette and her girlfriend invited me to get food with them at the Royal Fare a few times. So there was that at least. This provided a lovely distraction from my spiraling thoughts. But when I'm in my lonely room, I miss Divya even more.

As the third week begins, I'm determined to solve Divya's mystery and get out of here. All I gathered in the last week was from an overheard conversation between Barth and Ivor. Barth is planning a trip to another theme park for research, and Ivor was arguing with him about spending money they don't have. Barth assured him he had the finances under control. Not exactly a smoking gun. But I passed it along to Divya, all the same.

I also uncovered that Barth changed his locks, and new security cameras were installed yesterday. So, there's no way I'm doing any more recon near his office.

Harold needs to fix a rip on my costume before I get dressed, so my first stop is hair and makeup. Whether by coincidence or design, Tristian has rarely been here at the same time as me over the last several days, but this morning he is sitting in the room alone.

He lounges with one leg draped over the side of a chair, arms slung casually over the back.

"What"—I stifle a laugh despite myself—"is going on here?" I wave at him, appraising his new costume.

He's wearing black leather pants and a billowing black shirt, revealing a significant amount of chest. Black knee-high boots and a black leather duster finish the ensemble.

"I'm a pirate." He smirks, keeping the relaxed attitude. Prince Winthrop is all straight-laced and stiff posture. This pirate alter ego is anything but.

He hasn't smiled at me all week, at least offstage. My heart tightens.

Stop it, Imogen.

It's just a smile—an adorable smile. Still, you can find those on a toothpaste ad. Tristian Walsh is nothing special.

"Oh, really?" I keep my distance at the door. We've shared barely a handful of words lately. I'm cautious about what's unfolding but extremely curious, nonetheless.

"Didn't you read the lore? Arden disguises Winthrop as the pirate Captain Stormbreaker when he tires of royal life, so he can sneak among the people." He snatches black eyeliner off the table to smudge around his eyes.

"I remember. I just didn't know you played Stormbreaker." I step farther into the room, resting against the other chair, and pull my bottom lip between my teeth. "Am I on my own today?" Guess he finally decided to get rid of me altogether.

He tosses the eyeliner on the table as heavy tension fills the room. Averting his gaze, he drops it to the floor, his thumb presses into the countertop. "I've been a jerk."

I clamp my lips together to stop from interrupting.

"I wasn't with Aliana that night—I mean, I was, but not like you thought." His voice is thick, like he's forcing the words out. "I was in a funk and she was helping an old friend. That's it. That's all Aliana and I have ever been. She liked to play it off like we were a couple—and I didn't stop her because it was easier to let people think I was already taken. I wasn't ready to let anyone in and Aliana made the perfect shield. But we never were more than friends. I swear."

I shift back and forth on my tiptoes. When I confronted him, I expected him to tell me I was wrong—even if it was a lie. When he didn't, it felt like a knife in the back. It was an easy story to believe. He and Aliana have so much history they could probably fill a whole novel. Tristian and I are barely an opening line.

"Why did you let me think it was more?" I hate the dip in my voice, the ache that builds in my chest at his regretful tone.

"It was easier." His eyes flick up to find mine. "Imogen, I don't want to be here." His rough cadence feels like a hand reaching out in the desert for water.

"So you keep reminding me." I can't hold his stare. Instead, I focus past his shoulder.

A choppy breath escapes him. "You made me remember what I love about this place. But I can't forget the world outside of here. I have plans waiting for me."

Is he searching for an apology? Because he won't find one.

A muscle clicks in his jaw. "What I'm attempting to say is that I can't keep my emotions straight in my head." His voice softens. "But I shouldn't have taken it out on you. You were doing your job and enjoying it."

"My *job*. Right." I swallow hard. This is all a job, probably a detail I should remember. "Does that mean you won't ignore me anymore?"

He tilts his head, the pirate grin returning. "I couldn't ignore you if I tried. I promise to be less of a jerk." I lift an eyebrow and he chuckles. "I'll try, at any rate."

"Okay." I hold out my hand to shake on it. "But I make no promise not to profess my love for that which brings me joy."

"I sincerely hope you don't." His hand lingers in mine.

"So, you're a pirate." I pull away, shoving my fists into my tight pockets. "Where does that leave me?"

"I was thinking"—he grabs a garment bag off the back of

the door—"you might like to join me." Unzipping it, he pulls out a costume similar to his, only this one has a corset.

I run my hands over the soft leather. "I don't know anything about Pirate Arden." When I peek up, his gaze makes my cheeks flush.

"Technically, she's not in the story. So, how do you feel about going off script?"

My heartbeat ticks up as a sly grin crosses his face. "I've never stuck to a script in my life, but I didn't think that was your speed."

He draws the costume out fully and drapes it over my arms. "It isn't, but I need a change. Get dressed. A pirate's life awaits."

Tristian is the boss's son; he can break as many rules as he want (*see:* punching a guest). I'm not in the same boat. Still . . . like I'm going to turn down a little role-play.

He swallows hard when I return to hair and makeup after changing in the costume department. The black undershirt drapes over my arm, exposing my clavicle, shoulders, and upper back, as the black leather bodice and pants hug my curves. The elastic at the wrists makes the fabric ruffle over my hands.

I give him a shy grin. "Do you think you can help me finish lacing my corset? I couldn't get it, and Harold wasn't in the mood to help us go rogue."

His Adam's apple bobs up and down. "I—" He fumbles on his words, licking his lips. "I—yes."

I spin around to expose my half-laced corset strings. "In your line of work," I say as his fingers graze the exposed skin of my shoulder blades, "I'm sure this isn't the first corset you've laced."

I hope he doesn't notice the goose bumps he creates.

"Shockingly"—his voice is gravelly—"it is."

"Happy to be your first." I wink over my shoulder, my stomach whirling when I'm greeted with fire in his eyes. With a sharp breath, I whip my head forward again.

Imogen, what did we discuss not five minutes ago? Tristian is a bad idea.

Too bad those are my favorite kind.

Taking the laces, he tugs them tighter. My hands fly to the wall to keep steady. "Too tight?" he whispers.

"No." I'm breathless. "It's fine." The butterflies in my stomach twist tighter than the corset.

He works the strings in small movements; each pull brings me closer to him. Heat flushes my chest. "Imogen?"

"Huh?" I dip my head low.

"I'm done." He turns me around. "Not bad for my first time." Our faces are inches apart.

"Passable." I shrug, twirling from his grip, gulping in some fresh air.

Pierre is already at the castle, so we have to put on our own makeup. I apply mine quickly, already having become a pro. Lastly, I gingerly add red lipstick, then another layer for good measure.

"Where's my pirate wig?" I adjust my hair the way Pierre taught me.

Tristian hands me a long black wig with thick curls. His is black as well, pulled into a small ponytail at the base of his neck. I snort after he secures it.

"What?" His eyes narrow as he fiddles with the top.

"Nothing." I shake my head. "You don't look like you." This week, we were miles apart, but we have managed to slip back into old habits with just a few words.

We stand for a moment in heavy silence before he clears his throat. "Shall we?"

Yvette's brow creases in confusion when we arrive as pirates and not royalty. "I should probably be more concerned about this."

"Come now, Yvette." Tristian rests his hand on his sword. "Don't you think it's time for a little change?"

Yvette nods. "This place could use a refresh."

"Plus," I add, "you told me Keira Knightley in *Pirates* is your dream girl." We watched it a few days ago during a Fairytalers' movie night.

We enter the crowded Perilous Sea from the back entrance. Tristian takes my hand, the other on his sword. "Ready?" His shoulders relax, voice unburdened. Usually before we go onstage, his muscles are wound to the point of breaking, but not today.

"I don't have a name." I draw closer to him, so the guests who begin to notice two rogue pirates can't hear us.

"Make one up." He places a tendril of hair behind my ear.

I bite my lip. "Um, Ariel?"

"That one's taken." He nods at two little kids across the way who stare openly.

"Briar?"

"Briar, I like." He adjusts the leather duster. "Ready?"

"Always." Sweat forms on my lower back, the day's heat setting in. I squeeze his hand before he lets go and jumps on the rock near the water's edge.

“My good people of Carpathia.” He attempts a passable British accent. “I’m the famous Captain Stormbreaker you have undoubtedly heard so very much about.” He winks at a passing guest. Tristian and Garrick are twins, but this is the first time I notice how similar they are. He’s certainly channeling his brother.

A crowd forms around, as the dashing pirate continues, “I’d like to introduce you to my first mate, Briar. The best swordsman—sorry, woman—in all the land. No others dare cross her.” He puts his hand out, and I jump on the rock with him. “What do you say, love? Want to give ’em a show?”

I lean back and place my hand on my hip. “I don’t know, Captain. Are you prepared to lose in front of all these fine people?” I don’t try an accent because I’d embarrass myself.

“Aye, we’ll see about that.” He draws his sword, a slightly less bejeweled one than Winthrop owns—his stance less stiff. Royal guards taught Winthrop; this pirate learned on the seas.

I lick my lips, tension tugging at them as I take out my sword. When I was given it, no one asked if I knew how to use it. The question must run through Tristian’s head now, because he frowns as I adjust the weapon from hand to hand.

“Shall we?” I beam.

The distress falls from his features with a wink before he advances toward me, his sword hitting mine with a loud clang.

The Perilous Sea bustles with guests. They carry balloons and cotton candy, sweet scents overtaken by the occasional whiff of fish from the restaurant a few feet away.

Tristian's strikes are docile. So I hit harder. I lunge, sword whacking his, and the vibration trails down my arm. He grunts, stepping back. "You put up a good fight, milady."

Pressing my advantage, I push out a breath. My lungs burn as I increase my attack. "Not milady," I bellow, assuming the high ground on the rock. I'm careful of my footwork, so I don't plummet into the sea. "I'm a pirate. Keep your *milady* for the princess."

Sweat glistens on his forehead; he wipes it away with his sleeve. He smiles mischievously. I've never seen him have this much fun onstage. "Aye, love, a pirate you are."

I see my opening, and hit the bottom part of his sword, knocking it from his hand. He stumbles a few steps, eyes wide.

The point of my sword presses into his flushed chest. "Never get distracted on the high seas, Captain." My other hand rests on my hip. Cheers erupt from the crowd.

Winthrop would let me win, maybe even Tristian, but I'm not fighting them, and defeat is not Stormbreaker's style. He collects the fallen sword and returns to battle.

He gets the upper hand and edges my back into the railing. "Where did you learn to sword fight?" he whispers.

My lips graze his jaw as I angle my face to look at him. "Summer camp." My lungs heave with exhaustion. I wrap my hand around his sword. His eyes gleam as I push hard against his chest, spinning out of his hold.

"I'm afraid, Captain," I roar to the audience, "I tire of the teasing." I once again knock the sword from his grip, retrieving it from the ground before he can. "Do you surrender?" I hold a blade on either side of his neck.

Heat erupts over my skin as he surveys me. "Even a pirate knows when he is defeated." He dips into a deep bow. "The win is yours." The crowd applauds, and I beam, all Arden's pleasant contentment gone. I wave to the public before handing him his sword.

"When you want a rematch, Captain"—I drop my voice—"I'm all yours."

26

TRISTIAN

"Thank you, kind sea folk, for indulging a pirate." I return the sword to my sheath, my cheeks pink with the intensity in Imogen's eyes. "But now we must embark on an adventure. I dare say, where did we dock the ship?" I scan the land, squinting. The sun is high in the sky, the park bright with the colors of summer.

"There," shouts a person in the crowd, pointing to Pirate Adventure.

"Excellent eyes, mate. What say you, are you up for a voyage?" We could both use a quick dunk in the sea, if Imogen's flushed face is any indication.

Imogen and I part the crowd, our destination Pirate Adventure, several guests in tow behind.

"Hello, mate." I incline my head to the boy stationed as the ride attendant. The ride is busy, with the line reaching into the extended queue. "Me and the crew"—I point to the crowd behind us—"require passage on our ship. What say you? Will you help a fellow pirate get on board?"

The kid scrunches his face, tongue darting across his braces.

"Um . . ." He glances around, confused. "I could check with the captain." He indicates the booth a floor up, where the shift lead sits.

"No need. I am the captain." I puff my chest out. "So, what do you say?" He doesn't drop the scared expression, but lets us skip ahead.

"My dear citizens," I pronounce to the people in line for the next boat. "I'm afraid I must commandeer your ship. Do feel free to tell Prince Thornton it was I, Captain Stormbreaker, who stole this vessel." With a hearty bow, we jump into the ride vehicle.

"*Thornton* won't like that." Imogen slides across the bench, so that I can fit next to her.

"Exactly the point." How I lasted a week without apologizing to her is a miracle. Just this short time being back in her good graces is already making me breathe easier. I missed the way she lights up a room with her wit and smile. How she can just be standing there, doing nothing, and still she shines.

Imogen rests her hand on my leg. "Captain—the crew awaits your orders."

"Now, you ragtag crew of newly minted pirates." I glance over my shoulder. "Are you ready to sail the high seas? Let me hear an 'Aye, aye, Captain.'"

"Aye, aye, Captain," comes in response.

"This might be the coolest thing I've *ever* done." Imogen's smile rivals all the stars as the ride swallows us up.

"Now, listen here, you motley seafarers." I lay a hand behind Imogen's back, surveying the guests seated in the three rows behind us. A few have their phones to record our little performance—better make it good. "The first thing you need to know about being a pirate—the captain is always right." Imogen's lips twitch up at the side. "Aye?"

"Aye," echoes around the chamber. The ride ambles along on a slightly bumpy track hidden beneath the water. A cold breeze sweeps across us from a hidden fan, the smell of salt water pumping from a whining machine barely masking the chlorine. An eerie message plays, telling us to stay in our seats and keep our hands, feet, and legs inside the ride at all times. And, of course, the most important message: "Dead men tell no tales."

We glide through a dark cavern packed with lost treasures and skeletons. "This is what happened to the last crew that didn't listen to the captain." Imogen points to a lonely skull half-buried in the sand.

"Hold tight, there be rough waters ahead," I warn as a fake storm ramps up on the speakers and we sail down a short but steep hill. A large open village scene unfolds before us.

"Captain," Imogen says, turning to me, "I have a favor to ask the crew." The guests' attention focuses intently on us. "We want all the kingdoms to know better than to cross us, aye?"

"Aye." I'm curious where she is going. This is the first time in a long time I'm actually enjoying playing pretend.

She nods to the guests still clutching their phones. "So, if the crew would be so kind as to share far and wide the tales of our adventures, the captain would be much obliged." She leans in to whisper to me. "Go on, Captain; I know you have secrets to share with the crew."

We sail through the village facade, where scenes display pirates finding treasure and making themselves at home in the various taverns. I point out secrets about the ride. Most are made-up stories my brothers and I created, but we've said them for so long they've become fact. I identify the well where Garrick believes the ghost lives and the location of the buried treasure, the treasure being a time capsule Ivor, Garrick, and I planted when I was seven.

The guests' faces are alight with joy as the ride comes to a close, having discovered details they've missed before. What if I could do this all the time? Show the history of this place. It might not be Europe-level old, but there are plenty of years to explore. Don't get me wrong, I still want to travel the world, but I can use those trips as inspiration to further the rich storytelling people love about Fairytale Gardens. This might be the perfect compromise, so I can honor my dreams, while still participating in the family legacy Dad holds so dear.

"Thank you for crewing our ship." Imogen nods to the patrons as we exit the ride. I give them a hearty pirate wave. The riders from Pirate Adventure still follow behind us, a few more joining as we return to the center of the land.

"What say you, Briar—up for another show?"

"With you, of course."

We do more ad-libbing near the water's edge, a bit of a Q&A, showing off our pirate knowledge. Pride surges through me every time I catch Imogen admiring me from my peripheral vision. My chest puffs in response.

"Give her a kiss," someone yells from the crowd. The rest join in a chant.

My heart does a backflip at her shy smile. She doesn't speak, only shrugs.

"What do you say, love?" I whisper hoarsely. Before I can utter another word, she wraps her arm around my neck, pressing my mouth into hers—the world blurs. It's a stage kiss at first, close-lipped, but my hands find the small of her back, tugging her closer to me. Her lips soften against mine.

She tastes like honey and sunshine.

I've daydreamed about this more often than I should admit, but none of those fantasies compare to the real thing. The kiss is gentle, less for show and more real as we let the park disappear. I feel her smile against my lips and I match it. I run a hand over her cheek, pulling away so our noses touch and—

"What is going on here?" a voice booms from the crowd. Imogen leaps away from me, like she's been electrocuted. If my hammering heart is any indication, I might have been too. Ivor, or should I say Prince Thornton, stands in the middle of the crowd.

I run my finger over my lips. "Your Royal Highness." I give an exaggerated bow. "To what do we owe the pleasure?" The blood in my veins runs hot, a pink flush across my cheeks.

His jaw tightens as he tries to stay in character. "Pirates," he says, his words low, "aren't allowed in this land unless sanctioned by the king." I enjoy the struggle in his clipped words. He wants to yell at me as his brother, but he doesn't want to break the fairytale illusion.

"I'm sanctioned by Prince Winthrop," I drawl. "He has granted me passage through this land." Imogen watches this exchange with a pleased expression, but worry creases her brow. The impatient tapping against her lips increases with each glare Ivor shoots us.

"Prince Winthrop does not speak for the king. Come with me immediately." Ivor clenches his sword with white knuckles.

I tilt my head. "I don't know. I'm having a rather good time." And a pissed Ivor is a cherry on top.

"*Captain.*"

"Perhaps we should go with His Royal Highness," Imogen says. "We don't want any trouble with the king." These aren't the words of a pirate; they are hers. I know Ivor and Dad can't do much to me, but I don't want Imogen to get fired.

"Aye, love. My good people," I address the crowd. "It has been a pleasure. I'm sure we'll meet again."

"Not likely," Ivor says under his breath as we head toward the offstage exit. "What the hell was that?" My brother surfaces the moment we disappear from the guests' view.

"What was what?" I rip off my duster.

"That unplanned show in the middle of the park."

I take off my wig next. "If you'd bothered to read the marketing strategy I emailed you this morning, you'd have seen this is part of my plan to boost attendance. Impromptu shows around the park. I already activated ads about it. It's not my fault you can't keep up."

"You can't just implement things without permission, *Tristian*." He says my name slowly. "I'm in charge of guests' experiences. You can't just go out and do whatever you want."

I bare my teeth. "Oh, that's abundantly clear." My voice carries over the theme park sounds behind us. "If I could, I wouldn't be here right now."

"Would you excuse us?" Ivor turns to Imogen, who follows behind.

She glances at me. "I, uh, yeah—I'll go."

"Imogen, wait." I reach for her, but Ivor interrupts.

"He needs a minute."

I nod to Imogen, who runs off toward the main building.

My jaw muscles ache as I clamp down, speaking through gritted teeth. "Are you going to fire me?" I swivel to Ivor.

He crosses his arms. "Is that what you want? Are you trying to ruin yourself and the park?"

"I'm not trying to ruin anything. If you'd listened to a word I just said, I'm doing this *for* the park." I crack my knuckles, muscles quivering with anger.

"Why didn't you ask?"

I scoff. "Like you would have said yes?"

"You didn't give me a chance." The scar near his right eyebrow is more pronounced with his face fire-engine red from anger.

"I can tell you what would've happened. You would've said no because nothing ever changes around here. We are all stuck in this time loop, but, news flash, Ivor, everything has changed. Mom is dead, and nothing will bring her back. Especially not playing dress-up and going on like nothing has changed, like our customers don't have different needs and expectations than they did twenty years ago."

He opens his mouth to speak as I walk away.

When I get to the costume department, Imogen is already gone. Blood rushes in my ears, and my vision clouds as I put away my gear.

I'm halfway to my apartment before I make an abrupt pivot and head to her place.

Before Ivor interrupted us, the pirate outing was the most exhilarating day I've had in a long time. The kiss is probably what did it. It was a mistake. Not the pirate show—the guests enjoyed it—but kissing Imogen. It was pretend, but it shouldn't have happened regardless. Because now all I can think about is kissing her again.

I know what it felt like to ignore her the last week; I hated that. I don't think I can go back to that.

Reaching her door, I knock before I let my logic take over.

"Hi." Her smile lights up the gloom left by Ivor.

I rub the back of my neck. "Can I come in?"

"Yeah, of course." She steps to the side, and I enter, eyes rolling over the room. "Sorry, it's a little messy."

It smells like a convenience store, but a nice one. "Please, I live with Garrick. This is immaculate." She shuts the door, and we both stand in heavy silence.

"Do you want a drink?" she says at the same time I say, "I'm sorry about Ivor."

She waves it off. "Oh, it's okay. Yelling bosses don't faze me anymore. Water?" I nod, and she pours us each a glass. "Did he chew you out?"

Yes, family drama. Let's focus on that. It's only a matter of time before we have to address the kiss, but it can wait.

I sit at the dining table. "Yeah, he used his big brother voice and everything." I grip the cold glass.

"Sounds terrifying." She leans against the counter.

The tight coil in my chest lessens the longer I'm around her. "Ivor is'"—I run a hand over my face—"just like my father. He wants this place to stay exactly as it was."

"Change can be a good thing. Maybe you just need to stay on him, show him your ideas. This is your park, too." She runs her index finger over the rim of the glass. I concentrate on it to anchor myself in this moment.

"I don't know if I want this park to be mine." That towering truth hovers over me with everything I do.

"Then do you have a right to change it?" I frown at her candor. I should be used to it by now, but it still catches me off guard. "If you aren't going to stick around, do you have a right to say what happens to it? If you do *want* to stay, a hundred percent you do. I guess you just have to decide."

"Did you have fun today?" I ask, deftly changing the subject after a heavy beat of silence.

She looks down at her shorts and T-shirt. "Yeah, I did. Don't get me wrong, I love playing a princess, but the guests seemed to enjoy our off-the-page performance."

I tap a finger on the glass; the pirate rings I forgot to take off clink. "I tried to tell Ivor as much, but he wouldn't listen."

"So, make him listen. He's your big brother, but you aren't kids anymore."

"Was one of your past jobs a therapist?" I joke.

She smirks. "What else have you been working on?"

I blink in surprise. "That's the first time anyone has asked me that."

"Well, I'm all ears." She offers a half smile.

Warmth spreads across my chest and down into my gut, easing the acid left there by the conversation with Ivor. "I recently put up some billboards, and used our pictures from the photo shoot in a new ad at the airport." It took some magic, but I managed to get a shot where we looked semi-presentable.

"I knew you'd be great at marketing. Can I see?" Jumping off the counter, she sits down with me at the table, scooting her chair close.

I don't remember the last time someone showed interest in what I was doing. Her genuine smile sends me shooting into the sky, past the moon and into the stars.

27

IMOGEN

The last two days have been sadly uneventful. I ran into Barth in the hallway, and managed to snap a picture of a fancy gold watch and his designer suit. Both of which Divya said were not helpful, but if we're building a case of stolen money, surely we need to know where it's going?

Also, it's the best I could do. Which is giving me a case of nervous stomach, almost 24/7. Divya sent me here to find the smoking gun, and I'm failing her. I'm failing Tristian, too. Our chat the other day confirmed to me that Divya's article will be a light at the end of the tunnel for him to make his own future.

I was back to princess duties early today, but Tristian wasn't working. They saddled me with the off-brand Winthrop they use on Tristian's free days. In fact, I haven't seen him at all for two days. Maybe he finally followed his heart and left Fairytale Gardens.

Acid burns my stomach at the idea. I know that's what he wanted, and maybe our onstage kiss scared him away. I thought I would have merited a goodbye, at least.

My shift is over, and I leave my costume with Harold, depositing my tiara and ring into their box. I'm nearly three weeks into playing a princess, and I've got this royal persona down. It's easy to slip into Arden's skin. What's more surprising—I'm not bored yet. The only time I felt the itch to flee was when Tristian and I had our Aliana misunderstanding.

This job hasn't been perfect. The costume is hot, and my feet kill me by the end of each day, but those minor annoyances haven't bothered me.

Part of this I attribute to having an out. As soon as I get Divya's story sorted, I'll leave. The other credit goes to Tristian, obviously. He came off as grumpy to start—and still has those moments—but I see his hidden joy underneath his crabby outer shell.

I spot it when he forgets to hide his smile and actually allows himself to enjoy the moment. His *smile* is exactly what will get me in trouble. After our kiss, I planned to keep it professional by dialing the flirting down to a four. But I haven't seen him yet to implement the plan.

"Did you miss me?" Tristian leans against the wall near the break room. Delight forms in my chest at his relaxed smile, brown waves pushed off his forehead.

Why does he look better than when I saw him last?

Not wanting him to think I spent my time daydreaming about our kiss, I play coy. "Didn't even notice you were gone. The other Winthrop looks exactly like you."

I head toward the break room, but he catches my arm, warm fingers gently curling around my wrist. He grazes my face, tucking a fallen strand of hair behind my ear.

"Do you blush like this when he touches you?" He thumbs over my warm cheeks. I step closer to him, breath quickening as I tiptoe past the invisible line I tried to draw between us.

I swallow hard. "We didn't get that far."

"Good." He keeps his eyes on mine, ignoring the Fairytalers walking by.

"How was your time off?"

He breaks eye contact, gaze dropping to our feet. "I—it was okay." When he glances up, he's smiling. "Would you believe me if I said I actually kinda missed this place?"

I lean forward, our lips inches apart—the memory of his kiss tugs at my heart. "No," I whisper.

His laugh is warm and deep. I want to curl inside it. "Maybe not all of it, but certain parts called me back." We stay hovered in each other's orbit, neither making the next move.

Tristian fiddles with his leather belt, eyes downcast.

"Do you want to go on a date?" I blurt.

Omg, did I just say that out loud?

I've been thinking about what it might be like if we'd met as regular people, outside of the fairytale bubble, and what a date might look like for us. And then, as usual, I spoke before my brain could stop it.

He blinks at me in surprise.

I quickly backtrack. "Just kidding."

"Really? Because I was going to ask you the same thing." He scrapes a hand through his hair, brows dipping in disappointment.

"You were?" A phantom hand tightens its grip on my chest.

He nods. "So, if you weren't kidding . . ." A wonderful flush creeps up his neck. Lines crisscross his forehead, uncertainty coloring his blue eyes. "Would you go on a date with me, Imogen?" His voice is assured, despite his fidgeting.

I want to say yes, but I stall, holding the words captive on the tip of my tongue now that my brain has had time to catch up to my mouth. "Tristian." My heart aches, a deep pain I can't reach to rub away.

"I know it's sudden—maybe? And it's probably a terrible idea to mix business and pleasure," he rambles. "I've spent my whole life living someone else's story. I want to finally live mine. I don't want to pretend to kiss you as a pirate." His hand grazes my arm, making the hair stand on end. "I want to take you on a real date."

"I'll screw this up like I do everything else." I'm not sure if I'm talking about relationships or about Divya's potential story, which this could ruin—*will* ruin, knowing me.

"You don't screw everything up. I've been by your side for the better part of three weeks, and I can tell you, you're amazing."

Tears burn my eyes, and I swallow the lump in my throat. It was easier when he was grumpy.

He takes a deep breath, eyes clear, hands steady, as he takes mine. "So?"

I've made terrible decisions my whole life. *Why stop now?*

"Yes."

A brilliant smile crashes over his features, and my heart soars. Even if this is a horrible idea, it was worth it for the smile only for me. "Great." He scrubs a hand over his face. "I thought you were really going to say no after all that."

"I can always take it back."

He uncovers his face, eyes intense. "And break my heart? Imogen, you wouldn't dare." It's lighthearted, but I suddenly feel ice-cold.

"I have to go." I need to call Divya. "You have my number from the group chat Yvette started. Will you text me the details for the date?" I'm giddy just saying that.

He places a whisper of a kiss on the back of my hand. "I will."

I'm not sure if it's excitement or fear making me nauseous, but I'm doused in a cold sweat when I reach the apartment. I splash water on my face at the bathroom sink to regain composure before I call Divya.

Aliana is still in the park. I saw her queuing for a ride as I left. With the apartment to myself, I decide to sit in the living room for a change.

Divya answers on the first ring. "Why didn't you FaceTime me?"

The phone is on speaker as I balance it on my knee. "I thought you might be working. I didn't want to bother you."

And if you can't see my face, you might not discover I'm hiding a secret.

"No one cares." The call changes to FaceTime. "Great ceiling. You know popcorn is my favorite wall treatment."

"I want to give you the full experience." I switch the phone to my stomach, face still out of frame.

"*Imogen.*" She draws out my name.

"*Divya.*" I mimic her tone.

"What did you do?"

I feign hurt when I finally look into the camera. "I resent that accusation."

Earbuds poke out from inside dark strands of her thick braid cascading down her shoulder. "Bull. Spill it. I can literally cut the tension, and I'm hundreds of miles away. What did Prince Charming do?"

"Nothing." I bite my cheek until it hurts. "He asked me on a date." Technically, I asked first, but semantics. I scrunch my face in anticipation of the blowback—for her to reprimand me for risking the story.

Instead, she claps. "About time."

I frown. "You think this is a good idea?" Maybe I hoped Divya would talk me out of it. Be my excuse to bail.

"Imogen, it's clear by the way you talk about him. It was only a matter of time. I'm surprised it took this long." Crickets echo outside, the night relatively quiet for once. "Yes, one hundred percent it's a good idea. We need to get my story going, and I'm running out of time."

"Oh." My stomach drops. I should've known the other shoe was on its way down.

"Oh?" Her perfect, plucked eyebrow arches.

"I thought maybe . . ." She was excited for me to go on a

date. Describing it as a sneaky way to get info from him makes me wish I hadn't said yes.

"Wait." She points a pen at the phone. "Do you *like* him, like him?" I shrug, playing with a loose thread on my shirt. "You do, don't you?"

"Have you seen him?" I counter.

"You should go on a date, and"—she holds up her finger when I start to argue—"not just to get info from him, which is a nice side benefit. Because you actually like him. And you've known him longer than a week and are still interested. That's a record."

"Um, harsh." But not untrue. "Divya, if you write this story, he'll hate me." I can convince myself that he might be able to use the exposé as a way out of his fairytale responsibilities—but I'll still have lied to him about my reason for being here.

"Not necessarily. He might appreciate a well-written and researched exposé." I lift an eyebrow. "What? He might."

"But I doubt he'll appreciate that I was the one who orchestrated the takedown." I bite my cheek. "What if it compromises your story?"

She stops to study me. "Will you let it?"

Pain stabs in my chest. The familiar doubt creeps in. I can balance both, right? I'd never let anything risk my friendship with Divya. Especially a guy. Even if that guy is a literal Prince Charming. "No, of course not. I'm here for you."

Taps from her heels fill the silence. "Then I'm not worried. I'm more concerned this whole endeavor is useless." She drops her pen on the desk, it rolls off, hitting the floor, and she doesn't pick it up. "I've talked to every former Fairytaler from

Pixie Forest to the Perilous Sea. I've emailed and called every contact I can find related to those scam charities. All I got was vague, generic 'thank you for your interest' responses. Plus, we're talking about money in the tens of thousands, not millions. Law enforcement isn't going to bust down doors for that. Which makes me feel like a crappy friend since I forced you to go there and ruin your precious childhood memories for nothing."

My heart aches to see my confident friend so lost. "Stop it, Divya. You have never once been a crappy friend. Plus, you didn't kidnap me and drag me here in your trunk. I came and stayed of my own free will. Which I will do until we solve this."

Her elbows hit the desk with a thud, her head collapsing into her hands. "Imogen, there is steep competition for this cash reward. I need this to work, not just for the quick funds, but you know my family is counting on me to take care of them. This is the first step toward that. If you don't find anything by next week, I might have to scrap this story and find something else while there's still time."

I sit up. "I'd have to leave?" This is the only job in my entire life where the thought of quitting hasn't made me jump for joy.

She groans, barely lifting her head to respond. "You don't *have* to do anything." Her voice is weary. "You can keep the job for the summer. At least one of us will get something from this failed scheme."

If there's no story, Tristian wouldn't need to know what my real intentions were for coming here. I could pretend the story never happened. Then I wouldn't have to make a choice between friendship and romance. The thought thrills me, but the hopelessness in Divya's features sours that idea.

"I won't let that happen, Divya. I'll get you evidence." I know she smiles to placate me. "I will. You trusted me with this; I won't fail."

"I know you're trying your hardest." Her tone makes me grind my teeth.

"You don't need to say it like that." The phone burns under my vise grip.

"Like what?" Her brows pinch together.

I suck in a breath through my nose. "Like you always knew I'd fail."

She tilts her head. "Don't, Imogen. If I thought you couldn't do it, I wouldn't have asked. You're projecting your insecurities onto me." I focus on the side of the screen, not meeting her eyes. "You low-key always do this. You blame others—your bosses, coworkers, hot-dog hats—so you don't have to face you might be the one at fault."

My face stings from the invisible slap. The phone shakes as my grip tightens around it. "I'm here for you, Divya. I'm destroying a place I actually care about and a person I—" I stop myself short.

Divya closes her eyes, taking in a few breaths. "You are doing this for me, and I love you for it. I've always believed you could build a moon base, or cure the common cold—or whatever—if only you'd let yourself realize how talented and amazing you are, instead of fighting so hard against yourself." My eyes burn, but I refuse to let the tears fall. "Because you deserve the world; that's all I want for you."

Yelling at her would make me feel better. Throwing the phone across the room would also do the trick. But it wouldn't change the fact she's right. It's easier to think other people are the problem. Instead of telling her she's right, I say nothing.

"Why don't you search Barth's office again? If there's dirt to find, it'll be there," she says after a long pause.

"I told you already, they changed the locks and added cameras." My tone is clipped. "Barth's office is a no-fly zone."

"Then you need to figure where else Barth might hide something."

"Just because you want something to be true doesn't mean it is."

"Imogen, I know you love this job. And I regret asking you to go." I open my mouth to argue, but she keeps talking. "Not because I don't think you can help me. I regret it because I'm making you tear down a place you love." She pushes out her bottom lip, eyes glassy.

The anger fizzles out of me, the fire gone. "I owe you a million times over for all you've done over the years. There will be other jobs—there always are."

For the first time, that sentiment doesn't make me feel better. Fairytale Gardens might be my perfect fit, but it doesn't matter. I always ruin things just as they are getting good—it's inevitable that I'll end up burning it to the ground.

28

TRISTIAN

This is not how I thought our first date would unfold when I asked Imogen out yesterday. I was going to wear something nice, bring flowers. Impress her with a fancy dinner. It'd be the most romantic night I could create—not that I've had any experience with that, but I brushed up on tips online.

Best laid plans, however.

"Hey." My heart skips a beat when Imogen opens the door in a green-and-yellow palm leaf spaghetti-strap sundress. "You . . . look stunning."

"I opted to leave the crown at home tonight." She fiddles with the bag over her shoulder, bouncing from her right foot to the left. We spend all our days together, but the nervous energy from this shift in our dynamic is palpable. "Am I overdressed?" She motions to my jeans and T-shirt.

I rub across my jaw. "See, I planned the whole night—impressive stuff, you'd have been dazzled. Then I got a call from Ivor, and he desperately needed a babysitter since Garrick has to work late to cover the kitchen."

Her face drops. "You're canceling?"

"No, no," I say quickly, grabbing her hand. "Never. I did, however, have to change the plans slightly."

"Okay . . ." Her eyes narrow.

"How do you feel about seeing my nephew again? Bradley?"

"I remember." She nods.

Aliana's profile is visible from the kitchen as she stirs a pot. A car horn blares down below. I clear my throat. "We won't have to stay all night. I just told Ivor I'd watch him for a few hours." I glance at my shoes. It's been months since I even tried to go on a date—which was actually just a group thing at the movies. I forgot how terrible I am at one-on-one. "I screwed this up, didn't I?"

She lifts my chin. "Not yet." That twinkle in her gaze and reassurance in her tone makes everything better. "I'd love to help you babysit."

We walk down to the car and I realize this will be the first time we've been anywhere besides the park together. "I was going to take you to this Italian place. But Ivor usually has pizza rolls in the fridge."

"Really? He strikes me as a frozen vegetable kind of guy," she says as I open the passenger door of my car for her.

As we pull away, I slide my hand across the space between our seats to take hers—in what I hope is a cool move, and not shaky and sweaty like I feel inside. "He might surprise you."

"He's not the only one."

The sunset illuminates the sky in deep purples and oranges. She gazes out the window at it. "You know people complain about theme park food," she says, tapping against the glass. "But in my opinion, it's an underrated art."

"I grew up eating it. It was our summer staple, since I rarely left the park." Memories of Mom buying us corn dogs and turkey legs makes my chest seize. I grip the wheel tighter with my free hand.

"I know there are things you're probably dying to know about me," I say, before she notices my flushed cheeks. "Ask me anything."

She presses her lips together, studying me while I try to keep my eyes on the road. But the world outside might as well not exist with the way her attention focuses entirely on me.

"What happened on your first day playing prince? Were you *perfect* from the beginning?" I hear a tinge of disdain for the word *perfect*. And I don't know if it's about her or me.

"I hit someone on our first outing this summer. Do you think I'm always perfect?"

She laughs. "Oh my god, that will forever be my favorite memory. Do you think those guests really deleted the videos? I should've asked one to send me a copy."

The melodic tones of her laugh ease any apprehension. "I definitely wasn't perfect on my first day, for the record, but it wasn't the same for me. I've been in the park my whole life." I glance over to find Imogen staring at me, waiting for the rest of the story. "Then three years ago came the year I finally got to play a prince for the first time. I hate to admit it, but I was sure I'd be amazing."

"I'm glad to see how relatable you are in this story."

"Ha, just wait. Our whole life, my father made us feel like royalty. A screwed-up ideal to instill in children, I realize now. We knew Carpathia was pretend, but he said we ruled this land. The idea of ascending to my place as a prince felt normal. But my first day, I was horrible."

Her laugh makes my stomach drop, and my heart do things it hasn't done in a long time. Since Mom died, I've kept my heart away from anything that might make it feel too deeply. Right now, it's soaking up Imogen's attention like a dying man in the desert drinks water.

"I flubbed my lines. I nearly lost my sword any time I picked it up. Garrick roasted me for a week until he accidentally dropped his pants mid-show and made me promise a truce."

"Of course he did. It must be nice to have siblings. They're like built-in friends."

I bite my lip. Ivor is the first one that pops into my head. "It can be cool, but sometimes they're the actual worst because they know all the buttons to push that make you want to kill them."

"Still, you know they always have your back."

"Yeah, I guess they do."

We fill the rest of the short ride with easy conversation.

Ivor's house matches him perfectly. Two stories of brick in the suburbs with a white picket fence and matching stainless steel appliances. Okay, the fence isn't picket, but it is white. Ivor might only be twenty-six, but he has always been an old man at heart. He couldn't wait to grow up and start a family.

"It's Imogen, right?" James greets us when we arrive. "The new princess?"

"That's me." The smile is kind, but she twirls her hair around her fingers, a nervous tic I recognize.

"We already had plans, and I didn't want to cancel," I explain as we step inside. "I hope it's okay."

"Of course." James is more flexible than Ivor. "Bradley will be glad for more people to entertain. He's a little star in the making."

"Uncle T!" Bradley slams into me as he skids across the wood floor.

"Hey, kid." I rub the top of his head.

"Tristian"—Ivor crosses his arms—"you're late."

"It was my fault," Imogen says swiftly.

"I see. Well, we have to go. I left a list on the kitchen island with his schedule." Ivor and James hug Bradley and leave us alone.

"Schedule, huh?" I look at Bradley. "What's first?"

"Vegetables." He sticks out his tongue. "Did you bring your treasure?" He turns to Imogen.

She crouches so they're eye to eye. "I'm afraid those troublesome mermaids have stolen it. Help me get it back?"

"We need our weapons." Bradley hauls us to the living room. "We can use the vegetables to trap them."

"Great idea. But first, we need sustenance." I redirect him to the kitchen for dinner.

"Uncle T, you gotta hold still," Bradley says from across the living room after I've fed him peanut butter and jelly. "Don't move, or you'll die."

Bradley has me on the floor with an apple on my head . . . while he readies his bow and arrow a few feet away. The bow and arrow are plastic, so death is out of the question. But losing an eye? Very plausible. Luckily, I found safety goggles in the garage before we started.

"How long have you been an archer?" I try not to move as the bow tilts back and forth.

"Since Uncle G gave me the bow for my birthday." A solid three months. No worries, then. "Ready?"

"Nope." My shoulders tense to my ears.

"Come on, Tristian. Bradley is clearly a natural." Imogen fights a laugh. "Look at his posture."

"Aim," Bradley continues, unaware of the sweat on my brow.

"Maybe we should start with a can on a fence?" I suggest.

"Fire." He shoots the arrow off, and it lands with a gentle thud at my feet. He huffs—sounding an awful lot like his father. "I need to be closer."

"Why don't we sword fight? I'm good at that." I hold the apple on my head as he repositions.

"No, pleeeeeease. I want to do this. Daddy never plays with me."

I know the feeling, kid. "All right, move closer."

"I shall mourn you when he impales you." Imogen frowns dramatically from the couch.

"For years?" I glance at her while keeping an eye on Bradley resetting the bow.

"At least a solid three weeks. Black isn't my color." She's a good sport about all this, but I wish we were alone.

"No talking." There Bradley goes sounding like Ivor again.

He runs a few paces until I can reach out and touch him. He notches another arrow, squints, and lets go. The arrow hits me right in the eye—glad I got the goggles. I jerk my head to the side, and the apple topples off. "You did it." I stand with a cheer.

"An excellent marksman." Imogen claps. "Those mermaids will be no match for you."

"I did it?" He beams.

"Sure." His eyes were closed, so he doesn't know either way.

"Let's do it again. Can you film it for Papa and Daddy?" He turns his big round eyes on Imogen.

I jump in to save her. "It's late, kid. You need to go to bed."

"No," he groans. "Uncle G always lets me stay up late."

"He does?" I do my best impression of Ivor's stern voice.

"Yeah . . ." He avoids eye contact with me. I open my mouth to call him on his bull when the doorbell rings. "I'll get it," Bradley screams, and runs from the room.

I wrangle him to the side to see who's there. "Garrick?"

"Uncle G!" Bradley grabs his hand and drags him in.

Garrick dumps a plastic bag in my arms. "I snuck away early and, of course, I brought ice cream."

"Birthday cake flavor?" Bradley's eyes narrow, leaning back on his heels and using Garrick as a counterweight.

"Would your favorite uncle bring any other kind?" Garrick picks him up and heads toward the kitchen. "Imogen—hey."

"Hey." She takes a seat at the stools at the island.

I deposit the bag on the counter with a heavy plop. "Okay, we can have ice cream, just one scoop, and then bed." I hear Ivor's voice from my mouth as I collect the bowls.

"Okay, *Dad*," Garrick says.

It's more like three scoops later and a bath to eliminate the sticky ice cream that found its way everywhere, and I finally tuck Bradley into bed. This *date* has descended so far away from date territory that I'm not sure I can recover it, but I've had a good time, whatever it's turned into. Tonight's situation feels all too familiar: I make plans, and last minute my family ropes me into taking care of their needs instead.

But tonight, for the first time, it didn't feel like such a burden.

29

IMOGEN

"Why don't you two get out of here and finish this date properly?" Garrick says after Bradley is in bed. This wasn't the most conventional date, but I've never been the most traditional person.

I had a great time.

"We should wait for Ivor." Tristian glances around the tidy living room I cleaned while he was away. I wanted to snoop a little. Unfortunately, Ivor's house holds no dark secrets.

"I'll be here, and Bradley is asleep." Garrick flings himself onto the couch.

Tristian raises an eyebrow in question. I shrug. "I'm up for whatever."

Tristian scratches his neck, leaning against the headrest, when we get back in the car after leaving Ivor's. "What do you say we try to finish this date?"

My pulse accelerates as I study his profile. "What do you have in mind?" My voice is lower than I intend.

He tilts his head, eyes flashing to me. "Showing you my hidden talent. What did you have in mind?"

I clear my throat, straightening forward in my seat. "A hidden talent, huh? How can I say no." I hope the dark hides the flush up my chest.

The drive back to Fairytale Gardens is long enough for me to detail a hundred different scenarios I could walk into. But I never picked sneaking into the closed Royal Fare kitchen.

I remain at the door while he flips on the lights, then clicks buttons on the industrial oven. The kitchen is an ample open space with stainless steel worktops, and several ovens and fridges. The clean smell of lemons doesn't mask the lingering scent of fries and roasted meat underneath.

"So, your hidden talent is cooking?" I hop onto the counter to observe.

"I used to bake with my mom. She was amazing." He finishes preheating the oven before retrieving items from the fridge, and a few bowls from a shelf. Grabbing an apron from a hook, he ties the strings around his trim waist, the muscles tightening on his forearms.

While I watch him remove butter from the fridge, I'm aware this is no longer a pretend fairytale land or a babysitting gig. We're real people, on an actual date. It's easy to forget when you never leave the confines of Fairytale Gardens, but after our trip to the real world I'm nervous. Here, he's only Tristian, and I'm only Imogen.

Is that enough?

"What are you making?" Through the fabric of his thin gray T-shirt, I can make out the hard edges of his shoulder blades, the strong muscles mesmerizing. It's a Herculean task to form a coherent sentence.

"Well, we had such a five-star experience with the pizza rolls—I thought we needed an equally impressive follow-up." I never imagined Tristian as a chef, but I could get used to the apron.

Big fan, actually.

"I'm waiting with bated breath." I swing my legs, but my feet can't quite reach him at the stove.

He adds butter to the searing pan. "Brown butter"—he turns, grabbing my ankle—"toffee, chocolate chip cookies." I bend my leg to pull him toward me.

"That's an impressive number of syllables for a cookie." The words hitch as he traces the lines on my palms.

"I'm an impressive guy." His words are confident, but he's wearing his shy smile.

My arms slide around his neck as I scoot forward another centimeter on the counter. His eyes drop to my lips, and I smile in return.

"Can't let the butter burn." He steps away, twisting to cover the splotchy red spots on his neck. "Will you collect a few more items for me?"

I gather the ingredients he lists. "Did you ever work at the Royal Fare?"

"Other than the meet-and-greets, no. I've only been a face character." A small vertical line appears between his eyebrows as he focuses on the butter.

"Food service jobs are the worst." Out of all my jobs, I loathed those the most.

"I didn't see waitress or cook on your résumé." He swirls the butter around the saucepan. The kitchen fills with the nutty caramel aroma of the browning butter.

"Résumés should be about a page . . ." I lean against the counter next to him after measuring the ingredients. "If I listed all my jobs, I'd need a binder." I recall the name tags in my backpack and press my lips together. I don't have a name tag from Fairytale Gardens.

When this is over, what will I have to remember it by?

His mouth curves into a smile as I pull the strings around his waist to distract from my unpleasant thoughts. "Did you come to FTG because you ran out of jobs near home?" The butter has darkened, and he removes it from the stove to cool.

I swallow hard, drawing my attention to his eyes—the perfect shade of ocean blue. "That's exactly it."

Unlike the dining hall, the kitchen's lights are austere, made for function, not beauty. But right now, it's the most magical place I've ever been.

He leans over and whispers in my ear. "I'm glad you lost all those jobs because it brought you here." He picks up the pot and steps back to the cookie mix.

The kitchen warms with the hot oven. I draw my hair off my shoulders to get some air. "Hey, I didn't lose all of them. Some I gave away freely." I try to make a joke, but my words are thick. Moving to the opposite side of the counter, I lean on my elbows to watch.

I don't want to talk about me. This cozy setting and his alluring face might get me to spill more than I can afford. I change the subject back to him.

"Did you hang out in your dad's office a lot? Or was our meeting ten years ago all by chance?"

"If I wasn't on a ride or playing carnival games, I was always with my dad. I loved the old office because it had the best view. My brothers and I would pretend to survey our lands." He dips his head. "Silly, I know."

"That's not silly at all." It's really cute. Honestly.

"Too bad he moved backstage. All that old office is good for now is collecting dust and secrets."

I freeze, heart stopping cold. "Secrets?"

He shrugs, unaware of my sudden change, too focused on his task. "Dad is a pack rat. If he had anything to hide, it would be there." He finishes the mix and pushes the bowl between us. "Here, I need your help."

Okay, that is an important nugget of info. I don't want to process it right now. I know the second I tell Divya about it, she'll pester me nonstop until I go search that office. This could be the vital piece that cracks the case wide open—Divya can get her story and Tristian will finally have proof that his father is the villain he wants him to be, giving him the freedom to leave guilt-free. But where will that leave me?

I tuck my thoughts away for later.

He rolls the dough in his strong hands. "I used to sit in his office and lay all the reference pictures he took from his exploratory trips to Europe on the floor, walking through each one and imagining what it'd be like to visit."

I copy Tristian's lead, the sticky dough coating my palms. I scrape at it to get it off, dropping my ball on the baking sheet. Divya's voice in my head tells me to take advantage of this easy conversation to dig deeper. I open my mouth to ask about the charities, to probe him for intel. But as I watch his focused face, his hands deftly dividing each piece of dough into equal portions, I can't do it. It's not that I'm choosing him over Divya; that I think this is more important than her story. I'm just choosing to have a moment to just *be*.

He looks up at me, eyes warm, lips ticked up in a half smile. "What?"

My bottom lip tastes like chocolate when I rub them together. "Nothing. I just like watching you."

"I like watching you, too. In a non-creepy kinda way."

"Oh? I totally meant mine in a creepy way. Like Edward watching Bella as she sleeps level creep."

His soft laugh is like a sweater on a cold day.

We have ten minutes to kill when the cookies are in the oven. I've retaken my spot on the counter, and he settles a respectable distance in front of me. "So, tomorrow is training for the Starlight Ball." I hoped I'd make it this long before Divya's story broke.

He scratches his chin with his thumb. "Yeah."

"Are you going?"

"It's on my schedule."

I pull him closer. "I'll be there."

"Why do you think I'll show up?" The fire remains behind his eyes, but it softens, replaced by something I can't quite name. I intertwine our fingers, giving his hand a gentle squeeze. His eyes close slightly as his forehead dips toward me.

I'm tired of waiting, of being cautious.

Before my brain has time to stop me, I scoot forward to the edge of the counter. Our eyes lock and there's a brief moment of hesitation. He gives me an out—a second to back away.

Like that's going to happen.

"Will you kiss me already?" I sigh, and he laughs before his lips crash into mine, consuming all the wayward thoughts that never leave my tired mind. My pulse thrums against my flushed skin.

"You taste like chocolate." His voice vibrates against my mouth. The kitchen feels like someone turned the heater to the max. I can't keep my eyes open. I only want to feel him.

But I feel something else.

"Tristian. Crap." I shove him away.

"Did I—" He doesn't finish his sentence when he sees the flames. "Fire extinguisher." He points to the corner. I'm off the counter and skidding across the floor before I know it. I yank it down, but I've never used one before. He takes it in one deft motion and puts the fire out in seconds.

It was small—a dish towel too close to the stovetop. The hissing white foam from the extinguisher stops, followed by the beep of the oven timer. I let out a shaky laugh.

Tristian wipes his forehead with the back of his hand. We're both sweating.

"Why are you laughing?" He is, too.

"This is my second fire in three weeks." He lifts a brow and I press the back of my hand into my mouth as he removes the cookies—which look and smell divine. "Long story."

"I didn't plan on burning the park down as part of the date."

The cookies are gooey from the oven, but that doesn't stop me from sampling one. "I have that effect."

He brings my hand to his lips. "I bet," he says, kissing chocolate off my palm.

I'm in trouble.

We clean the remnants of the fire and the baking before Tristian walks me to my apartment.

"This was a good night—even with the fire." Tristian holds a to-go bag of cookies.

"It was, surprisingly."

"Ouch." He grabs his chest.

"No, I didn't mean because I thought you'd suck," I say quickly. "I'm not good at dates. I didn't doubt you." I doubted myself, my ability not to screw it up.

He cups my face, gaze intense, before he kisses me. I close my eyes and fall into this moment. It's less urgent than in the kitchen, but I feel it more intensely.

I block the thought that I might potentially ruin Fairytale Gardens, or he might hate me for it—will hate me for it—and kiss him harder to push away the worries for another day.

He staggers back before I'm ready to break the spell. "I don't want to call it a night," he says.

I muster a resistance I'm not accustomed to. "We have to be up early."

He nods, finally straightening. "You're right."

"A sentiment I don't hear often."

The way he smiles at me makes me weak in the knees. No one has ever looked at me like that. "I'll see you in the morning."

"Good night." I give him one last kiss before rushing inside.

I press a hand to my heated forehead as my heart pounds. I didn't want to get involved with Tristian in the first place. It clouds my judgment when it comes to helping Divya because now I can't deny how I feel about him. If I help Divya, I hurt him, and if I side with Tristian, I screw her chances of the future she's always wanted. No matter which path I pick, I'll lose someone.

30

IMOGEN

"What do you say?" I whisper in Tristian's ear. "After this, we go someplace. Just the two of us." It's early afternoon, and we find ourselves again in the castle training tower. But this time, we aren't alone. Today's lessons for the Starlight Ball includes all major characters—our understudies have taken over the park for the remainder of the day.

"I have a better idea," he counters. "Why don't we leave right now?"

After the date last night, I haven't stopped fantasizing about him. We have unfinished business I'd love to resume. I'd be horrified to see the pictures the guests took with us this morning at the meet-and-greet. We barely managed to keep our hands off each other. But a few well-placed glares from Yvette did the trick.

"I'm sure no one would miss us." Tristian runs a slow path over the back of my hand.

Aliana clears her throat next to me. "I've been a great sport about this." She waves her hand at us. "But I just ate lunch, and I don't want to hurl on my new leggings."

Tristian and I scoot apart marginally. She's not wrong about being a good sport. After I came home last night, she didn't comment on the date, other than to say it was nice to see Tristian smile again. I might have misjudged her.

Slightly.

Maria claps at the front of the room to silence the group. "All right, everyone. Welcome to training for the Starlight Ball." A spattering of applause echoes around the tower. "The opening weekend for the ball is in three days. This is one of the park's highest-grossing events and the most anticipated."

Tristian shifts next to me, his knuckles digging into the supple leather of his pants.

I rest my hand on his chest, his heartbeat a steady anchor under my palm. "Are you okay?" I drop my voice to keep the conversation between us. He grits his teeth but nods.

"Some of you have been characters in the ball before. However, last year there was some confusion over what were appropriate conversations with guests." Maria's narrowed eyes flash toward Garrick. "We have, therefore, decided we could all use a refresher." She motions to Michael, who's been nodding at every word. He clicks a remote, and her trusty projector turns on.

"God, it's nice not to be the one operating that ancient machine for once," Yvette mutters, leaning against the wall next to us. She's not on attendant duty since she's playing an elf for the ball.

Michael flips the lights off. "First, we'll watch footage from past Starlight Balls and go over the reason behind it in the lore." A few muffled groans come in reply.

The screen plays, and I elbow Tristian when his younger self pops up on-screen. "Look at you." He is gawky, with long limbs, shaggy hair, and braces. He must be twelve or thirteen.

He rubs his temple, a valiant attempt to conceal the blush streaked across his cheeks. "Not always the charming prince you see today."

"I don't know." I tilt my head. "You look pretty cute. I'm sure you broke hearts even then."

"Not likely." Garrick laughs to his left, followed by a grunt and a curse as Tristian kicks him in the shin.

The picture changes, and Barth Walsh is on-screen with their mother. Tristian's body stills, hand falling away from mine.

The video is a commercial showing all the activities the guests can do. I remember seeing it on TV and begging my mom to let us go. The ticket price includes special treats: notably a dinner at the Royal Fare, a firework display, and a stage show. Then, of course, the main draw: the ball itself. They encourage guests to wear their finest attire and come dance with the characters they know and love.

The commercial ends with the then Prince Winthrop and Princess Arden dancing together as the crowd disappears, and it's only them.

"As you can see," Maria says as the projector silences, "the Starlight Ball brings to life what we try to give a taste of every day in the park—a real-life fairytale."

"Guests pay a lot of money for this add-on ticket," Michael says. "We need top-notch performances."

"We don't have long, so no time to waste." Maria divides us into pairs to practice the dances.

"Leaders, take your partner's left hand and place your other on their waist." Maria demonstrates on Michael. Each couple gets to decide who they want to lead the dance. Since I'm a horrible dancer and Tristian has done this before, he takes control.

His warm fingers curl around mine, while his other hand rests gently on my waist at a respectable height.

Maria walks around, correcting people's stances. "The key is to make the guests believe the love between you is real." Tristian's eyes sparkle when I gaze into them. A born fairytale prince. I, however, am not sure if I put deodorant on this morning.

No, I did—pretty sure.

"Everyone, take a step closer to your partner. We aren't at a school dance; touching is allowed—appropriately," Maria adds to Garrick.

Tristian closes the distance between us until we're pressed together. "Is this okay?" he asks, voice low and rough, tickling the delicate space between my cheek and ear.

His body is solid against mine, the buttery leather of his costume soft against my skin. "Perfect." I nearly choke on the words, because it is, which freaks me out. I've never described being in someone's arms that way.

I let Tristian's firm yet gentle hold glide me around the room. It's going well until I'm supposed to step back when he moves forward, but my feet don't get the memo and I trample on his right foot. He cringes, hand squeezing my waist, but doesn't stop.

"Sorry." My chest tightens.

He shakes his head, deep lines between his eyes. "You're doing fine. My toes can take a few hits." This is good because I step on them several more times. I'm slightly better by the end of the thirty-minute dance lesson.

"A few more practices, and you'll be a pro." Tristian hands me water from the snack table.

"Your faith in me is unearned." But I'll be happy to do more practices if I can be close to him.

"You've earned my trust."

I choke, water spewing from my lips.

"You okay?" He strokes my back as I hack up a lung.

"Strong water," I manage to wheeze, my nods too vigorous. I slow them down. "I'm fine."

His trust in me might get this whole place exposed. Just when I think I can relax and separate Divya's story from my budding relationship—a reminder shoves me back into reality. It's always a balancing act when you get a partner to keep your friendships from suffering, but adding espionage takes it to a whole new level.

"Tristian, Imogen," Maria calls. "Please come to the front. As stars of the ball, you need to learn a special dance."

"Is it too late to invest in steel-toed shoes?" He winks, and my heart soars until it is yanked back by the chain that tethers me to the real reason I'm here—the thing that will likely be my undoing.

Maria takes my shoulders and forces them away from my ears, where they tense up. She pushes Tristian and me closer together. "This dance is a celebration of victory, of budding love." My eyes flick to Tristian, who is already gazing at me. "You need to be content in one another's arms. Okay?"

We nod.

"Now, Tristian, follow my lead." She takes Michael in her arms like a rag doll.

"Close your eyes if it's easier," Tristian whispers. "I won't lead you astray."

It is easier. I concentrate on the music and press of Tristian's warm fingers on my back, the way he taps out the counts on the back of my hand. The tension melts away from my rigid muscles.

"Excellent job," Maria cheers, and I open my eyes. It felt like only seconds had passed. "Practice a few dozen times, and you'll be ready for the ball."

His lips graze my forehead, a brief kiss left in the wake. "We make a good team."

I lean into him, the steady beat of his heart against me. I don't know what I want us to be. Or maybe that's a lie, one easy to repeat. If I want more with Tristian, I risk Divya's story, and hurting him and myself when everything blows up. Because it will.

"Good work, everyone," Maria says at the end of the two-hour practice. "I'll call you all to my office over the next few days to test you on your knowledge and dance skills." A collective groan rumbles through the room.

"I'm excited about the ball," I say as we leave the castle.

He stops near the Royal Fare back entrance. We inch closer as a few more people come down the stairs. He uses his thumb to scratch his jaw. "I haven't attended a ball since my mom died. It was her favorite event, her brainchild." A deep breath makes his shoulders sag. "It felt wrong having it without her."

"But?" I play with the buttons on his costume.

"But . . . I think she'd be happy for me to attend again." We stand in the quiet stairwell for a minute. An attempt to hold the moment a little longer. "I have to go to a dinner service. A VIP—they want the princes."

"Okay." Neither of us moves. I don't want to say goodbye. I could stand like this for the rest of the night, if he let me.

His lips brush mine. I whisper my wish into the soft kiss.

"Tristian, come on," Garrick yells from the doorway to the restaurant.

Tristian groans. "I'll see you later?"

"Yes."

I don't tell him my wish—barely let myself acknowledge it. I wish for time to stand still, for no articles. For just a few more moments of the perfect I've found.

Before I destroy it.

31

TRISTIAN

Travel alerts will be my villain origin story. I hover over the email from the summer program showing the idyllic places I should've been visiting. I know I should just delete it, but despite better judgment, I open it as I make my way to the castle to start the day.

I scroll through pictures of ancient ruins and lush greenery. A month ago, my hopes were high that I was finally on my way to where I'd always dreamed of going. But now I'm back in a crumbling castle made by my father, with no more history than the fast-food joint down the road.

Since yesterday, the chat has been nonstop about the Starlight Ball, all the Fairytalers excitedly anticipating the event. I watched Imogen glide through the movements of our dances with her fingers throughout dinner. As every second passed, the pressure in my head became unbearable. It's shoved me further and further into the ocean—my breath running out, with no way to get to the surface.

The worst part—I let myself be dragged under. At times, I forget all about the dream I'd been planning. Fairytale Gardens lured me in like always. Maybe no matter how hard I try, this is all I'll ever be.

"Hey, Tristian." Yvette looks up from her tablet as I walk into the stables. "You're early."

"Yeah." I scuff my polished boot, kicking a rock. I slept terribly last night, each toss and turn another stone weighing me down.

"Everything all right?" I don't know Yvette well, but even she picks up on my mood.

"Great." I force a smile as I clasp my hands together, nails digging into my skin. "Ready to play pretend."

Imogen arrives a few minutes after the call time—a habit of hers. She beams, and it makes my heart ache. I try to focus. She's one distraction I don't want to lose.

The carriage moves around the Village Center. We wave and smile as we have a dozen times. But today, my costume tugs at the seams and my arms can't move the way they're supposed to. I yank at my jacket to try and get comfortable, but the attempt is as hopeless as I am.

I dab at my sweat-covered forehead before taking Imogen's arm and leading her into the meet-and-greet. This is old hat by now. She's beautiful and perfect—like I knew she would be.

I'm spiraling. My whole body squirms as I try to say the words that should come easy. I'm not performing Shakespeare. The longer I stand with my back straight, Imogen's arm looped around mine, the worse I get.

"I need air." I stagger away from Imogen in the middle of the performance.

"Are you okay?" Worry colors her expression.

I can't speak. I just nod and disappear behind the back curtain. Swerving through the park, I ignore the guests calling my name. Blood rushes in my ears, smothering all the noise except my hammering heart. I reach Carpathia and take the stairs at the back entrance two at a time until I reach the castle roof.

It's a small space, barely enough for a few people to stand. I lean against the wall, glaring at the park as the warm sun bakes my neck. My tight chest constricts my lungs, each breath forced and ragged. The air is worse here, but at least the only eyes around are mine.

My phone buzzes—Yvette asking if I'm okay. I send a thumbs-up and shove the phone into my pocket.

I don't know what to do . . . because I want to stay. I want to go and hold Imogen in my arms and pretend with her—put on the crown and the sword. I want to be here. And that scares me more than leaving.

The magic waned when Mom got sick, and evaporated when she died. That was the final straw that pushed me to follow my dreams and pursue what I wanted, for a change. I thought staying would suck. But the longer I spend with my brothers, with Imogen, experiencing the park again through her eyes, the easier I find it.

I don't go back to the meet-and-greet or the one after. I ignore several texts from Imogen and my brothers. I stay on the roof until the sun is high in the sky and my skin might be burned to a crisp. By the time I get to the main building, it's early afternoon. My breath is steadier, my chest still tight, but at least my heart isn't about to jump from my body.

Imogen deserves an explanation. I just don't know how to give her one when I barely have one for myself. Our relationship status is as clear as the Perilous Sea, but *something* is developing.

I get a text from Harold to meet at the costume department for my final Starlight Ball fitting. The door is open when I arrive. Harold is working on the hem of Imogen's dress.

"Wow." The word slips from my mouth, and I'm not in my head for a moment.

"Do you like it?" Imogen runs a hand over her bare arm; unsure eyes search my face. I've been a jerk today. I want to kiss her worry away.

The top is a light-blue fabric, with sparkling silver stars splashed across it. The same blue material continues on the puffy skirt, topped by a soft silver tulle that swishes down to her feet. After living my entire life in this place, I've gotten good at describing gowns. But this one—*focus, Tristian.*

"You look—" I clear my throat to unclog my brain. "You look amazing."

She drops her gaze, fingers gliding over the skirt. "I've never worn an outfit so magical. I feel like a real fairytale princess."

I swallow hard. "Harold, you needed me?" I focus on him and not my pounding heart. Or the desire to run over and pull Imogen into my arms and tell her everything will be okay.

"Your costume is over there. Put it on. I need to see you two together."

I slip into the costume, a few stray pins pricking me. My outfit has less sparkle than hers but is still enhanced for the ball. The white jacket is trimmed with silver and blue down the length of the sleeve and along the edges, to match Imogen's dress. A silver sash hangs across the chest; metals and insignia for the rank of a Carpathian hero adorn the front. The white slacks are cut close to the leg, and I make a mental note to stand far away from Garrick. He cannot be trusted next to fabric this color.

"If I thought you resembled Prince Charming before . . ." Her eyes trace over me before she places out her hand. "Shall we?"

I raise an eyebrow.

"Harold wants us to dance. Make sure you don't trip over this balloon of a skirt." She swishes it for emphasis.

I take her gloved hand as her familiar shape melts into me. She watches her costume as we twirl around the room, and I take the opportunity to study her face: the stray tendrils of red hair that fall across her cheeks; the way her lips suck in when she concentrates on the steps, or mouths the counts in whispered breaths.

Imogen's swirling skirt makes soft music for us. And as we move, the costume shop and Harold fall away. Her eyes find mine halfway into the dance, and I hold them there.

Imogen is funny and intelligent, spontaneous and energetic—everything I wish I could be. A beauty and kindness that you find once in a lifetime.

"Harold, can you give us a minute?" Sweat builds on my forehead as panic radiates in my chest.

"I'll grab a drink from the break room."

Imogen frowns, and the line between her eyebrows deepens. "What's up?" she asks when we're alone.

I scratch my forehead with my thumb. "I'm sorry," I whisper, the words barely audible.

"For what?" She pulls my hands away from my face and into hers, glowing from the lights reflecting off the dress.

I rock back and forth, unable to meet her eyes the way I want. They call to me like a lighthouse in a storm, but I'm afraid.

She squeezes my hands, then moves her own up my arm until she grips my shoulders. "Hey, what's wrong? Please tell me. I can't read minds."

"I was a jerk today." The words surge out of me like a cork from a bottle. "I've been going through . . . the whole ball threw me for a loop I didn't expect. It brought up emotions I have been trying to suppress, and it isn't fair for you to take the brunt of them."

"Do you want to talk about it?"

"I don't know," I admit.

"If you do, I'm here." She bites her bottom lip.

I look at the ceiling to collect the words. "I got scared. The ball resurfaced all the reasons I wanted to leave this place, and then you . . ."

"I scared you?"

"Yeah—in a good way. Like the feeling right before you get on a roller coaster." I cup her face in my hands, thumbs smoothing over her cheeks. "I know we haven't known each other long, but I like you, Imogen, more than I've liked anything in a long time. And that terrifies me. I don't want to be here. I thought I hated FTG—maybe I still do, I don't know—I *do* know you make it better."

She shakes under my touch. "Why does that sound like a bad thing?" Lines crease her brow, and I kiss them away.

"You're a good thing. But I don't want to masquerade as a fake prince forever." The words ache as I let them out.

"You don't have to."

"Will you come with me? We can visit castles and bridges."

Confusion colors her features. "Castles and bridges?"

"First thing I thought of." My grin resembles more of a grimace. "You could come with me on my summer program to Europe. I don't know how, but we can figure it out, together."

"I . . ." She glances down, eyes glassy when she looks back up. "You don't want to go to those places with me. I'd break a vase neither of us could afford to replace. Then we'd end up in a dank medieval prison for life."

"It's hard to break a stone castle."

She smiles, but it's tight. "I'm good at breaking things." A single tear falls on her cheek, and I brush it away. "Can we just be here? Right now is good."

I nod, pulling her into a hug, ignoring the pins that are sticking into me from her dress. "I promise to be here right now with you." She nuzzles her face into my chest.

Acid still burns my insides. Marketing has been more fun than I thought it would be, and I'm actually really good at it. Could this be my way of making my mark here? Do I want that?

32

IMOGEN

I'm blissfully dreaming when my phone vibrates. Grumbling, I rub my eyes, and blink at the bright screen and room. I don't have princess duty today, but I am scheduled to help with Starlight Ball prep.

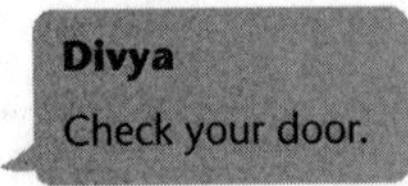

What now? Did Divya send me a spy care package, hoping that'll speed me along?

Aliana is already in the kitchen when I stumble out. I ignore her questioning eyes, swinging the front door open. "Divya?" My voice squeaks several octaves higher than usual.

"Surprise?" Divya stands on the welcome mat, wearing a bright yellow T-shirt embroidered with wildflowers, and a pair of denim shorts.

"What are you—" I cut my interrogation short when I remember Aliana is standing at the counter cutting watermelon.

"Who's your friend?" Aliana points the large knife in our direction. I doubt it's meant as a threat, but it makes my mouth dry.

I shove Divya behind me to block her from Aliana's view. "A friend." I snatch Divya, and haul her past Aliana's accusing stare and into my room, slamming the door with the grace of a bulldozer operated by a toddler. I let out a tense breath.

"What are you doing here?" My hair tangles at the base of my neck as I scratch at it. Grabbing a brush off the dresser, I comb through the snarls.

"I thought I'd come help. We're so close. We'll have this story set if we can get that smoking gun."

The brush yanks at my knots; pain follows each stroke.

"So, you think I can't handle it." My lips press into a thin line. Of course she figured she needed to rescue pathetic Imogen. It's too early to process this, since I haven't even had coffee.

But she's not wrong. *What have I actually accomplished?* Zilch.

"No, that's not it at all. I promise." She takes the brush and forces me to sit on the bed. Her fingers untangle the knots as she combs them smooth. "You haven't answered my texts for, like, three days. I didn't know what happened to you."

"That's not true, I . . ."

Wait, I swear I saw a message from her. But did I answer?

I try to dig myself out of this gaping hole. "See, my phone does this thing when I clear notifications, where it doesn't show I have unread messages—so I wasn't, in fact, ignoring you, I was just super busy with all my investigating that I didn't remember to reply."

"Well, I didn't know about this *tech* malfunction, and the big clock is ticking down, so I had to come see for myself everything was okay. Also, to make sure they didn't lock you away in the dungeon."

I look over my shoulder to stare her down. "You being here could blow our cover."

She crosses her arms, not backing down. "Imogen, I was worried this was all going to fall apart and I didn't see any other option when my only source was MIA."

Guilt gnaws at my insides. I really dropped the ball. "Okay, I'm sorry. But as you can see, I am very much alive. So, can you leave before someone recognizes you?"

Shaking her head, she resumes brushing my hair. "I'm here now. Aliana's already seen me, so I might as well get what I came for. Besides, the Walshes don't know me. We go to different schools, and by the time the story is published, we'll both be long gone."

"I love the confidence. You're speaking like you've already won. But that's beside the point. It's super risky." I have a good thing going, and while I am happy to see my best friend, her presence threatens all that I've built here.

"Fine. I was a little jealous, too, okay? You were having all the fun. I wanted in on the action. My favorite part of investigative reporting is fieldwork, getting my hands dirty."

The idea soothes the anger swirling in my chest, but does little for the pressure of failure churning in my gut. "You do hate to sit on the sidelines."

"Unless it's actual sports."

Ugh. She is already here and Aliana's seen her, so as long as we're careful she doesn't meet anyone else, we should be fine.

"What did you have in mind?" I curl my legs under me.

A long braid twists into a bun at the nape of her neck. "I want to go with you to see Barth's office."

"I told you we can't. He's got cameras galore now. It's too risky." Frowning, I massage my temples. "But maybe . . ." I haven't yet told her about Barth's old office.

"Spill it." Divya sighs. "I came all this way."

"Okay." I nod. "Barth used to have a different office, located in the park between the sea and the peaks. Tristian randomly mentioned that Barth could hide secrets there."

Divya's eyes widen. "Let's do some recon right now."

"I can't. I have work. But you can go. It'll be risky. The park has security and cameras."

"I'll figure it out." She has that ever-present air of cool. When I lapse into silence, she nudges my leg. "So . . . tell me about Prince Charming?"

"He has a name." I try to remain chill, dropping my eyes to the blanket to hide my blush.

She lifts a sculpted eyebrow.

"*Tristian* is a very nice guy."

"A very nice guy," Divya scoffs. "Please. Imogen, spill."

I fall onto the bed, Divya doing the same. I could lie and tell her it's a fling, a way to pass the time. And if this were a few weeks ago, that would've been the truth. Tristian was a distraction I didn't need but indulged in anyway. However, after getting to know him—the real person hidden behind the prince mask—I can't say that.

"I don't want him to get hurt." That's the most important truth. I'm still processing emotions I'm not versed in, but this one rings clear as a bell.

Divya leans up on her elbow. "Oh boy, you fell for Prince Charming."

"Well, he is very charming—when he wants to be, anyway." My chest surges with warmth when I picture his face, a smile lighting up his once-gloomy demeanor. Remembering the task at hand sours that joy.

"Who knew this story would also get you a boyfriend."

"He's not my boyfriend."

"He could be?" Divya studies me in the way only someone who knows you too well can.

"No, he can't." I push myself to the headboard. "I thought Tristian hated FTG and his father's control, but I've seen a change. This place holds so many of his memories—especially since his mom's death."

I drop my head to stare at my hands. "As much as he wants to be free of this place, I don't think destroying it will have the effect I hoped for. It won't give him freedom, it will just tarnish all the good memories. He's lost so much already, and I'm scheming to take away more." Not just with his family, but with me. When he thinks of the name Imogen, it will only conjure feelings of lies and heartache.

I shake off the melancholy before I look back at her. "I came here for your story and I intend to see it through. You *deserve* that money. But in the end, I can either have a boyfriend, or you can get the exposé. Both can't exist in the same world."

Deep frown lines mar her pretty face. "Maybe they can."

"Always the optimist." I wish she were right.

There's a beat of silence and I give her another smile, telling her without words I'll be fine. Which maybe I will—someday.

"Okay." She starts again, but a little more hesitant than before. "So I'll check out the park, and you go about your day normally. I'll let you know what I find, and we can execute our search when you finish work."

"You make this sound so serious."

"It is. I can feel the win within my grasp." Divya puts on her game face, and I know this is happening whether I want it or not.

33

TRISTIAN

I fixed things with Imogen yesterday. Who knew that expressing how you feel actually does lighten the weight on your back? I slept surprisingly well. Today the park is busy, as we finalize all the details for the Starlight Ball tomorrow. Garrick had the bright idea to volunteer us to help.

The ordinarily light cadence in his voice is stilted. "Mom would be happy to see you at the ball again. It's a nice way to honor her."

I fight the sudden sting of tears. "I miss her." It hurts to say the words, but holding them in cuts just as deep.

"Me too." I barely hear his response.

"We never talk about her." My insides tighten as I watch him. Garrick is always up to chat, but it's hard to get him to discuss anything serious when you want. He only does it on his terms.

"Do you want to?" He looks over at me.

I shrug.

"Any time you want to, we can." He squeezes my shoulder quickly. This is the Garrick who helped me home when I fell off my bike in third grade. The Garrick who told off a bully who called me a name. The one who actually cared about things.

When we were kids, Garrick used to become obsessed with things. He'd be so invested that it was the only thing he talked about. Sure, it annoyed the crap out of me sometimes, but the fire behind his eyes was contagious. Then after Mom, that fire vanished and he was still Garrick, but he'd been dulled.

Garrick wanting to talk about her again might be the hint of that spark coming back.

"Remember when we were, like, six, and I wanted to bake a castle cake for the Starlight Ball?" I try not to reminisce about Mom and how the park used to be, but I don't want to lose the good memories.

Garrick's lip twitches. "You mean the one Aldrich dropped on the ground and blamed me for?"

"Yeah . . . the way I remember it, *you* dropped the cake and blamed Aldrich for it." I was so proud of my lopsided, way oversprinkled cake. It was the first thing I made by myself.

"Weird, because the way I remember it, that never happened at all." He covers his mouth to conceal the grin as we approach the back lot.

We stop at a warehouse behind the main building where they store the larger props. Several groups have already set up decorating supplies at different stations.

"Tristian, Garrick, thanks for coming by," Michael greets us. "You guys can work over there." He points to an area near the open garage door.

Giant wood star cutouts lie sprawled on the cement floor. We've used them before, but they need a refresh. Imogen and Pierre paint two as we approach. My heartbeat quickens when I see Imogen smile, while she tucks a strand of loose hair behind her ear. It's like everything that I've been worrying about just disappears when she's there. I know she'll be the burst of sunshine I need to get through any cloudy day.

"Hey." I grab a star from the stack.

"Hi." Imogen's face lights up and I'm shooting to the moon.

A warmth unfurls in my chest as she beams at me. "Mind if I share your paint?"

She wipes her forehead, smearing blue across it. "Be my guest."

I dip my brush into the white paint, then swipe it on the star next to the one she's decorating. "Please tell me art is your hidden talent. Because I suck at this stuff." I sneak a quick kiss on her cheek as I lean over to get more paint.

Tiny specks dot her nose. "Not at all."

We're twenty minutes in when Garrick's attention reaches capacity. "You know what would make these stars better?" His hand hovers near the paint can.

"No." I reach for the paint, but I'm not fast enough.

"Splatters." Garrick dips a brush into the paint can and flicks it at me. White paint splashes across my apron.

Imogen lets out a yelp, jumping behind me to escape the pigmented waterfall. "Oh, you asked for it." I grab my brush and fling it at him. Blue covers the side of his face.

He turns to me, eyes alight. "It's on." A wicked grin graces his features as he throws the paint at us, using two brushes this time.

I seize the star closest to me, and Imogen and I hide behind it. I peek out. Garrick is distracted collecting another paint can.

"Now would be your chance to bail," I whisper to her, but she's already got a paintbrush in hand.

"So not happening."

The urge to kiss her overwhelms me, but I have a mission to accomplish first. Using Garrick's moment of distraction, I throw more blue.

"Are you kidding me?" Michael's eyes bulge on his bright red face as he takes in the scene.

A loud crack sounds as Garrick tosses an empty can over his shoulder. "It's called improvising." He moves on to purple.

"The stars!" Michael screams, while keeping his distance. The tiny clipboard he holds is his only defense.

"It adds character," Imogen chimes in, hair falling around her face. Her neck is covered in white paint, not to mention her clothes. But her huge grin is contagious.

"Ahh!" she screams as Garrick pops up on the side of the star.

"Surprise." He throws a handful of glitter.

"Here." Imogen passes me the blue paint bucket. She flings a paintbrush at Garrick's retreating form. I have lost mine in the chaos, so I use my hands to throw a fistful at him. He turns a lovely shade of blue. We stop a few minutes later when we run out of paint, and Michael looks like he might have a stroke.

"Are you okay?" I ask Imogen, who uses the back of her hand to squeegee purple pigment from her arms.

Her laugh is a dip in a cool ocean on a hot day. "I've always liked the color purple."

I wring out the front of my no longer white T-shirt. "Sorry about Garrick."

She waves away the comment, paint flying off her fingertips. "That was way more fun than real painting."

"Hmm." Someone clears their throat behind me.

I groan, resting my forehead against hers. "What?" I say without turning around.

"It's a safety hazard to leave this paint on the ground." Michael's worried tone kills the mood.

"We'll fix it. Sorry." Imogen pulls away to find a paper towel.

I join her on the ground. "Garrick made most of the mess. He should clean it up."

"I think he has his own problems." She nods to where Garrick has spilled a pile of glitter all over his shoes.

"He's never getting rid of that." The sight makes me feel much better about only cleaning paint.

We've managed to scrub the paint off the cement and source a few towels to clean ourselves. She scrubs over her neck, the paint smearing further across her skin.

I graze my finger over her cheek. "Glitter." I pull my hand away to show the shimmer.

"I might need you to walk around with me and do that all the time."

"Consider me hired."

"I call first dibs on the shower." Garrick throws a dirty towel at my face.

"I should go, too," Imogen says. "I'll have to clean the bathroom a few times after I'm done."

"Good luck!" Garrick whistles. I wish he'd take a hint and leave, but he stands at my side. Neither Imogen nor I move.

Garrick glances between us as he finally catches on. "Am I ruining a moment?"

"Sure, but what else is new?" I signal with my eyes for him to get out of here.

"Right, well—I'm going to go." Garrick gives a salute, heading toward the apartment.

"I do need to take a shower." Imogen picks dried paint off her arm.

"Can I walk you back?"

She nods, twisting her paint-covered fingers into mine. I'm unsure what I'm doing, but today I feel good.

34

IMOGEN

My arm wraps around his. Paint covers our bodies. It itches, but with Tristian by my side I don't care. I got a text from Divya twenty minutes ago that said she wanted me to meet her in the park, but I haven't responded. A jerk move, I know. She came all the way here and I promised to help her—which I will, but I'm just putting it off for a few more minutes. Plus, I need to make sure Tristian is somewhere he won't run into Divya.

Letting go has never been a problem for me. It's the holding on I struggle with. I never try to keep anything close to me. But I want to hold on to this for a lifetime. Hold on to him. We are two people on the brink, a roller coaster at the peak, the drop inevitable. All this will end, but that doesn't mean we can't enjoy the ride.

Tristian kisses the back of my hand as we walk. "I wish we could stay in this moment . . ." He trails off.

"Me too." The sun shines across the pool, the late afternoon air hot and muggy as the apartments loom ahead, mocking me that this time isn't meant to last.

"This moment doesn't require anything from us. Here we don't have to make any decisions." His words tumble out in a fast rhythm.

"What decisions?"

"Never mind. Let's not spoil this with the future."

I stiffen. "Yours or mine?" I want to say *ours*, but that future is even hazier.

He doesn't notice my body has stilled; he's in his head. "I was trying so hard these last few weeks to come up with a way I could still go to Europe. But the last couple of days, I've been thinking that staying here isn't as bad as I thought it would be. And who knew I'd actually like marketing. There might be a real chance I could use that platform to make some changes to FTG for the better." He scrubs his face. "I don't know what I'm saying."

The warmth inside me disappears, replaced by a cold dread. He was supposed to not care about what happened to the park. I counted on his apathy to make it easier to swallow my lies.

"So, you want to stay?" I try to keep my voice light as pain presses against my ribs. All he talked about is how horrible he found this place and his father's iron grip.

"Maybe. I don't know."

I want you to stay—the words almost leave me. I clamp my jaw tight. It'd be perfect. Spending every summer with him, in the first job I don't want to run from.

But it's a lie.

All I've built, with my job and with him, is based on falsehoods.

He takes my hand and kisses each of my fingertips as he speaks. "What are you thinking?" He jars me from the prison my brain was creating for me.

"I—" A huskiness fills my voice. "I want you to be happy, Tristian, more than anything."

Even if it's not with me.

I've searched so long for my perfect, I'd never want to be responsible for someone abandoning theirs.

"I'm ecstatic right now."

I let my whims and fancies dictate how long I stay or how quickly I flee in every aspect of my life. And, like always, my choices will leave all parties dissatisfied.

Except Divya. She has always been my constant.

While not like anything I've experienced before, this thing with Tristian won't last. We will likely fizzle out in a few weeks. I should leave before we have to watch it implode.

I wish the walk to the apartment were longer, so we could postpone the inevitable.

Despite the early summer heat, a chill runs down my spine. "Tristian." I stop at the top of the stairs to my apartment. I trace the lines of his forehead, the dip of his strong brow.

"What?" His hand in mine is more comforting.

"Thank you."

He laughs; the rumble vibrates through me. "You're more than welcome." I kiss him softly, memorizing it.

A throat clears behind us. "Sorry to interrupt," Divya says from my front door.

35

TRISTIAN

Imogen's eyes widen in shock as she takes in the girl at her door. "I thought you were still in the park?" Her voice is a mixture of delight stained with apprehension as she pulls away from me and toward the visitor.

The mystery girl swats a bug flying at her face. "I got tired of waiting." They speak with the undertones of two people with many years of friendship.

"I was going to text you. Oh—" Imogen steps back, brows furrowing as she looks at her friend. A silent conversation happens between them. "Uh, Tristian, this is . . ."

"D." The girl waves, staying by the door and sporting a pleasant smile. "So, this is the famous Tristian I've heard so much about."

Imogen's blush makes my chest swell with pride. "Go inside, D." Imogen graces me with a final kiss. "Goodbye."

I stay where I am until she's safely inside, then I start the short walk back to my place. The apartment grounds are quiet, the faint noises of the park a background hum. I didn't want to leave her. I wanted to go inside and keep talking, or maybe we could have watched a movie, whatever she wanted.

Closing my eyes, I picture her smile during the paint fight. If all I ever got was one memory, it could sustain me for a lifetime. But I hope I have many, many more. A warm tingle showers me—a lightness to my soul I've missed.

Garrick's laugh trails out through the thin walls before I open the door to our apartment. Aldrich's shouts of protest follow. I step inside, staying silent as I watch my brothers.

"So, did Imogen come to her senses and find better company?" Garrick says a minute later, eyes glued to the screen. "Dude—why is your horse trying to run me off the road?" You think they'd have had enough of sword fights and quests, but apparently that's just me.

"I'm sure you don't mean you." I perch on the arm of the couch.

Garrick shoots me a glance. "Pff, I'm clearly the best Walsh. It's just a genetic fact. I don't need to prove anything. Also, you're getting paint all over the couch. Not that I care, but I'm assuming Dad will charge you to have it cleaned."

"I'd take a shower, but I bet you used all the hot water." I note his hair is still wet.

"I—Garrick, what the heck?" Aldrich fumbles with the controller. "That's not fair."

Garrick grabs a chip with a shrug. "If the game lets me do it, it's fair."

"Anyway," Aldrich continues, ears tinged red. "Why didn't you and Imogen hang longer?"

Images flash before me. I shift forward. "She had a friend over, so I left."

"You could've invited them here," Garrick counters.

"Was I supposed to bring her home to this?" I wave at the screen. "It's basically a frat house."

Garrick kicks a controller on the floor. "We have extra. She could've joined."

"I left her at her apartment." It killed me to let her out of my arms.

"Did you shake her hand, too?" Garrick winks to Aldrich.

I slap the controller from his grip.

"Dude!"

"Sorry, hand slipped."

Aldrich and I share a grin.

Withdrawing my phone from my pocket, I click on the email confirmation for the summer program—my last chance of escape. The bold date stares at me like a ticking time bomb.

Maybe it doesn't have to be one or the other. Despite my protests, I'm enjoying my time here. I have been for a while. My stubborn ass took a while to realize that. If I can make my own choices and have this, I'd be willing to stick around Fairytale Gardens. Growing into my own person can help the park, too. We could both do with some changing.

I just need to convince Ivor and Dad that I won't run away if they let me off the leash. They have to let me have my own life and adventures. But I want to be with my brothers, too. That's what Mom would have wanted.

“What’s up?” Aldrich’s voice shakes me from my haze.

“What do you think about me trying to upgrade some things for this place?” I lean against the couch in an attempt to be casual as I tug at a loose thread on the arm.

Garrick pauses the game to give me a once-over. “Imogen’s really done a number on you, hasn’t she?” He smiles.

I chuck a pillow at his face, but he ducks.

“This has nothing to do with Imogen. I might want the marketing gig for real when I graduate. I actually liked what I’ve done and I’ve only just scratched the surface.”

The game ends, and Garrick throws his controller on the floor. “Why are you consulting us? We’re the props. We don’t make the decisions.”

“Speak for yourself.” Aldrich lies across the couch when Garrick gets up for a drink.

“I haven’t made any concrete plans—but if I do I’ll need your support. If it’s all three of us, they might listen.” Energy pumps through me, a drive I’m not sure I’ve ever felt.

“I guess I wouldn’t mind having you stick around.” Garrick kicks a foot up on the counter. “Plus, I liked the videos you and Imogen created—I can’t wait to see what you do next. And I look amazing in the billboard ad, so I guess you’re pretty good at your job. Although, with a face like mine, I made it easy for you.” He cracks a cheesy grin.

I stopped believing in fairytales because I assumed happily-ever-afters didn’t happen. That life was messed up, bad stuff happened, and then you died, often too soon. But Imogen yanked back the fog that crept over my vision. She opened my eyes so I could see that people—like my brothers—also think I might have a future here other than behind the prince mask. If this is what I do with no marketing training, who knows what I might accomplish if I fully invested myself.

For the first time in years, I see land beyond the sea I've been aimlessly drifting in.

36

IMOGEN

"I told you to wait in the park," I say, pushing the door open and all but shoving Divya inside. I head to the bathroom to get the itchy paint off me before I have to scrub my skin raw to remove it. Luckily, Aliana isn't in, so we're alone.

Divya's voice trickles in from the hallway. "You did not. I said I was going to do recon, and I did. When you didn't respond, I came looking for you. I didn't expect you and Tristian to be having a doorway make-out session."

"We weren't," I yell over the rushing water as I strip off my paint-stained clothes, before stopping and just getting right in with them on. They need a wash too. "So much for staying out of sight."

"I'm sorry, okay. It was a mistake. By the time I realized you were with Tristian, I was stuck. My options were either stay there and make the meeting brief and forgettable, or jump over the railing and run away like a prowler."

"I would've voted for option two." I squeeze the bottle of body wash all over me, rubbing it into my shirt and arms. Tristian only got a brief look at Divya—maybe he won't recall what she looked like. Aliana didn't say anything about knowing Divya, and we aren't friends, so I doubt she'll recognize her from school. But we're testing the limits of my plan to come out unscathed.

Divya plops onto the floor outside the bathroom door. "Whatever, it's done. Let's move on to more important things. Like you hurrying your butt up so we can head back into the park and snoop in Barth's old office."

I stop my cleaning, swallowing hard. "You found it?"

"I did, and I think I know how we can sneak in without being too noticeable. But it only works while the park is still open. So, get ready quickly. We have an hour."

I wish I had a reason to postpone this. Could I pretend my ankle is broken? No, Divya would never buy my lie, and also, I know this has to be done. The investigation is why this whole thing started, and I won't let my friend down.

"Okay, what's the plan?" I ask, once I'm dressed. Divya gives me a baseball cap that matches hers. We cross the back lot and go through the Fairytalers' entrance.

"All right. I marked where I saw security cameras." Divya withdraws a marked-up park map from her bag. She loves a plan. As much as this excursion gives me heart palpitations, I'm excited to have her here. "I believe I've found a blind spot." She points to the corner near the stairs. "If we wait there and come out when a large group passes by, we should be able to use them as cover and slip up the stairwell."

"Couple of questions. One: What if there isn't a large group going by? And two: How do we know there aren't security cameras in the stairwell?" I twist my shirt hem around my hands, squeezing them into fists. "I'll admit I was a little distracted the last time I was there with Tristian. Looking for security was the last thing on my list."

Divya smiles slyly. "Thanks for asking. I know there will be a crowd because the exit to White Out is adjacent, so we just need to wait for a group to leave. And I know there aren't cameras in the stairwell because I bribed a kid to say his little brother ran off and he thought he went up the stairs, so could security check the cameras. The guards said there are no cameras up there."

"*Some kid?*"

Divya pulls me away from a wayward child running with a turkey leg and toward the blind spot she mentioned. "This kid was good. Honestly, I might need to recruit him next time."

"Um, ouch. I'm like right here."

"Sorry. I love you, but he was good. Okay, shh. Now, we wait."

I wasn't talking, but I stay quiet. Following Divya's lead, I pull out my phone and pretend to stare at it, while we wait for a group to pass, so we can slip in.

"Someone is bound to recognize me," I hiss.

"Why do you think I got you the hat?" She pulls on the brim of her matching blue Fairytale Gardens baseball cap.

"Yes, a totally stellar disguise no one will see through." I smirk. She kicks me in the shin, and I wince.

Usually, Divya's confidence is enough to calm me, but it's not just the trespassing that raises my heart rate. My stomach aches, knowing our success will make Tristian think I betrayed him, that everything we shared was a con. Pain stabs at my chest when I think about the end of my fairytale.

Still, maybe it won't be so bad.

Tristian always said he wanted to leave. He's made that abundantly clear with every huff and groan uttered while we're onstage. Despite what he hinted at earlier today, his layover here was always meant to be temporary. No one would blame him for distancing himself from a sinking ship.

Still, I'll have to admit I lied from the beginning, and he won't appreciate that I . . . *Imogen, stop.* I shake my head, refocusing on the present.

I don't have time to spiral further because a large crowd exits the ride. Divya pulls me inside the mass, shuffling along until we see the break to the stairs and bound up them. My heart rages in my chest, but when no one yells at us to *get back here, you criminals,* I relax slightly.

We don't linger on the stairs. I copy what Tristian did the other night, but I'm not tall enough to reach, so Divya has to lift me to the top of the doorframe.

She shakes as she wraps her arms around my upper thighs. "Hurry up," she hisses. "I'm going to have a back spasm if I have to hold you any longer."

I'm worried it's not there, but I feel the metal slide under my hand. "Okay, put me down."

Divya wastes no time, and I hit hard into the wood floor with a thud. "Sorry," she whispers. I twist the key in the lock and quickly open the office door. "Wow, you weren't lying about the lack of security."

I close the door softly, not that it matters with all the noise from the park. "Tristian said his brothers snuck up here for more breaks."

"Are these pictures like the ones in the main office?" Divya walks along a dusty memorabilia wall I hadn't noticed the first time.

"Yeah—but this one ended several years ago. We won't find the new ones here."

"Oh, a safe. Perfect." Divya crouches to inspect the two-foot-tall metal box on the ground.

I lean on the dusty desk as she feels around the safe like she can find a loose bolt and pop it open. "I don't have the code."

"I'll try a few numbers. Some code an old guy would use." Divya tries the first number sequence.

The hall is silent, but my eyes drift toward the door every few seconds. The closed drapes let a little light into this dark hole, but I don't want to risk opening them more in case someone inside the park notices. "It needs five numbers, and you get four tries before it locks you out for twenty minutes."

She pauses, her face half shadowed. "How do you know this?"

I kick the sticker on the side with a company name. "They used this brand at the craft store I worked at. Trust me, I heard the managers complain about getting locked out enough times to know how it works."

"Okay, well"—she licks her lips—"I'll make sure I pick the four best."

I don't argue because I know she'll do it anyway. When it beeps after four tries and won't let her do more, I can't help myself. "I hate to say I told you so."

"You love saying it." She stands, jaw tight as her hands dig into her hips.

"Normally, yes, but not in a criminal situation." I peer around at the old boxes and metal cabinets. "Let's try the filing cabinet. That's where the charity ledgers are in his new office."

I take a deep breath. If Barth is a criminal, it's Divya's duty as a journalist to uncover it.

The filing cabinets look the same as the ones I saw in the other office, but if Tristian is right about his dad keeping secrets, this would be the place to do it. Divya removes dozens of file folders and spreads them on the floor. I help her examine the documents inside. It's a bunch of financials; most are familiar from my search in the new office. They must keep backups in here.

But several are new.

"He's embezzling." The flash on Divya's phone blinds me momentarily. She flips the pages over. "Look, this list is from a charity event the park hosted last year. These new charities had donations sent to an account in the Cayman Islands. These are the types of banks criminals use to hide money. And here . . ." She grabs another file and runs her finger down a column of figures, murmuring the numbers under her breath. "Bingo. Both were created two years ago. The same month those charities were started."

I bite my lip. I'm not an expert on the ins and outs of offshore banking, but something feels off. "I don't understand. None of these papers were in the other office."

"So? You said this was the secret stash." She doesn't glance up.

"But doesn't this seem too easy? There just happen to be documents with Barth's signature showing he gave money to fake charities? And look, these older papers are signed with black ink, but the new ones are in blue." I grab her phone when she doesn't answer. "Divya."

"It's just ink." Annoyance laces her clipped response.

"What if it's not?" I open a box to reveal a row of black fountain pens I spotted when I was here with Tristian and noticed the same brand in Barth's current office. "A man who keeps his writing this consistent is serious about what he uses—and these are all black ink."

Even in the dim light, I can see Divya's eye roll. "That doesn't mean anything. Maybe he didn't have his beloved pens on him that day?"

"Fine, okay, but if Barth wanted money, he could have given himself a raise. Why risk getting caught stealing?" I push, even as her confidence sows doubt in my theory.

"*Because* he wouldn't have to pay taxes on this money." Her tone further deflates me.

Still, I can't ignore the gut feeling that I'm onto something. "What if this is a setup?"

Divya frowns. "A setup? This isn't a Hollywood movie. Who would do that?"

I shrug. "I don't know. Shouldn't evidence be harder to find?"

"Criminals get sloppy when they think they've fooled everyone. That's why they get caught." She puts the files back together. "Imogen, I can tell when I've found my break. And this is it."

"Maybe if you—"

"Who would frame Barth?"

I bite my cheek. "I don't know." Tristian did say Barth likes the finer things, so maybe it's not that big a stretch that he would steal to maintain that lifestyle.

"This is it, Imogen. Trust me."

I stand, without helping her put away the files. "I'm not sure, Divya."

"Well, you don't have to be." She slams the cabinet closed harder than needed, the ting of metal on metal echoing in the silence. "This is my story, and I say I got my man."

Unease twists my stomach. "So, you're just done?"

"Yeah." She peeks into the silent hall. "I'll finalize the story when I get home. I pitched it to the editor at my internship, and he said he'd publish it if I cracked the case."

Once Divya publishes her article, my cover will be blown. I thought it would take her longer to get it written and then published. I assumed I'd be long gone before it hit the internet. Of course, I never thought I would make it this long at a job. She won't use my name, but I'll spill my guts if I look in Tristian's face.

37

IMOGEN

Tristian

I can't wait to see you.

Let's get away for a day this week.

I want to go someplace where it's just me and you.

My gut twists. He's been sending these sweet gems since this morning. At first, they made butterflies zoom around my stomach, but as I walk to the costume department, they turn my limbs numb with dread.

I feel like garbage.

Divya left a few hours ago, but I stayed hidden in my room. It'll take her a day or more to finalize the story. Tonight is the Starlight Ball, and she said I should enjoy one last hurrah before I leave.

I asked her not to publish the story until I have a chance to tell Tristian. He deserves to know. He might hate his dad and will probably hate me, but I owe him a heads-up.

"There's my princess." Harold grabs me when I step into

the costume department that evening. "We need to get you dressed ASAP."

Two days ago, I thought tonight would be the highlight of this job. Now I'm waiting for the axe to drop. I run a hand over the most magical dress I've ever worn. In the right light, I look like I'm made of stars.

Tristian's face brightens when I step from behind the curtain. His white military-style uniform is the epitome of princely fashion. "You're magnificent."

I drop my gaze, careful of my wig and crown. My throat tightens as I try to meet his adoring eyes, stopping halfway. It's like an emergency brake pulled while the train races at top speed. I can't look at him dead on.

He places a gloved hand out. "Are you ready, princess?"

I swallow the lump that threatens my air supply. If this is my last hurrah, I should enjoy it the best I can.

If it's even possible.

"With you at my side, always." It's meant to be the words of Princess Arden to Prince Winthrop, but it rings true to me.

He kisses my knuckles through my white silk gloves. A sharp pain cuts into my chest when his hooded eyes meet mine. It's the open, honest gaze of a guy ready to leap headfirst into the unknown.

How will I tell him what Divya and I found?

"Are you okay?" He cups my cheeks; worry clouds the hope. "You're pale. Is the corset too tight?" He motions to Harold, who runs over, grabbing at the laces.

I back away, hand pressed into my stomach. "I'm fine. A little nervous—that's all." It's not a total lie. "Let's go." I wipe away invisible dirt from the dress before taking Tristian's arm.

They transformed the park into the Starlight Ball with the hand-painted wood and paper stars. Beneath a thousand strings of fairy lights, sparkling pathways lead guests to hidden secret booths in the park. Large screens play a cartoon of the Carpathia royal family story around the lands.

We wait near the outdoor stage to officially begin the ball. Peeking out, I watch a giddy group of teens dressed in their finest ball gowns—likely leftover prom dresses. They twirl each other around, dancing through the crowd, bumping into others. No one cares. Everyone is joyful.

The Fairytalers aren't immune to the Starlight Ball magic. Employees dressed as foxes, birds, elves, and fairies parade around the outer rim of the guests, throwing glitter to the kids.

To the masses, it's a celebration. But to me, it's a funeral march.

"Welcome one and all to the Starlight Ball." The announcer's voice booms overhead. I startle, grabbing Tristian's arm. He places a soft kiss on my head, but I barely feel it through the wig.

"That's our cue," Ivor says, arm linked with Aliana's as they glide onto the stage. Tristian and I follow, Aldrich behind us and Garrick last.

We arrange ourselves on the thrones as the first show begins.

The fire-breathers represent the terrible blight Winthrop and Arden faced. A dancer dressed in gold swirls around them; fireworks burst from the back of the castle when the fire is defeated. The dancers use ribbons and flowy fabric, making arches across the sky. Despite the stunning performance, my eyes drift to the crowd below us.

It's difficult to see through the bright stage lights, but I catch glimpses of the audience surrounding the castle—dressed to the nines in gowns and period coats, or as fairies and elves. I see a few pirates as well.

If I squint and block out the ATM near the churro stand, I can pretend this is an actual ball. I've dreamed of happily-ever-afters and Prince Charmings, but I learned many years ago they don't exist. However, at Fairytale Gardens I've found a version of it. Not real, but close enough.

Still, like everything I've ever done—I'm about to ruin it.

Tristian breaks into applause next to me, and I follow suit. I ignored the last act, lost in my head.

"What a spectacular display," Ivor says to the crowd. "Thank you to all our performers." The audience claps again. "My wife and I are grateful you could join us on this special night to celebrate the great victory of my brother, Prince Winthrop, and his new bride, Princess Arden, along with the help of Sir Kendrick."

We stand and bow. Garrick adds a wink to the audience.

"And I'd be remiss if I did not show our thanks to the king." Ivor raises his arm to a window in the castle. A spotlight shines on Barth Walsh in full royal attire; he waves, face a practiced grin.

I may hold myself accountable for the inevitable fallout from Divya's exposé, but Barth is the real source of my trouble.

The problem: I'm not sure what to blame him for. I stand by what I said to Divya—I don't know if he's guilty. Surely there's a team behind the scenes, a board responsible for these kinds of decisions. He can't be operating alone. He might not even know what's going on.

Unless . . .

I glance up at the king, lording over his subjects. Fairytale Gardens is his entire life, from what Tristian has mentioned. How could he not know? Seeds of doubt blossom in my stomach.

If it's not him, and those documents were faked, who's the real bad guy?

"Now, please," Ivor says after the light dims and the king retreats. "Enjoy the festivities, and join us in an hour for dancing." Ivor gives a final wave, and we head offstage.

We have a thirty-minute meet-and-greet before heading to the Royal Fare. "Is your dad doing the meet-and-greet?" I whisper to Tristian as we take our position near the stage used for sword fights. All the face characters will meet in the same area tonight, and the elusive Barth Walsh has taken a spot next to Ivor.

"Looks like it." Tristian's jaw tightens.

"I didn't think he did them." I smile and wave at the guests in line, keeping my very bothered face unbothered.

"He doesn't, but I guess he figured he needed to make an appearance."

I don't talk about it any more because Tristian closes into his shell again, and with what I'm going to tell him later I want to enjoy the small moments of happiness.

Time passes in the blink of an eye, the whole night turning into a snow-covered blur. Maria comes to whisk us away to the Royal Fare restaurant to start the dance portion of the evening.

"Is it weird I'm excited about this?" I whisper as I lean into Tristian, relishing his body close to mine.

It could be the last time.

His fingers glide over my bare shoulders before he places them on the small of my back. "It's weirder *I'm* excited." The lights make his eyes sparkle like his crown.

"Really? *You?* Mr. Doesn't Believe in Fairytales Anymore?"

He smiles sweetly. "Maybe you convinced me."

I can only manage a grimace.

He spins me around, and I trip on his toes once before we fall into the rhythm. After a few beats, his strong arms are leading me. I'm not usually a follower, but I'd follow him anywhere.

"You're doing great," he murmurs in my ear after we make it through a tricky part.

I draw my hand away to brush the hair from his forehead before I place my hands on his shoulders. "This doesn't feel like real life."

"That's funny. Because for the first time, this place feels real."

"What do you mean?"

His eyes circle the room before they come back to me. "I thought this park was a facade, poorly covered in chipped paint. But you made it real, made me more than a pretend prince. You're the most real thing I've ever had."

A lump in my throat chokes out my next words. "Tristian, I need you to know everything with you and me is one hundred percent real. Please, remember that." I beg whoever is in the universe listening that he believes me, because once the story publishes even I wouldn't believe me.

Two lines crease between his eyebrows, a dark shadow on his hopeful face. "Imogen, what's up? You've been distracted tonight. Is everything okay?"

I smile, knowing it doesn't reach my eyes. I cut it off because a fake grin will only make things worse. The sigh I exhale buys me a few more seconds before I have to respond. "Everything is fine. I'm just in my feels tonight."

"Imogen—"

I cut him off with a kiss. "Let's not spoil a good night, okay?" The pleading in my voice edges on desperation, and I rein it back as best as possible.

The frown lines don't disappear as he nods. "I'm here for you, if you want to spill your secrets." It's a joke, but my insides turn to ice.

Secrets.

If only he knew.

Our eyes never leave each other, not until the dance finishes and the crowd applauds. We pull apart, waving, my heart racing in my chest.

"Everyone seems happy." I force lightness into my voice.

"So am I," he whispers into my ear. I loop both arms around his neck. He follows my lead, encircling my waist.

"Don't let Maria see us." I rake my fingers through the back of his waves.

"It's our ball. We can dance how we want. Besides, the crowd is supposed to believe we are madly in love." He tilts my chin, giving me the barest of kisses that burns to my toes. I let my body relax and rest my head on his chest. I could stay like this forever.

But forever will end sooner than I'd like.

38

TRISTIAN

I lean against the railing with my forearms to stare at the guests dancing below. The extra sparkle tonight hides the broken wood and chipped paint. Imogen's perfume—honey and spice—lingers where her body pressed against mine while we danced.

This is by far the best ball I've attended. As I watch the guests and the characters smile, it hits me—I feel Mom more in this moment, with the twinkling stars and giddy crowd, than I have in a long time. The ball keeps her memory alive.

"Remember one year when Mom had us make paper snowflakes and this place was so covered you could barely see the wood?" I turn to see Ivor holding out a cup to me.

I take a drink of the cold water. "And you took a nosedive off a ladder trying to help Dad hang them."

"You can still see the scar. I told James I got it saving an animal. Wanted to seem more heroic." We both chuckle, but it fades away, leaving an awkward silence.

"Tristian." Ivor shifts his feet back and forth, hands twisting around the hilt of his sword. "I'm glad you came." His eyes drop to the ground before looking back up.

"It was on my schedule." I try to joke, but an invisible hand squeezes my chest.

His laugh is as uncomfortable as I feel. "All the same, I know this isn't what you wanted for the summer, and I'm sorry for that—really. But I can't lie, I'm happy all of us are together."

My chin dips as I stare into my cup. "So am I." My voice is so low I'm not sure he heard me.

He places a hand on my shoulder, then draws me into a hug.

"Ivor . . ." I say into his fur cape.

"We suck at this, don't we?" He pulls away, messing up my hair as he rubs the back.

"Real human emotions?" I offer a half smile. Maybe it's the ball, the starlight mixed with the memory of Mom, that makes me actually listen to him.

"I was going to say *apologizing*. I want you here, Tristian. I always have and I always will. But maybe I didn't go about it the right way."

I swallow the lump in my throat, nodding. "Maybe neither of us did."

He rubs a hand across his beard. "Enjoy the party, T." He squeezes my shoulder again, turning to leave, but I stop him.

"Hey, Ivor?" For the first time in a long time, when I look at him I don't see Dad; I see my big brother. "Being back doesn't totally suck."

He smiles, nodding, as Imogen heads our way. "I don't think I deserve all the credit, but I'll take what I can get."

"Everything okay?" Imogen asks when she reaches me.

"Yeah, I think maybe it is." I kiss her softly. She smiles, but it's tight.

Imogen isn't herself tonight; that mask slipped into place to keep her secrets locked away. I want her to trust me enough to tell me. However, I don't want to push.

"This turned out better than I imagined." She rests her back against the guardrail to observe the characters.

I watch the lights dance off her pale skin. "I'm glad I celebrated the ball again." It's an odd sensation to mean it. A month ago, if you'd asked me if I'd be happy in full costume at a pretend ball I would've laughed in your face.

"I wish my mom was here to enjoy it." Heaviness creeps into my limbs, my body aching with regret at the lost years, with guilt for letting a part of me die along with her.

"She's here," Imogen says softly. "I'm sure." She squeezes my hand, green eyes filled with patience and—*damn.*

I swallow a surprise lump in my throat. "I hope so."

"I wish I could see the party from the guests' perspective." Her fingers trace the top of her dress, the light fabric floating across it.

"Let's do it."

"What?" She smiles, a laugh in her voice.

The brief surprise in her tone makes me long for more—to push that apprehension away. "What do you say? Ditch the wig—I'll lose the coat, and we go hide among the masses." I'm already undoing the sword from my belt.

"Someone is bound to notice us."

I cup her face. My lips hover over hers. "Maybe, but isn't

that part of the fun?" A fire lights her eyes, a spark she's been missing tonight.

She kisses me quickly. "Okay." We dump our accessories and make a run for the door. In all the chaos, no one stops us.

It's a different energy among the guests. It's truly magic. As I navigate Imogen through the crowd, I hear bits of conversation about how much they love the ball.

"I know the perfect place to see everything," I murmur against her ear.

We wait in line for Flight in the Clouds—this attraction sails you to the park's four corners on cables suspended in the sky. It's tight with her dress, but we manage to squeeze in.

She pushes her skirt aside to examine the park as the ride vehicle accelerates upward. "I could ride this forever," she whispers, more to herself.

Away from the others, my heart eases its racing—slightly. Every time I glance at her, it picks up again. "Ivor always brought his dates on this ride."

"Oh?" She raises an eyebrow.

"I used to think I'd do it one day."

"You didn't bring all your ladies here?"

"This place is special. There was never anyone I was close enough with to want to share it."

"You brought me." Her soft gaze studies me.

"Exactly." Other than my tower, this is my favorite spot in the park. A view from a different angle always gives a new perspective. Mom used to say that to fix a problem, look at it upside down. "It was the first ride I ever rode by myself."

She glances at me. The night's shadows cloak her features. "Not a Pixie kiddy ride?"

"If I did, I can't remember. This is the first one with a vivid memory. Probably because Ivor and Garrick said they'd ride with me, but as soon as I got on, they ran off."

"How old were you?"

"Four."

Worried lines crease her forehead. "I'm surprised they didn't scar you for life."

I play with hair fallen from her bun as I rest my arm behind her back. "Oh, I was traumatized for a good three years. I wouldn't come anywhere near this ride."

"What changed your mind?"

My other hand curls around the cool safety bar as I think. "My dad, actually. One day, before the park opened, he sat with me on the ride. We didn't go anywhere, just stayed for ten minutes, then left. The next day we did the same thing, and the one after, and the one after that. On the fifth day, I asked if we were ever going to ride it. He said whenever I was ready."

Tension radiates through my jaw. Remembering my dad, the man I used to admire, wanted to be—it's hard. I searched for him in the shell he is now for so long, but any trace has slipped away.

"And you rode it?"

I shake my head. "Not until the next day."

"He gave you the time and space to overcome your fear. Sounds like a good dad." Her voice breaks slightly on the last words.

If only he could have stayed one. "He was, or at least he used to do a better job at pretending." The ride descends as we head to Glacier Peaks. "Do you want to keep going?"

"Yes." She lays her head on my shoulder. Right now, with her arm curled around mine—I don't want anything else.

After the flight around the clouds, we end up back in Carpathia. The dense crowd pushes against us in this area as people stream in and out of the dance hall.

"Shouldn't we get back?" she asks, lips pressed close to my ear. "The fireworks are soon." Her green eyes dance with the colored lights.

Our fingers intertwine as I kiss her head. "I guess we should," I concede, even though it's the last thing I want to do.

Neither of us moves.

"Imogen." My hands cup her face, my thumb running over her chin. "I don't want what we have to be just a summer thing. I know it's early days, but you make me so happy. What if we—"

She reaches up and places a finger over my lips. "Shh. Let's just enjoy the moment and leave the rest for tomorrow. Okay?"

"Okay." I'm hoping we have plenty of tomorrows together.

I dip, and our lips meet halfway. Her warm, soft glow envelops me, my perfect elixir. Imogen's hands wrap around my waist, nails digging into my shirt, as I tug her closer to me. The noisy park gives way to a world where it's just the two of us.

The ball winds down, and the guests trickle out as the fairy lights turn off and the music dies away. "I can't believe it's over," she whispers.

"Did you want me to walk you back?"

Her eyes are watery when she looks at me, but she's smiling. "Any excuse to spend another minute with me, huh?"

"Guilty."

We drop off our costumes, and I try to make the walk back to her apartment last a little longer so this magical night will never end.

"Tristian . . ." The words trail off as we reach her door.

"Imogen." I squeeze her hands in mine.

"I need—" She looks around the darkened grounds, like she's searching for answers.

"What do you need? Tell me, and it's yours." I kiss her freckles, mapping my way across the foreign land I want to make my home.

She shakes her head as I pull away. "Never mind. It can wait."

I lift her chin. "You sure?"

"A thousand percent."

"I'll see you tomorrow?"

Her eyes are glistening again. "Of course."

I want to stay with her, let her wow me with her ability to make any situation better. But this summer is just getting started. We have all the time in the world.

39

IMOGEN

I'm going to tell Tristian everything.

At least that's what I tell myself as I get coffee and breakfast from the break room. Bad news is always easier to swallow with food. But as I make it across the *incredibly* short parking lot—I swear it's gotten smaller—my nerve is quickly slipping away. The sun is already up, the heat pressing, never having cooled from the night before. Dancing in Tristian's arms at the ball was everything I'd ever dreamed of, that elusive "perfect" I was starting to worry didn't actually exist outside of fiction.

Of course, it showed up when I wasn't trying to find it.

Last night, I was ready to spill my guts. The lies I've hidden were on the tip of my tongue. I wanted to give him a heads-up about his dad. But I choked. He was so hopeful that I couldn't burst that bubble just yet.

But a new day has dawned, and I don't want any more secrets. The pressure in my chest threatens to consume me the longer I keep him in the dark. He deserves to know—it's his family legacy at stake. And if Barth isn't responsible, I want to find out who is. That was the whole point of this endeavor—find the real bad guy. That'll be a lot easier to do with Tristian's help.

I reach for my phone to send Divya a quick text, asking when the article will publish, but I realize I left it at my apartment. It's fine. She said it would take at least a day. I just have to tell Tristian now, before it gets out.

"Hey," Tristian says, opening the door within seconds of my knock.

"Hi. I brought breakfast." I hold the coffee in one hand and the cheesy, meaty sandwiches in the other. I hope my voice doesn't give me away. I overcompensate with a huge grin. It all feels fake, but Tristian matches it.

God, this is so hard. I wish I could run away. Let the article be published and not care about the aftermath. But I can't. I'm invested. Ironically, that's what my parents hoped would happen this summer.

"You read my mind." He takes the breakfast and motions me in. "I'm starving. I was just going to text you."

The apartment is quiet. Garrick must not be here. "We don't have to be anywhere until tonight for the ball." He kisses me on the head before sitting at the dining table and digging into his sandwich. "Why don't we go somewhere today? You pick."

I want to spend all day with him, but reality awaits outside the door. The apartment's mugginess makes it hard to breathe. I slide into the seat opposite him, not touching my food.

"I'd love nothing more." All morning, I've thought of the best way to tell him about the charity fraud. Despite his insistence he hates his dad, it won't be easy to hear.

"We'll eat first because I know better than to keep you and food apart." He scoots the untouched sandwich closer to me.

I unwrap it to keep my hands busy. "You know me so well."

"I believe I do."

A chill attacks my body. Will the person he's gotten to know be enough to make up for my secrets?

Pulling apart the English muffin from the cheese, I practice a script in my head. I'll lay everything out. He'll probably hate me—I'd hate me. But Divya's story will publish whether I like it or not, so I have to be honest to get ahead of it. If the situation was reversed, I couldn't trust him after learning the truth. Let's hope he's more forgiving than me.

"This tastes even better than usual." He licks cheese off his fingers. "You should eat it while it's warm."

I pretend to focus on the eggs. "Mm-hmm." The lump in my throat gets tighter the longer I hold the words inside. I just need to rip it off like a bandage. "Tristian . . . I was going to say this last night."

His phone buzzes on the table.

"Do you need to get that?" I still can't look at him.

"No, it's just a text from Garrick. What were you saying?"

I push the sandwich around. "Well—"

His phone vibrates again, this time longer. "Crap, I should answer. Garrick doesn't ever call. It must be urgent."

I risk a glance up, nodding.

He swivels around, resting his lower back on the table. "Yeah?" he says. I hear the muffled voice on the other end but can't make out the words.

A beat of silence passes, followed by Tristian saying, "Send it to me."

He hangs up without a word. Back still to me, he scrolls through the phone, thumbs zooming over it at a furious pace.

"Tristian?" I say after several minutes have elapsed. "Is everything okay?" I abandon the breakfast and edge around the table to look at him.

He's gone pale, his mouth a thin line when he looks up, eyes hard. He doesn't say a word, just shoves the phone into my hand. On the screen is Divya's face, and in big, bold type, **FAIRYTALE SCANDAL: Founder of magical theme park caught stealing funds meant for charity.**

"Looks like your *friend* has been busy."

My blood turns to ice, the air in my lungs heavy as lead. "Tristian . . ." The words are barely a whisper. "I can explain."

I've never seen a heart shatter in real time, but I see Tristian's crack when I gaze into his face.

40

TRISTIAN

The room spins as the words fall into place—the black-and-white exposé. Scathing is the only way to put it. The accusations drill into my brain: Barth Walsh, responsible for embezzling tens of thousands of dollars meant for charitable organizations. My gut instinct is to deny it, and push for my father's innocence, but as the wheels turn it doesn't sound too far off the truth.

I dig my nails into my palms as I clench my fists. Just when I thought Dad couldn't scrape the bottom of the barrel any further.

"Tristian . . . I can explain." Imogen's timid voice is like nails on a chalkboard.

"Explain?" My hands shake as I rip the phone from her. "This is your friend, isn't it? The one I met the other night?" Blood pounds in my ears, and the bright room dims as my vision tunnels.

"Yes, but—"

"It says you came here to find evidence." My nostrils flare as I jab toward the park. "This job, everything you've done here, has been a lie."

She set me up.

"Divya wasn't supposed to run the story yet." Her eyes plead with me to understand. "I was going to tell you, Tristian—last night—then . . ."

"Are you blaming me?" I recognize someone trying to save their ass. Pain radiates through my neck as I grit my teeth.

Her face drops, eyes wide. "No, of course not. It's an explanation. I was literally about to spill my guts. Tell you that I believe Barth is innocent. I thought together we could find out who's really behind the charity fraud. It felt too easy finding the evidence. I was thinking—"

My humorless laugh cracks through the air as I cut her off. "Is that supposed to make it better?" She opens her mouth, but no sound comes out. I let her see me—parts of me I haven't opened to anyone. Ice slithers through my veins, turning my body hard. I was ready to throw away my future because of the lies she let me believe—the feelings she tricked me into thinking meant something.

Fake. Like everything else my life has been built on—a facade.

"Tristian." Her voice lures me in, even as the anger courses through me. "I'm *so* sorry." Her voice breaks on the last word.

"How could you?" Bitterness coats my tongue. I wish it were enraged, powerful. All I sound is hurt and wounded.

"I didn't mean for this to happen."

"Oh, really?" I put as much irritation into my words as I can muster. She tries to grab my arm, and I jerk, even as my traitorous body aches for her. "Because from what I've read, it says you took the job to find evidence."

She looks at the ceiling, throat bobbing as she swallows. "Yes, that's why I came here—but I didn't mean to fall for you. I never would've agreed if I knew at the start."

"How can I believe anything you say?" My heart pounds against my chest. I want to rip it out. "Do you hate us that much?"

Deep lines mar her forehead, eyes rimmed red as she fights back tears. "No, I don't hate you at all. I was helping a friend. I didn't think about the collateral damage." A few tears slip down her face. She wipes them away with a trembling hand.

I shake my head, the grip on my phone so tight it could snap. "You used me."

I've never been in love, never let myself fall that far for anyone. I'm not saying I was in love with Imogen, but I started to let myself feel more than I ever knew I could. This pain in my chest is why I never let love anywhere near me.

Losing Mom hurt, but it wasn't a betrayal. This hardening lump in my chest is what betrayal feels like, and I've felt it twice. First with my father, and now with Imogen.

"Tristian, I—"

"You didn't use me?" I push. I want to hear her admit what she did.

She hesitates. "I did," she says softly. "And I'm sorry. But you said yourself you were done with the park. So I thought—"

I slam my hand into the kitchen counter. The sound explodes through the quiet room. "It doesn't matter if I wanted to be here or not—so don't you dare try to spin my reasons as your excuse. You lied to me this whole time." A rushing fills my ears, my blood beating loud.

"I didn't—"

I level her with a stare.

"Not about everything." She tugs her hair. "Tristian, Divya has been my friend *forever*. She needs the prize money to save her family's restaurant."

"Well, congratulations, you ruined my family's legacy instead." She opens her mouth to counter my accusation, but gives up. "Why even bother to warn me? Why didn't you just slip out in the night?"

She stares at her hands, fingers white from her grip on them. "Because I don't believe Barth is responsible, and I thought you deserved to know."

"We could've worked together. I would've dealt with my dad—or whoever stole the money—but you took that choice away. The damage is done now. Whether my dad is guilty or not, once people read this, they'll always think that when they see the Walsh name. It's a lot easier to ruin a reputation than it is to fix one. The park may not survive this." The sharp pain deep in my chest surprises me. I care what happens to this place.

But it doesn't matter anymore.

"I . . . I don't know what more to say." She looks at me, face drained of color except for the small red patches on her cheeks.

I rub a hand over my face. "You don't need to say anything.

I don't care what happens anymore." The anger I felt moments ago seeps from me, leaving behind an empty husk.

"I have a whole world waiting for me. Who gives a crap what happens to a broken-down theme park. Guess you *did* do me a favor." I don't care what I have to do—I'm going on that summer program, even if I have to fake Dad's signature and deal with the consequences when they come. Time to take a page from Garrick's handbook. "You should go."

"Tristian—" she starts, but I open the apartment door, cutting her off.

"Go." I keep my unyielding stare on the doorframe. If I look her in the eye, I'll lose it. She hesitates, mouth opening and closing before she walks away.

I watch her go, and I hate myself for it. As she disappears, my brothers and father come into view, stalking across the parking lot toward the main building.

The world is red. Voices blur as I storm down the stairs and asphalt, the midmorning heat slamming into me.

"Tristian." Dad's voice rings loud when I reach them in the middle of the lot.

Despite what my father thinks, I've held my tongue all summer. I could've yelled when I realized this whole internship was a lie. Pitched a fit that they swindled me into donning the Winthrop costume. But I didn't.

But screw it. Gloves are off.

"Did you read the article?" Ivor asks. He stands next to Dad, while Garrick and Aldrich come to a stop slightly behind them. Good. Best to get it out with us all present.

Ivor continues without waiting for my answer. "An attack against us—"

"You might want to stop kissing ass. Or they might throw you on the coals next." I spit my words at him. We had a moment last night, a start at repairing what we had damaged, but right now, as the anger slithers back in, I don't care. I'm just so tired.

Garrick shoves his hands into his pockets. Aldrich bites his thumbnail, eyes darting to each of us.

"Tristian," Ivor begins, but I don't let him finish.

"Dad." I focus on him. Once the words leave my mouth, I can't take them back, but we have to know. "Did you really steal the charity money?" His eyes widen in shock—mouth opening and closing, with no words.

"Jesus, Tristian." Ivor steps into the space between Dad and me.

Dad catches up to the conversation. "You ungrateful child, how dare you accuse me of such a crime in my own park?" A pink flush covers his aging face.

"Is it true?" I press, so I don't lose my nerve.

"The lies in that filthy article are all unwarranted. I don't know who this mole is, but I'll have them sued for slander," Dad hisses.

They don't know it's Imogen. I mean, why would they? I was the only person who saw her friend. Without that, I wouldn't have connected the dots so quickly. This is my fault—partly anyway. I let Imogen get close, gave her the fuel. I open my mouth to reveal she's the traitor, but I stop before I speak. As angry as I am, I don't want to see her dragged away in cuffs.

Why can't these feelings just go away? I'm so mad at her, but I still care what happens to her.

"Do you believe them over your father?" Dad bares his teeth as he glares at me.

"You've been a terrible father for so long. I guess it wasn't a stretch." I focus back on the problem at hand. I always knew he liked to spend money to make himself seem more important—guess we know where he got it.

"Enough." Ivor tries to put a hand on my shoulder, but I swing out of his grip. "Tristian, this'll be a PR nightmare, without you causing more trouble."

"Causing trouble?" His words pierce me. We may have our differences, but he is my brother. I didn't think he'd be easy to convince, but I didn't expect him to accuse me of stirring the pot for kicks. "This is a legit concern. If it's all true, it could ruin your beloved fairytale."

"All I've ever done"—Dad straightens to full height—"is for this park and you boys. I would never put this place at risk."

"Come on, Tristian, you know Dad wouldn't do that." I double-take toward Garrick. Him, of all people, on Dad's side? "Whatever he's done—you know he loves this place."

"At least your brothers don't think so little of me." Dad shakes his head, eyes watery. A punch hollows my gut. "You are my sons. I'd never lie to you. I love you, all of you." He directs the last words at me.

“Tristian,” Aldrich pipes up. “I have your back, always. But what proof is there, really?”

I turn my head to the sky. The article had photos of documents with Dad’s signature. Imogen thought he might be innocent. And maybe it was too easy, or he’s just a terrible thief. Either way, I’m not sure I care anymore. My heart barely beats, despite the rush of blood in my ears; my chest is empty.

Dad scoffs. “Perhaps Tristian planned this all along. He’s made his position about FTG quite clear. He could have hired this journalist in a last effort to destroy us.”

Laughter bubbles up, hard jerks across my body. “Yeah, that’s it. Blame me. The ungrateful son strikes again.” I no longer care about containing my rage. “You preach about family, about legacy, but you’ve run it into the ground for years before this. Mom died, but we lost more than one parent that night. You stopped being our father. We needed you, and you copped out.”

Aldrich’s face pales, while Garrick stands impassive. Ivor shakes his head, dropping his gaze to the ground. None of them back me up, even though I know they agree.

“Boys, go to my office. I need a private word with Tristian.” Dad’s voice is low, barely tamed. Ivor and Garrick head inside without a backward glance to me, but Aldrich lingers. I nod for him to follow the others.

Once we’re alone in the parking lot, Dad tries to put a hand on my shoulder. I step away. “Tristian, I haven’t been the best father. I can admit to that. When your mother died, I lost everything—my happily-ever-after. Her death destroyed my fairytale."

I bite my cheek as he continues. "I dug a hole inside myself, and stayed there. Because it was safer than living in a world without her. That was unfair to you boys. But you and I are not so different. We both let grief and pain make choices for us."

My eyes sting, and I press my fingers into them to stop the tears. Perhaps these past two years it wasn't my father I couldn't stand to look at. It was myself reflected in him that stung. The guilt threatens to eat me from the inside, and all I want is for it to go away.

"Son." His eyes plead for understanding. "I didn't steal any money. Those accusations are false."

I shove my hands into my pockets. "It doesn't matter. It won't be my problem for long." His apology is two years too late. The part of me that might have once forgiven him has long since been covered with scar tissue too thick to pass through. "Do whatever you want with FTG. I don't care."

I head toward the apartment to put my new life into motion. I need to get out of here before I'm swallowed whole.

I knew when I walked through these gates a month ago it was all an act. But along the way, I let myself get swept into the fairytale, let pretend stories become real. That's the danger with losing yourself in a fictional world; it rips your heart out when it proves once again false.

41

IMOGEN

I stumble to my apartment. When I finally open the door, I don't bother to see if Aliana is there. I shake clothes I've abandoned on my bedroom floor, searching for my phone. With a thud, it falls from the pocket of some shorts. Then I'm back into the muggy outdoors before the squeaking door finishes its serenade.

Tristian is out front with his brothers and Barth, and there is no way I am getting anywhere near that. Blinking back tears, I skim Divya's story as I head into the park. Kids scream at their parents, tugging them in multiple directions—kettle corn and horse manure pepper the air as I pass near the stables.

The rumbustious park energy is the distraction I need. I slump onto a bench, consumed in Divya's words. If only she hadn't come. Tristian only knew I was involved because he recognized Divya. No one else saw her.

Ugh. Except Aliana.

It's only a matter of time before all of FTG knows, then. It was published an hour ago, and the online traction will soon leak into the park like oozing lava.

I rub small circles over the ache in my chest to collect myself before I call Divya. The phone rings several times, then cuts to voicemail. "Divya." I try to control my voice. "Call me ASAP." I grip the phone, knuckles white, as I stare at Fairytale Gardens. I don't know how long I sit, trying to clear my head.

It doesn't work. All I can see is the last look Tristian gave me.

The hurt on his face and anger at my betrayal cut deeper than any wound. What we were building was new; I've never felt this way. I'd have given him my whole heart, if he'd asked. But the disgust on his features made it clear any chance of that has disappeared.

And what will happen to Fairytale Gardens, now that people think Barth stole from charity? Who will do business with them or want to support their park? I killed two birds with one stone. For the first time in my life, I truly understand the meaning.

My phone buzzes with Divya's face, and I swipe a finger across the screen. "I thought you were going to wait?"

"Hello to you, too."

"*Divya.*"

She sighs. "I did wait, Imogen. I'm sorry, but once I submitted the story to the competition and my editor saw Barth's signatures on those papers, he wanted to run it ASAP—I couldn't retreat. The ball was already rolling down the hill. There was no stopping it."

My stomach clenches. "I asked you to hold off. I told you it might not be Barth—that we needed more evidence."

I don't know if additional evidence exists. Barth might be the criminal, but my gut still says otherwise. Then again, Divya has never trusted my instincts. No one has. I've made one terrible choice after another.

Why should she trust me?

"My future was on the line. I couldn't sit on it because you had second thoughts."

I want to be mad at her, even though she's right. I knew why I was here. I can't blame her for following through. I'm the idiot who went and fell for the owner's son.

"Imogen?"

The music for a carriage ride plays overhead. I don't turn to see who it is, if it's Tristian. That's a stupid thought.

Her voice softens. "I didn't know the story was running this morning. I would've given you a heads-up if I did."

I press my fingers to my lips. "I know."

"Are you headed home?"

"What?" I didn't think my stomach could drop any lower.

"With the story done and people catching on to your involvement, I assumed you'd head back." She's right. Everyone in the park will read the article soon enough.

What will Yvette think?

"I hadn't thought about it." I've left what feels like a million jobs, and with each one I happily gave them a middle finger salute on the way out. But glancing around the park, to its smiling guests, whimsical fanfare, and magic, the thought of walking out those gates forever brings tears to my eyes.

For the first time in my life, I didn't run away. I didn't self-sabotage a job or a relationship on purpose. I let myself care.

And I was happier than I've ever been. It was nice to have people rely on me and not screw it up. I've searched for perfection, for a place that feels right, and being here at Fairytale Gardens was as close as I've ever gotten.

"Tristian knows it was me."

"Oh, Imogen. I . . ." For once, Divya doesn't know what to say.

Fairytale Gardens felt like my *it*. Tristian, too. And in a single article, it vanished. My shoulders curve in as I lean on my knees. I use my hair to shield the park from view. "He thinks I backstabbed him. And he's right." Sadness should etch my voice, but it's flat.

"I'm sorry." She takes a breath like she's going to say more, but silence curls around us.

It'd be easy to blame Divya, but it's not her fault. "I'm not mad at you. I let myself get too involved." After I got to know Tristian, I couldn't help it. "It's for the best, anyway. I'd get bored soon, like always."

I wish that were true. Maybe if I say it enough, it will be.

I rub a hand across my face as I sit up. "I'm happy you won the competition. You're an amazing journalist and now you can save the restaurant. That's what's important." I always want the best for Divya.

"What are you going to do?" Divya says when the silence returns.

I don't have an answer for her.

Minutes slip into hours as I sit in Pixie Forest. The sun bakes my skin, but I don't notice. I'm not scheduled to work until tonight at the Starlight Ball, so no one wonders where

I am. No one cares that I'm sitting alone on this bench. My body is numb—a protection against the hammering behind the wall in my heart. If I let it open, I won't be able to breathe.

"Can you take a picture?"

I blink at the woman in a baseball cap. She holds out her phone.

"What?" My voice is raw.

"Uh." She second-guesses approaching me as she takes in my face. "Can you take a picture of my family?" She points to a middle-aged man and two kids.

"Sure." I nod. My joints ache from staying in one place for hours.

Still wary, she hands me the phone and joins her family, big smiles all around. My breath hitches, and the dam in my chest cracks as I snap the picture quickly, thrusting the phone back to her.

I stop before I enter the backstage area to center myself, refusing to have a public breakdown. I lean against a tree, fingers digging into the hard bark as the world spins. It might be off-kilter for many reasons, but I haven't eaten today and probably have heatstroke. I'm not hungry, but I should eat before crawling into my bed and crying myself to sleep.

Because it's coming—the fractured wall is too fragile to keep the tears in for much longer. The pounding behind my eyes blurs my vision. No one stops me on the way to the break room, and when I get inside I realize it's way later than I thought. It's pushing four.

I keep my head down, destination banana and chips.

The snippets of conversations around the room get louder as I walk through the tables—Fairytalers scroll through their phones, Divya's article on their screens. My hands shake as I reach for chips, spilling them all over the ground. No one notices, too absorbed in the scandal.

I wipe my forehead, cold sweat seeping down my back. I need to get out of here. Someone might know; they might recognize me as the traitor. And what if Tristian shows up?

I wish he would.

The thought thrills and terrifies me all at once. I want to explain further, but what more can I say? The image of his hurt face will haunt my dreams for a lifetime. The broken heart of the man I lov— *liked a lot*—shattered at my feet.

Food acquired, I start for the door.

Yvette's voice brings me to a standstill. "Imogen. Can we talk somewhere private?"

"Yes," I croak, crushing the chips in my fist. Is she about to yell at me, too? We walk into the hallway near the emergency exit. I debate running through it and not stopping until I'm home.

Her face is tight, but I wait for her words to deliver the final blow. "Please tell me it's not true?"

I suck in a breath. "I . . . it wasn't . . . I'm *sorry*."

She lets out a sigh, massaging her temple. "I'm supposed to come and fire you. Maria said you were the one who leaked all this stuff for the article. But I didn't believe her. Why?"

A vise grip squeezes my insides. "Yvette, it all got out of control. I didn't mean to hurt anyone." The rattle in my chest speeds up, a ticking time bomb to my inevitable meltdown.

"I know you, Imogen. You're not a bad person, but this . . ." She grabs my arm. "There's nothing I can do. You made your bed."

"So, I have to leave?" It's a pointless question, but I need to hear it out loud to make my feet work again. To know it's really over.

She nods, face solemn. "It's getting late, so Maria said you can stay the night, but you need to be gone first thing in the morning. And Imogen," she adds. "They're going to be watching you like a hawk now. Please don't go looking for more trouble."

Even after I might have ruined her livelihood, she's still looking out for me. *God*, this hurts worse than if she hated me. "I am sorry, Yvette. I really didn't mean for things to go down this way." It's a hollow excuse. I knew what I was doing the whole time—there was never going to be a different outcome.

"Goodbye, Imogen." She turns away and heads upstairs.

I bolt for the exit and don't stop until I'm in the apartment, my banana and chips dropped somewhere along the way.

I find refuge in my room. Crawling into my bed with my clothes still on, I pull the blanket over my head and let the tears flow.

I've had more jobs than I could count. I'm used to picking myself up and starting a new one, just like changing my shoes. It never bothered me before. But Fairytale Gardens changed me. A part of myself will remain at FTG, and I'm unsure what to do without it—without Tristian. I need to fix this.

42

IMOGEN

Sleep eluded me most of the night, except for the short bursts when it did show up with nightmares of Barth running away with money dressed like the Monopoly guy. As the dreams persisted, the more I convinced myself it must be true. Divya is the investigative reporter. I'm not even capable of keeping a job. What do I know? He probably did steal the cash.

The other dreams were worse. Visions of Tristian walking away over and over again as I stood frozen in place, unable to stop him.

I woke with a deep ache in my gut. A truth I can't deny stares me in the face. Nothing remains for me here. I'm not even sure what might be left of FTG, come this time next year. Social media is eating them alive. #boycottFTG is all over the socials. I wonder if Tristian's seen it? If he cares? I wish I could help, but I'm fresh out of ideas.

I call my parents early and ask them to come pick me up. Despite trying to hide it, I heard their disappointment. Not wanting to risk the security guards tossing me out, I told my parents to meet me at the gas station down the street.

I spare Fairytale Gardens one last glance as I roll my suitcase out of the parking lot and back to the real world. Back to finding another job I hate to get by. My eyes are puffy and swollen from the tears I cried all night, but they've dried up now.

The air outside is heavy when I reach the gas station. It's the dense heat that comes before a storm. The dark clouds gather, and I hope my parents show up soon. Leaning against the wall of the service station, I debate buying a snack when a familiar car pulls up to the tank in front of me.

"Milly? Hi." I smile. Then it fades just as quickly, when I remember the accusations against her boss.

"Imogen." Her voice is curt through tight lips. She glances at my suitcase. "Are you leaving?"

I wet my lips, pressure tight on my chest when I nod. "Yeah, it wasn't the right fit." Words have never felt so wrong, but it's a truth I need to believe to keep myself from collapsing into a puddle.

She frowns as she grips her purse strap. "Yes, well, that happens. I'll leave you to—"

"Grandma, can I get candy?" A kid around ten with shaggy brown hair pokes his head out from the back seat.

"Sure, honey. Go pick some." Milly hands him a twenty-dollar bill.

I watch the kid grin as he skips inside the gas station. "Your grandson?"

She nods brusquely. Milly always welcomed me, but her attitude now is cagey and standoffish. She must know I'm involved with the story.

I survey the kid inside through the windows, and the longer

I study him, the more I know I've seen him before. "Do you bring him to the park often?"

"Why?" She keeps her eyes down.

My suitcase tries to roll away, but I don't move to catch it. "He looks familiar. Has he come to a meet-and-greet?"

"No, no—he doesn't come to the park often. His father, Reed . . . No, I'm afraid it's been some time since he's visited."

My brow furrows as I try to place him. I know I've seen that kid. It's an itch in my brain I can't quite scratch.

"Well." She pulls the nozzle from her tank. "I should make sure he hasn't bought the whole store. Nice to see you, Imogen." She pivots quickly, heading inside.

I grab my suitcase from where it's landed in the driveway, but don't take my eyes off the kid. I watch them inside for a few moments, fingers tapping against my chin. They leave in a hurry, a trail of dirt in their wake.

As the dust settles—it hits me.

Fumbling for my phone, I drop it in the overgrown grass. I touch something wet as I retrieve it, but barely notice. I open my photos and scan the first days at FTG, zooming in on a picture within the picture.

It's Milly's grandson. He's the recipient, holding a check made out to the phony charity.

Wait. I can't jump to conclusions again.

I zoom in tighter on the kid's face, squinting to make sure I'm seeing this right. But after studying it, I can't deny it's the same kid. If the boy receiving donations is Milly's family, you'd think it would be a bigger deal. Like, *Oh, look at us helping our own*. But in all my digging, no one ever said—Milly included—that they were donating to family members of FTG.

Which means no one knows.

And Divya confirmed in her article that the money linked to these charities is held in sketchy offshore accounts.

Holy crap. Milly?

It's hard to believe, but she's got to be the one stealing the money. I didn't blink when I saw her fancy car because she wasn't anywhere on my radar, but now that makes sense how a receptionist affords a Range Rover. I just thought she was a nice old lady.

When they thought Barth's office was broken into, that probably tipped her off. Or it could've been when I showed interest in the charities. She has access to Barth's old office to plant the papers Divya and I found. It would've been so simple for her to cover her tracks by incriminating Barth. And with the reputation he has, it wasn't hard to believe.

I lean against the wall. I was right. Barth didn't steal the money; Milly framed him.

I have to fix this. Barth might be a terrible dad, but he's innocent. I send the picture to Divya with a brief message about what I saw and the names of Milly and her son. She doesn't respond, but I'm not going to sit and wait. I type out a quick text to my parents, telling them never mind on the pick-up, as I run back to FTG.

To correct the mistake I had a hand in, I'll need someone else's help.

I have no problem getting inside the property, which is great, but also makes sense why I was able to access so much stuff—security is probably something they should start addressing.

I called Tristian three times on the way—he sent me straight to voicemail. I try his apartment first, knowing it's futile. He's probably long gone, but I don't want to leave any stone unturned. I bang on the door. The sound echoes through the quiet apartment.

Stop two, then.

I'm breathless as I bound up the stairs to the costume department. "Why are you still here?" Yvette doesn't look mad, just tired.

"You haven't seen Tristian, have you?" The room spins as I try to steady my breathing.

She lets out a sigh. "No. But you have to—"

"I'm sorry, Yvette. I need to find Tristian." I broke him as much as I broke FTG. I want to make amends with both. What we had might not be salvageable, but I have to try.

"Imogen!" she yells after me.

If Yvette doesn't know his location, the next best bet is his brothers. I steel my nerves. I'm not sure they'll talk to me, but fortune favors the brave—and sometimes the stupid.

Ivor and Garrick are on the Knight School stage, and I wait in the back until they finish. My dry throat threatens to close by the time they complete the performance. I wipe my sweaty palms on my shorts. The jovial banter I heard onstage stops as they exit, heads hung low, swords dragging.

"Um . . . hi." I wave, trying for an innocent smile, but all I muster is a grimace.

"What the hell are you doing here?" Ivor's face pales.

"You have some nerve." Garrick tosses his sword onto a haystack, pulling off his gloves.

I hold up my hands in retreat. "Please, I need to talk to Tristian."

Garrick scoffs. They exchange a silent look.

"It's important." I'm not above begging.

Ivor steps closer, voice low. "You're lucky we don't call the cops and have you arrested for trespassing."

I drop my gaze. What did I expect? I'd call the cops on me, too. "He's not answering his phone." My words crack in a desperate plea.

"You broke his heart." Garrick doesn't meet my eyes. "Not to mention you tried to take our park down in the process. Just go."

The sentiment sends a chill down my spine, and I stumble away. "I am sorry—you might not believe me, but I am."

I square my shoulders.

There is one last option I can try—I'd rather eat glass, but my choices are stretched thin at this point.

The apartment smells like lemons when I reach the open door. Aliana is on her knees scrubbing the kitchen floor.

"That won't fix the Cheetos smell." I edge inside cautiously.

Aliana pushes her hair back with her arm. "I thought you'd be halfway to Canada by now."

"I'm not dodging the draft." I stay near the door. If she berates me too, I want a quick exit. She doesn't speak, just leans back on her heels.

I take a deep breath. "I know we aren't friends, but I need your help to find Tristian."

Aliana tilts her head, a sly smile gracing her face. "Actually, I kinda respect you. I gave you nothing but crap and you didn't back down."

I blink. "Really? You know I'm the reason the story about Barth is spreading like wildfire on the internet?"

"I know." She stands, tossing her yellow rubber gloves in a bucket. "Why do you want to find Tristian?"

My heart flips. The ache since yesterday fills every part of me. Still, a flicker of hope fights its way in. "I screwed up. I lied, and caused him and his family pain. But I want to fix it."

Her nails tap against the counter. "You care about him?"

"More than I've ever cared about a guy." The admission sends a warm glow over my skin, despite my heavy heart. A truth finally let free. A month ago, I wouldn't have believed that Aliana and I would have a heart-to-heart, but she isn't who I thought she was. Aliana might be a bit brusque, but she's not a terrible person.

She grabs her phone from her pocket. I watch her quietly as she sends the message. It takes several minutes, drenched in awkward silence, until she gets a response. "He's headed to the airport."

"When does he leave?"

"A few hours." Aliana grabs her keys from the table. "If we want to catch him, we should leave now. Come on."

"Wait. You're driving?" The stairs vibrate as I follow in her wake.

"Have you seen yourself?" She glances over her shoulder, cringing. "You're in no state to drive."

I pull her to a stop at the bottom of the stairs. "Why are you helping me?"

Her face softens. "You aren't the only one who loves a happy-ever-after."

43

TRISTIAN

Tyrone let me crash at his house last night. I couldn't stomach staying at the park any longer. After the fights with Imogen and Dad, I had to leave or I would've suffocated. I shoved all my belongings into my suitcase and ran.

I thought I could help guide FTG into a new era. But like all my stories, it ended as a tragedy. It's for the best. I should thank Imogen for exposing herself and the park for what they really were. I nearly gave up my future.

Garrick came by last night and forged Dad's signature on the permission slip, along with doing a remarkably accurate impression of Dad when he called the teacher in charge to sway them into letting me join the program a few days late. It worked. Garrick promised to cover for me as long as he could before Dad catches on. All I had to do was buy a plane ticket and meet the group in London—I drained my savings to do it, but it's worth it. I'm finally going to have the summer I want.

I thrust my toothbrush into my bag before I do a last scan over the room. Sleep failed me last night. I could blame the blinking sign outside my window from the karaoke bar or Tyrone's snoring, but I wouldn't have slept even without those. My head aches: the pressure escalates behind my eyes the longer I'm awake. I thank Tyrone, and accept some coffee to go, as my ride to the airport shows up.

I haven't answered my phone since I left. My brothers called a few times. Ivor to yell at me and then apologize. Aldrich—that one almost got me—didn't beg me to come home, just said he hoped that wherever I was, I was okay. It would've hurt less if he'd broken down and cried.

Ivor said in his voicemail that I was running away from my problems, and maybe he's right. I run a thumb over my passport. I've always thought I ached for adventure, a wanderlust for lands I've never seen. This little paper booklet was supposed to be my freedom, but am I using it as an excuse to run away from the pain? Or will pain follow, no matter what? I might as well suffer in ancient ruins rather than a dusty theme park.

But what if I'm making a huge mistake? I actually found something I enjoyed—marketing—and I'm giving it up just because it's at Fairytale Gardens.

Something Dad said before I left strikes me. *You and I are not so different. We both let grief and pain make choices for us.*

My phone buzzes, alerting me that my car is almost here. I just need to get to London. Then everything will feel right. It has to.

Imogen has called three times in the last twenty minutes. I sent those straight to voicemail. If I heard her voice, I wouldn't get on the plane. Then Aliana texted three simple words.

Aliana
Where are you?

I figured there was no harm in telling her. At least if my plane crashes and I'm lost on an invisible island, someone other than Garrick will know I am missing.

The driver makes minimal conversation on the way to the airport. My stomach churns the bitter coffee, the only thing in it besides the granola bar I ate last night. I'm about to set off on the journey I've always wanted. Strange, it doesn't feel like I thought it would. I'm numb from the inside out. The world is drained of color, muted despite the bright sunny day.

I collect my bag from the trunk and stare at the airport. I verify my flight on my phone before I head in to check my bag, enjoying the last dregs of fresh air and sunshine.

Only once I know where to go, I don't move.

The sounds of traffic and the smell of car exhaust surround me as I stare at my passport. I remember the day it came in the mail. I practically jumped through the roof when I opened it. My ticket to freedom, escape to anywhere I desire. As I study the tiny picture and the confirmation screen on my phone—for the first time, it feels like I'm running away.

"Tristian?"

The world halts. The noisy airport falls away, my beating heart louder than a jet engine. I pivot slowly to see Imogen.

She exits a car before it comes to a complete stop a few feet behind me. Strands of red hair fly about her head, catching the sun in a fiery kaleidoscope.

"Tristian," she says breathlessly as she bumps into a couple walking between us to the automatic doors.

"What are you . . ." The final words between us replay in my mind—shame coating her face as I uncovered the truth.

The numbness plaguing me all morning melts away to be replaced by anger and hurt—my fists clench as I step past her and into the air-conditioned airport. It's a short walk to the baggage drop-off, even quicker with my speed. I want as much distance between us as I can summon. My suitcase clicks loudly, like it's ready to pop open with the slightest impact—a feeling we share.

"Tristian," she calls after me, shoes slapping against the tiles as she jogs to catch up. "Can you—" She yanks at my shirt to make me stop before I get in line.

I rip my arm away. We might go unnoticed if this were a larger airport, but here we draw attention from more passengers than I'd like. "How did you know I was here?" My tone causes her to shrink away.

Gathering her resolve, she says, "Aliana."

I didn't see that coming.

She inches closer, and I move back several paces in return. "If you came to apologize, you tried that."

She licks her lips, the bottom one sucking in. My chest aches and I want to pull her close.

"I'm not here to apologize. Although I am sorry." She gives me a shaky smile, but swallows it when my face remains unreadable. Gripping her wrist with her other hand, she continues, "I'm not here to win you back; I'm here to help you."

"You've done enough." The bitter aftertaste of the coffee coats my throat. I can't meet her gaze and instead stare at the floor.

"No, I haven't." Her voice doesn't waver. "I let Divya run a story I knew in my gut was false. I left you in the dark when I should have asked for your help. I . . ." She huffs, and I peek up to see her glance at the ceiling, then at me.

An overhead announcement blares, and she waits for it to stop before resuming. "I never believed I'd find my perfect place. For every job I quit, I felt nothing when it ended. I simply moved on to the next. So I was confident when Divya's story came out, and I had to leave FTG, I'd feel the same way.

"I convinced myself I was destined to keep searching—even though FTG . . . and you . . . felt like home." She pauses, eyes glassy, before clearing her throat. "I was wrong. I don't want to lose any of it. I don't want to lose you, Tristian. I screwed up—*bad*. I know. Let me fix it. *Please*, I need to fix it."

The crowds around us thin, other than a few patrons who slow to watch on. My hands ache to reach for her. I shove them into my jacket pockets instead. Who am I if I walk back into her arms after what she did?

"I get you feel bad, but, Imogen, this isn't fixable."

Her face drops, and the hopefulness slides off. Still, she stays. "I wasn't talking about us—or not totally. I meant Fairytale Gardens. Your dad is innocent—"

"Imogen, we went—"

"It's Milly."

My mouth falls open. "*Milly?*" I squeeze my eyes shut.

"Yes, her grandson is the kid in all the pictures with the charities. She must have faked them and used her grandson as the poster boy. It makes sense. She would've had no problem getting into Barth's office to plant the documents we found. Either she did it after the incident with Barth's office door because she thought someone was snooping, or she planted them from the start to cover herself."

I scrub my hands over my face, placing pieces into a puzzle all the same color. "Okay, so what?"

"What do you mean, *so what*? We have to correct the article. Clear your family name." She takes my hands, warm and familiar.

"I can't." I pull away, not meeting her eyes because I can't stand to see the pain I know that movement will leave.

She releases a shaky breath. "I'm sorry I broke the Fairytale Gardens spell—that I may have ruined it. FTG is the only place I've wanted to stay when I've run my whole life. FTG is having a dark moment, but that happens right before the hero saves the day."

Tears burn my eyes, and I press my fingers into them. I look at Imogen, letting myself feel for the first time in the last twenty-four hours. "FTG was broken before you showed up—we all were." My voice cracks, but I don't care.

My gaze wanders around the open airport. "When I saw that article, part of me was relieved. If everyone saw my dad as terrible, no one would need an explanation for why I wanted to get away. I've felt only anger and guilt on top of grief for the last two years. It became such a comfortable place I forgot how to feel anything else." I thought the further I pushed FTG away, the less the grief could find ways in. But you can't trick grief away. "I'm sorry, Imogen. Some things can't be fixed."

The line clears, and it's now or never. I roll my bag up to the counter. As I lift it to the scale, Imogen grabs the other handle.

"Tristian Walsh—" the sadness in her voice is replaced by irritation—"let's put us aside for a second, shall we?"

The airline employee looks between us, confused.

"She's leaving." I attempt to remove Imogen's hand from the bag, but she holds tighter. "Imogen, let go."

"No. Give us a minute?" she says to the agent, yanking harder on my suitcase than expected, and I stumble with her.

"Imogen." My voice is low, barely contained, as I flush with impatience.

"Forget about you and me. This isn't about our relationship, it's about Fairytale Gardens. Your home, the place where so many memories with your mom were made, of summers with your brothers. You love FTG. Just give me a chance to save it. Please?" Her eyes plead with me.

"I'm supposed to give this all up?" I point to the airplanes out of sight. My heart aches, and I'm unsure if it's for the adventure I might miss or the family I left behind.

"If you can honestly look me in the eye and say you don't care what happens to FTG, that you're fine leaving it, then I'll walk away right now and never bother you again."

There is a stony resignation in her stare. I believe her. I could be done with FTG for good if I say a simple yes.

I swallow hard. The lump in my throat is all the words I've kept inside for two years. "My mom used to say home isn't a place, it's a feeling. That when you leave, you can't wait to get back. You ache every second you're away from it."

"And?" She prompts when I've gone silent.

"With my mom's death, we lost more than her. We lost the dreams we all had. As a family, we never took the time to process and figure out what this new life could be." I didn't realize how hard breathing was before. With my admission, I can fully exhale. "I thought leaving was my way of taking that back—but it was just another place to hide. I want to fix FTG."

FTG is so much more than a theme park; its history is rich and complicated—worthy of telling. I just needed to find my voice to be able to share it.

I'm going home.

"Where's your car?" My suitcase makes a *thud, thud, thud,* as I roll it out into the cement loading zone outside.

She waves at a silver sedan parked a few yards away. The moving car she jumped out of is still parked by the curb. Aliana leans her head over from the driver's side to yell out the passenger window: "Your carriage." The trunk pops open.

"When you said Aliana told you, I didn't think you meant she drove you." I stand stunned, so Imogen takes the case from my hand and throws it in the trunk.

"Well"—she slams it shut—"it's a long story."

"Not that long," Aliana says when I get into the passenger seat.

"True. I said I needed to find you, and she offered."

Aliana peels from the parking lot, tires screeching. I grip the door handle. "Why?"

Imogen and Aliana exchange looks in the rearview mirror. "I'm a sucker for a happily-ever-after." Aliana shrugs, nearly swiping another car.

I catch Imogen's reflection in the side mirror; it crumbles momentarily before she recovers. "I hope we can give FTG the happily-ever-after it deserves. Which is why Aliana and I put aside our differences." She catches me staring and offers a small smile. "We've got bigger things at stake—like saving the kingdom."

I didn't miss the part of Imogen's speech where she said she wanted to fix us. But repairing a broken kingdom is easier than a shattered heart.

I turn around in my seat. "Show me the picture of Milly's grandson."

"Do you know him?" Imogen asks.

I look at the photo of a preteen kid. "I don't think so."

Aliana glances over. I grab the wheel to keep us in our lane. "I've seen him," Aliana says. "Not this summer, but yeah, that's her grandkid. I'd bet money on it."

"Is that enough proof?" I ask, passing the phone back to Imogen.

"I'm working on it." She leaves it at that.

The drive gives me time to formulate what I'll say to my dad. It's been a long time coming. I'm tired of grief coloring my life. I thought I chose for myself by leaving, but that was another decision made with pain.

I watch Imogen in the back seat from the mirror. She stares out at the fields, mumbling a silent melody. Maybe I'm a fool for listening to her, but I don't think so. We both let fear trick us into mistakes.

The first step is to forgive.

Do I forgive Imogen for a choice she made without all the facts? I know her well enough to know she'd never do anything with malicious intent. But is that enough for me to look past it?

I know I need to forgive myself for not coming to terms with the pain left by my mother's death. Forgive Ivor for coping the only way he knew how. And I owe my father a chance to let me forgive him. My heart broke when I left Imogen yesterday, and I've only known her for a month. My father lost his wife of thirty years. That pain is unimaginable.

44

IMOGEN

Aliana drops us at the main building with a skeptical *good luck.* Tristian's family agreed to meet in Barth's office, so we make our way there.

"What do you want me to do?" I pause at the bottom of the stairs. It was my idea to save FTG, but I'm not sure where my part in that lies. My text thread with Divya is more one-sided than I'd like, as she tries to find dirt on Milly and her son. She said she'll send any info as soon as she gets it, and the wait is killing my nerves.

Tristian's gaze wanders over the pictures on the walls, memories documenting his entire life. "You should come in, since you actually saw Milly and her grandson."

I nod, bottom lip worried between my teeth. Being in a room with the Walshes after what I've done is not on the top of my list, but for him, I'd go anywhere.

"It was messed up you lied to me." Tristian stops when we reach the third floor.

My heart hammers against my ribs. "I know."

"But it was the push I needed to remember what was

important." A calm surrender washes over his face as his shoulders relax and his arms hang loose at his sides.

Brow furrowing, I try to keep the prickling tears at bay. "I have one more piece of unsolicited advice before we go in: don't forget every once in a while, it's okay to believe in fairytales. To let yourself get swept away in them, especially when the world is crumbling around you." He frowns. I motion to the park. "Your dad buried himself in this fairytale. Don't hate him for how he copes with it all. But make sure you tell him you need him."

Milly's desk is empty when we pass it to knock on Barth's door. Tristian's gaze lingers on it for only a moment, jaw muscles tightening.

"Come in!" Barth's voice rings through the door. A crypt-like shadow blankets FTG today, everyone waiting for a pin to drop.

"Tristian." His face softens when he sees him, then hardens when I follow behind. "What is she doing here?" Dark circles hang heavy under his eyes. His shoulders sag as he reclines in his desk chair.

"She wants to help." Tristian defends me. My heart soars at the gesture. Maybe there's a possibility that what we had might not be over.

Ivor and Aldrich sit in front of the desk, while Garrick perches against the window.

"She's done plenty already," Ivor hisses through gritted teeth.

"Enough. Let's listen to what they have to offer," Barth says. His voice is edged in uncertainty, not the disdain I expected. I'm taken aback by the words. I'm partly responsible for destroying his reputation; I pictured him tossing me out the first chance he got.

"Thanks," Tristian replies, frowning as we trade glances. I stay quiet beside him, hands gripping my phone like it's a life raft, but I offer an encouraging smile.

He scratches the back of his neck. His brothers watch the exchange in silence. "Dad, I know you didn't steal the money."

"Is that so?"

"It was Milly," Tristian says. I stiffen as the ripple of the accusation spreads across their faces.

"What?" Ivor's eyes widen in shock. "Tristian, come on, that's—"

Barth holds up his hand to silence him. "I'd like some hard evidence before we accuse a respected member of FTG."

Tristian nods to me.

All right, Imogen. Time to fix this.

I lick my lips, pulling up the photo on my phone. "Um, this kid with the giant check is Milly's grandson. I saw him at the gas station today. And it makes sense since she'd have access to plant fake documents with your signature."

Barth shakes his head. "I've known Milly for as long as Tristian has been alive. She isn't capable of this."

"With all due respect, Mr. Walsh, didn't you find it strange that she had a fancy new car?" I push, attempting confidence, but Barth's stony exterior makes it difficult.

"And the trips," Tristian adds. "How did she afford the one to Bora Bora?"

"I don't scrutinize every aspect of my employees' spending. I'm sure—" He stops when I gasp. "What now?"

My fingers shake as I enlarge the picture Divya just sent. "You wanted proof. Here you go." I slide my phone across the desk to Barth. "I gave Divya Milly's name and her son Reed's. Turns out Reed is a busy guy. He has a couple of aliases that connect back to the bank accounts Divya found for the charities."

Tightness tugs at my chest as Barth studies my phone, squinting at it with a frown. "This is a legitimate source?"

I release a deep breath. "If Divya said it, then yes."

"She wasn't so good with the first source," Ivor mutters.

"Everyone's allowed one mistake," Tristian says. I glance at him with hopeful eyes and a wordless thank-you as I take my phone back.

Barth laces his fingers into a steeple grip, bringing it to his lips. "Milly hit hard times a few years ago. I wanted to help, but the park wasn't making enough profit to give her a raise. Then two years ago, her situation suddenly got better. She said her son made some good investments. I'm sorry to say I didn't push it further."

"So, are you turning her in?" Garrick asks from the window. "This is Milly we're talking about."

"It pains me to think about it, but it is a crime." Barth taps his fingers to his lips. "Milly is a good person. She doesn't deserve to go to prison for her son's mistakes. What will your friend do with this info?" His attention turns back to me.

"Bring it to the authorities with a revised article."

"Then it's out of our hands."

"I'm sorry." I look at each of them in turn, before retreating to the ground. "I didn't mean for this to happen—well, I knew about the story, but I love FTG. I wish I'd handled it better." Maybe it wasn't as simple as choosing between my loyalty to Divya and my relationship with Tristian. I could have found a better solution. Rubbing at the pain in my chest, I finally gather the courage to meet their faces again.

Barth's eyes are glassy when he looks at me. "You're not the only person in this room who's made too many mistakes to count. You boys didn't deserve to lose your father just because he lost his wife."

The cloud that hung around Tristian lifts, like he's seeing his dad for the first time in forever. I squeeze his hand without a thought, relieved.

"I was never good with facts or truth. I thrived on stories." Barth makes a slow pan around the room to each of his sons. "The rest was your mother's doing. I didn't know how to pick up the slack when we lost her. I owe you boys an apology."

Aldrich plays with his T-shirt, rubbing his face against his shoulder to hide the tears.

"I didn't help." Tristian offers an apology. "I had so much anger rotting away inside. I needed someone to blame for Mom's death, and you made the perfect scapegoat." He steps forward and extends his hand across the desk. "I'm sorry, Dad."

Barth stares at it a moment before coming around the desk and drawing Tristian into a hug. He stiffens, but when Barth doesn't let go, he gives in. Tristian lifts his eyes to Ivor. "Ivor, I'm sorry for how I treated you, too. I know Mom's passing wasn't easy on you either."

Ivor's normally stoic face softens. "It's in the past. Consider it forgotten."

My throat is thick with restrained tears, having witnessed a moment between Tristian and his family I know they all deserved a long time ago.

Sniffles fill the room. "Your apology isn't needed, son. I let you down in more ways than I could ever count." Barth pulls away, putting a hand on Ivor's and Aldrich's shoulders. "Fairytale Gardens means nothing without you boys to share it with. Get over here." He motions to Garrick, who moves to sit on the edge of the desk.

"We've been stuck in a repeating pattern that's worn us into the ground for two years. That ends today." Barth eyes Tristian, then nods. "Tristian was right. This park is stagnant, and I want to fix it. First order of business—Tristian, you're fired."

"What?" he sputters, face flushing. "After all that, you're firing me?"

His brothers and I are equally confused. "I am." Barth smiles. "Your services as Prince Winthrop are no longer needed. You'll be too busy anyhow, as our lead, and only, marketing intern. Or if you still want to go on your summer program, we can make that work, too. Just know, once you graduate college—should you still want it—you can take over as head of marketing. I've seen how you thrive in that position. You're incredible."

Tristian sags against Aldrich's chair. "Head of marketing?"

Barth moves to the window, opening the shades. "You have the skills—and I saw what you and your princess did with the social media stuff. That was with no schooling; imagine what you'll be able to do once you have a degree." He motions to me. "You might need a partner. Imogen, are you up for the task?"

I open my mouth and close it again, settling with a nod. This is their moment and I don't feel right adding my words. But dizziness washes over me, knowing I'd have the family's blessing to stay.

Stay. The words are an answer to a wish my heart has whispered since I left all those years ago.

Tristian leans onto his knees. "What if I still want to play a prince—on weekends maybe?"

"I'll keep your armor shiny." Garrick smirks.

"My offer stands to any of you." Barth looks at each of them in turn. "This is your park and it's better when we're all together. If you see a place for improvement or want a change, speak up."

Tristian gives his dad a hug before he leads me out of the room.

"So . . ." I trail off as we stand by Milly's empty desk.

Tristian rubs at his face before looking at me. "I thought all I was, was a toy crown and a costume. Fairytale Gardens is built from words in a storybook, but it's not fake. It's real to every person who walks through those gates. It's real to my brothers and me. And together, we can build a new story where everyone fits in."

I smile tentatively. "I'm glad." The congratulatory words don't hide the tightness in my voice. The park is saved—or on the way anyhow, but there's a story still unfolding with us that I'd really love to know the ending to.

We stand in awkward silence. My brain spins a million miles an hour, flipping through everything I want to say, not knowing which is correct.

"Imogen—" he starts, as I say, "Tristian, we—"

"You go." He nods.

I take a deep breath and stare at my feet, wringing my hands together before meeting his eyes. My pulse ticks up and my words come out in a quick stream. "I got you to come back on the promise of saving FTG, and I meant that, but I can't lie; I had another motive. Life is short, Tristian. I don't want you to let grief consume what little time we all have. You're the most amazing person I've ever met—and I've met Taylor Swift." I place a hand on his cheek to ground myself to him.

"I could apologize a thousand times, and it'd never be enough—I get it, really I do. I'll say it one more time and hope you can feel everything inside that one word." I struck a flame to my last job and I didn't shed one tear. I thought that was my fate. That no matter where I went I was destined to ruin it. And FTG almost followed the same course, but I stopped it—I fixed it.

"I'm *sorry.*" Tears pool in my eyes, blurring my vision before I blink them away. "I don't want to lose us."

Tristian leans into my touch, kissing my palm. "You made a mistake, a big one, but I screwed up too. The truth is, if you had told me your plan from the beginning, I wouldn't have cared, might have helped. Not telling me was the best thing that could have happened. It gave me a chance to fall in love with FTG again."

He places his hand over mine against his face. "Imogen, you changed everything. Reminded me what made FTG special and why I loved it. You believed I was more than a fake prince, and having someone believe in you when you've long since lost faith in yourself is the most powerful magic we have in this world."

"But I—"

Tristian lifts an eyebrow. "I'm in the middle of accepting your apology. Don't you want to hear it?"

I press my lips together, smiling with a nod. My racing pulse isn't from despair, but in celebration.

"You messed up, and you know it. But this whole thing spiraled out of your control. Trust me, I've been there too. What we had together isn't something I'm willing to throw away. So, what do you say we start this over? I need you to promise that from now on, no more lies."

A weight lifts from my shoulders as I bat away tears. "I promise I'll always tell you the truth, even when it's hard."

Tristian and I have both spent too long on the run, the adventure we thought we'd find always on the next horizon. It's time we stopped and smelled the roses.

Warmth spreads across my chest as he pulls me into his arms. My lips quirk up, and he kisses the corners.

He rests his forehead against mine. "Thank you."

"For what?" My voice is a whisper against his lips.

"Making me believe in happily-ever-after again."

Lying to myself and others was how I made it through. I want to try a new path. I thought my happy ending would be perfect, but I was wrong. Perfect doesn't make you happy; there is no beauty without a few thorns. The effort is what makes it worth it. The key was finding something that made the hard parts pale in comparison to the best bits. And Tristian is the best of all of it.

EPILOGUE

IMOGEN

"Who thought it would be a good idea to make Garrick Santa?" I slide on my fur-lined cloak as we leave the costume department and head toward the park.

Tristian fastens the clasps on his new red vest and carefully smooths out the nonexistent wrinkles. "He took the outfit and wrote himself on the schedule. We didn't actually give him the job."

It's been five months since Divya published the story about Barth and Fairytale Gardens. Five months of righting the wrong I was complicit in. It wasn't easy. I know from experience gaining back broken trust doesn't happen overnight. But together with his brothers, Barth, and Divya, Tristian and I have created a Fairytale Gardens we can all be proud of.

That started with clearing Barth's name. He didn't want to implicate Milly and was adamant Divya do her best to keep the blame off her when she wrote a follow-up story. The truth was a blow to Divya's pride—she wasn't used to being wrong. But she wouldn't be responsible for accusing an innocent man.

The company wasn't happy when Divya had to confess she messed up, but they let her keep the prize money because they respected her admitting the mistake and promised to give her space to right the mistake—plus Divya had the inside knowledge to get all the details.

Milly folded without much pressure. Her son masterminded the whole scheme. They both face criminal charges. Unfortunately, the damage to the park was done. That's where Divya's third article came into play, and some fine marketing strategies from Tristian and me.

The third story was more successful than her first and second. So much so, it became a series of stories the website published over the next three months. That also allowed Divya to earn a little extra money to help the family restaurant stay afloat.

Divya, with her incredible words, and me, with my fairytale touch, brought to life what truly makes Fairytale Gardens successful: the people. Both the guests who enjoyed the fairytale and the Fairytalers who made it possible.

We started a campaign for people to share their experiences at Fairytale Gardens. It took hundreds of emails, phone calls, internet searches, and hashtags, but we gathered people worldwide. Each person with a memory near and dear to their heart tied to this park—magic they felt every time they stepped through the gates—was welcome to submit a story for publication.

Attendance soared in the days following the stories. It wasn't a magical fix. There are rough weeks, but the people see Fairytale Gardens as more than the charity scandal. And we already have plans for next summer, to bring a new fairytale to the park.

"Here." Tristian slides on Arden's ring, kissing my knuckles before he releases my hands. My heart still skips a beat, knowing he's mine. "Ready?"

I slip on the white fur-trimmed gloves as the park comes into view. "Absolutely." It's early November; the unrelenting summer heat has disappeared. A faint dusting of snow covers the bottom of my dress as we reach the castle.

Fairytale Gardens used to close for the winter. But with a bit of brainstorming, we came up with a way to keep it going. "Welcome one and all," the announcer booms as we step onto the castle stage overlooking the Village Center. Aldrich and Aliana walk arm in arm ahead of us. His character recently got a princess. Most of the regulars are back to work over Christmas break. Since Aliana played chauffeur to my apology all those months ago, we have begun a tentative friendship—saying hi to each other in the hallway at school, and other baby steps. Once you get past the bristly exterior, she's not too bad.

Ivor follows behind them in his new role as Prince Royce, the latest addition to the royal family. Along with his partner, Prince Marlo. Still the best with a crowd, Ivor does the introductions. "We are happy to have you join us for the most magical time of year in the kingdom of Carpathia, known far and wide for their magical Christmas markets."

We wave onstage as holiday music plays. The park's transformation to a winter wonderland includes garlands and fake snow, a glittering ice-skating rink where the Perilous Sea lives in the summer. We set up Christmas booths throughout the Village Center to sell local goods and treats.

Fairytale Gardens is more magical than usual.

We debated with Ivor on whether Carpathia would celebrate Christmas, given it's a fictional land. In the end, they decided it was their fairytale, and anything was possible.

Barth watches from the sidelines. I didn't interact with him much before this whole ordeal—and from what I know, I'm glad I didn't. The Barth I've gotten to know since is kind, if a bit aloof. I admire his newly found dedication to his sons. There are still things to work through—two years is a long time to hold on to anger—but they're doing it as a family.

"The royal family of Carpathia is happy to welcome a special guest, all the way from a far-off land: Santa Claus." Garrick, dressed in a full red suit and white beard, comes out with a reindeer in tow.

"Thank you," Tristian whispers into my ear, lips brushing my skin as we step offstage. The park is officially open for the day. We have meet-and-greets and carriage rides to get to, but we take a moment to ourselves.

"For what?" I slip my hands under his cloak to press closer for warmth.

He grabs a cup of hot chocolate on a table near the stage, taking a sip. "I would've lost this without you."

"If it wasn't for me, you might not have had to save it." We moved past the undercover fiasco, but guilt stabs my gut when I think about it.

Snow catches on his eyelashes. "You made me fall in love with Fairytale Gardens again by letting me fall in love with you."

I lift onto my toes, kissing him. He tastes like chocolate and peppermint. "You're so welcome." I tingle head to toe whenever he looks at me, face full of love and contentment.

He laughs against my mouth. "Too kind." He places a kiss on the tip of my nose.

"Oh." I step away with a sly grin. "I almost forgot. I have a surprise for you." I reach into my skirt's deep pockets to withdraw a red envelope.

"It's not Christmas yet." He raises an eyebrow.

"I wanted to give it to you early. Open it." I bite my lip, bouncing on the balls of my feet as he rips it open.

His brow furrows while he reads the letter twice before looking at me. "A plane ticket?"

"I know you used all your savings for that flight you never got to take, so I worked my magic and got them to give you a voucher." I really laid on the acting thick with the airline hotline. "It's good to use wherever you want to go."

"I love you, Imogen Rogers." His eyes are glassy.

This moment is perfect—I know it deep inside. I've searched for this my whole life. I realize not all the moments before this were perfect, and the ones after won't be either, but that doesn't matter. I don't need perfect as long as I'm with him.

And we all lived happily ever after—did you expect anything different? This is a fairytale, after all.

Acknowledgments

Happily-ever-afters do come true, even if they take fifteen years to get there. I created and shelved so many stories along the way. Queried agents and got close, queried agents and didn't get anywhere—I thought the dream of seeing a published book I wrote in my hands would never happen. But this little book about a fairytale theme park, a girl who started a fire, and a boy who wanted to fly away is the story that finally made me a published author. And sure, this isn't the end, not for me or Fairytale Gardens, but still, it feels an awful lot like happily-ever-after.

I wouldn't be where I am today without my mom. She's read every book I've written (even the terrible first drafts that will never see the light of day) and has loved every one of them. Without her support and belief in me I wouldn't be the person I am today. Thank you to my dad, who has supported my dream of being a writer and is always there when I need him. My grandma never got to see this book, but she asked me every day if my autobiography would be in bookstores soon—so although I'm still not writing an autobiography, I'm sure she'd be proud.

To my wonderful agent Hannah Todd for her love and dedication to this story and my career—I couldn't ask for a better partner. And to all the people at Madeleine Milburn Literary who supported this book. My fabulous editor, India Chambers, whose guidance in this process was a true gift. Thank you, Mollie Schofield, for keeping this process moving so smoothly, and to everyone at Penguin who has shown such excitement and dedication for this book—you made my dreams come true. Thank you, Lowri Ribbons, for being the first champion of this story. Thank you to Sara Schonfeld and the team at Harper for being the wonderful US home for *Enchanted to Meet You*, and to my agent, Jemiscoe Chambers-Black, for making it happen.

I am in love with the cover of this book and owe that to the outstanding cover artist, Louisa Cannell, who was able to bring the world and characters of Enchanted to life.

To all the amazing people who read drafts of this story from the very beginning and helped shape it into what it is. And to those who have supported me for many long years and always been my cheerleaders: Alyssa, Anna, Desiree, Elizabeth, Scarlette, and my Shakespearean Sisters. To my AMM mentors, Livy and Rochelle, your guidance was invaluable.